Coffee Breaks

by

Eva Reddy

2013

ISBN - 10: 0992384117

ISBN - 13: 978-0-9923841-1-1

1st Edition: December, 2013.

Disclaimer:

This is a work of fiction. The characters, their names and the places depicted are entirely the product of the author's imagination. Any resemblance to actual persons or places is completely coincidental.

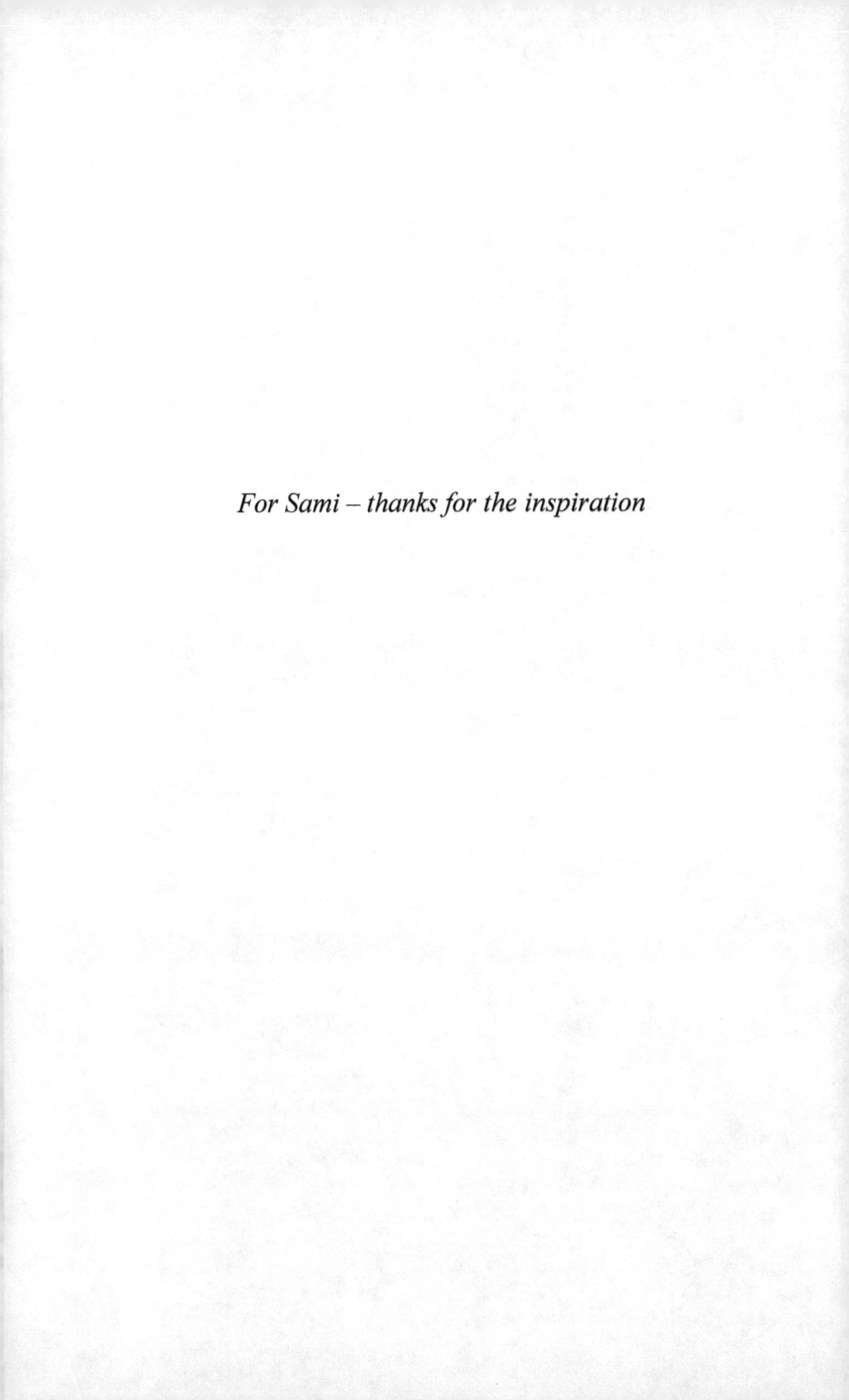

For Sami – thanks for the inspiration

Acknowledgments

Eva would like to take this opportunity to thank all those who have helped in the writing of this book, either wittingly or not.

Much appreciation goes to Emma and Suzi for their surprising level of patience and understanding throughout the process of preparing this collection of stories. I'd like special recognition for Suzi's assistance (and insistence) with editing the final draft in readiness for publication. She taught me much and made me a better writer. Thank you, so much.

Also many thanks go to Em for providing the 'last line of defense' in reading the final edit prior to publication.

Acknowledgements

Contents

Coffee Break

Matilda took in a deep breath and sighed as she turned the page of the newspaper she was reading. *No news is good news,* she thought. *I should stop reading; it's too depressing.* She absently reached for her coffee cup from the counter at the café where she took her afternoon break on most days. She lifted the cup and ferried it toward her mouth, stopping just before the cup met her lips. She paused in that way for several seconds while reading each of the news headlines on the page to see if there was a story there that took her interest.

"Would you like my muffin, too?" a strange woman's voice asked of her. Matilda looked up from her paper with a puzzled expression and took in the sight of a handsome, smiling woman staring straight at her through a dazzling set of blue eyes. "That's my coffee you've picked up by mistake," she laughed easily.

Matilda looked at the counter to see her own cup of coffee still sitting on the saucer where she'd left it. "Oh, my goodness. I'm so sorry," Matilda exclaimed, horrified at her error she said, "allow me to buy you a replacement."

"No need," the smiling woman stated, "but I would like it back." Her smile was genuine and

1

warm, showing off a set of bright white teeth framed by plump pink lips. Matilda was so mesmerized by the smile and the thought of kissing those luscious lips that she neglected to hand the prized cup of coffee back to its' rightful owner. It was not until the smile began to recede that the spell was broken enough for Matilda to realize that she still had a firm hold on the other woman's coffee.

"I….oh…..yes, sorry." She released the cup into the waiting grip of its' true owner. Smiling and then pulling a face to express her embarrassment Matilda said, "Silly me," she giggled shyly and looked away from the other woman's face and straight at her ample bosom. Matilda's mouth watered as again she slipped away from reality for a few seconds to consider what it would be like to delve her tongue into such a snug fitting cleavage. *Behave yourself,* she thought, blinking hard, trying to quickly shake off the obsession and flashed a look back up at the woman's face. *Too late! She caught me!* Clearing her throat, she turned back toward the counter and attempted to lose herself back into her newspaper while turning a particularly deep shade of crimson. *Fuck!*

"An easy mistake when you're distracted," the slightly taller woman empathized. "No harm done."

Matilda made to look up and then found she was too embarrassed to look the other woman in the eye. She tried to smile but even that failed her as her face began flush red again.

"Anything take your interest?" The woman said as she ran her fingers through her short cropped brunette hair.

Matilda's eyes widened. She continued to stare at her newspaper shocked by this woman's brazen candor. "Sorry?" she said and this time she did look up.

"In the paper, anything worth reading?" The brunette asked as she broke a small piece from her muffin and popped it into her mouth.

Matilda began breathing again and with relief stated, "Just more doom and gloom. I don't know why I bother really," she said as she turned another leaf and pretended to be scanning the page. She could feel the blue eyes upon her and her skin tingled as if it had been lightly stroked.

"My name is Chase, by-the-way."

Matilda looked up at Chase's face, returned the smile she found there, and said, "Matilda."

"Nice to meet you Matilda," Chase said looking into Matilda's soft brown eyes. Then taking in Matilda's curly, shoulder-length, dark brown hair. *One or two greys,* she thought as she contemplated the wayward bangs, maybe 30 to 35.

Matilda picked up her own cup and gave a little giggle as she lifted it in a silent toast to Chase and then took a self-conscious sip.

Chase smiled and took the opportunity for a clandestine scrutiny of Matilda's slight form and petite breasts. *She likes the outdoors; she has a slight tan.* She allowed her eyes to drift down Matilda's white sundress, lightly toned legs and sandals. Looking back up as Matilda replaced her cup onto its saucer.

"Do you work around here?" asked Matilda.

"I live and work from my home. It's just around the corner."

"Oh," Matilda answered with interest. "How fortunate to be able to work from home. What is it that you do?"

"I'm a sex therapist," Chase stated and watched for Matilda's reaction. Matilda seemed stunned momentarily, needing a few moments to contemplate the answer she'd been given. Her face awash with one expression after another as she quickly glanced around the café at nothing in particular. Her lips were slightly pursed as though she were about to start speaking but had changed her mind. Then she closed her mouth with a slightly audible gnash of her teeth; unable to think of what to say next.

Chase gave Matilda a few more seconds to compose herself and then stated, "You might consider me a Gigola; a lady's lady."

"Oh!" Matilda said in a far more delighted manner than she was comfortable with. Embarrassed again she looked back down at her newspaper. She shook her head a little from side to side, as she chastised herself, *That was smooth, Matilda. Well, done.*

4

Chase went back to her muffin and coffee while Matilda looked at her from the corner of her eye as she pretended to continue to read her newspaper. Chase was lean and muscular. *Wow! She must really work-out!* Matilda thought as her eyes studied the Gigola with greater and greater appreciation. Matilda's breathing deepened as she studied the stretch of the black singlet across Chase's breasts. Then her gaze lingered on the small amount of skin visible where the singlet didn't cover the small of Chase's back each time she leant forward at the counter to sip at her coffee. Chase's ass was perched on the front half of the counter stool. Her jeans gaped a little near her exposed spine and Matilda could feel herself being drawn to lean over to look into the little grotto. She blinked hard again in an effort to steel herself from the compulsion to touch Chase's skin and squirmed a little on her stool, as her frustration presented as a wave of excitement that roiled between her thighs. She closed her eyes and rocked forward a little on her stool to place a small amount of pressure against her clit; needing to ease some of her excitement. She breathed out heavily with the slight release the motion had offered and opened her eyes. Again, looking out the corner of her eye at Chase, she let her eyes drift lower, to Chase's crotch. She stared for some time at the slightly raised zipper area. She felt her nipples harden against her bodice when she imagined herself unzipping Chase's jeans and pressing her face into the opening.

She cleared her throat lightly, took a deep breath in an attempt at composure before asking, "So...uh-hmm... much work on?"

Chase smiled broadly and said, "Bit slow...at the moment." And then lowered her voice a few tones and added, "But that's the way I like it....slow." She let her eyes drift over Matilda's body again. Smiling when Matilda blushed and shivered and notably began breathing more deeply. Then she turned back to the waitress and called, "Bill please," pointing at Matilda's coffee as well as her own order to indicate a combined payment. She placed some notes on the counter and said, "Keep the change," before sliding from the stool.

She took Matilda's newspaper and when Matilda looked up; looked into her eyes with confidence. Keeping Matilda's gaze, Chase smiled more and more broadly while folding the newspaper and laying it back on the counter. Then, taking Matilda's hand and pulling her to her feet, she asked, "Your place or mine?"

Matilda was speechless. Try as she might to put a simple sentence together – managed nothing more than, "Umm..."

"Mine then," stated Chase and tugged her along by the hand out of the café and into the street. After a short walk around the corner, Chase stopped and opened a waist-high wrought iron gate and entered the front yard of an old Federation-style house. She gestured for Matilda to enter along the front path to the porch steps. Chase closed the gate and checked the letterbox while Matilda took in the sight of the magnificent home.

"Wow!" said Matilda, "Business must be good." Chase smiled and again took Matilda by the hand and led her up the few steps to the front door. As she opened the fly-wire door, a maid wearing a French maid's outfit, opened the heavy wooden front door and allowed them in.

"Welcome home, Chase. Is 'zere anysing you will be needing 'zis afternoon?" asked the maid with a French accent.

"Yes, a cheese board and a bottle of....." replied Chase as she looked at Matilda questioningly, "...white? .....No.... Red." Matilda nodded and the maid hurried away.

Chase led Matilda into the living room and offered her a seat on the couch. Matilda sat and Chase sat down beside her on the three-seater. They looked at each other for a few moments. Slowly, wordlessly, leaning ever closer together. Looking from each other's eyes, to each other's lips. Their lips parted and Chase moistened hers with her tongue. The sight caused Matilda to moan quietly and then moisten her own lips in the same way. Just as their lips were about to touch, they were distracted by the sound of clinking glasses and a quiet knock at the door. They instantly sat up straight and Chase said, "Come in, Suz."

The petite little maid quickly entered and placed a pine board ladened with cheese wedges and accompaniments onto the ornately carved, heavy, jarrah coffee table. Then she placed a small tray with an opened bottle of Merlot and two wine glasses next to the cheeseboard. Having ensured the nibbles were within easy reach of both women, Suzette straightened and asked, "Should I pour 'ze wine, Chase?"

"No, thank you, Suzette. I'll let this one breathe for a few minutes first." Suzette nodded and quickly left the room and stopped to shut the paneled doors as went.

Matilda studied the bounty on the table before her, pouted slightly before looking at Chase from the corner of her eye.

"What?" Chase asked.

"If you have all this at home, why do you need to go to a café?" Matilda asked.

Chase looked thoughtfully at Matilda for a moment before answering, "The café is good for drumming up potential business opportunities." She looked Matilda up and down and then looked into her eyes for long moments.

Matilda nodded and this time the blush was for the sexual attraction she felt toward the woman next to her. She looked appreciatively at Chase's breasts and then back up to Chase's full pink lips. She watched as Chase reached over to the cheese platter, picked up the cheese knife and cut a small portion of Brie. Turning the knife over between her fingers and jabbing the portion with the curled points of the knife's blade, Chase pressed it against a shelled pistachio, embedding the nut into the cheese. Then she picked up a bite-sized cracker, and used it to knock the cheese from the knife. Matilda watched as Chase offered the cracker; brushing it over Matilda's soft lips and enticing her to part them so Chase could pop the treat into her mouth.

"Mmm," Matilda approved. "Delicious."

Chase looked at Matilda seductively and said, "Yes, I think you might be right."

The corner of Matilda's mouth curled into a fleeting smile. Chase was a little confused as to why it had disappeared so soon.

Matilda looked at the cheeseboard while she swallowed her treat and said, "I should ask, how much?"

Chase reached over and took hold of Matilda's small, smooth hands and said, "You say that as if you may not be able to afford it. We both know that isn't true."

Matilda smiled and nodded.

Chase took the bottle of Merlot and half-filled each of the glasses. While she did so, Matilda looked around the room. It was delightfully furnished. Aside from the brown suede couch she and Chase were sitting on and the jarrah coffee table in front of them, there was an antique looking Grandfather clock against the wall next to the doorway they'd stepped through to enter the living room. The next wall, situated behind the couch, had two large windows, draped in fine lace curtains with colorful swags and tails above. The room was light and yet private. In front of the windows was a medium sized jarrah table with two ornately carved jarrah chairs. On the side wall, next to the table were shelves of leather bound books interspersed with ornaments; making what could have been a boring looking library, somehow very attractive. On the wall opposite the windows and in front of the couch, was a fireplace and above its mantle; a large ornately framed mirror, cleverly reflecting the light from the windows and making the room seem large and light and airy.

Chase picked up the wine glasses and handed one to Matilda. "To new friendships and business partners."

Matilda lightly tapped her glass to Chase's and they simultaneously sipped to seal their toast. Matilda once again noticed the crotch of Chase's jeans and shivered. She placed her wine glass down on the table and watched as Chase did the same. Long moments passed as they each surveyed the other's body. Looking back up at the same time, they leaned in and their lips touched. Tenderly at first. A light, still kiss. Each feeling the life breath of the other tickle the skin on their cheek. Matilda growled softly when Chase opened her lips and licked her softly, slowly, gently. Matilda opened her mouth to growl again and Chase pressed forward and probed with her tongue using sensual strokes of discovery across Matilda's tongue and the insides of her cheeks. As Chase's tongue retreated, Matilda was compelled to follow after it with her own. Licking and lapping at the taste of the wine on Chase's lips.

Chase ran her hands up Matilda's arms and held her shoulders to press against the kiss more deliberately. Matilda raised her left hand and cupped Chase's breast. The nipple already distended and hard to her touch. Chase groaned with pleasure as Matilda took hold of and gently twisted her nipple through her singlet.

Chase ran her hands down Matilda's back, caressing her while shuffling her body closer and again probing Matilda's mouth with her tongue.

Matilda unfastened Chase's bra through her singlet in a quick, decisive movement and Chase stopped kissing her for the few seconds it took to offer Matilda a surprised but congratulatory look. Matilda giggled and Chase swallowed the last of that delightful sound with a passionate kiss.

Chase ran her fingers through Matilda's hair, tickling her neck and causing her to shiver with excitement. Then she ran her fingers down Matilda's back, catching hold of the dress zipper on the way.

Matilda lowered her arms to put her hands in under Chase's singlet and as she did so, the top half of her dress slipped away from her shoulders; exposing her breasts. Chase immediately cupped the small mounds, one in each hand and squeezed them lightly and then ran the knuckles of each hand over the nipples making them rigid and raised.

"Oh, yes." Matilda managed, as she moved from kissing Chase's mouth, to resting her head on her shoulder. She could tell by the contours she was feeling with her fingers under the singlet, that Chase had a very muscular abdomen. The vision she had in her mind of them made her suddenly wet and hot. Her clit pulsated, causing her to slowly writhe her hips back and forth.

Chase took hold of the hem of her singlet and pulled it and her bra off and over her head in one easy movement. Matilda could now see the muscle tone, not only of Chase's stomach, but also in her pert breasts and contoured shoulders and arms. She leant forward to take one of Chase's nipples into her mouth. She struggled to untangle her arms from her own dress as she reached for Chase's other breast. Chase helped free Matilda from the dress and as Matilda momentarily lifted her hips; Chase pushed the dress down her legs toward the floor.

Matilda was now only wearing her panties and sandals. Chase rhythmically ran her palms over Matilda's back while Matilda hungrily suckled at Chase's nipples. Alternating from one to the other, while Chase's breathing became more ragged as her excitement grew. Chase felt every swipe of Matilda's tongue across her nipple as if it were a lap at her clit.

Matilda reached down and undid the button on Chase's jeans. Kissing her way down Chase's abdomen to Chase's belly button. Plunging into it with her tongue while she unzipped Chase's jeans and reached into Chase's underwear. Finding exactly what she'd hoped for, she extracted the rock-hard bulge before kissing her way further down Chase's muscular abdomen. Matilda slid her body to the floor, kneeling in front of Chase and nestled herself comfortably between Chase's strong thighs. Matilda looked up into Chase's bottomless pools of blue just before she opened her mouth and took in the head of Chase's cock. She murmured approval at the taste of wild strawberries and cream. Chase thrust her hips up slowly and almost orgasmed from downward pressure as Matilda pressed her mouth down onto her cock again.

"Mmm," Matilda murmured, releasing her oral grip and then looking up at Chase said, "I need this in me."

Chase immediately stood and lifted Matilda from the floor, holding her close as Matilda wrapped her legs around Chase's waist. Chase carried the little woman over to the medium-sized table near the windows and laid her down upon it. Kissing her while feverishly removing her underwear. Matilda wrapped her legs around

Chase again and used her toes to lever off her sandals; allowing them to drop to the floor. Chase moved Matilda's buttocks closer to the edge of the table and slowly inserted her cock. She bent over Matilda and licked and sucked at her nipples while gently increasing the pressure with her cock, driving it slowly deeper.

Matilda groaned, "Mmm, I need it all the way in, Chase. All the way!" She tightened her legs around Chase's waist and struggled to push her hips up and into her.

"Hang on a minute," Chase whispered. She stood, careful to ensure her cock remained inside of Matilda, as she grasped the frame under the table-top and pulled the table toward the wall between the two windows.

Once the table was in position, Chase lifted Matilda's legs and encouraged her to brace her feet against the wall.

"Oh, very clever." Matilda said with an approving giggle and raised her hips to encourage Chase to continue with inserting her cock. Chase complied leaning in to take Matilda by the shoulders to help with driving the cock slowly inward. Matilda looked down the front of her own body to watch as Chase drove her cock into her. Chase still had her jeans hitched over her hips and the straps of her apparatus were, for the most part, hidden. Matilda purred as she watched Chase's slow rhythmic thrusts. The breasts above her swaying with that same rhythm. The muscles twitching and rolling with each thrust. Matilda reached down and began to fondle her own breasts. Squeezing them mercilessly. She grasped her nipples, rolling them and twisting them between her fingers. She became so wet that she could hear the wet sounds of her pussy lathering Chase's cock with every stroke in and out. In and out.

Chase mumbled approval at watching Matilda's hands working her own breasts, *She likes them to be fondled a little rough.* "That's so hot!" Chase left one hand at Matilda's shoulder; holding her in place and ensuring she didn't slip up the table and away from her thrusting cock. With the other she slipped her thumb down between her and Matilda, running it up and down over Matilda's clit. Matilda screamed her delight and began pumping her hips harder and faster.

Matilda was so wet that Chase's thumb glided effortlessly across the tight bundle of nerves. *I could come just watching this,* Chase thought as she took in the view of Matilda: her tongue licking her lips as she moaned and screamed her delight, her hands twirling her own taught nipples while her hips thrust upward, and her chest heaved from the exertion.

Matilda shouted, "Oh, Chase. Faster!" she gulped, "harder! Deeper!" She was breathing heavily, raggedly, "Ohhhhh! .....Fuck! ....you're good at this," she screamed, as she broke into a sweat and groaned long and throatily. Suddenly, she stiffened. She threw her head back and grasped Chase with her legs, wrapping them back around her waist and holding on tight. The vice-like grip of Matilda's legs effectively held Chase's cock inside her to the hilt. "Faster! HARDER!" she screamed and Chase realized she was talking about her thumb working back and forth across Matilda's clit. Chase did as commanded and Matilda cried out, "Ahhhhhh! YESSSSSS..........!" as her hips spasmed with the last throes of orgasm. "YESSS! YESSS!"

Matilda suddenly reached down and grasped Chase's wrist to remove her thumb from her clit. Her other hand reaching high, holding the nape of Chase's neck and pulling her down for a long, languid kiss. Chase was still inside Matilda as she kissed her cheeks, her forehead, her nose and then her chin. Then a row of tiny little kisses to her neck, nuzzling at Matilda while she groaned with approval. She chuckled as she kissed her way around her neck to the other side and nuzzled again. Once again, Matilda moaned her appreciation.

Chase placed her hands on Matilda's breasts and fondled the small mounds, soon feeling the nipples harden against her palms. She kissed her way back to Matilda's mouth. Then, licking lightly on Matilda's lips with her protruding tongue, Chase enticed Matilda to open her mouth. She plunged in with her tongue to again explore Matilda's taste. Soon, she found herself becoming aroused from Matilda's biting lightly on her tongue. She felt her body shudder and probed even more deeply into Matilda's mouth. Chase's arousal was becoming apparent to Matilda by the renewed thrusting of her hips.

Matilda motioned for Chase to stand straight and then remove her cock. Matilda sat up on the table and demanded, "Sit on the chair." She pointed to one of the two ornately carved chairs at the table.

As Chase moved to comply, Matilda grabbed hold of the waistband of Chase's jeans and started forcing them down. Chase sat and then removed her boots, jeans and briefs. Now she, too, was naked.

Matilda straddled Chase and slowly inserted the cock into her pussy. She knew that the downward pressure would press against Chase's clit. So she tightened the muscles of her vagina to create as much resistance as possible, pressing the base of the cock hard against Chase's clit for a prolonged, sensual insertion. Chase groaned loudly as she watched the cock disappearing into Matilda.

Once fully inserted, Matilda cupped Chase's chin and lifted until their eyes met. "I want to see you come. I want you to look at me when you come. Don't look away and don't close your eyes."

Chase's eyes were half-closed just from this first sensation of her hardness being inserted into

Matilda's straddled pussy. She thought she might come with the very next thrust; the pleasure of it was so intense. She lightly ran her hands down Matilda's sides and rested her hands on her hips.

Matilda lifted her weight from Chase's lap and allowed Chase's cock to partially withdraw from her. She ran her hands up Chase's arms, brushing the sides of Chase's breasts with her wrists as they passed, on their way to Chase's neck. Matilda ran her fingers through the short hair at the back of Chase's head and Chase closed her eyes from the enjoyment of Matilda's touch. "Open your eyes," Matilda said. "Keep them open and looking into mine."

Chase struggled, but complied and then struggled again as Matilda began to slowly lower herself onto her cock once more. Chase groaned loudly and wanted to look down to watch again but stopped herself. She continued looking into Matilda's eyes as requested.

Matilda began moving upward again and Chase became aware that sweat was dripping down the sides of her own face, running down her neck and chest. The intensity of the experience and the strain of keeping her eyes open, taking their toll on her stamina.

Matilda moved her hands down Chase's neck, over her shoulders and reached her breasts just in time for another slow downward compression. Matilda cupped Chase's breasts and massaged them between her palms and fingers.

Another downward thrust and Chase began breathing so heavily she needed to open her mouth to suck in more air.

Matilda slowly moved her body upward and then very slowly thrust down again while caressing Chase's nipples. Chase's groans became louder and again her eyes almost closed but she managed to force them open once more.

Matilda's movements continued, slow and rhythmic. Up and down while pressing and squeezing and tweaking Chase's nipples between thumb and fingers.

Chase started to murmur, "Oh.....fuck me, Matilda.....Fuck me." The sensations so overwhelming, they caused her to catch her breath from time to time. Then again breathing deeply, rapidly, trying to gulp in more air. Matilda maintained her speed, slowly pressing down while tensing the muscles of her vagina, pushing down on the cock, pushing it hard against Chase's clit. She continued to squeeze Chase's nipples and stare into her blue eyes.

"Matilda......OH! ....FUCK!" Chase's eyes started to close and again she had to force them to stay open. "Matilda....I'm.....com...ming." Matilda stopped playing with Chase's nipples and placed her hands on the sides of Chase's face. Holding her face up and looking into her eyes while continuing her slow dance on Chase's lap. She looked deeply into Chase's eyes. They were glazed over; she was coming. Still Chase kept her gaze on Matilda's dark   brown   eyes.   "Oh! ....Matilda.......this.....feels.....amazing,"   she managed as she held Matilda's hips hard in place against her thrusting hips. During the final throes of orgasm, Matilda dropped her head forward and kissed Chase thoroughly; thrusting her tongue into Chase's mouth. Allowing Chase to finally, close her eyes.

Slowly the thrusting hips eased and Chase sat wasted on the chair. Her chest was heaving and sweat poured from every pore of her body.

Matilda held Chase's head between her breasts while waiting for the last few thrusts of Chase's hips. She kissed Chase's face and nuzzled at her neck and ears. She purred her delight at Chase's long-lasting orgasm. After some time she lifted her weight and allowed Chase's cock to fall away, before reseating herself on Chase's lap.

Chase lifted her head and looked again into Matilda's eyes. She so obviously wanted to express her feelings, but Matilda knew that couldn't be allowed to happen. Matilda just smiled while petting Chase's forehead and in a gentle tone she said, "Shushhhhh. It's okay." Again, she cuddled Chase's head to her breast, enjoying the feeling of Chase's still panting breaths against her skin. "Shushhh."

She kissed Chase's forehead and nuzzled her hair; breathing in the scent of her. *Even her perspiration smells good. I could sit here holding her like this all day.*

Chase began to recover and started moving her hands up and down Matilda's body, appreciating her subtle curves.

Matilda leant back to gaze again at Chase's eyes for a moment while she moved her hips and positioned her legs between Chase's. She allowed her body to slide down Chase's front to kneel on the floor between her thighs. Her hands slid down Chase's front at the same time, although they stopped to linger at Chase's breasts. With her head in Chase's lap, Matilda opened her mouth and nibbled at Chase's cock. She relished the scent – her own scent – and the taste of her own pussy on Chase, and then settled in to lick up and savor her own juices.

She moved her hands down Chase's body, tickling the flesh of Chase's abdomen as they descended. One hand taking hold of the shaft and bending it to the side to allow her better access to the treasured fluids, while the other hand continued to tickle Chase's muscular abs. Changing hands, Matilda twisted the shaft to the opposite side and noisily lapped up the last of the slick fluids.

"Mmm," she said as she licked her lips and began moving her hand up and down the shaft. She observed the small movements Chase made with her hips. Chase was ensuring the base of the shaft met its target. Matilda pointed the shaft forward and a little more toward her. She felt great satisfaction as she acknowledging Chase's delight at her having found the sweet-spot. *That's handy,* she thought, *now if I can suck it at the same time...* Matilda dropped her head down and took the cock into her mouth.

"Slowly, Matilda. That's right." Chase panted and threw her head back. "Oh, yes, yes. Just like that." Matilda smiled and stopped to lick at the insides of Chase's thighs, causing Chase to flinch with ecstasy from the light touches. "Oh........Matilda......"

Letting out a loud groan, Chase opened her mouth wide to allow her to breathe more deeply, and uttered, "Slow down, Matilda....or I'll come too soon.....make it last for me, lover." *Did I just call her lover? Oh, my, but she is so good at this. I should be paying her.*

Matilda slowed the rhythm of her hand and leant in and opened her mouth. Chase looked down and watched as Matilda took the head of the cock into her mouth while murmuring little sounds of her enjoyment. Chase became even more aroused, watching Matilda's head bobbing slowly up and down. "Suck it, Matilda. Suck my cock!"

Matilda moved both hands back up Chase's body and took a nipple between each thumb and forefinger. She began rhythmically pressing and pulling until she heard Chase groan, "Oh, Matilda, that feels *so* good." Unable to sit still, Chase thrust and writhed her hips a little. She placed her hands either side of Matilda's head, adjusting the angle of each downward thrust of Matilda's mouth, and further enhancing the sensations for her clit.

Matilda's hands cupped Chase's breasts and thumbed at her erect nipples. Again Chase struggled to resist thrusting her hips. Her heart was pounding in her chest and her breathing became more and more rapid. Her clit pulsated in time with every heartbeat. She was mesmerized by Matilda's every move. By every sound from Matilda's mouth, sucking and licking while murmuring with delight.

Chase felt her clit swell to almost bursting, as Matilda sucked her cock to its tip, releasing it for the time it took to noisily nibble and bite and suck at its sides. Listening to the sounds of Matilda's sucking and licking at her slippery cock, Chase felt the first twinges of her approaching orgasm. *Clever girl. Slowing down a little and making it last longer.*

Matilda licked down each side of Chase's cock, then opened her mouth wide and bit down hard on its tip. She moved her head downward and forced the butt of the cock hard onto Chase's clit. Matilda squeezed Chase's nipples between her fingers and Chase gave a deep throated groan.

Matilda released the grip with her teeth and relaxed the muscles in her throat, allowing the cock to probe deeply. As she pushed her lips down the full length of the shaft, Chase – still holding Matilda's head – held her breath. She was well aware of how deeply her cock was delving into Matilda's mouth. *Fuck me! She can Deep Throat!* thought Chase as her eyes opened wide and she slowly exclaimed, "Oh, Matilda. That's so fucking hot."

Matilda slowly lifted her head. When the cock left her throat she breathed in deeply and then chortled while exhaling. She giggled when she released the cock from her lips and watched it wobble to and fro. She looked up at Chase with a sexy smile; a knowing look in her eye. *Did I just surprise the Gigola?*

Then returning her attention to the tip of Chase's cock, Matilda touched the tip of it with her tongue. Moving it in small, slow circles. She lowered her head again and opened her mouth to take Chase's cock once more. Chase groaned out loud again. Now, completely unable to prevent her hips from bucking against Matilda's mouth as she watched her cock being slowly reinserted. Matilda's lips moving rhythmically up and down its full length; the erotic scene driving Chase wild. Chase held Matilda's head and ran her fingers through Matilda's wavy hair. Then, winding the locks around her fingers, she pulled Matilda's head up and down her cock. Faster, then faster again. Matilda was intuitively reading Chase's every move and instinctively riding Chase's undulating hips.

"OH!   MATILDA!!" Chase   shouted, "Coming......again!!!" Matilda squeezed Chase's nipples, further heightening Chase's orgasm. "Ohhhh! ......Fuuuuck!" Chase called as her whole body twitched and bucked. Chase threw her head back, "OH!!!.....Yes!!!!" she said closing her eyes and pressing Matilda's head down into her groin. Holding rigid for the last few seconds of her orgasm and then collapsing, limp on the chair.

Matilda scrambled back up to sit in Chase's lap. Chase's torso heaved through each gasping breath while Matilda showered her with hundreds of little kisses on her neck and chin.

Chase strained to roll her head forward and kissed Matilda softly on her lips before resting her head on Matilda's shoulder. She wrapped her arms around the little woman and breathing heavily into her neck, while softly groaning with each exhaled breath.

Chase slowly recovered and then giggled. She knew it sounded childish, but she couldn't help it and giggled again. Matilda leaned back and looked at her a little puzzled at first. When Chase giggled again, Matilda couldn't help but join her. Then they stilled and looked seriously into each other's eyes for a few moments, before each attempting to stifle yet another giggle. Finally, the giggling, too, subsided.

Matilda sighed and Chase nodded. They both got up from the chair. Each a little stiff and sore from their exertions. Slowly, they dressed while offering each other warm smiles of mutual appreciation.

They took the time to sit together and ate most of the cheeseboard and drank some of the wine. Chase leaned in for another kiss and Matilda offered her mouth gladly. For a few long moments, they re-explored each other's mouths thoroughly. Just as Chase was about to reach out to hold Matilda, Matilda sat bolt upright and said, "Oh, no you don't! I have a business meeting tonight and I haven't even started getting ready for it." Then her gaze toward Chase softened as she reluctantly stated, "I'm afraid I'll have to go."

"Oh," said Chase, suddenly aware that she had taken her kiss further than she'd planned. She exhaled deeply and said, "Okay, then. I'll see you to the door."

Matilda smiled and nodded and they both rose to walk out into the entry. In the middle of the entry hall was a small ornate table, situated between the living room door and the heavy wooden exterior door. On the table was an eftpos machine and a delicately carved wooden cashbox with a key in its lock.

The table hadn't been there when they walked in and Matilda looked at it for a moment in puzzlement. Then it occurred to her that she needed to ante-up.

"Oh, yes, of course," she said as she took her handbag from her shoulder and began rummaging through it to retrieve her credit card.

"No charge!" insisted Chase, holding her hand over the opening to Matilda's bag and preventing her from being able to remove her wallet.

"No, Chase, that wasn't the deal." Matilda retorted.

"Next time." Chase said kissing Matilda lightly on the cheek. "Next time or there won't be a next time." Chase whispered in Matilda's ear.

"Oh," said Matilda, shivering from the feel of Chase's breath so close to her still sensitive skin. "Okay." She looked up at Chase. Her breath taken by those bottomless, blue eyes smiling warmly at her. She smiled back and walked to the door.

As she walked away, she could sense Chase's eyes checking out her receding form, and she liked it. She liked it a lot.

Suzette appeared as if from nowhere. A look that might have been a frown on her face as she opened the door to let Matilda out.

"Thank you," said Matilda as she passed. The maid nodded slightly as Matilda passed and closed the door behind her.

Walking down the path, Matilda could feel Chase's attention on her once again. At the gate she stopped and turned to find Chase watching her through the window. Matilda gave her a little wave and Chase returned it and smiled. Matilda turned and left after closing the gate behind her.

She smiled to herself as she walked back toward the café thinking she should go home to shower and change before her meeting. Then she smiled again; this time, at the very fact that she needed to go home to shower and change. She felt a spring in her step that hadn't been there in a very, very long time and she was pleased that her easy smile was there to stay.

The End

Heebie-Jeebies

I'll share with you a little secret of mine – I'm terrified of spiders! And when I say terrified, I mean *TERRIFIED!* They give me the heebie-jeebies.

Stop smiling!

Last night while my wife was out I was fishing through a basket of clean washing to find a clean work shirt. I like to have myself organized for the next day because I wake up so early and I don't like to disturb the girls (my wife and daughter), by moving through the house in the dark trying to find clothes, etc. So, as I was saying I am delving into a basket of washing and out crawls a spider! A big, fat fuckin' furry one. (A cold shiver runs down my spine and I still cringe with the memory).

I let out the loudest girlie scream that you have ever heard in your life. As the high pitched squeal leaves my mouth I start jumping around like a freaking lunatic, calling out for the missus frantically. However, there is no answer. It's at that moment that I realize: A. the spider is sitting on the top of the washing pile which is right in the middle of the doorway between me and the rest of the house, so I'm cornered in the laundry with nowhere to run; and, B. My wife isn't home! Mother Fucker!

I freeze. My whole body – still – like a statue. It's staring back at me. I slide my hand down to my pocket making a silent prayer that my phone is in there so I can call the wife and she can come and save me from this evil creepy crawly. Bugger! Bugger! Shit! Piss! Fuck! My phone is on the kitchen counter.

So, there I am, wondering if I can stay there and stare at the spider for as long as it takes for my wife to return home. I decide I'm being a big fucking idiot and I need to harden-the-fuck-up and take on this creature. Well, that's the moment the spider chooses to lunge at me. I swear to God, dear reader, it's like the spider heard my thoughts and said, "Yeah, right lady. Take this you pussy!" I squeal again and do my little jumping-up-and-down jig-like dance. I mean, I swear to you, I think a little bit of pee may have come out!

So, after another five minutes of calming myself down, giving myself a little pep talk on how if I can't kill one fucking spider what kind of butch can I call myself, I grab a shoe and take my best spider whacking stance for attack. Five, four, three, two, one…. Attack! Except I whack so hard that the spider flies up into the air! I track that mother fucker through the air like it's all going in slow motion; like in a movie. As it lands on the ground – no joke – that little bastard does a side to side movement like some kinda fucking footballer.

It's at that moment that I see my opportunity and…splat!

I place my hand on my chest because my heart is pounding a hundred miles an hour. Then the reality of what had just happened sets in. I take a deep breath and push my shoulders back. I'm feeling very pleased with myself and think of how proud the missus will be of me. So… I step over the 'evil-doer' and go grab my phone and call the wife so I can tell her how big my balls are! She doesn't answer and I'm a little let down and a bit distracted as I walk back to the laundry. Just as I'm about to leave a message for her the spider convulses and does a little, "Help me, I'm dying," motion with its legs. So, of course, I scream – again – drop the phone and with the shoe I did not even realize I was still holding in my hand, I splat the fucking thing into a gazillion tiny pieces! Bang! Bang! Bang!

Sitting on the floor, I'm wondering if I should continue with my braveness and clean up the mashed mess of a spider, or – cringe – leave it for my wife, when my phone starts to ring, scaring the bejesus out of me and causing my over-used heart muscle to palpitate once again. I see 'lover' on the screen, (the wife is programmed into my phone as lover), and so I answer the phone. The poor woman is a frantic mess; one step away from calling the cops because of the huge 'scream' I left on her voice mail followed by an engaged signal. Out of relief-from-fear for our daughter and me, she is furious at me for scaring her senseless. She's on her way home and I've ruined her night out. But, once I tell the story about the events that occurred leading up to my message she is able to laugh with me, or should I say, laugh at me!

When she gets home, I show her my trophy smeared on the laundry floor. She shakes her head and bravely cleans up the mess with a tissue while I stand at a safe distance in the hallway. She laughs at me when I jump back as she walks past me toward the kitchen bin with the pieces of the critter in a tissue.

Hey! Stop smiling!

I go back to fishing for a clean shirt, keeping a close eye in case my spider has family with a vendetta. I start pulling out the shirt I'm after and didn't notice the wife come back into the laundry until she gently took an unfair advantage of me being bent over the laundry basket. I let out another one of them girl-screams – hang my head, how embarrassing. My wife laughs as she cuddles me with her apology. You gotta give me my due; I'd just been through a frightening experience.

Anyway, while she's giving me this comforting cuddle, I can't help but notice she's got a whopping big set of tits. She looks great having been all dressed-up for going out and she smells like heaven. It's understandable that I would want to press my face into that cleavage and not give a fuck if I died there from suffocation.

Turns out, tonight, that's her 'on-button.' My wife has on-buttons – something I do or touch that gets her horny. Big grin. Problem is that it changes from one day to the next. So...what gets her horny today, might get her cranky tomorrow. I call that her 'off-button.' Heaven fuckin' help you if you hit her off-button, that's all I need to say about that. Tonight, I got lucky.

She lifts my face out of her melons and plants a wet one on me while she marches me backwards to our bedroom. I don't take a lot of convincing when it comes to sex, so by the time we make it through the bedroom door, I'm gagging for it.

She can't rip my clothes off fast enough and throws me down on our bed. I want to help her out of her dress, but she grabs my hands and holds them above my head. That's code for, 'stop interferin' and let me have my own way.' Experience has taught me, 'never get between a lesbian in a dress and her code,' so I imitate a starfish and wait to be rewarded for my obedience.

She starts by planting another one of those insanely passionate kisses on me. Now, my tongue is the only means I have left of releasing my passion on her. I work it hard in her mouth and do my best to wrap it around her tongue because it's the only way I have of caressing her. My lips are doin' their best to keep up with the passion of her kiss and try as I might, I can't kiss her deep enough to show her how much she means to me. I don't know how she does this, but she uses her kiss to get me hot and interested and then, she uses it to calm and control me like nothing else can. I'll do anything she wants, however she wants, just so long as she keeps that wonderful mouth on me.

She's touching me, everywhere but the most important bits, and when she's got me twitching and hungry for her touch she slows and softens her kisses. She controls me completely and she knows it. She starts to give me short, soft kisses on my lips and cheeks, on my nose and forehead. She looks at me all meaningful and gee-whiz but she can hold my attention with those amazing amber eyes. She lets out a low chuckle as she places loads of little light kisses on my face. Each time she chuckles, lots of her tickling breaths play against my skin, machine-gun style, and then kisses me deeply again.

My breathing is deep and ragged, I'm straining to keep from touching her and she knows that, too. She chuckles low again as she kisses down my neck and across my chest. My skin puckers up into goose-bumps and I shiver at the touch of her breaths as well as her lips. She's getting-off on making me squirm. "Bitch!" I whisper lovingly and she chuckles low again.

She lets the weight of her breasts brush lightly over my tummy as she slowly kisses and licks at the skin around my nipples. Then she stops and blows on my nipple and it puckers up as if at her silent command. My chest is heaving and

I can't quite wriggle close enough to get my nipple into her mouth. She chuckles again as she kisses and tickles the skin on my other breast, being careful not to touch the nipple. Then she blows gently and that nipple too, rises into a hard peak just short of her lips.

I push upward with that side of my body, trying to get my nipple into her mouth. I felt myself get wet when she relented, parted her lips and accepted my nipple into her mouth. I couldn't help but groan loudly. My reward was a long time coming and the feel of her lips and tongue on my nipple was exquisite. She chuckles low and my skin goose-bumps again at the tickle of her breath.

"Shush!" she warns low and sweet. (I'm at risk of waking our two-year-old). I have to bite my lip as she starts teasing me again.

She begins to kiss and lick her way back to the first nipple, but it's already puckered up from the goose-bumps she gave me before. She blows on it anyway and it rises more; painfully puckering toward her lips. I cry-out with a mix of discomfort and delight and my hips thrust up and down as if in sympathy. I gulp and bite my lip again out of frustration. When she parts her lips and takes my nipple into her mouth; I melt and moan as she again, chuckles. Her breaths are tickling my skin even more than before. I hadn't realized I'd done it; but I've got my hands in her hair and I'm holding her to my breast as my hips are trying to press up against her. She takes my hands, one at a time, and returns them to their position above my head. *Oh yeah!* I remind myself, *Starfish*.

I squirm and make a strange little squeal because of the strain, the effort, to behave myself as my lover wishes. My girlie sounds are a turn-on for her and she chuckles low as she kisses lightly all over my tummy. Her breaths and her hair are tickling my skin. My hips are pumping in response to her every touch; every tickle of her breath.

My pussy needs her touch and I have no control over my body as she kisses across my groin and the tops of my legs. It's as though I'm chasing her with my pussy, trying to catch her mouth. She giggles and lifts her head high so she can watch my comedy of movements.

My clit is swollen rock-hard and if she doesn't go down on me soon I'm gonna come without her even touching it. I'm breathing so hard, my chest is obscuring my vision of her each time I breathe in. I have to keep licking my lips because my rapid breathing keeps drying them out. I can only keep my hands above my head if I ball them into tight fists and drive them into the pillow. I have to keep my mouth open because breathing through my nose isn't giving me enough air. But now that my mouth is open I'm groaning loud enough to wake our daughter. I resort to biting my tongue to keep quiet while my lover, my wife, the center of my world, starts gently nibbling the insides of my thighs. She chuckles and each breath against my skin causes me to clench the muscles in my pussy. It's as if she's touching me there anyway; every clench of my muscles moving my clit in a way that her tongue or her lips might.

Okay, so now I'm groaning with each change of breath in and out. I know I'm loud and her saying, "Shush!" isn't helping anymore. I need her mouth on my clit. I need her fingers in my pussy. I need her tongue to lick away my frustration and give me release. And I need it, NOW! I chase her mouth with my pussy and cry-out each time I miss. She chuckles as she watches my wet pussy bounce around just out of reach of her face. Her chuckling breaths are now repeating against my wetness and the sensation is driving me completely wild. She looks me in the eye – a serious look – one that says, *behave*, without making a sound. Then she looks at my pussy, opens her mouth and moves toward me. I swear, I was coming even before her lips encircled my salty lips and sucked all of it deep inside her mouth. Her tongue sought out and found my clit and I was lost in that moment for what felt like hours. When I finally drew another breath, I realized her fingers were deep inside me and I started coming all over again. I looked down at her with all the love and devotion I have for her and realize, I have both hands full of her hair, pulling her face tightly to my pussy. I let go and it's her turn to groan with relief.

I don't know how she knows it. Maybe it's from twelve years of practice at making love to me. I don't know. But she knows exactly how to make me come and come and come again, and then, she knows exactly when to stop.

When she rips off her dress and moves her body up and lies on top of me and cuddles every part of my body with every part of hers – well – it just doesn't get any better than that.

Okay. Now you can smile.

The End

Déjà Vu

Matilda sat at the counter of the café holding open her newspaper and reading a short human interest story. *Not nearly enough of these 'feel good' stories are printed anymore. At least not ones with a happy ending like this one*, she smiled to herself. Occasionally, she would lean forward and reach for her coffee cup, taking a sip as she turned to the next page. Each time she returned her cup to its saucer on the countertop, she would take the opportunity to look around the café: scanning the faces of the patrons; searching for one in particular. *If I don't see her today; I'll call*, she thought to herself and then grimaced. *I hope that doesn't make me look too needy.*

She'd been back in town almost a week and had taken her afternoon coffee at the same café each day. She had only a few more days to go and she would be flying out again. *To Mongolia of all places*, she thought as she shook her head. *A week to get into the mine site and a week to get back out, just to do three days-worth of work!* She shook her head again and then returned to her newspaper, browsing an advertisement for a therapeutic massage service at a local day spa. *Mmm, maybe that's all I'm needing.* She took another sip from her cup and again scanned the room for new faces.

"Looking for me?" A softly spoken voice came from behind her. For a moment she thought it may have been only her imagination and then she acknowledged that unmistakable scent of expensive cologne – the scent of Chase. She shivered as the owner of the scent bent to whisper in her ear, "….I hope." Matilda gasped as the tickle of breath in her ear and on her neck coursed through her body, clutching at her center and making her wet.

She closed her eyes and swallowed hard as her chest heaved. She turned to speak. Looking into bottomless blue eyes she opened her mouth and…forgot what she was about to say. She was lost in the hunger in those eyes; in the expression that promised a pleasure she could already feel on her skin.

Only when the eyes shifted their focus to the open newspaper page in her lap, was Matilda able to compose herself enough to say, "Actually…. Yes, I was." Then she too, looked down at the paper, now too self-conscious to risk looking back into those eyes.

"Interested in a Day Spa?" asked Chase as she moved to sit on the counter-stool next to Matilda's. She motioned to the waitress for coffee and nodded her appreciation to find it already on its way to her.

"No!" said Matilda, shaking her head, "But the massage menu was taking my interest."

"Really," said Chase with piqued interest as she returned her cup to its saucer on the countertop. "I know a good masseuse, if you're interested in a recommendation?"

"Let me guess?" retorted Matilda finally able to look Chase in the eye again. The upturned corners of Chase's mouth catching her attention and causing her to realize that the face was in fact, even more beautiful than she'd remembered.

"You'd be wrong." Chase smiled genuinely, showing off her white teeth framed by soft pink lips. She fiddled at the back pocket of her jeans and quickly thumbed a number into the mobile phone she'd retrieved from there. "Suzette! I'll be needing Helga this afternoon." She didn't wait for an answer before ending the call and slipping the phone back into her jeans pocket.

Matilda tried to refrain from studying the crotch of Chase's jeans while Chase was distracted with her phone. "Not today, I'm afraid." Chase said softly. Matilda looked up quickly and then – embarrassed to realize that she had been sprung for her studious gaze – quickly looked back at her newspaper and blushed a deep crimson. "Are you disappointed?" asked Chase, watching for Matilda's response over the rim of her coffee cup. She took a quick sip and replaced the cup without taking her eyes from Matilda.

Matilda smiled and breathed in deeply, still not able to look up from her paper. She shook her head slowly, "No, I was just…curious." She shrugged and then shivered as she squeezed her thighs together while reminiscing over their previous encounter. She sighed inwardly and felt her nipples tighten and swell against the bodice of her sundress. Exhaling a shaky breath she flicked a long curl from her face and looked again into Chase's eyes. "I'm glad to see you again." She smiled almost timidly as her eyes moved quickly over the features of Chase's face. The perfectly arching dark eyebrows; the high cheekbones; the delightfully protruding lips that transformed before her eyes, into a crooked smile of satisfaction. Matilda looked back to Chase's depthless pools of blue and smiled, too.

"Well," said Chase as she reached again for her coffee cup. She took a large swallow while she waited for the waitress behind the counter to turn back their way. Catching her gaze Chase motioned for a combined bill.

"Oh, you don't have to do that." Matilda said as she took her purse from her leather handbag. "It's my turn anyway." She removed some notes from her purse and placed them on the counter. "Keep the change," she said as she smiled and waved to the waitress.

They both stood and Chase took Matilda by the hand as she led the way out of the Café. Matilda couldn't help her smile, or her heart thumping against her chest. She looked down at their clasped hands and smiled even more broadly as she followed the line of Chase's arm. She watched the muscular bicep ripple as Chase tugged her along and wove their way through the mass of tables between them and the door. The armhole of Chase's tank top showed just the beginnings of the curve of a breast and betrayed the braless state beneath. Matilda took in Chase's slim form as she willingly followed along behind. She took the time to appreciate how sexy Chase's ass looked in those jeans and noted each buttock taking a turn at bobbing up slightly as she walked along. *Oh, she is so hot! And I am so horny!*

Out on the street, Chase turned in the opposite direction of her house. "Where are we going?" Matilda asked, suddenly alarmed that she might not be spending any intimate time with Chase.

"I was actually on my way to the store when I looked in through the window of the café and saw you. If you're not in a huge hurry, I'll just stop and pick up a few things before we head back?" Chase pointed at the supermarket on the next corner.

"Of course," said Matilda and motioned for Chase to lead-on.

As they walked about the supermarket with Chase consulting a list that she'd produced from the front pocket of her jeans, Matilda had a feeling she'd not felt before with anyone. There was something about sharing this activity with Chase that she found…appealing. A sense of…ordinariness. *Yes. Ordinary couples would do this together with no sense of value for the completeness it offers their lives together. The sort of thing you'd only miss if you didn't have it,* she thought sadly.

Oblivious to Matilda's musings, Chase smiled at having found the can she'd been looking for and dropped it into her basket before draping an arm carelessly over Matilda's shoulder. Matilda smiled and felt her eyes become half-lidded at the exhilaration of that moment. *I would love to get used to this.*

The shop order fitted neatly into a single bag at the checkout, leaving Chase with a free hand to offer Matilda. Matilda took it keenly as Chase tugged her alongside and together they left the store. The walk to Chase's house was more an afternoon stroll as Chase asked after Matilda's movements since they'd last been together. Once again, Matilda had feelings of appreciation for the ordinariness of it all.

They entered through the front gate at Chase's house and Matilda intuitively took the shopping bag from Chase to allow her the use of both hands to check the mailbox. That done, they walked in silent synchronicity up the steps and across the porch to the front door.

As they neared the door it opened. Matilda was about to offer a greeting, expecting Suzette to be holding the door for them. She was surprised to see a blonde haired woman with a large bosom in a white uniform.

Chase immediately performed the introduction, "Ah! Helga. This is Matilda. Matilda, please say hello to Helga – your masseuse."

Helga smiled warmly and looked Matilda up and down, assessing her, as she said in a thick Swedish accent, "I am pleasing to be make you acquaintance, damen." She bowed her head and made a slight curtsey.

Matilda smiled, returned the greeting and then stopped suddenly, momentarily awash with a curious sense of déjà vu. "Have we met before?" she asked politely.

Helga shook her head as she moved back from the doorway and made more room for the pair to enter the house.

"I 'ave not 'ad you pleasure, lilla damen," Helga answered in her sing-song accent.

Matilda tried to hide her spontaneous smile for the woman's broken English. "Don't mind me, I'm obviously confused," waving her hand dismissively as she passed the buxom woman and crossed the threshold.

Chase took the bag of shopping from Matilda and held it up for Helga. She took it as well as the mail as it was passed to her. "I vill take deez, damen."

"Thank you, Helga. I assume everything is in readiness for us?"

"Ja, damen. In der living room, if you please?" Helga hurried off down the central hallway, toward what Matilda thought must have been the kitchen.

Chase nodded and took Matilda's hand, tugging gently to encourage her to follow, passed the stoop of the staircase on the right and through the doorway of the living room on the left. The room looked much the same as the last time they were in it. Only this time, in place of the medium-sized carved jarrah table, was a professional looking massage table. A clean towel draped over cushioned-top almost hid the shelf underneath, allowing Matilda to see that there were some things on the shelf, but not what they were.

Music played quietly, accompanied by a soothing Gregorian-style chant. Although Matilda could not place the music, she was aware that she liked it and found it calming. *How does she do this? How does she always know exactly how to put me at ease?*

The two carved chairs belonging to the table were still there. They were placed to one side, nearer the windows and, next to them, the small table usually used for the eftpos machine near the front door when it was time to settle the account. On this table was a small platter of cheese, fruit, nuts and crackers, as well as a bottle of that lovely red wine Matilda and Chase had shared the last time they were in this room. Again, the thought of their last meeting caused a surge of sensations through Matilda's body, culminating between her legs and causing her to shiver and catch her breath.

Chase stopped to close the living room doors while Matilda walked over to the massage table and ran her hand over its surface; shifting the towel as she went. The table surface was soft leather that felt as though it had been coated with a layer of thin oil. Matilda drew her fingers to her nose and appreciated the aromatic scent. She was unable to discern its' exact composition, *Cinnamon, perhaps, but something else as well.* Then she noticed the oil warmer at the head of the massage table. *Ah! That's probably where the other aroma is coming from.* "Mmm, what a delightful aroma."

"We need to get you ready for your massage," Chase said as she motioned to take Matilda's handbag from her. Matilda allowed the straps of the bag to fall from her shoulder and handed over the bag. Chase placed it on the table and then facing Matilda, reached around to unbutton the sundress at Matilda's back, bringing their bodies closer together. Chase managed to undo the first button and moved to undo the second before she was distracted by Matilda's closeness. She stood motionless as she studied Matilda's face. Looking longingly into Matilda's eyes. Then allowing her gaze to dart about

Matilda's face, taking in the fair skin; the faint freckles across her nose and cheeks; the deep rich pink lips that were parting slightly; the deep pink tongue tip that slowly moistened them.

Chase became aware that she too, was moistening her lips in a mindless mimic. "Matilda," she whispered as she lowered her head and brushed her lips softly against Matilda's.

Matilda groaned lightly and ran her hands up Chase's sides and cupped her breasts through her yellow tank top. Chase's nipples hardened and pressed against Matilda's palms.

Chase leaned against Matilda's hands and deepened their kiss. Her tongue tip traced Matilda's lips in a silent request for entry.

Matilda groaned again as she opened her mouth to suck Chase's tongue inside. Their breathing became rapid as each pressed their hips forward into the other searching for some measure of release.

Chase broke the kiss and Matilda rested her head against Chase's chest. Her eyes closed as Chase kissed her hair and held her close. Matilda moved her hands to Chase's back and immersed herself in the pleasure of just being held.

They stood that way, gently swaying together for a few more moments before Chase said, "Matilda?"

"Mmm?" replied Matilda.

"The massage?"

Matilda breathed in Chase's scent and then nodded. "Yes, of course," she said as she turned to allow Chase to undo the remainder of the buttons on her sundress.

Chase held one of the shoulder straps as she allowed the dress to fall almost to the floor. She knelt slightly to help Matilda step out of the dress and then carefully laid it on top of the towel on the table. Matilda turned back to face Chase. She was not wearing a bra. Her small white breasts were exposed and Chase could not take her eyes away from Matilda's raised and hardened nipples. She leaned forward and gently kissed each one as she slipped Matilda's panties over her hips and let them fall to the floor. She kissed her way down past Matilda's belly-button and nuzzled the small triangle of brunette curls as she blindly felt for and retrieved the panties.

Matilda held Chase's head with both hands as she pressed Chase's face into her. She needed Chase. She needed her mouth on her. She needed Chase's tongue on her clit. Matilda's heart rate leapt and her breathing became shallow and rapid. "Oh, Chase. Fuck me, please!"

Chase chuckled soft and low, "Not yet, Princess," She said and then stood quickly, reaching out to hold Matilda as she wavered off balance. Chuckling again, Chase said, "We'd better get you on the table." Chase pushed the towel and clothes aside and supported Matilda while she sat down on the massage table. Chase stooped again. This time to remove Matilda's sandals. She placed them together on the floor and then pushed them safely away, under the massage table. Standing again, Chase neatly folded Matilda's few pieces of clothing and placed them and her handbag on the back of the couch near to the other side of the room.

She returned to the massage table with one of the cushions from the couch for Matilda to use as a pillow as she lay on her back. Chase took the towel and draped it across Matilda to cover her from her breasts to mid-thigh. Matilda smiled appreciatively at Chase's concern for her modesty. Chase smiled back and then walked to the small table and selected a few pieces of fruit from the platter. She popped a grape into her mouth and walked back to Matilda. She held a large strawberry just above Matilda's lips and watched as she took a bite. A small amount of the strawberry's juice found its way to Matilda's chin and Chase leant over her, licking up the fluid and then kissing the moistened spot. Matilda murmured in delight at the flavorsome fruit and Chase smiled with satisfaction. Turning, Chase returned to the little table. Matilda wondered which piece of fruit Chase would select for her next and was surprised when Chase sat down on a chair instead and leaned forward to open a small drawer at the front of the little table. She reached in and withdrew a small bell, rang it and then returned it to the open drawer.

Matilda watched as Chase lifted the wine bottle revealing two wine glasses that had been hidden behind the bottle. Chase filled both glasses and after replacing the bottle on the table, picked up one of the glasses and inhaled the aroma. Her approval was evident by her pleased expression and a purring sigh. She picked up another grape, this one had its stalk still attached. She stood and walked to Matilda while carefully dipping the grape into the wine.

Matilda smiled as Chase approached and carefully lifted the grape out of the wine. Matilda opened her mouth, expecting the grape to be popped in. Instead, Chase held the grape just above Matilda's lips and allowed the wine to drip from it onto her tongue. A sole drip remained on the base of the grape and Matilda stretched out her long tongue to lick it away. She smiled as she noted Chase's raised eyebrow and look of surprise. Chase dipped the grape into the wineglass once more and again watched the drips fall to Matilda's long tongue. Chase heard the door to the living room open and looked up to see Helga enter. She looked back down to Matilda and held the grape to her lips. Matilda grasped the grape between her teeth and waited while Chase plucked the stalk away. Chase nodded to Helga and retook her seat near the little table.

Helga nodded to Matilda as she reached under the table and retrieved a sanitary wipe. She quickly worked the wipe over her hands, between her fingers and around her nails. Once she'd disposed of the wipe, she rubbed her hands together; using the friction to both dry and warm her hands.

The buxom blonde then moved to the head of the table and dipped her fingers into the fragrant oil there; first one hand, then the other, before rubbing her hands together again. When she was pleased with the coating of oil, she moved to Matilda's side, picked up her hand and quickly massaged the oil into it. Helga's fingers were strong and her movements practiced and logical as she massaged Matilda's entire hand from wrist to fingers with equal pressure and attention.

Matilda breathed in deeply and closed her eyes as she exhaled and gave herself over to Helga's soothing ministrations.

Helga returned Matilda's hand to rest comfortably at her side. Then she quickly returned to the oil warmer and richly lathered each of her fingers and palms, before moving to the other side of the massage table, and administering equal attention to Matilda's other hand.

Helga moved back to the warmer for what was to become a predictable ritual. She evenly coated her hands in a quick and skilled manner, before walking to the foot of the massage table. She started at the ankle and deftly massaged Matilda's entire foot down to her toes with that same methodical attention. This time Helga collected a sanitary wipe on her way to the oil warmer. Cleansing her hands before dipping one hand after the other; working the oil into a warm lather before shifting back to the foot of the table and massaging Matilda's other foot.

Another sanitary wipe on her way to oil warmer, Helga looked at Chase, who had been nibbling on cheese and crackers and sipping at her wine, and lifted her chin in query.

"Roll over onto your tummy, Matilda." Chase said with a little wink at Helga. Matilda turned her head and directed a sleepy gaze in Chase's direction. "Let Helga massage your back and get you really relaxed," explained Chase as she placed her glass back onto the little table next to her.

Matilda rolled over as Helga held the towel in place for her and then removed the pillow from under her head; returning it to the couch. Matilda fidgeted to get comfortable and placed her face down though the table's cut-away. She tucked her arms into her sides and was pleasantly surprised at just how comfortable this position was. Below her face, under the table, a mirror was positioned and tilted slightly to one side. She thought she could see Chase in it – walking about the room. Then a hand appeared and grasped the edge of the mirror. She immediately recognized the hand as Chase's as it adjusted the angle of the mirror and then moved away. She watched in the mirror as Chase returned to her seat and sat down.

Chase turned, picked up her wine glass and faced back toward Matilda, spying her face in the mirror, she raised her glass to Matilda and smiled before taking a sip of the wine.

Helga returned to the oil warmer at the head of the massage table and said calmly, "Und now ve begin." She reached over to move Matilda's hair away from her neck and clip it in a bundle at the back of her head. After recoating her hands, she coated Matilda's shoulders and neck with the warm, pleasing oil.

"Mmmm," Matilda breathed, closing her eyes. When she opened them again, she could see Chase, wineglass in one hand and circling her own nipple with the forefinger of the other. Matilda groaned again, but this time it was not because of the therapeutic pressure being applied by Helga's skilled fingers.

Chase looked back at Matilda and smiled – a very naughty smile – as Matilda groaned again. When her nipple was easily discernible as a raised and hardened protuberance through her tank top, Chase stopped, swapped her wineglass to the other hand and began circling her other nipple.

Matilda licked her dried lips and groaned lightly again as Chase gave her yet another naughty and self-satisfied smile. Matilda could feel her own nipples hardening in sympathy and her body felt as though it were vibrating slightly from her breasts down to her center.

Helga reached out and moved Matilda's arms up and rested them on the table above Matilda's head. Coating her hands again with the warm and fragrant oil; she set about massaging both of Matilda's arms at the same time. Matilda broke out in goose bumps and Helga looked over at Chase to nod and smile.

Noting Helga's silent feedback, Chase grinned and reached to the table to retrieve a strawberry. She dipped it into the wine and then held it up as she tilted her head back and caught the drips of wine on her tongue. Moving her tongue up and down suggestively before retracting it back into her mouth. She looked at Matilda in the mirror and took a slow sensual bite from the fruit savoring as she chewed and swallowed. Then she licked the remainder of the piece of fruit watching as Matilda tongue moistened her lips again before swallowing hard. Chase could see that Matilda had begun to breathe more heavily. She smirked as she popped the rest of the strawberry into her mouth, took one more little sip of the wine and then placed her glass back onto the table.

Helga reached over Matilda's head and began to massage her ribs and sides, brushing at the sides of Matilda's breasts as she went.

Matilda closed her eyes for a moment, she could feel herself becoming wet and could not determine if it were more from Chase's behavior or Helga's. When she opened her eyes again,

Chase was sitting with her legs apart. Massaging her own center through her tight fitting jeans. Matilda moaned a little more loudly and before she could stop herself had pressed her hips down against the table.

Chase smiled at her success and then reached down and undid her sandals giving Matilda a view of her cleavage and breasts, untamed in their braless state. Having undone the clasps of her sandals, Chase kicked them off and as she slowly sat up again, she allowed her hands to trace the insides of her legs all the way back to her crotch. She closed her eyes against the pleasure of kneading her center with the fingertips of both hands. Chase's chest heaved and she opened her mouth to release a throaty groan as she allowed her head to drop back for a moment.

Helga lifted the towel and folded it over so that only Matilda's ass was covered by it. It tickled Matilda's skin as Helga moved the towel causing Matilda to quiver with delight at the sensation. When Helga's hands began to massage her back, they were warm and slippery with oil.

Matilda watched in her mirror as Chase moved her hands to unclasp the button of her own jeans, revealing her belly button. Both hands then moved up to circle her own nipples, so very lightly, with just the tips of her fingers. Again Matilda was unable to prevent herself from driving her hips against the surface of the massage table. Once each nipple was again excited and bulging, Chase let her hands slip down her front and while one held one side of her jeans, the other unfastened its zipper. She pressed each fold aside to give Matilda a view of the tender skin beneath and then delved in deeply with her right hand. She slipped her fingers in under her thong and cleaved her own folds. Her face told the story of the pleasure she was able to give herself, and when her left hand made its way under her tank top to her right nipple, she groaned again.

Helga's hands left Matilda's back. It was a few seconds before Matilda even noticed. When she did she held her breath, expecting her towel to be completely removed. When Helga's hands returned they were warm and slippery again, but on Matilda's left leg – not her buttocks.

Matilda returned her attention to Chase who now had her tank top pushed up under her armpits; exposing both breasts. She watched as Chase moved both hands to her breasts, cupping them and pushing them upward. Chase spread her fingers as she slipped both hands over her breasts, catching her nipples between her fingers. She watched herself massage her own breasts; squeezing her nipples and rolling them between her fingers. Her hips rose upward in response and Matilda's hips moved in unison.

Chase allowed her breasts to slip from her fingers as she crossed her arms, smoothing the skin from her breasts to her armpits, catching her tank top and lifting it up and over her head. She held the tank top high for a few seconds and then let it drop to the floor behind her chair.

Bending her elbows, she placed her hands in her short brunette hair while lolling her head about to feel her fingers pushing through the short strands. Her breasts were bobbing here and there, as if in a dance of their own, in time with the chanting and the music.

Helga left momentarily, but this time Matilda predicted she would be returning to her right leg with warm, oily hands. She was not disappointed, or distracted from Chase who was now standing and swaying her hips in time to the music. She watched Chase pushing her hands slowly down over her hips; moving her jeans a little downward. Then smoothing her hands back over every exposed curve of her body while moving in an erotic trancelike dance.

Turning to face away from Matilda, Chase allowed her jeans to fall halfway down her buttocks while swaying her hips to and fro. Her yellow thong was evident above and between her buttocks as she slowly bent forward. Never missing a beat with her swaying dance moves, she pushed the jeans down over her hips and past her knees. The thong was wet and clinging to every fold of Chase's pussy, which seemed to Matilda, to be dancing, too.

Chase stepped out of the jeans and as she danced and turned back toward Matilda. She hooked her thumbs into the thong and stretched them out to the sides before lowering them enough to expose the beginnings of a triangle of short cropped curls.

Matilda hadn't noticed that Helga had stopped massaging until she felt the towel being completely removed. She held her breath. Unable to take her eyes from Chase, she waited with immense anticipation for what would come next. When her masseuse returned, Matilda quickly relaxed when the warm oily hands on her buttocks felt surprisingly welcomed.

Chase continued to run her hands over her own body, caressing every curve in just the way Matilda would, if she were able.

Chase hooked her thumbs in the thong again and this time worked them down and over her thighs, until it fell to the floor. When Chase ran her fingers through the thatch of curls and between her legs, Matilda was certain she could feel that caress as if it were on her own flesh. Every movement of Chase's fingers over her own folds, felt as if she were being touched in that very same way. And then she realized, *I am being touched in that very same way.* Helga was touching her.

Matilda's eyes widened as she looked at Chase in her mirror. *Does she know? Has she noticed yet?*

Chase offered a seductive wink and smiled, "Just relax, Matilda. Give yourself up to it."

Matilda took a deep breath and complied. She relaxed herself again more quickly than she would have thought possible and surmised that it was due to the massage that Helga had so expertly administered. Or perhaps she was drunk on the heady fragrance of the aromatic oil. The more she relaxed, the more daring the massage Helga was now concentrating on her buttocks and the backs of her thighs.

Chase continued to sway her hips to the music and Matilda was once again mesmerized by the erotic dance. Chase ran her hands over her own body clutching at her breasts and roughly tweaking each of her nipples between forefinger and thumb. She swayed her head and moaned her self-approval as she turned and slowly danced her way back to the chair. Still swaying her hips she bent over and leant her weight on the chair.

Matilda watched, spellbound as Chase arched her back and spread her legs wide, completely exposing her pussy to Matilda's mirror. Chase was swaying her hips in time to the music as she reached between her legs with one hand and ran a finger from her wet center forward to her clit. She breathed out heavily, as did Matilda, when Helga replicated the fingering stroke.

Chase circled her clit with her fingertip and then slowly traced her folds. Matilda became completely aroused by Helga mimicking those same caresses she was watching Chase perform, on herself.

Matilda held her breath and her mouth opened in anticipation, as she watched Chase move her finger toward and then into her own vagina. The sensation of that penetration was incredible. Matilda was so wet and the stimulation so welcome, that she began to yelp every time she exhaled.

Helga moved Matilda's right leg, bending it at the knee and encouraging her to tuck it under her body slightly. Matilda's sex was now completely exposed allowing Helga to penetrate her more deeply and more purposefully.

Chase worked her finger in and out, in and out; breathing rapidly and hissing her excitement. Her legs began to quiver as though they may crumble from beneath her at any moment. She obviously had no choice but to turn and sit on the chair. She looked over to Matilda and seeing that Helga had repositioned Matilda's leg; lifted her own right leg, hugged it to her chest, resting her foot on the seat of the chair. Once again exposing the full view of her pussy to Matilda.

Chase reached into the table drawer, which had been left open after returning the bell, and retrieved a 7" dildo. She held it to her mouth and licked it, heavily coating it with saliva before lowering it to her pussy. Helga slowly removed her finger from Matilda's pussy and then suspended all movement at her entrance. Chase looked up at Matilda with that same naughty smile as she slowly pressed the dildo into herself. At the same time, Helga re-entered Matilda with an identical slow thrust, firstly with two fingers and in unison with Chase's motions, added a third.

Matilda groaned loudly, "Oh, yes, that's so good. Just like that."

Chase threaded her right arm between the thigh and calf of her raised leg and took control of the phallus, working it in and out with shorter but faster thrusts. Her freed hand was now able to stroke her clit. She made a small inverted 'v' shape with her first two fingers, sliding them one each side of her clit and closing them together to administer an exquisite pressure.

Helga pressed her other hand against Matilda's hip in an effort to slide it under Matilda's body. Matilda lifted her hip and gave Helga the access she needed to slip her hand in underneath. She pressed the hood of Matilda's clit together and gently squeezed while still moving the fingers of her other hand in and out of Matilda's pussy.

"Mmmm." Both Matilda and Chase exclaimed in accord. Each began breathing more rapidly.

"Faster," Chase demanded of Helga. "I'm getting close."

"Oh! Me too," grunted Matilda. "Faster! Please!" she strained, "Faster!"

Chase hastened, moving the dildo in and out of herself so quickly her hand was almost a blur. The sounds of her wet pussy sucking at the phallus with each outward motion drove Matilda to point of orgasm. Helga braced herself and pounded her fingers deeply and more quickly into Matilda while continuing to caress Matilda's clit with her other hand.

Chase threw her head back and lifted her hips slightly from the chair; screaming with her rush of orgasm. "Matilda!"

"YES!" Matilda screamed, "YES! I'm coming!" Her body jolting uncontrollably. Her hands slipping under her body, grasping her nipples and squeezing them mercilessly. "Oh! Yes!" she screamed as immediately, a second rush of orgasm filled her. She held her breath and writhed: her eyes closed, her face flushed, her sweat dripping onto the mirror below.

Finally, Matilda's body relaxed instantly and completely. She was able to take a deep breath and whisper, "Ohhhhhh, yeaaahhhh!" She opened her eyes, looked into her mirror at Chase and beamed.

Chase shuddered. Her spine tingled and goose bumps appeared on her skin. Her chest heaved and after a few moments, she recovered enough to offer Matilda another of those naughty smiles.

Helga slowly removed her hands and quickly covered Matilda with the towel. "I am returning in moments wid robes," she explained as she left the room.

Matilda slowly pushed herself up onto an elbow and looked over at Chase. She shook her head slightly as she gazed at Chase in wonderment. Her smile broadening, she raised her free arm and with her palm facing upper-most and simply said, "Wow!" before breathing out heavily and letting her arm collapse back to her side.

When Helga returned, Chase had managed to stand and ready herself to accept the heated robe and pull it on for herself, while Helga helped Matilda to sit up and enrobe. Helga collected the towel from the massage table and hurried over to the small table to close its drawer. Then, stooping with the towel over her hand, Helga collected the dildo that Chase's pussy had spat onto the floor in her previous throes of orgasm, quickly wrapping and tucking the package under her arm. Helga then re-positioned the chairs at the table so that Matilda and Chase could sit in comfort and share the remainder of the platter and wine together. A final, professional nod to Chase, and Helga ushered her towel-wrapped package from the room and closed the doors behind her.

Chase walked over to Matilda and pressed her body between Matilda's legs. Reaching behind Matilda's head, Chase released the hair clip and placed it on the massage table next to Matilda. Then she gently tussled Matilda's hair back into those curly ringlets that framed her face. Looking into Matilda's eyes, Chase held Matilda's face between her palms while she leant in and kissed her deeply. Her tongue slowly, passionately explored Matilda's mouth. She reached around and grabbed Matilda's ass, pulling Matilda toward herself and pressing Matilda's crotch hard against her abdomen at the edge of the table.

Matilda wrapped her arms around Chase's neck and squirmed in the embrace, pulling her head slightly away from Chase's kiss to allow her to tilt her head the other way and enjoy the passion of the kiss anew.

Chase mumbled against Matilda's lips, "Time for one more?"

Matilda chased Chase's mouth, not yet ready to relinquish the strong probing tongue and soft, moist lips. She sucked Chase's tongue into her mouth and bit down provocatively on its shaft.

Chase moaned with the pleasure of the sensation of Matilda's teeth against such delicate tissues. Then withdrew it, just long enough to entreat, "Please say 'yes'," before plunging her tongue into Matilda's mouth again. Chase cupped Matilda's ass again and pressed herself hard against Matilda's pussy.

Matilda ran her hands up and down Chase's back as she wrapped her legs about Chase's body and pulled herself in closer. Squeezing chase with her legs allowed Matilda to maintain that wonderful pressure against her swollen pussy.

Matilda's hips began undulating with her increasing desire.

"Yes," she managed, gasping for breath in such a fervent embrace.

Chase pushed her hands in under Matilda's robe, exposing Matilda's breasts slightly as she slid her hands around behind Matilda and cupped her buttocks again. She squeezed, pulling Matilda toward herself while smoothly undulating her hips in time with the music. Chase's abdomen was sliding against Matilda's wet pussy.

Matilda moaned and dropped her head to Chase's shoulder.

Chase grabbed hard at Matilda's ass again and Matilda threw her head back and cried out aloud; the ache of Chase's grasp heightening her arousal.

Matilda further opened her robe and lifting a breast, held it up while she roughly grasped a handful of Chase's short cropped hair and dragged her mouth to a hard and waiting nipple. "Suck it!" Matilda demanded.

Chase took the nipple into her mouth and sucked hard.

"Bite it!" Matilda rasped, jerking Chase's head by her hair.

Chase moved a hand around to cup Matilda's other breast. Discovering a distended nipple there, Chase squeezed it roughly between her fingers and the palm of her hand. She became so wet, she could feel her fluids moistening the insides of her upper thighs. "Oh, yeah!" she managed with Matilda's nipple held firmly between her teeth; flicking her tongue back and forth across its apex.

Matilda gasped, exhaled quickly and then gasped again. "On your knees!" she screamed and Chase immediately knelt and sniffed at Matilda's thatch of curls. Matilda used both hands to grasp handfuls of Chase's hair and thrust Chase's face between her legs. "Lick it!" She bellowed. Chase's legs quivered with her arousal. She licked at Matilda's pussy, struggling to maintain her concentration as she pressed her own thighs together; squeezing her engorged clit. She groaned loudly into Matilda's pussy and forced herself to perform for Matilda, even though unable to prevent herself from writhing her own hips in an attempt to relieve her throbbing center.

Chase managed to think clearly enough to continue her finger-play over Matilda's nipple. Moving her other hand so as to be able to cup both breasts while working her tongue over Matilda's clit.

"Tongue fuck me!" commanded Matilda in a deep growl, now using Chase's hair to pull and push Chase's face to and fro. Chase poked her tongue out as hard as far as she could and, as best she was able under Matilda's punishing pace; wiggled its tip in strong strokes against the insides of Matilda's vagina. She was rewarded by Matilda's high-pitched gasps and groans.

The motion of tonguing Matilda's pussy played well for Chase. It allowed her to maneuver her own clit to better use the pressure her thighs produced. In this way Chase was able to squeeze her own clit with each forward thrust.

Chase became overwhelmed with the sensations: Matilda's tightly pursed nipples pressed, one against each palm; Matilda's groaning, gasping breath blowing the hair about the top of her scalp; Matilda's pulsing pussy sucking at her face and tongue with each change in direction; the hot-pain at her temples from Matilda's relentless grip on her hair; and, her own, throbbing clit, sliding amongst the wetness at her center, straining with each clutch of pressure from her thighs pressing together.

"Suck me!" Matilda demanded and pulled Chase's face hard against her pussy. Chase complied, but that last command – *'Suck me,'* – was such a turn-on for her. The expression echoed in her ears, and trickled down her body like warm syrup. Those words – *'Suck me,'* – caressed her own folds and vibrated against her clit, melting her into orgasm. Chase's hips halted their writhing pattern and she held her breath. She was coming, and coming in a way that washed over her entire body like a mild but tremendously welcomed electric shock that seemed to make time itself stand still.

When Chase finally snorted in a gasping breath, she realized that she was still sucking

Matilda's luscious, salty lips. When she looked up at Matilda's face, all she could see was Matilda's throat and lurching breasts. Matilda's head was thrown back. Then Chase realized Matilda's thighs were pressed in a vice-like grip against the sides of her face and Matilda's hands were firmly pressing Chase's head against her pussy.

Matilda was coming.

Chase had no idea when Matilda had succumbed to orgasm, but she *was still* coming; a prolonged rumbling moan gurgling in her throat.

Suddenly, the moaning stopped and Chase was thrown to the floor. When she looked back up, Matilda sat gripping the edge of the massage table: her eyes closed, her mouth open and her chest heaving.

Chase scrambled to her feet while quickly running her fingers through her hair in an attempt to calm her tender scalp. She pressed her hips between Matilda's thighs and wrapped her arms around the obviously drained body.

Matilda rested her head on Chase's shoulder as sweat poured from her brow. She rested there with her eyes closed while Chase gently stroked her hair and rubbed her back until her breathing slowed to normal.

Chase leaned back and Matilda looked up into eyes that held concern for her. Matilda smiled and reached up for a kiss. Tender, soft lips claimed hers, moistening and rejuvenating her own.

Chase pulled her down from the table and they finished the kiss standing and swaying together, in time to the music.

Taking Matilda's hand, Chase led her to the table and sat her on a chair. They chatted like best friends and shared their fill of the wine and nibbles.

Reluctantly, Matilda motioned at having to leave. Chase helped her dress, holding her clothes out for her and steadying her as stepped back into her panties. Then Chase knelt to the floor and slipped Matilda's sandals back onto her feet and fastening the buckles.

While still on her knees, Chase held Matilda closely to her, nuzzling her through her clothing.

"Stop!" said Matilda, "You'll get me all horny again and I feel so wonderfully sated at the moment."

Chase smiled and shrugged, "Oh yes, that's right! I forget sometimes that the service is for you, not me." She climbed back to her feet, suitably chagrined and offered, "Can't blame a girl for loving her job, can you?"

Matilda almost snorted in her laughter. She held her hand gently to Chase's face and rubbed her check with her thumb. Looking back and forth from one eye to the other she eventually stated, "You are such a find." She smiled a contented smile before collecting her handbag and fixing her hair and makeup in the mirror above the fireplace. When she was happy with her reflection, she returned to her seat at the little table with her wallet in hand.

Chase opened the drawer of the little table and pulled out the eftpos machine. She fingered a few buttons before handing it to Matilda who had her card out and ready.

Matilda pressed her visa card into the machine and then looked at the little screen, confused she said, "Oh, Chase, you haven't entered the fee."

"I'll leave that to you," Chase returned. "You set the amount. Whatever you feel the service was worth."

Matilda looked perplexed for a moment and then shrugged, "Very well." She made her selections and finalized the account before removing her card and handing the machine back to Chase.

Chase motioned to the door and then opened it for Matilda as though she were royalty. Matilda was charmed and smiled with appreciation.

Suzette was waiting by the front door to let her out. As she neared, Matilda looked at her intently. The little French maid seemed a little unnerved by the scrutiny. "All is well? No? Madame?" she asked.

Matilda looked back at Chase and rolled her eyes.

Chase bit her lip trying to hold back a smile and then chortled, "Would you believe they're twins?"

"Right!" said Matilda incredulously, "One born in France and the other in Sweden?" She looked back at Suzette and smiled as she walked past her and out the door, down the steps and out through the little front gate. Pulling it to behind her she stopped, smiled even more broadly and waved at the two women still standing at the threshold of the open door.

Suzette looked sideways at Chase as they waved back and discreetly asked, "Did we please her, mademoiselle?"

Chase glanced momentarily at Suzette and simply asked, "Can you say, 'Bali' in the time it takes to pack a bag, Little One?"

Matilda began her walk down the street recognizing the return of that confident spring in her step and easy smile on her face, *Mongolia*, she thought, *no problem!*

The End

First True Love

I can't remember a time when I wouldn't have considered myself to be gay. My friends often speak of how they were confused about their sexuality during adolescence. I have a very vivid memory of a wet dream I had about the time I noticed my first pubic hair. It involved one of my girlfriends from school. I spent the next twelve months secretly drooling over this young girl. Quite often she would catch me staring at her and tell me off for daydreaming. Little did she realize at the time that I was musing over the things I wanted so desperately to do to her body.

I dreamt of us going out on a picnic in a field of long green grass, delightfully speckled with outcrops of daisies and daffodils. Both of us lying naked on a soft woolen blanket and kept warm by a temperate sun. Occasionally, a gentle breeze would pass over us, tickling our skin and tantalizing our nipples to full erection. I would run my fingers through her long blonde hair while she moved her head a little with each loving stroke, and quietly groan her approval. We would kiss with warm, wet passion as we drew our bodies closer together. Ecstasy – as we allowed our nipples to touch and our legs to entwine, and then, at the most critical moment...my mum would wake me up for school. Why is it; I never quite made it to the best part in any dream? Sexual frustration became my way of life.

I never hated myself or doubted my feelings. Being gay was very natural to me. I was well aware of society's distaste of homosexuality (a taboo in the 70's) and even though I couldn't understand why people should feel that way, I was prepared to allow others to have their own opinions; after all, I had mine. Others were the ones with the 'acceptance problems,' not me, and it would be futile for me to take on their problems as my own. In short, I felt comfortable about myself. Not once did I wonder if I were abnormal nor did I ever believe it to be a fleeting thing or a stage I would grow out of as my mother may have wished for me. I was gay and that was that!

Perhaps I was more fortunate than most in that my mother was very supportive toward me. Although I'd never told her how I felt, she obviously just knew. Our chat about the "birds and bees" consisted of five minutes on heterosexual sex; maybe fifteen on menstruation; and thanks to my leading questions, a good half hour on homosexuality. She told me her opinion was that: "It takes all kinds to make up this world" and that basically, she would prefer the company of a kindly homosexual than a man who considered himself to be "God's gift to women." She told me she believed that homosexuals were not mentally deficient nor sexually depraved – just people who'd made a different set of choices. She said she felt that so long as they're not hurting or purposely offending anyone else, it was fine by her. (A surprisingly lenient opinion for the time and one that I was to test to its limits as the years wore on). She concluded our 'heart to heart' with one of her favorite adages: "If it feels right – it can't be wrong – for you".

Quite often I would have girlfriends from school stay over on weekends. Actually, every weekend. Sometimes two or three at a time. Mass orgies you're thinking? No, unfortunately not. However we would give each other these terrific body massages with Johnson's Baby Oil while listening to the latest hits on my stereo. We would feed each other chocolate and huddle closely together while we watched the Friday night "Creature Feature." If we cooked cakes it wasn't unusual to taste-test the mixture from each other's fingers. Strangely enough, my fingers were always heavily coated.

One night, not long after my fourteenth birthday, the girl I'd been drooling over for so long slept with me with only a pair of knickers on. Even though it was a hot night, I cuddled up to her and fondled her breast, it felt so good. Inexperience and a lack of confidence prevented it from going any further. She stayed quite often after that. We'd shower together and wash each other. Occasionally she would let me kiss her and always we would sleep together, naked, gently fondling one another until we drifted off to sleep. In retrospect, I guess it was all fairly tame and I was no doubt ignorant and clumsy, but at the time I was floating on cloud nine.

Eventually, my friends and I left school to go to technical college or to pursue job opportunities while I went on to university. Gradually we drifted apart and by the end of the following year I had no further contact with any of them. Including my blonde sweetheart who had decided by then to spend her nights with a boy from her college.

The beginning of the next year soon became enormously depressing. While I had plenty of opportunities to go out with different people I more often chose not to. Hanging out with heterosexual friends tended to bore me quickly. I spent some of my spare time with a workmate of my mother's. A gay woman. Although nothing was to happen between us she was helpful in providing me with literature about Lesbians. I readily took her into my confidence and she was always prepared to listen when I needed to talk.

Second semester became more interesting when we got a replacement professor for one of my classes. It was a small class, only eight students, which provided us with a perfect opportunity to have a very casual student/teacher rapport. This teacher was a stunning woman. Always perfectly groomed and attired in the very latest of fashion. She was regularly taken to task by the Dean over the clothes she wore and would laughingly share with our little class about how much "shit" she was in for what she was wearing that day. There was something very different and daring about this woman. We "clicked" immediately, her and I. She appreciated my sense of humor and encouraged me to employ it during our classes. If she drove past me on the way home she would sound her car-horn and wave goodbye to me. If we passed each other on campus she would always stop and make casual conversation. If she was organizing any special projects; I was the first she would ask for help. I enjoyed her classes most of all: the mutual respect; her passion for teaching; and, her ability to keep her students attentive and eager to learn.

However, our class, perhaps due to its size, was a little too casual. As we neared the end of semester we found ourselves running out of time to complete the required curriculum. In an effort to make up time it was decided that we would all congregate at her house for a film-study. The date and the time were set and we were all a little curious about this woman. If this was how she dressed, imagine what her house must look like.

The house was entirely the opposite of what I had anticipated. It was an old-style limestone town-house with French polished floors and a spiral staircase. Everything was neat and tidy, clean and shinning. It was obvious that a lot of thought had gone into the décor to ensure that it was in harmony with the era of the turn-of-the-century town-house. The reception room came off the entry hall and it was a beautiful room. A plush leather and carved wood Chesterfield lounge suite was situated in front of a blazing fireplace and between the lounge and the fire was a large oval-shaped shag-pile rug. In the center of the rug was a carved occasional table where she had set up the projector.

Eventually, the last few members of the class arrived and we were ready to begin. The projector was turned on and the lights were turned off. She focused the picture on the white wall and sat down beside me, laying her arm across the back of the lounge, and inexplicably, I snuggled into her side. A few minutes into the film she moved her arm across the back of the lounge and draped her hand over my shoulder. I looked up at her, stunned by this public display of affection. Many seconds passed before she casually turned her head and looked me straight in the eyes. Her eyes danced with the reflection of the flickering firelight as she breathed in deeply and exhaled heavily, holding my gaze throughout. Then, just as casually as before, she returned her gaze to the film and moved her arm back up the lounge. Her fingers, however, were still resting lightly on my shoulder. I was incapable of paying attention to anything other than her. I was ultra-aware of her every breath; every blink of an eyelid; every cautious squeeze of my shoulder. The first reel came to an end. The lights came on and she skillfully pretended that she needed her arm on the back of the lounge for support while she rose to her feet. While she was busy preparing the second, and last, reel for viewing, the other students chatted and laughed. I studied each of their faces. *Did any of them see what had happened? Apparently not. Was it all in my imagination? Was I making more of an innocent show of friendliness than I should? Yes, I must have been.*

She started the second reel of the film, the lights went off and she returned to my side and seemed to snuggle in close to me. After a while she draped her hand over my shoulder again and then, motioned with the tips of her fingers for me to lean into her as I had done before. My heart raced. It was pounding so loudly I was sure it was audible.

The second reel finished and out came the wine and cheese as we entered into discussion. After about an hour many of the class members began to leave and as the numbers dwindled, we set about cleaning up; packing away the projector; and ferrying the empty glasses and cheese platters to the kitchen. Finally, the lounge was tidied and I set about doing the dishes in the kitchen as the last of the class members left to go home – possibly not even aware I was still there.

She came back to the kitchen laughing as she told me about the car loads of youths waving and yelling at each other as they hung out of windows. She laughed and after a few moments, giggled to herself again and turned to face me. She became serious and stood studying my face.

"I should get going too," I said suddenly feeling a little uncomfortable. "It's getting late. Do you mind if I use your phone to call for a taxi?"

"It's not that late," she said glancing at the watch on her wrist. Then giving me a sideways look through that beautiful blonde hair, she asked, "Just stay for a cup of coffee and a chat? It's not like you have a class tomorrow or anything." She put the kettle on the stove and then looked at me as she pressed, "Okay?"

My heart was leaping out of my chest as I managed to choke out a feeble, "Okay."

I finished up the dishes and she smiled at me saying casually, "Take a seat back on the lounge and I'll bring it in."

I returned to my seat on the Chesterfield and watched the dancing fire and tried to calm my pounding heart while I waited. Shortly after, she came in carrying two cups of coffee and placed them on the occasional table. I made mention of how beautiful her home was and she explained a little about the many renovations she'd made. We spoke of many things and eventually the topic of conversation moved to members of the faculty. She made it more than obvious that the only members she wanted to make comment about were the females. Then of course, the obvious question. "So. Who's your favorite professor?

To which I naturally answered, "You, of course!"

"Why?" she asked, flicking her long blonde, curly hair over her shoulder. She placed her elbow on the back of the lounge and rested the side of her face in the palm of her hand.

I felt my face flush with immediate embarrassment as I stumbled over my answer. "Well…. 'cause you're fun,…" My mouth when dry, "…easy to talk to…." Clearing my throat and turning an even deep shade of red, "…you….dress nice….um…."

She chuckled, took my hand and placed it on her knee as she sidled closer to me and placed her arm around my shoulder. Silence. All I could do was stare at my hand resting on her knee – the flickering glow from the fire dancing on my fingers. I wanted to say something – the right thing – but I couldn't move, certainly not even enough to talk.

She placed her fingertips on my chin and gently motioned for me to look at her. I turned my head and gazed straight into her beautiful ice-blue eyes. She was heavenly. Femininely divine. A faultless complexion adorned with long dark-brown eyelashes, high cheek bones and lips that looked moist and inviting. The fire-lit room with its low lighting created the most romantic atmosphere and then she slowly leaned in and kissed me, softly, just for a moment. "Is it alright?" she asked.

"Yes… It's wonderful," I replied, my shaky voice betraying my nervous anxiety. She looked at my lips and I knew she was going to kiss me again. This kiss was so soft and tender – so warm. As our tongues touched a flood of warmth coursed through me, melting me, making my body grow so limp that I needed her arms to hold me upright. She held me close to her, running her hands up and down my back and charging my body with an almost electric exhilaration that culminated between my legs.

Our kissing session no doubt lasted some time, but even in retrospect, if it had lasted an eternity, it would not have been long enough. Her kisses were so sweet, tender and caring. Evoking emotions and sensations that were so all-consuming; saturating me in an ocean of euphoric bliss. She allowed her tongue to wander. Gently swirling up and down my neck and in and out of my ear. My self-consciousness faded more and more with every kiss. My hands became more and more animated and I found myself struggling to pull her white shirt-tail from her beige pants. She stopped kissing me, staring into my eyes. My heart sank as I dealt with the thought that I may have taken things too far.

"You've done this before, haven't you?" Her voice held a hint of surprise.

"Sort of."

"Who with?"

"You wouldn't know her," I said as I looked away.

"So how far did you go?" She smiled broadly. I didn't like the inflection of her tone. It made me feel even more anxious and self-conscious.

"Not far enough!" I answered as I stood and walked over to the fireplace. It had died down considerably, so I began stoking and placing more wood on it. I was a little annoyed at the inquisition. What did it matter what I'd done and who with? I glanced over my shoulder at her to see she was still sitting on the lounge. Unnecessarily stoking the fire became a good excuse not to look at her while I spoke. "I don't know if I can do everything right…. I've read a lot in books but," then my heart sank further still, *Had I given her a false impression of my sexual prowess?* "Do you only like virgins or something?" *Should I confide that, essentially, I am?*

"No," she chuckled heartily. "I didn't mean to offend you. Besides, I'm your teacher. I already know how good you are at putting theory into practice. You've nothing to worry about." She smiled broadly again as she sat forward, spread her legs and held her arms out to me saying, "Come here silly."

I moved from kneeling beside the fire to kneeling in front of her. She held me close to her and spoke softly into my ear. "You need only do what you feel you want to. Just do what you're comfortable with and if I do something you don't like, you can tell me to stop."

She began to cover my neck with tiny, wet, tender kisses. I shivered with excitement as she kissed her way back up to my ear and whispered, "It's your body. You have every right to say 'no.'" Placing her hands on my shoulders she gently pushed me away until once again I was looking into those beautiful blue eyes. "What do you want to do?" she asked.

Well! It seemed like I had been waiting an eternity for just this moment. The atmosphere couldn't have been more perfect – more electric. The woman couldn't have been more beautiful and here she was: offering me everything; assuming nothing. No pressure. No need to worry about performing to expectation. No fear. My self-consciousness had abated and my anxiety had welled into an incredibly wet intensity between my legs. The decision wasn't hard to make. "I want to make love to you." For a second my head seemed to buzz and I thought I might faint. I had to remind myself, *Breathe you idiot!*

She took her hands from my shoulders and said, "I'm all yours."

She sat back in the lounge and waited for my next move. I nervously unbuttoned her blouse and exposed her breasts. An all-over tan and no bra, *This woman is a knock-out,* I thought as I leaned forward and kissed her on the lips passionately, delving my tongue deeply into her mouth, while I tickled both sides of her neck with the tips of my fingers. I leaned away from her, just far enough to get her face into focus. Her eyes were closed and her rate of breathing had increased dramatically. I ran my fingertips down her neck, tickling as they moved over her chest and followed the curve of her well-rounded breasts. Then using only index fingers I ticked at her mushroom pink, up-turned nipples with slow circular motions until they became fully erect. Leaning forward I sucked her left nipple gently into my mouth, trying hard to remember to, at the same time, roll her right nipple between my thumb and forefinger. *Okay, that's about the sum total of my previous experience, right there. And let's face it my delivery isn't exactly smooth. Is she going to tell me to stop because I'm not good enough at it?* I heard her groan with pleasure and then she held the back of my neck with one hand and ran her the fingers of the other through my hair.

I released my oral grip, "Tell me what you want?" I asked as I moved to her other nipple and began sucking and licking it. I'd read that line in one of my books. *That ought to get me out of trouble.*

"Oh! That's beautiful." She replied impelling me to suck and lick more intently. I tried unsuccessfully to undo her trousers. She mused over my struggle for a while and then said in a soft, melodious tone, "Here. Let me."

I moved back a little and watched as she undid them, lifted her hips and pushed them down as far as her knees. She sat back on the lounge and looked up at me, "Take them off," she instructed. I placed one hand behind the back of each knee and reveled in the smoothness of her skin as I drew my palms down her calves moving her trousers downward at the same time to her ankles. One at a time, I lifted her legs and cupped her heel in my hand as I pushed the material away and off her foot with the back of my hand.

She leaned forward in order to remove her blouse; a slinky jiggle of her shoulders was all that was required to make it slip over her shoulders and down her arms. She held the blouse out to the side of the lounge and casually dropped it to the floor. I reached across and dropped her trousers on top of it. I leaned back on my haunches to return my attention to her and froze. My heart must have beating noticeably against my chest as I suddenly realized that she was sitting on the lounge, completely naked. My mind began to race, *What the fuck do I do, now? Don't stare at her, you idiot! Okay, just breathe.*

Her soft, velvety skin glowed in the firelight. Her eyes had deepened in color and yet remained surprisingly transparent, in a way that only blue eyes can do – truly sensuous in their depth. Looking into them was like looking into her soul. Her high cheek bones gave her face a constantly pleased expression. My gaze moved to her slightly parted lips. They seemed poised; ready to speak. I glanced back at her eyes. They had a knowing expression about them and I realized, *She knows she has a beautiful face and body and she's pleased that I'm taking the time to fully appreciate it.*

She relaxed her body further back into the lounge and spread her legs a little more so that I could see her pussy as well. Again I become conscious of staring, *Don't stare! Don't stare!* Her shoulders were broad and mildly muscular, as were her arms. Her perfectly proportioned, golden brown breasts moved voluptuously up and down with her breathing. Her flat stomach provided an erotic platter for her oval-shaped bellybutton. *Do I dare to look at her pussy? No, not yet!*

The tan on her feet was uneven. She obviously wore thongs or sandals while she was in the sun. Her legs were long, golden-brown and muscular. I noticed the tan on the inside of her thighs was lighter than the tan on the rest of her leg. *A natural, all over tan?* My eyes followed her thighs to her warm, wet pussy which was partly concealed by a thick thatch of blonde hair. *So she is a natural blonde, then.*

"Take your clothes off," she said without demand. I hesitated for a few seconds, startled by her sudden use of speech. I was self-conscious with the knowledge that my body was nothing in comparison to hers. She smiled at me and I stood while she watched with overt excitement as I too, stripped – naked.

   She held her arms out to me again and drew me down to sit on her knee. We kissed with heated passion and she motioned for me to lift one leg up onto the lounge. Having ensured my comfort she moved her hand down between my legs and began massaging my clit with slow circular strokes. My pussy was very wet and slippery. It was easy for her to slip her fingers in; working them in and out with deep rhythmical strokes. I kissed her strongly and rolled one of her nipples between my thumb and forefinger. She moved her fingers in and out of me faster and faster. I groaned loudly unable to contain my excitement and my body began to quiver uncontrollably. Nothing had ever felt this good before. I groaned loudly again as she delved her fingers as deeply as she could reach inside me and wriggled them against the wall of my vagina, almost violently. At the same time she ran her thumb skillfully back and forth across my clit. Waves of warmth engulfed me as I experienced my first G-spot orgasm. I'd had orgasms before. Lots of them – all on my own, of course – they were…not like this! This was definitely different, less intense perhaps but lasting much, much longer than the next orgasm I suddenly became aware my clit was giving me. This woman had, in effect, made me come twice in two entirely different ways, within a split second of each other.

I wanted to kiss her. I wanted to hold her tightly to me. I wanted to tell her how good I felt, but my rapid breathing and jelly-like appendages made that impossible. Instead, I rested my head on her shoulder while she held me and gently stroked my skin causing yet more involuntary shudders from body.

After a while, I'd recovered enough to sit up and say, "I want to make you feel this good." I looked into her deepening blue, caring eyes as I made my suggestion. "I just want to do whatever comes to mind. I want to see if it all comes to me naturally." She looked a little confused. *Was that too profound?* "Just….don't tell me what to do, okay?" I asked.

"Fine," she said with a shrug of her shoulders. I stood up and took hold of the occasional table and moved it a little closer to the lounge. Then I stood in front of her, lifting one of her legs and resting her foot on the table. I knelt on the rug, lined myself up between her knees and lifted her other leg, once again resting her foot on the table.

She was smiling, "Oh, very good," she said as she moved her pelvis forward, resting the cheeks of her backside near the edge of the lounge. I began to lick the inside of her thighs, swapping from one leg to the other, moving further and further up toward her pussy. I licked the very top of her thigh and then circumnavigated her thick blonde bush, eventually licking the very top of her other thigh. A slow sideways movement and I was licking her labia, gently tickling them with the tip of my tongue. I hesitated momentarily - scared that I might not do it right and that I must be clumsy. My desire and excitement soon quashed any reservations I had as I became enthralled by what I was doing. I allowed my tongue to soften and I pushed my face into her pussy, heavily coating my skin with her wetness. I started feverishly licking and sucking – I lost all sense-of-self. Without thinking, I drove my tongue deeply into her vagina, quickly moving it in and out. She groaned as though enjoying it.

I quickly discovered that by listening to her breathing and her occasional groans, by glancing up at her face every now and then and by feeling the muscle flexes in her legs, I could assess the effect I was having on her. I moved from her vagina to concentrate on her clit, licking it with gentle rhythmic motions. Swirling my tongue over it and then sucking and licking fervently. I began playfully attempting to pick the most surprising moment to delve my tongue deeply into her vagina again; working it in and out quickly, deeply, purposefully. Coating my tongue, my face with her juices; working them up over her clit, allowing my tongue to slip and glide readily back and forth.

"Oh yes," she said throatily and then her urgent plea, "faster."

Her pussy was sweet tasting, the single most beautiful culinary delight of my life. I was entranced. If my life had ended within the next few seconds it wouldn't have mattered. I had found my Utopia. I couldn't have felt more pleased with myself. I had achieved my highest goal. I was making love to a woman and she was enjoying it. Moreover, she was letting me know it with every spontaneous jerk of her body: with her writhing; her moaning; with her fingers digging deeply into the muscles in my shoulders; with her gasping breaths and heaving chest.

Knowing what to do seemed to come easily to me. I was doing what came naturally to me and the truth of it could not be more obvious – *I was born to be gay*. No doubts, no remorse – only absolute certainty. As though I had brought myself from the deepest depths of the sea and overcome the struggle to break the ocean's surface and find the warmth of the sun. To find enlightenment, but more importantly – self approval. The only opinion that counts is my own. As long as I am comfortable with who I am – nothing else matters. This is my life. This is my lifestyle. This is the way I am meant to be. A long winded description? Perhaps. And yet this realization dawned on me in seconds. As if something deep inside of me said, *Yes. This is right! Give it everything you've got.* So I did. Delving my tongue into her vagina even more deeply than before. She let out a deep throaty groan of approval, clasped my head in both her hands and pushed my face hard against her sex.

"Faster," her voice a high-pitch. Her need becoming more urgent. Both of us lost in our lust as she jerked her pelvis against me in pulsating motions. Our actions becoming more and more feverish with every second. I was amazed by my stamina. But it was so easy. Never had I wanted to do anything with such passion; such meaning. My euphoria letting me believe that I had performed with such perfection; as if it had been planned to happen that way and I was blindly following an exact blueprint of passion. And then it dawned on me – pain – if this woman presses any harder my nose will break. Just as I was wondering what I could do to relieve some of the pain, she groaned loudly, almost a prolonged scream as she approached the final throws of her orgasm. Finally, she let go of my head and collapsed across the lounge.

The fire had burned low again but the soft lighting provided enough of a glow for me to see my way to the kitchen where I poured out the last of the wine. I returned to the lounge room. She still lay across the lounge, her chest heaving from exertion. Lazily, she lifted an arm as though to wipe imaginary beads of sweat from her brow with the back of her hand. I lifted her head and brought the rim of the glass to her lips. She swallowed a mouthful and then slowly opened her eyes. She studied my face for a few moments and then smiled a little as she wrapped her hand around the back of my neck and pulled me closer to her for a long, soft, tender kiss. As we stopped kissing I lifted myself away from her and she took the glass of wine from my hand. She moved her body a little further up the lounge so that she could rest her upper back on the arm rest.

I dipped my index finger into the wine and allowed some droplets to fall from my finger onto her right nipple. She giggled a little and then said, "Suck it." I leaned over and sucked her wine-flavored nipple deeply into my mouth. She exhaled heavily as she ran the fingers of her right-hand through my hair. I surrendered her nipple to watch as she carefully sprinkled a few drops from the glass onto her left nipple, "Now this one," she said, and I happily obliged. When I had finished sucking the wine from her breast she carefully made a trail of droplets down her flat, well-tanned abdomen. The droplets slowly joined together to make a tiny rivulet forming a well of wine in her belly button. I followed the trail of wine with my tongue and lapped at her bellybutton much as a cat would lick at a tiny saucer of milk. After licking-up the last of the wine I lifted my head to look at her face. She lifted the glass to her lips, swallowed the last of the wine and then pointed to her mouth, "Now here," she said. I moved forward and she held me tightly as we kissed.

The fire had all but died and the air was beginning to chill. I shivered and goose-bumps appeared on the surface of both our skins. Cuddling so closely, being as one, it amused me that my shiver should transfer to her so readily, causing her to shiver in empathy. I rose to my feet. "It's getting cold. I'll get the fire going again."

"No, don't bother," she said, "let's go upstairs." She got up from the lounge and took hold of my hand, leading the way in the semi-dark, out of the lounge room through the entry hall, up the spiral staircase and along the hallway to her bedroom.

It was a large room. Tastefully furnished with antique furniture. The center piece of the bedroom was a large four-poster bed. On the bed, an abundance of satin-covered pillows and cushions in varying hues of pink and lilac. The bed quilt was made of a pure white velvety material in a patchwork design of diagonally textured stripes, so as to produce a chequered effect. The room was lit by two small wall lamps situated either side of the bed. They were dimmed, and gave the room a romantic atmosphere. Against the far wall was a large antique wardrobe with twin oval mirrors. On the opposite wall to the bed and beneath the window, was a beautiful antique two-seater chair with a cushioned seat and carved wooden back. I could imagine her sitting on it, her arm resting on the window sill, looking out at the ocean just a few streets away. Against the wall with the door, through which we'd entered the room, was a magnificent antique dressing table with an enormous mirror and three sets of three drawers. Each drawer was adorned with old fashioned brass handles. Every piece of furniture was lacquered solid oak, complemented by pale lilac walls. There were three white rugs on the French polished floor, one on either side of the bed and the other at the end of the bed. They were similar to, though smaller than, the one in the lounge room.

I was so awed by the room's beauty that it took a while to realize that it was very warm. Another quick look at the walls confirmed that there was no fireplace. "Why is it so warm in here?" I turned to see her smile as she closed the door and then pointed to the wall heater situated high above the wall lamps. It was glowing, brightly, obviously set on high. It was as though everything had been pre-planned. "Were you expecting someone?" I asked as I motioned at the heater and the dimmed lamps as evidence.

She moved toward me and held me tightly from behind and replied, "Be prepared." She kissed me softly on the neck and I quivered with delight. She placed her hands on my shoulders and gently persuaded me to face her. We kissed passionately as she pushed forward against me. She guided me back toward the bed, until I felt the side against the back of my legs. I sat down on the edge and, still kissing me, she lowered me backwards until I was resting comfortably against the cushions.

My breathing rate was increasing, assisted by the way that she was delving her tongue in and out of my mouth. She lowered her body on top of me and began licking and gently sucking my neck. I ran my hands over the smooth tanned skin of her back and buttocks. Her body shuddered a little. She moved her swirling tongue down the side of my neck and across my chest where she began sucking my nipples. She alternated from one nipple to the other until she had brought them both to full erection. Satisfied with her efforts she made a wet trail with her tongue down my abdomen to the thick thatch below. I consciously felt my heart begin to race when she started gently biting me. Gently nibbling so as not to hurt but hard enough to excite me.

"Do you want me to lick your clit?" she asked and then went back to her nibbling.

"Yes!" I whispered.

"Do you want me to fuck you with my tongue?" she asked teasingly.

"Yes!!" I responded a little louder.

"Do you want to eat my pussy?" She asked provocatively.

I lifted my head to look at her as I nodded and replied throatily, "Mm-hmm." I dragged myself to the middle of the bed and she climbed on top of me, lowering her pussy to my face and then pressing her face between my legs. I wrapped my arms around her waist and plunged my tongue into her wet and slippery pussy. She tightly wrapped her lips around my clit and sucked it deeply into her mouth, allowing her to expose and tantalize the entirety of my clit with her well-practiced tongue. My body became charged with waves of warmth that radiated from my groin, spreading spasmodically and uncontrollably through me, culminating in Technicolor splashes behind my eyes – clitoral orgasm.

Quick to learn from this seasoned lover of women, I sucked her clit deep into my mouth. Pressing my lips firmly around her clit to ensure that I would not lose my grip, I began swirling my tongue around and around over its surface. Slowly at first and gradually quickening the pace.

She started licking my clit again, this time more feverishly. I wasn't certain that I really wanted her to be there, since I'd just had an orgasm. I tried to pull away from her while still swirling my tongue around her clit as fast as I could. Once again, she sucked my clit into her mouth, licking and sucking on me at the same rate as I was licking and sucking on her. Our love-making becoming more and more urgent. She groaned loudly and our bodies shuddered violently as we came almost simultaneously.

I felt certain that I could not come again. She broadened her tongue and pressed it down on the skin above my clit and so, covering my clit completely with its own hood. (Protecting my clit from being touched directly by her tongue). She applied pressure and again I considered jerking away, but then, lights danced behind my eyes, my brain shut down and I was lost in a world of wonder. An orgasm more intense and lasting much longer than any before it. I forgot to breathe and unable to scream my pleasure aloud, I seemed to scream inside my head. My heart pounding and my body writhing with a will of its own; the orgasm went on and on. Somehow, intuitively, she knew exactly when to stop and if it's possible to completely collapse when already laying on one's back, I did so.

We lay motionless for some time. Both our bodies bathed in sweat, heaving with our fight for life's breath and incapable of speaking.

She released a long almost inaudible groan as she used what was left of her strength to roll off of me. There we lay trapped by fatigue. Our bodies motionless, save for our still heaving chests.

Eventually she moved to lay by my side and snuggled her head into my shoulder, we both drifted off to sleep.

The End

e-Sex

Oh crikey! My ass hurts something shocking! thought Matilda as she tried to get out of the taxi in front of her Hotel in Calhoun, Hong Kong. *How on earth am I going to be ready for a meeting tonight with representatives from the Mongol General Authority for Boarder Protection and the Chinese Ministries for National Security and Foreign Exports Affairs.* She winced as she moved her body sideways toward the door and again as she swung her legs out through the opening door and readied to alight. The doorman looked at her with concern and offered a hand to help her stand.

"Thank you – xie xie," Matilda said gratefully as she let the young man assist her to her feet. "Awhhhh!" she gave a short groan as she strained to straighten her body. *I'll be fine once I start moving,* she told herself as she forced one foot in front of the other and entered the hotel lobby. Her bags whizzed past her on a luggage trolley and she wished she could catch a ride with them to the reception area. *All I need is a bath,* she thought, *and a good strong coffee.* She began to move more easily just in time to stand at the reception desk.

"Your room is ready, Madam. May I escort you?"

Matilda turned around to see an immaculately dressed young woman standing behind her. The badge on her lapel said, 'Ah Kum, Guest Liaison.' Matilda smiled when she read the name, meaning *'Good as Gold,'* and mused that this woman might be an omen of impending success and simply acknowledged her with, "Please."

Ah Kum nodded and with utmost politeness said, "Please follow me." She turned to lead the way, signaling for the Bellhop to hold the elevator door for them. When they entered the elevator, Ah Kum pressed a key-card into a slot on the same panel as the numbered buttons for each floor and then pressed the button marked 'Tree Peony Suite'.

Matilda smiled, relieved that her Personal Assistant, Tammy, had managed to book her the room she'd hoped for. Matilda had had no doubt that she would arrive from her business trip to Mongolia physically drained and so had wanted her two day hotel stay in Hong Kong to be as comfortable as possible.

When the doors opened directly into the suite, a short Chinese man in a heavy, white, double breasted jacket with gold buttons and black dress pants stood in the room waiting for them. He immediately bowed his head as Ah Kum introduced him to Matilda. "Chaoxiang, will be your butler throughout your stay, Madame Matilda."

"Please, allow me to take your coat Madame." Chaoxiang helped Matilda out of her jacket as Ah Kum and the bellhop bowed together politely before re-entering the elevator.

"Thank you, Chaoxiang." Matilda smiled again as she considered the name meaning *'expecting fortune'* and couldn't help but consider it another positive sign for this evening's meeting.

"I have made coffee, Madame. If you like, I can serve you in the lounge area?" Chaoxiang said with a smile.

That's it! thought Matilda, *Things are definitely falling into place for me today.* "Thank you, yes, Chaoxiang. I need to sit down, I'm exhausted."

Serving the coffee, Chaoxiang asked, "Should I begin to run a bath, Madame?"

"Yes, please, Chaoxiang." She could smell the aroma of the coffee as it was being poured into the cup and knew it was going to be good, even before she tasted it. She lifted the cup to her lips, closed her eyes and took a slow, grateful sip. "Oh, *yes*," she whispered and snuggled back into the lounge to savor each sip in comfort.

Chaoxiang busied himself with running the aromatic bath and unpacking Matilda's bags. As he tucked the last of her clothing into the dresser in the bedroom he stopped at the wardrobe and withdrew the evening gown that Tammy had sent directly to the hotel. She'd also sent along with it, a bag of accessories and make up. He held the gown high and took it into the lounge where Matilda was sitting with her eyes still closed, sipping at her coffee.

"Excuse me, Madame. This evening gown arrived for you, today. If you are to wear it tonight, I will need to take a few moments to steam it for you and remove the wrinkles."

"Yes, please. I will need it for dinner this evening," Matilda confirmed as she moved forward in her seat to inspect the material.

"I will pour you more coffee, first," said Chaoxiang, noticing that her cup was almost empty. Matilda sighed with an appreciative smile as Chaoxiang refilled her cup.

While he was gone, Matilda did a mental stock-take of her body parts in order of most painful to least. She was trying to decide if her toes hurt more than her fingers as Chaoxiang returned. *That was quick,* she thought, *I haven't even finished my coffee.*

He'd returned with the dress in perfect condition. She watched as he hung it in the bedroom before hurrying to the bathroom to check on the bathwater. When he came out of the bathroom, he had a fluffy bathrobe and slippers in hand. He set them out in the bedroom before returning to the lounge area and announcing, "Your bath is ready, Madame." He ushered her to the bedroom to change into the robe and when she came out he quickly collected her clothing, along with a bag of clothes that he'd found in her luggage, asking, "If these are soiled, Madame, may I launder them for you?"

"Yes please, Chaoxiang, thank you," Matilda graciously accepted. As much as she enjoyed and truly believed she'd earned the butler service on this trip, she felt a guilty pleasure for it, as well as astonishment for the excessiveness of the service in Asia.

She closed the door of the bathroom, slipped out of her robe and into the warm aromatic water in the tub. Reclining and then relaxing quickly as the medicinal herbs infused in the water began to untie the knots in every muscle of her body. She smiled to herself, let her head loll back, and closed her eyes as she breathed in the rich aroma of the bathwater. *Mmmm, definitely better than the smell of horse manure,* she giggled to herself and began to relive some of the events of the previous six weeks. She had met and worked with officials from what seemed like almost every ministry in the Mongol government. *Oh, let's see: the National Development and Innovation Committee; Foreign Investment and Foreign Trade Agency; the Mineral Resources Authority; the Ministry of Environment; and oh, it just went on and on,* she shook her head, trying to lose the frustration of it all. There had been many, many meetings with department heads and legal advisors; all keen to get everything right for the signing of the contracts due now in just a few weeks' time. She was certain that some of the departments wanted a meeting with her and her advisors, simply to appear to have had some involvement in setting up the mining venture. This was a massive undertaking, a highly beneficial contract for Mongolia's economy as well as serving to ensure the continuing popularity of the Mongol Prime Minister. *Soon the Foreign Affairs Ministers for Australia, Mongolia and China will all get together and shake hands for the cameras and pretend like it was them that made the whole thing happen.* It's true. The figureheads always took all the glory and the people in the background doing all the hard work were always forgotten. *Still,* she thought, *I'm not in it for the kudos, I'm in it for the money.* She chortled softly to herself and pondered the enormous sum of money she was being paid to broker this venture. It had been at the behest of the Australian Foreign Affairs Minister than Matilda had accepted the brokerage contract in the first place; and he was right, she was the best person for the job. Being a small statured woman, spearheading negotiations in the company of small statured Asian men; the need for time-consuming-posturing was non-existent. She was able to win acceptance for her role quickly among her Mongol counterparts and get down to the grass-root necessities for the mining venture immediately. Her polite but competent style generally had each government official eager to display an equal level of competence and enthusiasm in assisting her to accomplish her goals.

Matilda moved slightly in the tub, noting that the soreness of her muscles was at last, abating. She sighed as she rubbed at a particularly sore spot on her arm and recollected the manner in which she'd arrived at that soreness – the trip to Goldie's proposed mine site.

The site is currently accessible only on horseback – a round trip that had taken the best part of three weeks to complete with her entourage of guides, advisors and engineers. She recalled her arrival at the base of the Altai Mountains just over three weeks ago.

Matilda had noticed a helicopter at the base camp when she'd arrived and, when she was introduced to her horse, Yeti, asked if the helicopter could be hired instead.

"When we get up to the mine site you'll be disappointed at how little we've managed to haul in up there," explained Jack, the site engineer. "The winds up in these mountains are so severe, we've only been able to use the chopper a half dozen times in the last eight months and even then it was dangerous.

Everything we try to do here is frustrated by limited accessibility."

"Ouch!" yelped Matilda as she spun on her heel while grasping at the pain in her arm. "Don't tell me. Yeti means biter or something doesn't it?" The mare was a small horse, practically a pony and picked especially for Matilda because of her petiteness.

"Naughty dog," one of the guides translated as he was walking past.

"Dog?" Matilda asked, her face contorted from the pain she was still trying to rub from her arm.

"Small, like dog," he chuckled as walked away.

Matilda and Yeti battled each other's will for the full eight days it took to climb that mountain. Yeti would try to turn her head to bite Matilda on the leg requiring Matilda to be constantly vigilant. The track was thin, winding and often fell away down the mountain to one side. Often times, Yeti would bite a nearby horse and cause a raucous and frightening melee on a cliff edged section of the track. Soon, others refused to ride near Yeti, meaning there was little opportunity for Matilda to have conversation. When it was time to take a break or make camp for the night, Yeti would begin to walk sideways as Matilda attempted to dismount, causing Matilda to fall off backwards. When it was time to mount-up again, Yeti would begin to trot off just before Matilda was able to commit her weight to the stirrup.

One morning, as Matilda was saddling Yeti and attempting to avoid being bitten, she failed to notice Yeti intentionally bloating her midriff as the girth strap was being tightened. Matilda was aware that some of her companions were watching her and smiling as she saddled her horse and thought it was due to the way she could skillfully dodge yet another bite attempt from Yeti. She cheerfully speculated their attention might lead to a more companionable day on the trail. She tentatively placed her foot in the stirrup and was pleased when Yeti did not break into a trot. Quickly, she committed her weight to the stirrup hoping to scramble up into the saddle without incident. As she did so, Yeti relaxed her midriff and the girth strap slackened. The saddle slipped around and under Yeti's girth, unceremoniously depositing Matilda flat on her back, looking up at her upturned saddle dangling under her horse. Each of her companions roared with laughter. Aware that Matilda was at risk, the guides raced in and pulled Matilda out from under her horse and not a moment too soon either, as Matilda escaped by the narrowest of margins from being urinated upon by the surly mare.

"Right! That's it!" yelled an infuriated Matilda, "The minute we get to this mine site, your name is 'Stew' and I don't care if that means I have to wait eight months for a chopper ride back down this mountain!"

Matilda stretched in the bath and moaned softly with the relief of being able to do so without pain. She shifted for comfort and returned to her recollections.

When they'd arrived at the mine site, Matilda could see that little had been achieved. *Understandably so, as well*, she thought. She completed her assessment in just over two days.

"You're cutting through your work at a staggering pace," Jack noted with a pleased smile.

"Helps that I'm still too sore to sit," laughed Matilda, "I feel as though I'm still walking with my legs bowed around that silly little horse," she sighed. Then looking intently at Jack asked, "Doesn't show does it?"

"A little," he laughed. They spent the remainder of the third day discussing the requirements for building an access road to the mine site. "Obviously, a heavy-load capacity roadway will be needed before much more can be realistically achieved here." Jack offered as much as he could for Matilda to grasp the engineering requirements. Matilda seemed as though she found all of his information and ideas useful, but he had to be honest about his area of expertise. "Roads, well, especially mountain roads, are not my specialty," Jack disclaimed near the end of their long conversation. "The engineer you really need for this job is the one who built that access road through the Kimberley – what was her name – I can't remember it now. The one that Goldie had the hots for but couldn't get."

Matilda's ears pricked up immediately, "Goldie set her sights on a pussy and it got away?"

"Yep." Jack nodded his head while smiling broadly. "Goldie tried to make as though it didn't really bother her, but you could tell, she was gagging for that girl." Then the smile disappeared from his face as he recalled his last meeting with his boss at her home and he almost looked somber as he added, "Goldie's daughter was telling me that Goldie's love-sick for this woman. Like; she might actually be The One."

"Oh, and this woman isn't interested in Goldie at all?" Matilda asked with compassion.

"Yeah, she was. Well, according to the assistant we shared back then," Jack recalled as he shoved his hands in his pockets to try and save them from the cold. "Apparently, her contract was coming to an end and she didn't want to complicate things while she renegotiated. Seems she's interested in doing a bridge in India for another company. It'll be good for her career if she can get it, too." Jack shivered as another gust of cold whirled in on them. "But I tell you Matilda, this woman is dynamite. I wish I could remember her name. She really knows her stuff. See if you can get her for this job, will ya?"

Matilda nodded, "Sure, Jack. If you want her, she must be good."

Matilda smiled and giggled softly to herself as she moved again without pain. *Mmmm, pain's gone,* she noted. *Must be time to get out of this bath.*

♀♀♀♀♀

When Matilda emerged from the bathroom, Chaoxiang informed her, "I have plugged in your mobile phone and your tablet, Madame. They will soon be recharged."

"Xie xie, Chaoxiang," Matilda bowed her head in customary style for appreciation.

"Is there anything else you need, Madame?"

"No. I'll be heading out for dinner in a couple of hours and won't be back from that until very late tonight."

Chaoxiang nodded and bowed with respect, "Please, press the button marked 'Butler' on your room phone when you need me again, Madame. Whatever the time."

"Thanks, Chaoxiang." She smiled as she watched the butler leave the suite.

The lighting in the suite was subtle and relaxing. She could easily sit on the couch and drift off to sleep. But that was not what she needed. She walked to the array of switches at the bar and flicked on all of the lights. *Wake up!* she ordered herself as she began to prepare for her dinner meeting.

♀♀♀♀♀

Matilda sipped her coffee while she appreciated her view of the harbor from her suite window. Chaoxiang busied himself with serving her breakfast as quietly as he could. Matilda was on the speaker phone to Tammy keeping her up to date with the negotiations, "…well what else could I do? I couldn't tell him the name Matilda meant 'strong in battle', not when we're in the midst of negotiations and his name means 'plums'."

Tammy giggled, "So what did you end up telling him your name meant?"

"Dances by billabong," Matilda confessed and they both roared with laughter. Matilda went on to give Tammy a list of her needs for the next part of her business trip. Then she began ordering her next lot of research requirements. "So that trip to China is confirmed, now. I'll need you to organize flights, etcetera."

"Can you stay in Hong Kong an extra day, to give me time to get you everything you'll need?" Tammy asked. It sounded as though she were shuffling papers and typing on a keyboard at her end.

"Okay," Matilda said quickly as she thought, *Yes! Women's Market, here I come!*

"I'll send your e-ticket and itinerary to you by tomorrow afternoon, along with the information you'll need to read up on before your next meeting," Tammy said with confidence.

"Great! Last night's meeting has dropped everything into place just beautifully," Matilda said excitedly.

"So, can I set up the meeting with The Gold Digger, now?" asked Tammy.

"You bet!" Matilda said with confidence. "You're a legend, you know? Thanks, Tam." Matilda poked the phone and ended the call. Smiling broadly at the breakfast before her, she exclaimed happily, "Oh, Chaoxiang, did you cook this?"

"Yes, Madame. Would not be fresh enough, otherwise," he smiled with pride and refilled her coffee cup with freshly brewed coffee. That and the smell of the freshly cut fruit at the center of table made Matilda's mouth water.

"Mmmm, tastes fabulous," said Matilda once she'd swallowed her first mouthful. "I'll be staying another day, Chaoxiang, can you organize for me to keep this suite?"

"Certainly, Madame," he assured her.

"Excellent. I'd love to have this same breakfast tomorrow, Chaoxiang, if you're still working?" she asked cautiously.

"I will be happy to extend my shift for you, Madame. Will there be anything more?" he asked as he returned the coffee pot to its keeper.

"Yes," Matilda said excitedly, "I'll need a car and driver for the day. I'm going shopping." He bowed and quickly left the room to make the arrangements for her.

♀♀♀♀♀

The elevator doors opened and Matilda stepped out with the bellhop, whose arms were loaded with bags and boxes from her day's shopping. Chaoxiang directed the bellhop to the bedroom and instructed him as to where to place Matilda's shopping. Then he moved to the lounge area and poured a coffee for Matilda.

Matilda was astonished. "How did you....I've only just...." Then she smiled and quickly sat before the filled cup. "Thank you, Chaoxiang."

"You're welcome, Madame Matilda. I had instructed the doorman to ring me upon your return. You have been out all day. I thought you would enjoy a cup by now."

"Chaoxiang, I'm going to have to pack you in my luggage and smuggle you back to Australia with me." Matilda said as she kicked off her shoes and rubbed at her sore feet.

"Should I run a therapeutic bath for you, Madame?"

"Oh, yes, please," Matilda accepted eagerly.

The bellhop left and Chaoxiang hung and stowed Matilda's shopping while he waited for the bath to fill. By the time he'd returned to Matilda's side in the lounge, he had the bath ready and a bathrobe and slippers set out for her in the bedroom. Matilda finished the last of her coffee while he reported that her bath was prepared and that he would leave until she called him back to order her evening meal.

I could get used to this, Matilda thought as she went into her room to ready for her bath.

♀♀♀♀♀

Bathed, fed and comfortable, Matilda sat on the lounge and went through her day's emails on her tablet. She caught her breath when she saw one was from Chase. It said, simply: *Missing you! Missing me?* Under the message was a URL link. Highly curious she tapped on the link and within a few seconds a notice came up outlining an hourly charge for the service she was signing into. She tapped the 'Continue' applet. Next, came a request for her credit card details. For a just a second she stopped to ponder. Then she thought to herself,

I've got to see what's worth charging for. Matilda entered her card number and tapped, 'Continue.'

Chase was smiling back at her. At first Matilda thought it must have been a recording, but when Chase said, "You look a whole lot more relaxed than I was expecting." Matilda realized, it was a real-time connection.

"Chase!" Matilda said in delighted surprise.

"Hi there, Sexy," Chase greeted with a cheeky smile. "How's it all going?"

"Oh, Chase. It's been a tough couple of months, I can tell you. Especially during the trip to the mine-site." She filled Chase in on her business trip to date.

"Lonely out on the trail, eh?" quipped Chase. "Did you dream about me nights?"

Matilda blushed, cleared her throat and changed the subject, "I went shopping today."

"Oohh! Show me what you got?" Chase asked with keen interest.

"Oh, I..." Matilda looked confused as to how she would operate the tablet camera and share pictures of her booty.

"Go into the bed room, Matilda. Set up the tablet on a pillow against the bedhead and do 'a fashion show' for me," suggested Chase.

"Okay," agreed Matilda with a smile. It took some adjustments and further instructions from Chase to set up the tablet for the exercise, but when Matilda started showing off her bargains, she found herself thoroughly enjoying the interchange. It was like having a best friend sharing in the excitement of the bargain hunt. Matilda's petite body made it easy for her to fit into the outfits worn by the Chinese and Thai women of Hong Kong. She'd managed to find some exquisite dresses in fine silks and satins. Chase's reaction to her while modeling the outfits made Matilda feel pretty and sexy. Just the therapy she'd needed after so many weeks of working long hours with very few days off.

"I really liked that aqua evening gown the best, Matilda." Chase said at the completion of the exercise. "It really sets off the highlights in your hair. Put it on again, with stockings and a garter belt and those cream high-heels. Put your hair up in a clip and wear that thin little silk scarf; the creamy-colored one." Matilda put on the outfit and paraded it in view of Chase. "Which handbag?" Chase asked.

"Oh," said Matilda, "I got a small one, today…." She moved in and out of view a few times, saying something that was nothing more than unintelligible mumbling to Chase and then, appeared with the outfit complete. "Well?" asked Matilda while doing a slow twirl in frame.

"Absolutely, stunning." Chase replied honestly. "Wait! I've got something for you."

Matilda turned back to face the tablet, puzzled. Then music started playing and Chase came back into shot.

"Dance for me, Matilda. Let me see how you'd look on the dance floor in that outfit." Chase sounded hungry for Matilda and it made Matilda shiver a little with excitement.

"Okay," Matilda smiled wryly and began to sway her hips a little in time to the music.

"Make me hot for you, Matilda. Shake that cute tush of yours at me. Make me wish I could reach out and touch your ass."

Matilda giggled and gyrated her hips, provocatively wriggling her ass at the tablet. Turning, she held out her handbag and then slowly lowered her arm and let it slide off over her wrist and onto the floor. She closed her eyes and began to slowly rotate on the spot while running her hands up her sides; lifting the evening gown a little and showing off some of the garter belt she wore underneath. She slowly ran her hands up over her breasts.

"Those are my hands on your breasts, Matilda," Chase spoke low, slow and husky. Matilda smiled and squeezed her breasts and groaned. "Pinch your nipples for me, Matilda. I want to see how that dress looks on you when your nipples are erect. I want to see how you'd look in that outfit when you're hot for me." As Matilda began to pinch and pull at her nipples, Chase continued, "Tweak them into rock-hard little peaks for me, Matilda." Matilda got them hard for Chase and enjoyed their feel against her palms for a few moments before moving her hands down and pressing them between her legs. Her lips parted and she opened her eyes to look at Chase. Seeing Chase watching her with an obvious gleam of excitement she smiled and concentrated on her dancing. She was rotating slowly and running her hands over her body, then lifting her arms above her head, she seductively swayed for the camera.

"Is this what you'd like to see, Chase?" Matilda asked as she began to turn toward the camera again, "And if I *were* hot for you, how would you let me know you liked it?" She looked at Chase through eyes filled with lust.

Chase moved back from her computer to give the camera a wider shot of her. For the first time, Matilda noted the bed behind Chase.

"Are we in your bedroom?" Matilda asked.

"Yes, we are," Chase replied.

"I've never been in your bedroom before," Matilda stated.

"Then I'll be sure and make this a memorable occasion for you, Matilda," Chase said pointedly. "You wanna know how I'd show you I liked it when you're turned on in your sexy new dress?" Chase sat on the end of her bed and spread her legs. She pressed two fingers against her center through her Chinos and squirmed for the touch. She closed her eyes and moaned. Then opened them and looked back at Matilda. "Dance, Matilda. You're on the dance floor, dancing for me and it's a private show."

Matilda's color reddened and her lips parted as she resumed dancing, slowly. Her eyes were glued to her tablet. Glued to watching Chase enjoying touching herself.

"Take off your scarf, Matilda. Slow and sexy. Make it part of your dance. Make me hot for you." Matilda slowly pulled at the half-hitch of her scarf. The sheer silk fabric caressed her skin as it slowly slid about her neck.

"Mmmm," said Matilda, closing her eyes again. "That feels good."

"That's my breath on your skin, Matilda," Chase stated suggestively. "That's me circling your beautiful body and breathing against your skin." Matilda's nipples hardened again and danced under the cool, soft fabric of her gown.

Matilda held the scarf so it tickled at her small cleavage. "Mmmm," she repeated and opened her eyes to look at Chase, "I love it when you breathe into my cleavage," she said in an enticing tone. "Like my new perfume?"

"Intoxicating," answered Chase as she slowly rubbed at her clit through her trousers and watched Matilda brush the skin of her arms and shoulders with her scarf. The expression on Matilda's face told of the pleasurable sensations the scarf provided. Matilda continued to dance as she wrapped and twirled the scarf around her wrists and danced with them above her head as though she were tied to an imaginary rafter. "Oh,

Matilda! You're such a tease, girl," Chase commented.

Matilda smiled and held her arms out toward the tablet, loosening the ties and allowing the scarf to fall to the floor. She danced and watched as Chase undid the two top buttons of her shirt and pushed her hand in under her bra.

"I'm getting my nipples ready for you to suck, Matilda. It's your reward for the sexy dance with the scarf."

Matilda again pressed her hands to her center, pressing at her clit in answer to its throbbing at Chase's suggestions. She swallowed hard as she watched Chase's hand move under her shirt material and rolled her head back with her enjoyment of the touch.

"Undo your hair clip, Matilda. Tussle your hair for me while you dance," Chase requested, still playing with her nipple. Matilda undid her hair clip while she danced and held her hair in place with one hand while she used the hairclip to tickle a path down her neck and around her breasts. She used it to draw the outline of her erect nipples before holding it out and dropping it too, to the floor. Then, she ran the fingers of both hands through her hair while rolling her head from side to side; enjoying the massage to her scalp.

When she looked back at the tablet, Chase was changing hands to cup and tweak her other breast, "I got that nipple ready for you now, Matilda. Close your eyes and pop the tip of your finger into your mouth. Keep dancing and suck my nipple for me. Suck it hard Matilda. Make me sing with the feel of your teeth on the tip of my nipple. Bite me, baby. Make me wet for you." Matilda did as instructed and continued to dance slowly and seductively.

While she bit and sucked on a fingertip of one hand, the other traveled down her body and again pressed against her clit. She moaned out loud and the movements of her dance were to ensure the best sensations from her fingertips pressing against her center.

"Don't you come yet, Matilda!" Chase cautioned, "You can't come until I say you can." Matilda gasped, the instruction making her want to press against herself again. Making her want to come – the very thing she'd been told not to do. She squirmed and tried to dance with the tops of her legs pressed together. Her skin tone darkened further and she released the finger from her teeth so that she could use her hands to squeeze both her breasts. She began sighing and moaning with the intensity of the throbbing between her legs. After a few minutes, she found herself better able to comply with her instructions and opened her eyes. Settling a little from her overexcitement, she returned to her seductive dancing while watching Chase's face beam with delight.

"Run your hands up and down your sides, Matilda. I want to feel your shapely hips." As Matilda moved her hands over her body, Chase said, "Those are my hands feeling you Matilda. Those are my hands worshipping your shapely form. You have such sexy hips, Matilda. I love to run my hands over them, and around your waist." Matilda started smoothing her hands about her waist and hips, feeling the hardness of the newly earned muscle – hard won on that trek up and back down that mountain range in Mongolia.

"That tiny little waist of yours, Matilda. It's so sexy, especially when I run my hands from your waist to your hips and back again. I love feeling you. I love caressing your sexy little body." Matilda began to slide a hand down to her pussy and Chase said, "No, Matilda. You can't touch your clit yet. You can't touch it again until I say you can."

Matilda exhaled loudly with frustration. Then she watched as Chase pulled her hand out of her shirt and undid her Chinos. She slid her hand down into her pants and began to massage herself between the legs.

"Oh!" Matilda protested with a whimper. "That's not fair, Chase. I'm so fucking horny."

"Mmmm, this feels *so* good Matilda. This is you touching me and you're *really* fucking good at it, too." Chase breathed in deeply so that her chest heaved and her breasts thrust forward. She smoothed the palm of her free hand over her breasts, moving from one to the other. "Oh, Matilda. That feels *so* good."

Matilda was entranced. Without thinking her hands moved down toward her pussy again.

"Uh-uh-ah!" Chase sang in caution. "No, you don't, Matilda. Not yet, not until I say." Matilda moved her hands back to her breasts and squeezed them again, hard.

"Put one foot up onto the bed, Matilda" Chase instructed, "Run your hands down over your leg and remove your shoe." Matilda slowly moved her hands down one leg and dragged the fabric of her dress up past the tops of her stockings before lifting one leg up onto the bed. She played her fingers over her upper leg, playing with the straps of her garter. Slowly, she moved her hands down over her calf before removing the shoe – sweeping it over the side of the bed and onto the floor. Then, starting at her toes she moved her hands slowly up and over her calf again.

"Very sexy, Matilda. You can touch yourself now, lift your dress and let me watch you press your fingers against your clit. Slowly now, very slowly."

Matilda gratefully complied. Her lips opened and a groan escaped them the moment she pressed her fingers against herself.

"That's enough!" demanded Chase. "Take off the other shoe, nice and slow, Little One." Matilda moved in time to the music and tickled the skin beneath her stocking as she raised her other leg onto the bed and slowly reached down and removed her shoe. When she looked back at the tablet, Chase was undoing the rest of the buttons on her shirt. Matilda again moved her hands toward her pussy and stopped herself just before she made contact with her clit. She made a slight whimper and asked, "May I touch myself, now?"

"Not yet!" said Chase as she reached behind herself and undid her bra.

"Oh, Chase, please?" Matilda implored.

"Just a second," Chase said, calmly as she pulled her bra up and allowed her breasts to descend into view.

"Oh, wow!" Matilda said as she watched the ample bosom bounce into view.

"Now!" said Chase and Matilda touched her clit through her underwear. "That's enough!" insisted Chase. Matilda's face contorted as though in pain but she did as instructed. "How horny are you, Matilda?" Chase asked.

"Unbelievably horny, Chase. Can I do it again?"

"Not yet," taunted Chase. "Undo your stockings and remove them, Matilda. Just like you did with the shoes." Matilda did her slow dance, while she watched Chase slowly remove her shirt and bra; doing a seated version of the dance in time to the music. Her breathing became shallow and rapid as she watched Chase, still seated on the bed, moisten her fingers between her legs and smear the wetness over her nipples.

"You make me wet, just looking at you in that outfit, Matilda." Chase was excited as she watched Matilda remove her stockings. She wet her fingers with the fluids between her legs again and smeared another layer onto her nipples.

When Matilda had removed her stockings, she asked, "Can I touch myself again, Chase? I did as you asked." Matilda's voice was almost a whisper between her rasping breaths.

"Yes, but watch this while you're doing it," instructed Chase and with that, she lifted a breast toward her chin and then reached out with a surprisingly long tongue and licked her pussy's juices from her nipple.

Matilda groaned and pressed hard against her clit. "Oh, that's gonna make me come."

"No!" exclaimed Chase. "You're not allowed to come, yet. Touch yourself and watch what I'm doing, but don't come."

Matilda nodded and groaned loudly as Chase lifted and licked her other nipple with apparent ease. "Oh! Fuck me!" Matilda said, in her husky whisper.

"Stop touching yourself, Matilda. Dance for me some more. Do your slow hip-sway for me again. You make me hot with that move, you know?" Chase pushed a hand down into her pants and moved it around while Matilda stood at the base of her bed and danced.

"Take off your dress, Matilda," Chase requested as she swapped hands in her pants and sucked and licked at her sticky fingers. Matilda moaned and squeezed her thighs together, thrilled by the vision of Chase eating her own juices.

"This is you I'm eating, Matilda. This is your wetness on my fingers, mmmm." Chase lapped and licked at each of her sticky, wet fingers and savored their flavor while Matilda squirmed and moaned as she danced her way out of her dress; sliding it down over her hips and toward the floor. She stepped out of it and kicked it out of her way as she continued to dance for Chase.

"Is this what you wanted to see, Lover," asked Matilda as she ran her palms over her naked breasts, cupped and squeezed them. Then she took both nipples between her fingertips and teased them into peaks. She looked up at Chase with a pleased look and said, "I'll be allowed to touch myself for doing that for you, won't I?"

Chase nodded and said, "You're one hot little Venus, aren't you? Sure, touch yourself Matilda. A nice slow circle or two of your fingers over your clit. Go on." Chase brushed a hand over her chest, breasts and abdomen as she strained her hips and moved the fingers of her other hand lower and lower into her pants. Then she seemed to be moving her fingers in and out of her pussy. She looked back to Matilda's image on her computer screen and watched as Matilda enjoyed smoothing her fingertips over her clit through her panties.

"That's enough, Matilda. You'll make yourself come in a moment, I can see it on your face."

Matilda smiled at Chase before sighing, "Yes, you're right." She stopped touching her clit through her underwear and brushed her fingers lightly over her abdomen. Watching Chase get closer and closer to release, Matilda complained, "Hey! If I'm not allowed to come, neither are you!"

Chase laughed and removed her hand from her pants, "I was wondering how long you'd let me get away with that." She stood and removed her trousers and sat back on the end of the bed. Now completely naked before Matilda.

"Oh, Chase. I'm gonna come just looking at you like that. I have to touch myself again."

"No!" insisted Chase, "Not yet, Matilda. Take off your garter belt and panties. Dance your way out of them for me." Chase sat back on the bed and propped herself up with pillows as she watched Matilda dance her way to total nakedness.

"Now sit on the end of the bed Matilda. Spread your legs wide and let me see everything you've got down there."

Matilda climbed onto the bed and straddled the tablet. "Show me yours," Matilda insisted and Chase spread her legs wide.

"Touch yourself Matilda and don't take your eyes away from me." Matilda reached between her legs and brushed her fingers up and down her pussy.

"Those are my fingers touching you like that, Matilda. Those are my fingers making you wet and causing you to twitch and moan."

"Oh, yeah," breathed Matilda as she shivered with the enjoyment of her touch.

"Stick a finger into your pussy for me Matilda. Get it good and wet. That's it, work it in and out, just like that. That's my finger in your pussy now, Matilda. That's me making you wet." Matilda moaned loudly as she watched Chase touch herself and listened to her dirty-talk.

"Paint your clit with some of that juice, Matilda. Make yourself wet and slick all over your pussy. Use all of your fingers and spread that cream around for me. Stick your fingers into yourself again and get more of that slippery cream out and spread it around. Yeah, that's the way, that's making me so hot for you, watching you fuck yourself like that."

Matilda watched as Chase led by example. Each instruction she received was a reflection of the acts Chase was performing on herself. "Oh, Chase, this is….this is something else. I'm high on this, I feel like I'm tripping."

"That's me touching you, Matilda. That's my fingers in your pussy, pressing deeper. Get them in there as deep as you can, Matilda. I want to touch you deep inside. Oh, your fingers are saturated. I can see them gleaming. You're creaming yourself everywhere. Mmm, good girl. I can hear how wet you are. I can hear the sounds of your wet pussy sucking on your fingers as you move them in and out. Smear some of that on your clit." Matilda followed her instructions and groaned, "Mmmm, you liked that didn't you?"

"Yes," nodded Matilda, watching as Chase also smeared her cream over her clit. "I'm so close. Please don't stop. Please let me keep touching my clit."

"Sure, Matilda. Watch me and copy what I'm doing. I'm close too. I'm creaming myself everywhere, just like you are. Draw circles over your clit, Matilda, and spread your legs nice and wide for me. Expose as much of your clit as you can and smear those juices all over it." Chase began to move her hips up and down in steady rhythm with the strokes over her clit.

"Mmmm, move your hips like this, Matilda. I can see your clit bulging under your wet fingers. You're going to come like this. You're going to come watching me like this. You're going to come with me watching you and touching you."

Matilda was breathing hard, she licked her lips as she watched the juices drip down Chase's pussy. Chase was enjoying this as much as she was. "Oh, Chase. I want to come now. Please let me come, please, please."

"Use your free hand to twist your nipples, Matilda. Keep circling your wet clit with your fingers and squeeze your nipples as well. I'm gonna tweak my nipples too. And I know as soon as I do I'm gonna come. Come with me, Matilda." Matilda moved her hand from one nipple to the other, pressing and twisting the hardened peaks, while swirling her fingers around and around on her clit. Her hips were jolting and twitching. Her clit was throbbing in time with her stroking fingers. She tweaked her nipples hard and when she heard Chase scream with her orgasm, she quickly followed.

"Ahh! Ohh! Chase. I'm…Oh!"

"Me…too!" Chase managed.

They writhed on their fingers and groaned and cried out with their ecstasy. Each heightening their joy with the sight of the other in orgasm. Each watching the other come on their screens. Each looking straight into the pussy of the other; watching the contractions and repose of each other's vaginas. Each seeing the fluids glisten and moisten and spread with the travel of each stroke of their fingers.

Matilda collapsed onto her side on the bed; her chest heaving from her exertion. Her eyes riveted to her tablet as she watched Chase continue to orgasm for several more seconds.

When Chase's hips relaxed and her hand stilled between her legs, she lay seemingly exhausted, gulping in huge breaths of air. After a minute or so, she looked toward her computer screen to see Matilda's calm, captivated expression. Chase lifted her knees and let her legs drape open wide. Thus, allowing Matilda to take in the view for however long she wanted.

"That was un-fucking-believable," said Matilda with a smile. "I'm so glad you made contact with me." She blinked several times to control the emotion that had started to well in her eyes. Then she stared at Chase's pussy for the longest time, motionless and speechless.

When she did finally look into Chase's eyes, Chase suggested, "You look tired, Matilda. I'll go and let you hit the sack, okay?"

Matilda yawned as if on cue. "Oh, dear!" She exclaimed in apology. "Yes. You're right. I should get some sleep. It all starts again tomorrow when Tammy sends me her research."

"One more thing before you go, Matilda?" requested Chase.

Matilda yawned again, "Sure. What is it?"

"The pony? Yeti? You didn't really eat her did you?"

Matilda laughed and shook her head as her mind drifted back to that last morning at the mine-site. "No," she giggled. "When it was time to make our way back down the mountain trail, I met with the others in the center of the compound. They all collected their horses and began to mount-up. A few riders cleared the way for me to see, Yeti. She was standing with one of her front hooves lifted high and I figured she was getting ready to start kicking me in the shins. I sighed and my whole body just sagged – I was already beginning to dread the trip back down. I decided to take a deep breath and resign myself to her. I expecting the worst as I walked over to her, but, she put her hoof down onto the ground and walked over to me. Met me, halfway. When she nuzzled my hand, without biting me, for the first time since we'd met, my heart went out to her. The guide said, 'she hates climbing the mountain; she loves going back down.'" Matilda giggled and for a few moments she was mesmerized as Chase smiled broadly back at her. Matilda continued, "I'm still walking like I've got bowed legs, though. Each time I think I've recovered, the soreness returns."

Chase laughed along with her, "Well it sure didn't show in your sexy dancing."

"You're required to have your legs parted for sexy dancing, Chase. The bow in them isn't apparent then."

Chase laughed warmly and said, "Goodnight, Little One and good luck in China."

"Goodnight," said Matilda. She reached forward, tapped 'exit' and Chase was gone.

She climbed in between the sheets thinking, *Now that's just what the doctor ordered,* and quickly drifted into a deep slumber.

The End

The End

The Anniversary Gift

Claire and Flynn walked into the nightclub together. It had been five years since they'd last ventured into this dark, loud, people-packed club where they'd first met ten years previously. Back then, they were regulars at the club; popular and recognized on sight by every staff member. The club manager in those days would often invite them upstairs to the VIP lounge where they would enjoy complimentary drinks and table service while watching the lively crowd below pulse and undulate to the rhythms of the house DJ.

The music playing as they entered the now tired and seedy looking club was completely unrecognizable to them. Claire looked at Flynn with a wry smile and Flynn returned it. Wordlessly, they were able to communicate their thoughts. *Yes, they were getting older and they were both feeling like it at that moment.*

The bar staff were all young and scantily dressed in the latest of what looked to be a twist on Goth fashion. Not one was a face from their past. Even the club manager they'd known for so long had been replaced by a younger man with multiple colors in his hair and clothes that fitted him only where they touched. Looking around the crowd, Flynn realized that almost all of the butches were wearing clothing that looked several sizes too large for them. She smiled and took Claire's hand as she led the way to the bar.

Claire took a seat at a small counter table near the bar as Flynn waited to be served her order of two light beers. Claire looked about the crowd thinking, *Even just five years ago, I would have been greeted by a half-dozen girlfriends by now. All wanting me to introduce them to Flynn.* She surveyed the crowd in a full circle around her. *They all wanted Flynn back then,* recollected Claire as she smiled to herself and then looked over at her lover of ten years. She was still striking to look at today. Claire noted that the young women at the tables nearby were taking good long looks at Flynn. They were looking her up and down and bringing her to the attention of friends next to them. Then commenting and giggling their appraisals to one another and outwardly appreciating the tall, slim, physically fit Aphrodite that was Flynn. *Well, some things never change,* Claire thought and then took-in for herself, that fine form of woman.

She gasped with shock and looked around quickly when she was roughly bumped into by a couple squeezing through the crowd.

"Sorry," they each offered as they pushed past her.

Claire smiled her forgiveness and appreciated the dresses the femme couple were wearing. *They're probably the best dressed in the club*, Claire thought to herself. Claire looked down at her own party dress and wondered if she might be a little overdressed by comparison to other patrons. She'd hoped to be dancing tonight and so decided to wear her cool, cream crepe Georgette dress with its sheer, layered fabric, over a white body hugging slip; cream high heels and a matching clutch bag. She wore the gold necklace that Flynn had given to her on their first anniversary. It had a single pearl high-mounted in a teardrop setting. Tonight she had her auburn curls tamed into a bun on top of her head showing off the matching pearl earrings that Flynn had given her earlier in the evening, for their tenth anniversary.

Flynn collected their drinks and started looking about for Claire. She wore tailored black slacks and a cream silk shirt with its long sleeves rolled up a few times. Tonight she wore patent leather Doc Martens with a low heel so as not to tower over Claire's tiny frame any more than she had to. Flynn never wore a lot of jewelry and tonight was no exception: a watch, her wedding ring, and around her neck, a simple leather thong with a small 'infinity' pendant inserted into it. The talisman catching what little light filtered through and drawing focus to Flynn's ample bosom and olive skin. She wore her black hair in a single, short pony tail, tied loosely at the nape of her neck – 'pirate-style', she called it. Claire giggled out loud as she recalled Flynn's humorous 'pirate antics' as she showed off her new hairstyle before they'd left the house that evening.

Claire raised her hand and waved to catch Flynn's attention and when the deep blue eyes looked in her direction, followed by a smile full of perfect white teeth, Claire caught her breath. Flynn looked and walked toward her exactly as she had done, ten years before. Claire was as spellbound by the vision of her tonight, as she had been that very first time.

Flynn handed Claire the small bottle and immediately clinked her own bottle against it, "A toast!" she spoke loudly above the music, "To the next ten years with you, Claire."

Claire smiled, and clinked the bottles again, calling back, "And the ten after that, for eternity." She pointed at the infinity symbol at Flynn's throat; their symbol for a commitment to spending eternity together in this life and the next. Flynn nodded and they both drank to their toasts.

Flynn moved to stand behind Claire who was still sitting on her stool and cuddled her in one arm, while she sipped at her beer and watched the crowd at the nightclub. "Was it always this loud?" she asked and Claire nodded before taking another swallow from her beer. Flynn continued her observation of the crowd and determined, "There is no one here we know." Claire shook her head and snuggled back into Flynn.

Flynn looked down and watched the hem of Claire's dress ride up higher on her thigh as she leaned back against her. Claire's legs were crossed and her sheer stockings made her legs look tanned and smooth. Flynn had to stop herself from reaching out and running her hand up Claire's leg and under the hem of her short dress. Claire reached up and cupped the side of Flynn's face with the palm of her hand. Flynn turned her face to kiss Claire's palm and when she looked back at Claire's legs, she could see that Claire was wearing lace-top stockings; meaning Claire was wearing a suspender belt underneath her dress. *Now I want to run my hand up there even more,* Flynn thought. She didn't of course. Claire wouldn't have liked that, even in such a dark nightclub.

By the time they had finished their drinks they had gotten used to the music and the crowd and were feeling more comfortable. The dry ice had cleared from the dance floor and Claire exclaimed, "The stage is still there, Flynn, look!"

"Oh yeah!" said Flynn, "that's where we had our first dance."

"That's where we first kissed," said Claire simultaneously.

"Shall we?" Flynn asked and offered her arm to help Claire down from the high barstool. Claire nodded with a keen smile and they made their way onto the dance floor and then up the few stairs and onto the stage.

They danced together as if the last ten years had yet to pass. Everything seemed the same –

even the music didn't seem so different to them anymore. It didn't matter that they knew no one. They were oblivious to everything and everyone but each other while they were dancing, anyway.

Claire watched Flynn moving her fit body in time to the music and began to recall that first night. The first time they'd met at this very nightclub...

All the girls were hanging around Flynn: wanting to talk to her; wanting to dance with her; wanting Flynn to ask them home. Each time Flynn came back from the dance floor another girl would ask her to dance. Claire had decided that the competition was far too fierce and resigned herself to just admiring this woman from afar, but after an hour or so and quite possibly a dozen different dance partners, Flynn had struck-up a conversation with Claire. However, just as the conversation got interesting, another girl came along and asked Flynn to dance. Flynn seemed to seek Claire out each time she returned from the dance floor and just when Claire had begun to expect Flynn to return to her and start up their conversation again. Flynn grabbed her hand and said, "Quick!

Let's get up and dance, before we get interrupted again."

Claire giggled out loud and was comforted that the music was loud enough to drown out her overly exuberant, girlish laughter. The other girls stopped to stare. Not because Claire was going to dance with Flynn, but because Flynn had asked her to, and was leading her to the dance floor; holding her hand and obviously keen to dance with Claire. Every other time Flynn had followed another to the dance floor, after having been asked by the girl leading her there. Claire was aware of their gawking looks of surprise and it made her feel special. She smiled broadly, and even though she wanted to act nonchalant, she could not hide her happiness.

There was very little room on the dance floor and Flynn was keen not to get overly familiar with Claire too soon. She really liked this woman and didn't want to scare her off. She took Claire's hand and led her up the steps and onto the stage area where there were fewer people and giving them more room to dance. It also gave Flynn a better opportunity to check out Claire's form. The front of this stage area was better lit than the back and they danced there together, in full view of their other friends for almost half an hour without stopping. Flynn would often lean in close to talk into Claire's ear. Claire more often than not would simply answer with a nod or shake of her head. All of her girlfriends wished they were her. She could feel their constant gazes burning into her. She knew they were scrutinizing every move the two of them made and jealously envying her apparent ease in holding Flynn's attention.

Claire had her brownish-red locks cut into an inverted bob, (a craze of the early 2000s) a straight bob at the front with a shorter layered effect at the back. She had to use copious amounts of straightening gel to tame her wild curls and waves and maintain that straight-haired look. When Flynn gently reached up to slide her fingers around Claire's neck and hold her while she spoke into her ear, her fingers were clearly visible – to all of their friends – at the back of Claire's neck, where the hair was cut shorter. Flynn repeated the move a few times, holding Claire closer to her while she talked into Claire's ear. Claire knew this spontaneous contact from Flynn would be causing her friends to turn green with envy. So she smiled and looked around for a moment toward the table where her friends stood watching them. Immediately all her girlfriends reached for their drinks and looked away from her direction in lame attempts to pretend they'd not been staring. Claire giggled to herself and as she turned back to face forward, to her surprise, her lips brushed against Flynn's. A comedic error on both their parts; Flynn had leaned forward to speak in Claire's ear just as Claire had smugly turned back to face Flynn. Their lips had met by accident and yet, neither could bear to relinquish the resulting kiss.

Flynn's other hand moved to hold Claire's waist and pull her closer as their kiss deepened. Claire rested her palms flat and motionless against Flynn's chest and welcomed the cautious expression of affection that Flynn was pressing against her lips. A moment later, Claire pulled away from the kiss. Flynn became immediately concerned that she'd moved things along too quickly and said into Claire's ear, "Are you okay?"

"They're watching us." Claire answered, admitting that she'd begun to feel self-conscious.

Flynn looked around, and being taller than most, identified a dimly lit part of the stage where they could dance without scrutiny from their table of friends. Flynn pulled Claire to the more secluded location, and as the DJ played a number that lovers could choose to dance closely to, held Claire closer; humming along to the music as they swayed together.

The next song played was also one they could choose to dance closely to. Claire enjoyed the smell of Flynn's cologne mingled with her perspiration from dancing. She mused that Flynn might smell like that all over and momentarily envisioned them both in her bedroom, on her bed, naked. She imagined them staring at each other while laying upon crumpled sheets with that smell – the smell of Flynn's cologne mingled with their perspiration – heavy in the air. When her mind returned to moment she found herself looking up at Flynn as Flynn leaned down for another kiss. This one was a little less cautious. Flynn's lips were slightly parted encouraging Claire to do the same. When she did, Flynn touched just the tip of her tongue to Claire's lips. Fleetingly, Flynn pressed just the tip of her tongue into Claire's mouth. Claire followed up with a gentle touch of her own tongue to Flynn's lips. She felt instantly aroused when Flynn's tongue returned and touched on hers.

Not wanting to have Claire become self-conscious again, Flynn ended the kiss. She looked into Claire's dark brown eyes and smiled almost shyly before leaning in for one more quick and gentle kiss. Holding Claire close to her, they again swayed together in time to the music.

The next song was a faster number and they smiled at each other in acknowledgement before separating and returning to their earlier dance moves. Another dance-track and Flynn asked, "Want a drink?" Claire nodded and Flynn took her hand and led her back to their table of friends.

This time Flynn kept her arm around Claire's shoulder as they struck up a new conversation. No one interrupted. No one asked Flynn to dance again that night. When Claire at last looked around at her friends, they all gave her warm smiles and cheerful gestures, indicating their pleasure at her victory in making such a fine catch as Flynn.

"Want a drink?"

Claire was slightly startled as Flynn's question brought her back from dreamily recalling that first night. Flynn was leaning in close, waiting for Claire's answer. Claire looked up into her lover's face and pressed her lips against Flynn's. Flynn's hands immediately smoothed their way about Claire's waist to grasp hold and draw the little woman to her. When Claire broke the kiss, Flynn looked confused and then remembered, *Claire doesn't like the limelight or lengthy displays of affection in public.* She looked around and danced Claire into that same dimly lit corner of the stage. Dancing closely to Claire, Flynn gently took hold of Claire's neck with both hands. The fingertips of each hand touching at the back of Claire's neck and her thumbs and palms cradling Claire's jaw. She leaned in slowly as Claire flattened her palms against Flynn's chest. Flynn gently claimed the lips that still made her heart pound with excitement. *I love her so much,* she thought as she parted her lips slightly and pressed just the tip of her tongue into Claire's mouth. Claire touched her tongue to Flynn's and that familiar stirring between her legs caused her to exhale heavily.

Claire pulled away from the kiss and looked deeply into Flynn's eyes. Usually, they were blue, but in this dim light they looked dark gray. She raised her hand and lovingly brushed her fingers down Flynn's cheek. The music changed to a faster pace and the spell was broken. Claire nodded and Flynn led her to the bar for another drink.

"We'll go home after this one." Claire suggested and Flynn nodded in agreement.

The evening had been lovely. They'd dined together at their favorite restaurant before going on their trip-down-memory-lane, ending at the nightclub they used to frequent in their youth. It had been enjoyable to relive some of that earlier time together; sharing anecdotes and laughing over and over as they reminisced together. But it was time to go home. If they left it too much longer, it would be prime-time at the taxi rank and they'd be in for a long wait for a cab-ride home. As Claire continued to scan the crowd, Flynn reminisced about that cab ride they'd taken home together that first night they'd met...

> "I'm two suburbs away. Is your place closer or is mine?" asked Claire as she and Flynn climbed into the cab.

"Yours is closer," answered Flynn.

Claire gave the driver her address and sat back in the cab for the short trip home. When they arrived, Claire gave the cab driver double his fare and asked, "Could you wait a few minutes, my friend needs you to continue on to take her home?"

"Sure!" agreed the driver as he took her money.

They alighted from the cab and Flynn walked Claire to her front door. Claire pushed her key into the lock and as she turned it said, "I hope you're not too disappointed by my not inviting you in." She allowed the door to open slightly as she turned to meet Flynn's gaze. "You might be wishing you'd gone home with one of the other girls now, I suppose. I hope I didn't give you the wrong impression."

Flynn took Claire into her arms and kissed her deeply. She ran her hands up and down Claire's back and when she moved away, Claire was left panting for breath.

"I'm not disappointed in the slightest," returned Flynn as she moved back toward the footpath,

"...but since I know where you live, why don't I pick you up for coffee tomorrow afternoon?" Flynn smiled as Claire looked her up and down, perhaps assessing her sincerity. If Claire changed her mind and asked her in, Flynn would jump at the opportunity. The fact that she didn't, however, made her all the more interested in dating this little woman.

"Two?" Claire suggested.

"It's a date." Flynn smiled victorious and walked back to quickly peck Claire lightly on the cheek before saying, "Goodnight."

"Goodnight," replied Claire as she watched Flynn walk back to the cab.

"I'm ready. How 'bout you?" Claire asked.

Flynn blinked repeatedly and brought her attention back to Claire, sitting at the counter table next to her in the nightclub. "Sure," Flynn answered and took one last swig from her beer bottle before helping Claire down from her barstool.

They walked out of the nightclub, down the stairs and onto the sidewalk and then, each turned to walk in the opposite direction of the other. Flynn looked back over her shoulder to see Claire walking away from her. She turned about and hurried to catch her up. "The taxi rank is back the other way," Flynn stated, pointing over her shoulder with her thumb.

"I thought we'd take the train," Claire said through a smile.

The house they had purchased together was just a few minutes' walk from their local train station. It was a warm, cloudless night and a moonlit stroll to their home would be a romantic end to their evening out. Flynn hooked her arm about Claire's and fell-in-step with her as they walked along in companionable silence.

The walk to the train station from the nightclub was just long enough for Flynn to recall the train ride home they'd shared after they'd been out to celebrate their first anniversary. Nine years had passed since that late night train ride together...

Flynn had had a bit too much to drink and as they were the only ones on the platform, she wanted to kiss and cuddle Claire while they waited for the train. She had been hungrily eyeing Claire all night, thinking how hot she looked in her height of fashion outfit. Claire was wearing a particularly revealing jade green suit. The top finished well short of her waistline and the little matching skirt left much of her midriff and almost all of her legs on display. Her reddish hair was still cut short – not quite touching her shoulders. She had by this time, dispensed with the hair-straightening products that never really managed to tame her wild curls and waves and so, allowed her hair to set its own style. Flynn enjoyed the feel of those curls and bangs as they slipped through her fingers. Even though Claire was wearing high-heeled shoes, she still barely came up to Flynn's shoulder height as Flynn enveloped her in her arms and held her in a firm embrace and kissed her passionately. Flynn seemed highly amused when Claire complained of her concern that they may be seen on the security cameras installed on the platform and insisted that Flynn 'behave' herself.

"We are in public, you know?" Claire sounded cross, but it was hard to stay angry at Flynn when she wore that silly grin of self-satisfaction and swayed on her feet from the effects of alcohol.

"It's not my fault," Flynn slurred, "If you weren't so gorgeous, I wouldn't get so turned on when I look at you. So, it's your fault." Flynn leaned in toward Claire with a smug smile, "Give us a kiss, Gorgeous."

Claire giggled as Flynn puckered up and leaned in closer. "Oh, Flynn. That's a face only a mother could love," she said dodging the incoming kiss and gently slapping Flynn on the arm. "Behave yourself!" Actually that wasn't true – Claire loved that face very much. She also enjoyed Flynn's drunken attentions, although preferably not in public. Flynn always seemed more in touch with her emotions when she'd had a few, and those emotions generally manifested themselves: firstly as a loving devotion for Claire; and then, as an insatiable lust for her. Flynn was fast moving into the lust stage as they waited for the train.

Flynn leaned her weight against a transit information sign and looked Claire up and down. *Yep*, thought Claire, *definitely at the lust stage now*. To her relief, the sound of the train approaching broke the silence between them. She held out her hand for Flynn so she could help her to stand upright from her leaning position.

When the train stopped at the station, Flynn said, "Oh good. It's an old carriage." *No cameras*, she thought to herself. "Let's sit upstairs." They climbed the stairs to find the top level deserted. Flynn sprawled into the middle of a two-seater and stretched her arms out atop the backrest. She spread her legs wide to give Claire plenty of room to slip in and sit facing her, in the two-seater opposite.

Claire sat upright with her sexy legs crossed and Flynn's sparkling blue eyes were captivated by her. Claire could feel Flynn's lustful gaze burning into her. She tried to concentrate on the passing scene outside the window but Flynn's commanding gaze kept drawing her attention again and again. No matter how hard she tried to ignore Flynn's scrutiny, she was compelled to keep looking back to her. She knew this look from Flynn. She knew what it meant. The moment they walked in through their front door: Flynn would be holding her, kissing her, undressing her, making love to her. Claire's skin shivered in anticipation of the lovemaking to come.

"Do you have any idea how hot you are?" Flynn asked.

"Only when you look at me like that," answered Claire timidly. In truth, she wondered how well Flynn *could* see her, given her drunken state and the poor lighting of the old carriage they travelled in.

Flynn's hungry eyes dropped to Claire's breasts and then down lower. "Your body is just...I need to see more," Flynn got out hungrily.

Claire laughed incredulously, "There's practically nothing of my outfit as it is. I think you can see plenty enough already."

"Show me, Claire."

Claire followed Flynn's gaze down to her crotch. She couldn't explain why, but she suddenly became wet and felt her clit swell. She squirmed slightly in her seat and for a moment pondered giving Flynn what she'd asked for. She looked back up at Flynn to find her head cocked to one side and slowly lowering her torso in an attempt to look up the hem of her skirt.

"Flynn!" she chastised and pulled the hem of her skirt down as far as she could.

Flynn licked her lips and her eyes settled on Claire's lap. "The carriage is empty. We're alone."

Claire knew Flynn to be telling the truth but had to look around and make sure of it anyway. "We're on a public train!" she protested.

"Pull your skirt up and let me see between your legs." Flynn's voice sounded deep and husky. It made Claire's skin quiver whenever Flynn used that sexy, husky voice, but all her good upbringing; all her senses of right and wrong were screaming for her to maintain her decorum. She squirmed slightly in her seat again, needing to find some small release for her fast swelling clit. Claire was embarrassed when Flynn noticed and chuckled at what she recognized as the beginnings of success.

"You've got a lovely pussy, babe. No one can see you but me and I've been good all night. You could give me this as a reward."

Claire uncrossed her legs but firmly held her knees together. She cleared her throat and sat upright in her seat before looking back out the window as the train rolled to a stop for the next station.

Flynn held her breath, hoping not to hear footfalls on the stairs. None came and the train ride resumed.

Claire looked back at Flynn to find her still staring at her crotch.

"You've got a beautiful pussy, Claire. It's begging for me to lick it, isn't it? You can't wait for me to make you scream with my tongue."

"Flynn, no!" Claire sounded exasperated.

"Okay, I'll save that for when we get home, but it wouldn't hurt for you to just show it to me now." Flynn's gaze was fixed on the hem of Claire's skirt. "Just lift your skirt for me. Just a little, babe. Come on."

Claire began to breathe more heavily. She couldn't help it. It was as if every word Flynn said in that low, sexy voice was stroking her clit, making her wet, eroding her resolve. She bit her lip and took one more look about the carriage.

"Do it, Claire. Let me look between your legs. I won't touch you. I just want to look at you." Flynn didn't raise her blue eyes as she implored. She licked her lips and raised an eyebrow as Claire reached down, hooked her fingers under the light material and slowly lifted her skirt up, almost exposing her crotch to Flynn.

"A little more," she urged softly. "A little more…that's it, good girl." she praised.

Claire swallowed hard and released her throbbing lip from between her teeth. She breathed deeply and fought the urge to squirm and squeeze her clit between her thighs. Her heart was beating fast. As fast as the clickety-clack of the train on its tracks.

"Spread your legs for me, cutie." Flynn said low and lustfully.

Claire's eyes widened, obviously concerned by the request. However, the enjoyment on Flynn's face made her want to comply. Claire felt so conflicted. Her lover was truly excited by the idea of being able to bend her will and convince her to act out of character. Claire wanted to make this fantasy come true for Flynn, but…I don't know. She began to panic until Flynn's voice comforted her again.

"You're so hot, Claire. You've got a sexy little pussy. I need to see between your legs, honey. Spread them for me, please!"

"Just this once," Claire said in a hoarse whisper and slowly allowed her knees to part.

Flynn's mouth opened in awe, she was transfixed by Claire's slow movements. She heard Claire gulp hard between breaths, even over the clickety-clack of the train. Flynn copied, gulping too, and ran her pink tongue over her lips again in anticipation.

"A little more," she begged. She could now see the crotch of Claire's matching panties. "Part them a little more, Claire. Mmmm, good, good!" She smiled and licked her lips again.

Claire slipped down in her seat in what she felt was a shameless effort to give Flynn a better view.

"I can see your panties, but I want you to show me your pussy. Spread those sexy legs nice and wide, hon." Flynn wanted to look up and study the emotions written on Claire's face, but was afraid of ruining the moment by embarrassing her. "Raise your skirt a little bit more....Mmmm," she crooned appreciatively, "good girl."

Claire smiled a little self-conscious smile and quickly looked about the carriage again. She was becoming more and more motivated to obey her lovers every word. Flynn's voice was becoming hypnotic and she could sense her excitement building along with Flynn's.

"Now pull your panties to one side and show me your pussy."

Claire gaped at Flynn and gulped audibly as her lips parted from the shock of Flynn's request. She shook her head slightly about to speak her protest when Flynn beseeched her.

"It's just the two of us here, Claire. This is just so hot. I can feel my clit pounding against my briefs. C'mon babe, do it for me?" Flynn was breathing deep and hard, rubbing the insides of her thighs and licking her lips. All the while, her gaze was fixed between Claire's legs. "C'mon, hon. Let me look at you. Let me see that gorgeous pussy of yours. I can see you're already wet for me. You want to show me. I can tell by your breathing. You're just as excited as I am, aren't you?" Flynn licked her lips again. "Go on! Pull your panties to one side. Just a little look for me, babe?"

Claire hesitated. Her brow furrowed and yet, to her absolute dismay, she was incredibly turned-on by the request.

"C'mon, hon," came Flynn's persuading tone. "Show me. Let me look at you. Let me…that's it…yes!"

Claire's hand began to slowly move toward the wet strip of fabric between her legs. Flynn's eyes were locked on, watching for Claire to uncover her prize. Claire's fingers took hold of the edge of her panties and paused.

"Oh, babe! You got my heart pounding. Don't stop now! Let me see. Show me your wet pussy."

Claire gave the carriage another quick look before staring back at Flynn. Flynn's blue eyes were wide and fixed between her thighs. Flynn's face was full of expectant enthusiasm and lust. Claire took a deep breath and slowly pulled the fabric aside.

Claire's pussy was small, tightly trimmed and her delicate pink lips were glistening with slick wetness. She watched as Flynn studied her with overt hunger and worried what she would do if Flynn were to lunge face first between her legs. Causing her even more stress was her awareness that the train had begun to slow for the next station.

"Keep your legs spread," demanded Flynn when the train had stopped. Claire froze. "Oh baby, you're beautiful," the butch breathed as she thought, *I've never seen anything more erotic than Claire with her legs spread on a train seat, with her panties pulled to one side showing me her most intimate and secret part of her body.* "You look so sexy, spread out for me like that."

Claire's eyes were darting from side to side. She strained to hear if anyone was coming up the stairs as the train left the station. Then came the sound she'd been dreading; someone was walking up the stairs. Claire's eyes widened. Her fingers released the elastic of her panties, which immediately snapped back into place. She dropped her skirt back into her lap and slammed her thighs together just as a tired man in a gray suit finished climbing the stairs and sat down at the other end of the carriage with his back to them. Claire clutched her chest. Her heart was pounding and her face was flushed. She looked back up at Flynn and then held her face in her hands. She was mortified.

Flynn jumped over to sit next to Claire and comforted her from her state of blatant panic. She put her arm around her little lover and whispered into her ear, "Fuck! You're so beautiful and I am so incredibly lucky." She lightly flicked the tip of her tongue over the edge of Claire's ear. When Claire quivered Flynn whispered, "You're so, so sexy, cutie. You've made me so hard and wet."

Claire smiled and snuggled into Flynn who seemed to be sobering by the second. She shivered when Flynn gently nibbled her earlobe and then realized her fear had abated, but her heart was still pounding.

"My nipples are so hard. I can't wait to get you home so I can lick your sweet little pussy. I know you need it baby. Don't worry. I'll take care of you. I'll take care of your sweet little pussy." Flynn could feel Claire's body relaxing as she spoke.

Claire turned to whisper into Flynn's ear, "I have never been so turned-on in my life. I want you. I'll do anything you tell me."

Music to my ears, thought Flynn as she continued to comfort and whisper to Claire until they reached the next train station – their destination.

"Run!" Shouted Claire, scaring Flynn out of her daydream.

Flynn looked about with surprise as Claire grabbed her hand and pulled her quickly down the stairs at the station just as their train rolled in to a stop.

They hurried aboard with only a second to spare before the doors closed and the train rolled off again. *Huh!* thought Flynn smiling to herself. *One of the old carriages, I didn't think they used these on this line anymore.* Claire was still holding her hand as they climbed the stairs to the upper deck. They looked about as they entered and found one young couple seated together at one end. The young man seemed to Claire, to be clumsily and hurriedly adjusting his clothing. She heard Flynn giggle and then felt her lover tug her by the arm to the opposite end of the carriage. Flynn motioned for Claire to sit in a two-seater and then sat next to her, facing away from the young couple. Flynn put her arm about Claire's shoulder and looked out the window as the train sped along its tracks.

"Were they doing what I think they were doing?" Claire asked through a grin as she snuggled in under Flynn's long, strong arm.

"Yes," whispered Flynn into Claire's ear. She lingered in that position and took the opportunity to breath in the perfumed aroma of Claire's hair. She breathed out heavily onto Claire's neck and Claire shivered.

Claire quickly moved to the opposite two-seater and sat facing Flynn. She was sitting in the middle of the seat to ensure there was no room for Flynn to move and sit either side of her. Flynn shrugged and looked a little confused, certain that she'd done nothing to warrant being brushed off in this way.

Claire looked over Flynn's shoulder and could see the other couple now also sitting facing away from them at the other end of the carriage. She slowly kicked off her right shoe and brushed her stocking-covered toes up and down Flynn's leg. She looked up to see Flynn watching her every move with pleased surprise. They caught this train every other week together, but not usually at this time of the night and not usually with so few passengers aboard. This carriage, an older style, had no security monitors and very poor light managed to seep through the old, carbon stained light fittings. Claire could see the entire carriage from where she sat and often looked toward the far end at the other couple, to ensure they were not under any scrutiny.

Flynn swallowed hard as Claire moved Flynn's knee aside with her toes. Claire reached with her toes toward Flynn's other leg, to run her foot up and down the inside thigh. Flynn shuffled into the middle of her seat so Claire could reach her leg more easily. She smiled and wriggled her eyebrows as she looked up into Claire's dark-brown eyes. It seemed to Flynn that those eyes were full of mischief. Flynn knew this look of Claire's. She knew what it meant and her smile broadened. She didn't know what Claire had in mind, but she was convinced it would be both discrete and enjoyable.

Now that Claire could reach Flynn more easily she slipped off her other shoe and began gently kneading Flynn's inner thighs with both feet. Flynn stretched her arms up over the backrest, holding on while she wriggled her buttocks forward slightly in her seat, hopeful that Claire might dare to massage her groin through her clothing.

Claire smirked at Flynn's obvious invitation and catching her eye, mouthed, *Hussy.*

Flynn giggled and quickly covered her mouth trying to stifle the sound before it could carry up the carriage to the other couple. Flynn looked at Claire with questioning eyes. She was concerned she had drawn the young couple's attention, knowing that Claire would not appreciate it. Claire quickly assessed the other couple and seeing that they'd not taken any notice, alleviated Flynn's concern with a quick shake of her head before returning to her Ashi-Anma style massage.

Flynn's smile became a permanent fixture on her face. Her eyes flicked back and forth from Claire's face to the pulsating massage she was receiving to her legs as Claire moved closer, ever closer, to her pussy. Her breathing picked up pace and she could hear her heartbeat pounding in her ears. Claire was close to massaging her pussy; the toes now skirting the outer edge of Flynn's groin through the material of her slacks. Flynn bit her lip. She was concerned that she would cry out when Claire touched her pussy through her clothes and give away their game. Claire would stop if Flynn made the slightest noise – she knew that. She had to control her breathing, she had to refrain from outburst and she had to keep a cool demeanor, if she was to ensure that Claire continued her foreplay. Flynn needed Claire to touch her. She could feel her distended clit pressing against the seam of her slacks and she was beginning to feel a desperation for the touch of Claire's toes. She was certain that her face had reddened; she felt hot and beads of sweat were starting to form on her forehead and top lip.

"Mmmm," breathed Flynn quietly.

"Shush," whispered Claire.

Flynn looked up into Claire's eyes but she didn't really see her through them. She was far too absorbed by the feelings growing between her legs.

The train began to slow and the intensity of Claire's ministrations lessened slightly as Claire closely watched the young couple at the other end of the carriage. She stopped and feigned crossing her legs as the young couple stood and moved toward the stairwell.

Flynn breathed out heavily, managing to stifle an agitated groan as she read the look in Claire's eyes to mean, 'their carriage companions were on the move'. She closed her eyes and tried to breathe in and out more slowly with limited success. She could hear the young couple making their way down the stairs to the lower level as the train pulled into the next station.

"Oh, fuck me, Claire!" she exclaimed lowly, "That was *such* a turn-on."

"Shush!" insisted Claire, listening for footfalls coming up the stairs.

Flynn did her best to hold her breath, imploring whatever cosmic force that might have the power to grant her wish, for just two more stops without an audience in their carriage.

For the moment her wish was granted and the train pulled quickly away from the station with no one making their way upstairs.

If it is possible to look gleefully naughty, that was the look on Claire's face. Flynn looked her up and down, waiting, hoping for Claire to restart her uncharacteristic, risk-filled sex-play. She swallowed hard as Claire lifted first her right foot, then her left and rested the soles of her stocking covered feet on top of Flynn's knees. She felt a downward pressure as Claire coaxed her to spread her legs wider. This had the added benefit – from Flynn's perspective – of also spreading Claire's legs, giving Flynn full view of Claire's lace-top stockings, held in place by her garter thong. She followed the white strap atop Claire's tanned leg to the white thong that Claire wore under her party dress. Flynn's breathing hitched and she licked her lips as she stared at Claire's pussy, covered only by a very thin strip of white material.

Claire smiled widely and giggled at the besotted expression on Flynn's face. Flynn was distracted by the delightful sound of Claire's amusement just long enough for her to glance up and say, "What?" and then return her gaze to Claire's pussy.

Claire shook her head slightly from side to side, "So predictable," she stated. She glanced momentarily at the stairwell to ensure no one was about to join them. Then, keeping her gaze locked onto Flynn's face, reached down and pulled her thong to one side; exposing her glistening, wet pussy.

"Oh, Claire." Flynn murmured with immense appreciation.

Claire chuckled low and sexy as she reached down with her other hand and touched herself, running her index finger inside the fold between her outer and inner lips. "Mmmm," said Claire, "that feels good."

Flynn's mouth fell open and her eyes widened. She sat in stunned silence for a long moment. Finally, alternating between smiles and gaping shock she gasped, "Claire!" Her look was incredulous as her eyes quickly flitted back and forth from Claire's eyes to her pussy.

Claire closed her eyes as she reached to press her middle finger into her vagina, "Mmmm," she moaned, "I love it when you finger me like this," she opened her eyes and was pleased to find Flynn's mouth and eyes still wide open with astonishment. Claire removed her finger from her pussy and slowly raised it to her own mouth, watching Flynn intently as she slowly licked and then sucked it. "Mmmm," she mumbled as she moved her other hand to her center and began to trace her fingers around and around her wet folds.

Flynn had begun to breathe very heavily and finally managed, "Have you lost your mind?"

"No." replied Claire softly. "Have you lost your nerve?"

Flynn stared at Claire's hand moving sensuously around her sensitive folds. She was speechless. This was not at all like the timid, well-mannered woman who'd given her heart cause to beat for the last ten years. *Well, it's pounding now,*

Flynn thought. She could hear her heart beating inside her ears and was certain, that should she look down at her chest, it would be thrumming against the fabric of her silk shirt. *Was Claire possessed?* she wondered as she looked up into the eyes of a woman with a mission. "Mmmm," Claire moaned again, "I've been thinking of doing this all night. I'm *so* wet Flynn. I'm *so* horny." Claire breathed in and out deeply as she spoke. Her voice was breathy and barely audible.

Flynn raised her hand as though to reach forward and touch the wet beauty before her.

"Uh-uh-ah!" Claire sang, rocking the finger she'd been sucking and licking back and forth in front of Flynn's face. Flynn sat back against her seat and draped her arms across the top of the backrest. She resigned herself to doing exactly as Claire instructed.

"What do you want me to do?" Flynn asked.

"Watch the show," said Claire. Then smiling provocatively, she added, "Touch yourself if you like."

Flynn's mouth dropped open with shock once more. *This can't be my Claire saying this.* "I can't believe this is happening. It's like a dream. It's a dream come true." Flynn rambled as she watched Claire's fingertip tracing large circles around her inner lips. She could see Claire's wetness increasing before her eyes and recognized Claire's scent of sexual arousal. Suddenly, the train began to slow again as it pulled into the next station. "Oh no!" Flynn said, almost in a panic. She wasn't ready for this to end. She knew if a passenger climbed the stairs to their carriage, Claire would stop her sex-show and immediately return to traveling in her usual quiet compliance of socially acceptable behavior. She looked up at Claire's face, worried that Claire was about to shut-down the show, but Claire simply shrugged and regularly looked over toward the carriage entrance. Her legs were still spread wide and her finger was still exploring her pussy; circling her clit and delving into her vagina.

Flynn watched Claire touching herself and at the same time listened carefully for footfalls. Her heart was pounding and so was her clit. The suspense of not knowing if they were about to be interrupted, if Claire was going to continue with her self-touching display, heightened Flynn's arousal. Just watching Claire continue, in such a tense atmosphere caused Flynn's clit to swell to such an extent, she couldn't help reaching down to touch herself through the fabric of her slacks. Flynn's hips moved slightly with the torment of impending orgasm. She was distracted by her thoughts of copying Claire's finger-action with her tongue when they got home. Claire obviously enjoyed this slow, prolonged, circling motion around her inner lips. And so, Flynn was keen to try mirroring the action with the tip of her tongue the moment they got through the front door of their home.

The train moved off again and both of them breathed a sigh of relief when no one came up the stairs. They were both pleased at being able to continue with their sex-game.

Claire dropped her other hand back down between her legs and held herself open for Flynn to view. When Flynn licked her lips hungrily, Claire responded with a soft and sexy chuckle and then held the hood of her clit back with one hand while slowly circling around her it with the other. She quickly became very wet and scooped up some of her wetness with a finger to use as a lubricant over her clit.

Flynn licked her lips, wanting to lick up some of those fluids for herself, but knowing Claire would not let her help herself here. Flynn gently thrust her hips forward and enjoyed the sensation of the pressure from her fingers and the seam of her slacks as she pressed down against her clit. "Mmmm, Claire I'm going to come watching you do that," she divulged.

Claire smiled wide as she breathed heavily, "I'm almost there myself." She began to stroke her clit quickly with her second finger. "Mmmm, I'm very close," she said as she slipped down slightly in her seat and spread her legs as wide as she could to give Flynn an even better view.

"Oh, Claire! You're so beautiful. I love you *so* much!" exclaimed Flynn as she massaged her pussy through her slacks.

"Happy Anniversary, darling," said Claire between panting breaths. "Now fuck me!"

Flynn could hardly believe her ears. Her eyes and mouth opened wide with shock, "Wha...okay!" She quickly wet her fingers in her mouth and leant forward to slowly push into Claire's wet and throbbing pussy. As she did so, the seam of Flynn's slacks pressed delightfully against her engorged clit and she slowly slipped into orgasm. The feel of Claire's wet pussy against her fingers! The feel of the seam of her slacks pressing against her clit! The risk of a passenger or train attendant climbing the stairs and catching them out! The sight of Claire's finger playing over her own swollen nub of nerve endings! The look of intense pleasure on Claire's face! The smell of Claire's sex in the air! All of these, gave Flynn the most intense and long-lasting orgasm she could ever recall having.

Flynn closed her eyes against the intensity of her orgasm for just a moment and was forced to re-open them when she heard Claire groaning out aloud. As her orgasm slowly abated, Claire's arrived, and Flynn savored the sight of Claire in the throes of her own release. Claire's face flushed with color and her eyes half closed as she stared across at Flynn. She was groaning loudly and her breaths hitched with every thrust of her hips against Flynn's fingers. Flynn quickly looked around at the stairwell, concerned that Claire's cries would bring unwanted attention, but none came and Claire quieted.

Claire looked relaxed in her slumped position across from Flynn. Flynn could feel the muscles of Claire's pussy spasming against her fingers. She knew from years of loving this woman to keep her fingers completely still and allow Claire to enjoy the last fleeting twinges of her orgasm. When Claire removed her own fingers, she sat panting heavily, staring at Flynn. Flynn knew that now was the best time to slowly, gently, remove her fingers from Claire's intensely sensitive vagina.

While Claire watched, Flynn re-positioned Claire's thong to cover her pussy and then licked Claire's juices from her glistening fingers. Claire licked her dried lips as she watched Flynn enjoy the flavor and scent of her fingers. When Flynn had finished, Claire struggled to sit upright and adjust her clothing. Flynn moved across and sat next to Claire and helped her sit up and shuffle over.

"Thank you for my anniversary present, Sweetheart," said Flynn sincerely. She gathered Claire in her arms and held her tight, "It was a wonderful surprise."

Claire gave a soft, sexy laugh, "Ten years is a special anniversary. I wanted my gift to you to be unforgettable."

"Unforgettable is right!" said Flynn as she leaned down to claim Claire's lips and gently press her tongue into Claire's mouth. The kiss was gentle, loving and long. Broken only by the sensation of the train slowing as it neared the next station.

"C'mon," said Flynn, "This is our stop. I can't wait to get you home and thank you properly for my gift."

Claire quickly slipped her feet back into her high heels. Together they rose and arm in arm alighted the train. They continued to gaze lovingly at each other they made their way from the train station to their home.

The End

Pennys from Heaven

Matilda took a quick sip from her coffee cup before restoring it to its saucer. She had been sitting at her favorite spot at the café counter with her newspaper still folded neatly in front of her. She was distracted; wanting to call Chase but not really having the time needed to organize a meeting before now. *Shit! Why didn't I call her from the airport yesterday? She might have been able to fit me in today,* she chastised herself as she looked around the café and then sighed her frustration. *Don't be ridiculous!* she scolded herself, *She's not going to magically make an appearance just because you're horny.*

She looked back down at her coffee cup, picked up the teaspoon and absently stirred her coffee. To a casual observer she would look as though studying the contents of the cup when in fact her gaze was absent; her mind elsewhere. *It would have been nice to celebrate my success in Mongolia and China with a good romp in the sack with someone who really knows what they're doing.* She smiled inwardly, *Not that we've actually ever made it as far as the bedroom.* A quiet giggle escaped her lips as she returned the teaspoon to the saucer, picked up her cup and forced herself to stop smiling long enough to take another sip of her coffee.

The smile returned only to slowly subside. She huffed audibly and couldn't help herself but to look around the café again. The waitress walked over to Matilda; reading her glances about the café as a need for service. "Can I get you something else?" she asked politely.

"No, thank you." Matilda replied, "I was actually just looking for a friend. I *will* pay my bill though," she decided, reaching into her handbag for her wallet.

"Chase?" asked the waitress.

Matilda's head snapped up and she looked pointedly at the waitress. The young woman was smiling back at her warmly. "Well, yes – as a matter of fact," Matilda nodded, resuming her search for her wallet. She found it and pulled it from the bag.

"I saw her driving toward the supermarket as I arrived to start my shift about 15 minutes ago. I'll bet she's still there. I hope she's meeting you here again afterwards," said the young waitress as she reached to accept the notes that Matilda offered, "…she always leaves me a good tip." The young woman smiled bemusedly before heading for the till with the cash.

Matilda's heart had leapt into her mouth. She quickly stuffed her wallet back into her handbag and slipped down from the stool. If Chase was taking time-out for shopping she might be available after all. *Only one way to find out,* she thought as she quickly left the café and made her way to the corner store.

♀♀♀♀♀

The small inner-city supermarket was busy as Matilda started walking up and down the aisles in search of Chase. *Please let her still be here!* She made a point of looking at the checkouts each time an isle offered a clear view to the front of store. She was still scrutinizing the last checkout as she rounded a display and began walking down another aisle. *Nope, she's not at the checkouts,* she concluded as she turned to look where she was going. Then, just a short distance before her, was her quarry. Chase was slowly pushing a shopping trolley toward her and looking from side to side at the products on the shelves.

Matilda stopped dead in her tracks and took in the view of the slight but strong and muscular form. Chase's short dark hair combed to stand upright from her head. Matilda could almost feel the cool shiny strands against her fingers and smell the sweet fragrance of Chase's shampoo. She watched the muscles ripple in Chase's arm as she reached out a hand and selected a packet of Tampons from the shelf, checked the label and then tossed it into her trolley. Matilda licked her lips, thinking, *Mmmm, she might be bleeding.*

Just then Chase suddenly looked in her direction and Matilda scrambled to make as though she was selecting a product from the shelf next to her.

"Hello, there!" greeted Chase, immediately making her way toward Matilda. "Fancy meeting you here," Chase offered a wide smile of genuine delight.

"Oh," said Matilda. "Hi, Chase. I was just doing a bit of...last minute shopping, you know..." attempting to act nonchalant. "I just needed to pick up some...." she waved at the shelf near to her before looking as if to pick up a product from the shelf.

"Condoms?" Chase questioned.

Matilda was dumbstruck as she finally acknowledged the products on the shelf she had just motioned toward and felt herself begin to deflate and redden. "Ah!...well!...no!" She felt awkward and words failed her. She closed her eyes, grimacing momentarily, and then opened them again. She took a deep breath and rolled her eyes before exhaling heavily and declaring, "Okay, so I'll admit I came here looking for you."

"Well, you found me," Chase managed through a giggle. "What can I do for you?"

Matilda looked down at the floor, tilted her head and flushed deeper still.

"Oh," said Chase. "I'm sure I can help you out with that." She moved closer to Matilda and placed her hand on her shoulder before sensuously running her fingers down the length of Matilda's arm.

Matilda slowly let her eyes drift up, appreciating Chase's body. Her slightly worn work boots. Her faded blue jeans, and her...bulging crotch. Matilda's heart threatened to burst from her chest it started beating so wildly. Her mouth went dry and her breath became shallow and rapid. She licked her parched lips and struggled to move her gaze above Chase's belt buckle. When she did she found Chase was wearing a white 'V' neck T-shirt and her nipples were clearly visible as raised nubs through the fabric.

Chase allowed her fingers to tickle the skin on Matilda's arm as they traveled back up to Matilda's shoulder. Finally Matilda managed to look upon Chase's face. Just then, Chase smiled, a sexy smile, as she noted her touch had elicited a shiver from Matilda. Satisfied, Chase moved her hand back to her trolley, "I've almost finished. Want to share my trolley for....your....shopping?" she gestured toward the small boxes of rubbers.

"I....actually, I don't need anything from here except you." Matilda said sidling up and falling into step with Chase. They smiled knowingly at each other and then continued on with Chase's shopping.

Matilda studied the contents of Chase's trolley. Mostly cans and easy-heat dinners. "Has Suzette gone on a holiday?" she enquired.

Chase looked at Matilda with soft blue eyes and replied, "No, I'm going on a sleep over. Want to come with me?"

"Absolutely!" Matilda responded immediately, *Coming with you is* exactly *what I've got in mind.*

Matilda brought Chase up to speed on the outcome her recent work trip abroad while they finished-up the shopping and made their way through the checkout. Matilda continued to speak and Chase managed to interject with the odd question of interest while she led the way to her Jeep Wrangler Sport Soft Top in the car park.

"Did you drive here?" Chase asked.

"No, I walked," answered Matilda easily.

"Oh, good," said Chase, packing the last of her shopping bags into the back of the Jeep. "You can ride with me, then."

Matilda smiled and nodded and Chase took her hand. Leading her to the passenger side of the vehicle, she opened the door to usher Matilda in. Matilda nodded her appreciation of the courtesy and then realized Chase was standing there waiting to help her climb into the vehicle. Not especially easy in her tight-fitting black skirt and high-heels.

"The easiest way is to put your right foot there," Chase said pointing to the forward base of the door frame, "and hold on to the hand grip with your right-hand and just lift yourself in."

Matilda attempted to follow her instructions only to find her skirt was just a little too tight to permit her right leg to reach the step. Chase reached down and helped by lifting the hem of Matilda's skirt to allow Matilda a wider range of movement. Foot on the step, Matilda lifted her body weight with her right arm as instructed and just as she was to hoist her backside into the seat, her high-heel slipped on the door frame. Matilda squealed softly for fear of falling just as Chase pressed her body weight against her and held her fast.

Chase was looking directly into her eyes. Their lips were all but touching and Matilda felt another shiver rise through her body as she realized Chase's bulging crotch was pressed against her pussy.

Chase swallowed hard and reached around and grasped Matilda by her buttocks, squeezing the tiny woman against her. When Matilda gasped, her breath tickled the skin on Chase's face as Chase leaned in and kissed her. The kiss was soft, gentle. Chase's rate of breathing was increasing as she broke the kiss, gazed at Matilda for a moment and then kissed her again.

Matilda moaned with the pleasure of Chase's slowly undulating hips. She reached and struggled to pull her skirt up to allow fuller contact with Chase's bulging crotch.

Chase lifted Matilda to help her sit her rear on the seat which freed her hands to help with lifting the skirt. Then she fumbled for her zipper and lowered it while Matilda reached under her skirt and pulled her panties to one side. Chase dipped her hand into her briefs and freed the cock she'd been packing.

Seeing the object of her desire, Matilda murmured, "Fuck, yeah!" She watched as Chase's fingers slipped down its shaft to push the fabric of her briefs out of the way. The maneuver caused the cock to wobble and Matilda groaned loudly, "Fuck me, Chase."

Chase leant in against Matilda and the tip of her cock found its target.

Matilda shuddered, her desire was so intense she could feel herself become dripping wet, "Fuck me, Chase!" she said a little louder.

"Shhh!" Chase whispered and quickly looked about the car park to make certain they hadn't attracted any unwanted attention. She wrapped her arms around Matilda and pulled her slowly closer; slowly, onto her cock.

"Mmm, yeah!" Matilda exclaimed throatily.

Chase leaned in again to kiss Matilda. Probing Matilda's mouth with her tongue in time with her pumping hips. Matilda tasted sweet, hot and wet.

Matilda tried to suck on Chase's tongue, knowing the action would help to keep her groans less audible to the public passing unawares close by. Still, she couldn't help but to make gasping, yelps and moans. It'd had been too long since the last time Chase had held her, kissed her, fucked her. She held on to Chase's shoulders and wrapped her legs as best she could around Chase's hips. She managed to move one hand down the front of Chase's top and lightly scratched the very tip of Chase's engorged nipple through her T-shirt and bra with the nail of her index finger.

Chase groaned loudly for her achingly erect nipple and pumped her hips faster still.

Matilda enjoyed the speed control playing with Chase's nipple provided and increased her attention accordingly. Then swapped to pay the same attention to the other nipple. Again, she was delighted with the affect it was having on Chase.

Chase pounded her pelvis into Matilda with all her might. Now if she could just stop Matilda from attracting every living sole in the general vicinity with the noise she was making. She stretched to kiss Matilda more passionately in an effort to stifle her cries of appreciation. She held Matilda tightly with one arm and moved to cup Matilda's breast with her free hand, catching Matilda's nipple between her thumb and first finger through the fine fabric of her blouse. At that instant Matilda's hips thrust forward and her legs tightened around Chase's hips. Her breathing stopped and started with a whimper, one after another after another.

Chase pressed hard up against Matilda's pussy and squeezed Matilda tightly to her, holding her there. Pulsating her thumb and first finger against Matilda's nipple and stroking Matilda's tongue with her own.

In that instant, Matilda threw her head back and let out a low throaty growl. She held her breath and tensed the muscles of her vagina, savoring the last of her orgasm.

Then she lifted her head to look into Chase's soft blue eyes while she waited for her breathing to quieten. Then she kissed Chase lightly on her nose, followed by her forehead, and finally her lips before stating, "You have no idea how badly I needed that." A moment later she released Chase from the vice-like grip of her thighs and wiped the sweat from her brow with the back of her hand.

"Welcome home." Chase smiled and kissed her deeply while she slowly withdrew from Matilda's soft, wet pussy.

"Mmmm," Matilda moaned, "you better put that away before we have to start again."

Chase gave a quiet little laugh and said, "Let's hit the road then."

♀♀♀♀♀

They drove through the city, making small-talk and taking some thirty minutes to reach the outer suburbs. It would have taken twice that time if they were in peak hour traffic. Matilda did most of the talking and rarely took her eyes from Chase. She delighted in every bump in the road and the resulting bounce in Chase's bosom. She appreciated the muscles that rippled in Chase's arms each time she changed gear or turned the wheel. She ogled the bulge of Chase's crotch and the way it moved each time Chase depressed the clutch or brake pedal.

The open highway meant traffic conditions became less and less complicated and they were soon speeding out of the city limits. Chase sat comfortably draping one hand over the gearstick while the other loosely gripped the wheel.

Matilda leaned over the short distance between them and placed her hand on Chase's thigh. Chase looked down at the touch and moved her hand from the gearstick to cover Matilda's hand on her leg. She took a second or two to look at Matilda and smile before returning her attention to the road.

Matilda slipped her hand out from under Chase's and ran her fingers down the inside of Chase's thigh. Chase placed her hand over Matilda's again, this time to grip and lift the smaller hand. Matilda was expecting to have her hand placed in a more neutral zone, but instead, Chase placed Matilda's hand on her crotch. She encouraged Matilda to squeeze the cock beneath the denim while Chase momentarily raised her hips against the pressure.

Matilda reached across with her other hand and unfastened Chase's belt buckle and then the button beneath it. She felt for and found the zipper slider and slowly pushed it all the way down. She reached in and pushed the denim aside pressing her hand down and cupping between Chase's legs. Chase lifted her hips momentarily and allowed Matilda to make more room for her hand by pushing her jeans downward a little.

Taking a deep breath Chase moaned softly as she felt Matilda's fingers lift the waistband of her briefs. She licked her lips and swallowed hard as Matilda slipped out of her seatbelt and leant across to lower her head into her lap.

When Matilda exposed Chase's cock she could smell her own scent on it and when she licked at the ripples near its tip, she could taste herself, her own nectar still apparent on it. She salivated in anticipation of licking the phallus clean.

Chase reached down and operated the lever to let the seat move back a notch to provide Matilda with a little more room between her and the steering wheel. Matilda moaned to signal her approval at the comfort provided. She rewarded Chase by placing downward pressure on the cock with her hand; the base of which was pressing down against Chase's clit.

Matilda leisurely moved her head back and forth, licking the full length of Chase's cock. Lapping loudly and sucking up every last morsel as she went. She began moving her hand up and down letting her fingers stroke Chase's slit through her briefs.

Chase looked down at Matilda's head making side to side movements in her lap. Licking loudly and unashamedly as she sucked and lapped at her cock. The way Matilda was stroking her slit, Chase could almost swear it was Matilda's head movements causing those sensations; as if she could really feel Matilda's mouth on her cock. She groaned and pushed her hips up slightly while forcing herself to look back at the road.

Matilda licked all around Chase's cock as far and low as her tongue could reach. She pushed against the material of Chase's jeans in an effort to get more access. Chase lifted her hips enough to allow Matilda to shift her briefs and jeans down her thighs a little more.

Matilda had just enough access now to be able to suck and stimulate as she pleased. The fabric of the briefs no longer a barrier as she resumed stroking Chase's slit with her fingers. When she began licking and sucking Chase's cock again, Chase groaned and her breathing accelerated. Matilda lifted her head from Chase's lap and looked at the pert and upright cock that waved in her face. She opened her mouth and took it in. She moaned with satisfaction, using her mouth to press the base of cock down, knowing it would place pressure against Chase's clit. Slowly she began taking Chase in and out of her mouth. Each time she pressed down on Chase's cock she ran her fingers down Chase's slit. Then running her fingers upward, every time her mouth moved to the cock's tip.

Chase kept looking down into her lap, watching Matilda's head slowly bobbing up and down against her, feeling as though she could really feel Matilda's mouth on her.

Chase decided she had to pull the SUV over before she had an accident. She indicated to use the emergency stopping lane and silently praised the Jeep's four wheel drive as she drove up over the curb and behind some shrubs and bushes growing at the side of the road. Once stopped, she reached down for the lever once more, letting the seat back a few more notches. Rummaging for another lever she allowed the seat back recline to a more comfortable position.

Matilda sucked Chase's cock to its tip – knowing that Chase could see her every action now – and licked the shaft with a broadly flattened tongue. As she licked upwards, she ran her fingers up Chase's slit. Then she opened her mouth and went down on Chase again, pressing the base against Chase's clit while at the same time running her fingers down Chase's slit. Sucking and lifting her head, stroking Chase's slit upward, licking down the side of Chase's cock as she was slipping her fingers downward again.

Chase was soaking wet and those juices were soaking away into the fabric of her briefs. Matilda scooped up as much of the fluid as she could and smoothed them over Chase's cock. A slight tinge of red smeared here and there.

"Oh, shit! I should change that tampon," Chase admitted.

"It's okay," Matilda calmed her. "It's only a little bit and your briefs are black. Don't worry." With that Matilda sucked the cock deeply into her mouth. Returning her fingers to Chase's slit and sliding them down as she pressed the base of the cock onto Chase's clit.

"Oh, Matilda. You little gem," Chase breathed through a grin.

Matilda made a low guttural chortle and then returned her attention to Chase's cock, slit and clit. Sucking up to the tip of the cock and moving her fingers up Chase's slit and then back down again with both her mouth and her fingers, applying pressure to Chase's clit. Matilda started to increase the speed and pressure a little with each cycle of the process. She was sucking and groaning with pleasure.

Chase brushed Matilda's hair away from her face so as not to obscure her view of the artful blowjob she was getting from Matilda.

Matilda opened her eyes and looked into Chase's bottomless blue ones. Sucking her cock to its tip, Matilda said quickly, "Tweak your nipples for me."

Chase lifted her T-shirt and undid her bra, smoothing her hands over her breasts and pushing her clothing upward and out of the way. Giving

Matilda a full view of her tits. Chase massaged her breasts for a while enjoying watching Matilda's head bobbing up and down ever faster on her cock while also seeing herself play with her own breasts. The sensations were overwhelming her. She could feel her climax approaching quickly.

Matilda slid her fingers up Chase's slit and hurriedly recoated the cock with Chase's pink-hued juices. Quickly licking her fingers before stroking Chase's slit again. Matilda sucked the cock hungrily, excited by the taste of Chase's juices on her cock, pressing it down onto Chase's clit. Matilda regularly looked up at Chase, watching her even more intently as Chase played with her own heaving breasts. When Chase began tweaking her nipples between her thumbs and forefingers, Matilda took Chase's cock deep in to her mouth, relaxed her throat and pushed it all the way down until the entire cock was swallowed. The downward pressure thrust the base of the cock against Chase's clit. She pushed her fingers up Chase's slit and pressed Chase's clit further into the base of the cock.

Chase opened her mouth, she may have been going to say something to Matilda, but when she felt that pressure on her clit not only from the base of her strap-on, but also from Matilda's fingers – effectively wedging her clit between them – her eyebrows lifted as if in surprise and then she screamed with her orgasm. Her legs shook with the intensity of the sensations. She could not take her eyes away from the erotic scene of Matilda's face pressed deeply into her lap.

When Matilda's mouth rode back up the shaft of her cock, Chase began pumping her hips, gasping and writhing and coming again as she watched herself pump her cock in and out of Matilda's mouth. She was squeezing and tweaking her own nipples harder and harder and coming against the pressure of Matilda's skillful fingers still pressing her clit against the base of the cock. Her orgasm washed over her time and again; a series of buzzing and tingling shock waves moving over her flesh.

Then Chase was only aware that her chest was heaving and she was moaning and groaning loudly, saying over and over, "Oh, Matilda! Oh, Matilda!"

When she finally stilled, Matilda kissed her way up Chase's torso and suckled on her nipples. Chase groaned and lifting her hips, surprised to feel aroused again so soon. Matilda had a firm grasp on her cock and started slowly moving her hand up and down its shaft.

Chase watched Matilda's hand work her cock and said, "You know I can always come again," she panted, "but it's gonna take a while to recover from an orgasm like that."

Matilda continued to suck Chase's nipples while she thought seriously about removing her panties and straddling Chase. She longed to feel Chase's cock fill her again, but she knew that would only lead to her also wanting to suck more cock. They needed to get to their destination and the sooner the better.

She sighed and reluctantly moved back to her own seat. "How much further do we have to go?"

"Another 20 minutes," said Chase as reached in the back for the trenching tool and the packet of tampons. "...but I have to make use of these bushes first." She took her bottle of water from her drink holder, opened the door and disappeared into the brush.

Matilda straightened her clothing and checked her hair and lipstick in the mirror.

By the time Chase climbed back into the Wrangler, Matilda was a picture of innocence. The sight of Matilda and the smell of her freshly applied fragrance hanging in the air made Chase smirk. *Such a Princess,* she thought as she started the engine and beat a track back to the road.

♀♀♀♀♀

Fifteen minutes later, Chase turned off the main highway and wound her way down a series of smaller and smaller roads, before turning onto what appeared to Matilda to be nothing but a dirt track. Chase pulled up at a gate and got out to open it.

She climbed back into the Jeep and excitedly announced, "We're here," before driving forward just far enough to be able to alight and close the gate behind them.

Here where? Thought Matilda as she looked down the bumpy track. *There's nothing here.*

Chase climbed back in and looked very pleased, "You're going to love this."

Matilda looked sideways at Chase and then cast her gaze out the side window to hide her uncertainty as they drove slowly around a bumpy bend and then down a steep embankment. Matilda was worrying if the little Wrangler would be able to take the steep climb out when it was time to leave.

Just past a grove of trees, the track turned onto a level section of ground just above a flowing creek. Nestled in amongst some Gum Trees was a small stone walled bungalow, surrounded by verandah. Chase pulled up in front of it and said, "Isn't it just perfect?"

"Oh, just," said Matilda feigning enthusiasm. *There's more verandah than house.*

They collected the supplies from the back of the Jeep and walked to the front door. Chase opened it without a key and walked straight into the kitchen.

Matilda followed and placed her load of shopping bags onto the kitchen bench. She looked around the bungalow as Chase searched through the shopping bags and finding what she was after, took toilet paper from one of the bags and made her way down a hallway saying, "Just need to take care of a little housekeeping and we'll be set."

Matilda sighed and continued to look around. The bungalow was tastefully furnished and the kitchen was actually very pretty although quaint with its old fashioned Meters wood fired oven and lacey country-style curtains in the windows. She looked out through the window and noticed two rocking chairs on the verandah. Just in front of them a few steps down to a walkway which led down to the creek. Here and there, where the sun peaked through the trees, were outcrops of colorful wildflowers. Birds flitted by and landed on the verandah's balustrade, twittering and dancing and then flying off together just as a Magpie trilled its' beautiful song. *Maybe it* is *perfect, just as she said,* thought Matilda.

And then it *was* perfect, as two strong arms gently wrapped about her and soft, wet lips lightly touched on her neck. "What are you thinking?" asked Chase.

"It's beautiful here," replied Matilda honestly, turning in the circle of Chase's arms. She ran her hands around Chase's waist and rested her head against Chase's bosom. As Chase ran her fingers through Matilda's hair, Matilda stated, "It's just perfect."

"Mmm, I got a local lady to come in and clean this morning, but there's a few things that I think need attention. I don't usually bring company with me when I head up here."

"I'll put the groceries away, while you go...." Matilda stopped in midsentence as she heard a mobile ring. She reached for her mobile phone only to realize that it was Chase's pants pocket that was ringing and not her handbag.

"Huh!" said Chase, fishing in her pocket for her phone. "That's another thing that's different, we don't usually get mobile coverage out here either." As she finally untangled the phone from her pocket, it stopped ringing and then beeped to signal a new message. "I usually have to trek up to the top of the embankment to check for messages."

Matilda began to check the kitchen cupboards and fridge for places to stow the shopping while Chase walked away checking her phone message, "Oh, by the way, Chase," Matilda called after her, "I need to be back in the city by mid-afternoon tomorrow. I've got to prepare for an important business meeting."

Chase read the message on her phone. '[*I've booked you out for tomorrow night. A car will be here to pick you at 7 sharp. Suz*].'

"Yes, okay," Chase smiled, "That works in well with me."

♀♀♀♀♀

Matilda rocked herself gently in the rocking chair on the verandah of Chase's hideaway in the bush. Occasionally, she would stop rocking just

197

long enough to take a sip of the coffee she'd placed on the table between the twin rockers. It wasn't a quiet setting at all; the birds chirping and calling even drowned out the sound of the running creek at the bottom of the hill. A gentle breeze tickled her skin and played in her hair as she thought, *this is as relaxed as I've felt since.....mmm....since Chase took care of me in Hong Kong.* She chuckled softly to herself as she relived some of those moments spent in her hotel room in Calhoun.

Just then she heard the kitchen door open and waited for Chase to walk around the corner of the verandah. "Hey, good lookin'," she said as Chase slowly approached her. Matilda studied Chase; struck by the calmness with which Chase ambled along the verandah, *she is so...self-assured, so strong and yet, so relaxed.* Chase had showered and changed, now wearing a black tank-top and blue jeans. As Matilda eyed her crotch area, she realized that Chase was no longer sporting her strap-on.

"Well, you look very comfortable." Chase smiled as she appreciated Matilda's relaxed body language, as she gently rocked in the chair. "So, am I still in your 'good books' even after bringing you here?"

"Oh yes!" Matilda nodded easily, "The only thing that worries me is how your little four-wheel-drive is going to make it back up that hill."

"No need for worry, Matilda. I've got that down to a fine art these days," Chase said waving off Matilda's concern as she sat in the other rocking chair.

Matilda caught a whiff of Chase's freshly shampooed hair and made a mental note for herself to press her face into those soft, shiny, short strands at the very next opportunity. She imagined them tickling her face while she deeply breathed in that scent. Her eyes drifted down, taking in Chase's amazingly bottomless blue eyes. Her luscious pink lips that smiled even as she spoke. Her strong, muscular neck and shoulders, and ample bosom.

"....so I took a shower, I hope you didn't mind the wait?"

Matilda suddenly realized Chase had been talking while she had been daydreaming. She blinked herself back to alertness. "Not at all," she recovered. "I had noticed you were carrying a lighter load," Matilda smirked as she pointed at Chase's crotch.

Chase looked down to follow Matilda's direction and laughed, "Yes, Penny had a date with a sanitary bucket. She's still drying-off in the bathroom."

"Penny! You named your poker, Penny? Penny the Penis?" Matilda chortled before taking another sip of her coffee.

"No! Penny Stick," Chase retorted indignantly.

Matilda almost choked trying to complete her swallow and then doubled over laughing. A mental image of a hard, pink, phallic-shaped, musk-flavored candy cane, pictured large in her mind. Her mother used to call them "penny-sticks" and buy them for her as a child. She looked up at Chase, covered her mouth with the tips of her fingers as if in apology and laughed some more at the supercilious grin on Chase's face. She continued to giggle, as she gestured and attempted to make comment with regard to her 'fellatio-styled antics' during their earlier road trip. Eventually, breathless from laughter, she managed to compose herself enough to clear her throat and say, "Ahem. Yes. Apt name for her." Unable to keep-a-straight-face, she snorted loudly and giggled some more.

Chase giggled with her, finding Matilda's humor enjoyable. The sound of her laughter was intoxicating; compelling even. She wanted to make Matilda laugh some more so she could hear that delightful sound again and again.

"So, what's next?" Matilda asked as she kicked off her high-heels and pushed them under the rocking chair with her toes.

"As it happens, I'm running a bath for you as we speak. In fact, I had better go and check on it," she said, starting to stand. As she walked back up the verandah she tossed back over her shoulder to Matilda, "Come into the bathroom when you're ready."

♀♀♀♀♀

Matilda finished her coffee and dropped off her cup and saucer to the kitchen on her way through to the bathroom. Walking down the hallway that came off of the lounge room and following the sound of running water. As she went, she took the time to look into the remaining rooms of the house: two bedrooms, a bathroom, toilet and laundry. *Mmm, compact but functional,* she thought as she pushed the door of the bathroom open.

Inside Chase stood bent over the old-fashioned Esperanza bathtub situated at the center of the room. Behind her was a walk-in twin shower screened only by an almost invisible glass sheet wall. To Matilda's left were twin vanities and on her right, a number of towels hung over towel rails and closer to the doorway was a diamond pattern of four coat hooks. An unusual layout, that struck Matilda as being logical and pleasing to the eye. She turned to close the bathroom door and mused momentarily at Penny Stick hanging there from a hook on the back of it; erect and ready.

Chase had changed again and was now wearing a sheer, three quarter sleeve, creamy yellow robe which left Matilda in no doubt she was completely naked underneath. Chase finished stirring her hand through the water and turned off the taps situated at the foot of the tub. She turned to welcome Matilda.

The Esperanza's high back beckoned Matilda to indulge herself; to lounge back and soak, in ergonomic comfort. She walked to Chase's outstretched arms, pressing her hands to Chase's chest and reveled in the security of the strong embrace. She drew in a deep breath and breathed out heavily as strong fingers moved through her thick wavy hair and gently massaged her scalp. She closed her eyes and rested her head against Chase's cleavage, just above her own fingertips and gave herself over to Chase completely.

Chase smoothed her hands over Matilda's shoulder blades, down to the small of her back and then cupped her buttocks, holding Matilda against her while kissing the top of her head.

Matilda sighed and nuzzled the cleavage with her face as Chase began to tug at her blouse and free it and the chemise from her skirt. Chase reached under the hem of the undergarment and gently ran her fingers over the skin on the small of Matilda's back. Matilda murmured appreciatively when Chase lightly ran her fingers around Matilda's waist and began to slowly undo the buttons of her blouse. When Matilda moved her body slightly away from Chase to allow access to the remainder of the buttons, Chase reached up with a single finger, angling Matilda's jaw upward, so that she could lean in and press her lips to Matilda's. She tickled Matilda's neck and chest; her fingertip following the neckline of Matilda's blouse to the top button, undoing it effortlessly.

Chase reached in under the unbuttoned blouse and gently fondled Matilda's small breasts through the smooth fabric of her chemise. She ran her palms over Matilda's upper body to cup and hold the back of her head while she deepened the kiss, pressing her tongue between Matilda's waiting lips. They luxuriated in that kiss for many moments as Chase slowly pushed Matilda's unbuttoned blouse over her shoulders and down her arms, letting it fall the floor. Matilda pushed her hands up Chase's chest, over her shoulders and interlocked her fingers behind Chase's neck. Chase raised her hands to Matilda's torso and slipped them under the chemise. She smoothed her fingers up the sides of Matilda's body, carrying the chemise up with her wrists; breaking their kiss just long enough for the garment to pass over Matilda's head. Matilda, hands held loosely above her head was now naked from the waist up.

Chase wrapped her arms around Matilda and cuddled her close. Her hands moved caressingly back and forth over Matilda's back and buttocks as they kissed deeply once more. Then, allowing one hand to fall toward the small of Matilda's back, Chase unbuttoned the waistband of the skirt and slid the zipper open. The skirt fell away and Chase marveled at the feel of bare buttocks afforded by Matilda's lacey thong.

Breaking their kiss, Chase leaned back and looked upon Matilda's face. Matilda's eyes expressed her relaxed state and the upturn at the corners of her mouth told Chase that she was wielding her magic well.

Chase kissed Matilda's forehead softly, then her chin and the apex of her sternum. She kissed the soft skin of her tummy as she hooked Matilda's thong with both thumbs and pushed them lower.

Matilda separated her legs slightly to allow the tiny piece of lace to slip over her inside thighs as Chase squatted before her, moving the panties still lower. Chase leaned in, pressing her nose to Matilda's center, to breathe in the heady scent as Matilda stepped out of her last stitch of clothing. Drawing another deep breath, Chase took her last opportunity to bask in Matilda's scent before it was washed away. Matilda pressed her center to Chase's face, groaning as she exhaled slowly. Holding Chase's head to her she encouraged Chase to kiss and tongue her slit.

Chase opened her mouth wide and wrapped her lips around the area her tongue had moistened and sucked in the juices. She felt her own wetness increasing when she heard Matilda moan, "Oh, yes," and felt Matilda's fingers toying with her hair. She wrapped her arms around Matilda's legs and grasped the cheeks of her ass. She pressed the little woman against her, sucking Matilda's salty lips and clit deeply into her mouth. Holding Matilda in place with the suction of her mouth, Chase ran her tongue in small circles over Matilda's clit.

Matilda hissed as she inhaled and said, "Faster! Suck it! Lick it and suck it faster!"

Chase complied and held Matilda fast as the little woman began to shake and waver. Matilda let go of Chase's head and reached behind her. Locking her elbows, she leant hard against the tub, holding the weight of her upper body and giving herself a better view of Chase's face pressed against her wetness.

"I'm about to come! Oh! Faster!"

Chase sucked and licked for all she was worth, holding Matilda's weight up by her butt cheeks and preventing her from crumbling to the floor. "Oh, Chase!" Matilda screamed, "I'm – oh, Chase!"

Trembling, breathing heavily, Matilda came long and hard into Chase's mouth. She let her head fall back for the last few moments of her orgasm and growled out her ecstasy. Chase could feel Matilda's flesh shrinking from her mouth and sucked harder in an attempt to ensure none of the sweet nectar of Matilda's orgasm escaped her waiting tongue.

"Oh!" Matilda exclaimed as she snapped her head forward and looked down into Chase's eyes. Chase stopped and gently kissed the triangle of pubic hair on Matilda's mound while Matilda slowly took her own body weight with her legs.

Chase quickly kissed her way up Matilda's torso. Wrapping Matilda in her arms, she looked deeply into her eyes as though searching for something important there. She held Matilda tightly for a few moments before closing her eyes and gently kissing her lips. She gently explored Matilda's mouth with her tongue until Matilda's breathing began to slow and she seemed steadier on her feet.

"Hop into the bath, Sweetheart," Chase encouraged, holding Matilda's arm to steady her while she stepped over its high sides. "Not too hot?" Chase checked with her before allowing Matilda to sit down.

"No, it's perfect. Everything is perfect, thank you." Matilda smiled warmly and allowed herself to be lost in the depth of Chase's eyes.

Chase held Matilda's gaze as she soaped up a Loofah slice and skillfully exfoliated the soles and heels of Matilda's feet. Matilda leaned against the backrest of the Esperanza and let her body slip under the warm soothing water. Having attended to Matilda's feet, Chase traded the Loofah for a Mesh Pouf richly lathered with soap and laced with essential oils. Matilda delighted in holding up each of her legs in turn, turning and twisting them to control the length and depth of attention Chase paid to the task of bathing them. As Chase neared Matilda's pussy, she smeared the soapy ball along the crease of her groin and Matilda gladly rolled over to allow Chase access to wash her buttock. They then repeated the process for the other side. Chase grinned as she acknowledged Matilda's enjoyment. *I'm not certain which of us is enjoying this the most,* she thought as she completed the task and lowered Matilda's leg into the water.

Moving up the side of the bath, she kissed Matilda on the forehead and said, "Scoot forward a bit and let me in." Then she stood upright and slowly pulled at the tie of her robe.

Matilda watched, mouth gaping, as the knot gave way and the robe parted. A jiggle or two of Chase's shoulders and the sheer fabric fell away leaving her naked. Matilda grabbed the sides of the bath and pulled herself forward while Chase stepped in behind her with the lathered Mesh Pouf. Chase held the sides of the bath while she threaded her legs either side of Matilda and lowered herself into the water. Once Chase was seated comfortably against the backrest, Matilda leaned back and snuggled up between Chase's legs and arms.

Chase washed Matilda's arms and armpits and again Matilda controlled the attentions with twists and turns, rises and falls. Chase didn't need a bath, of course, but it was a sexy way to complete the wash attendant process. She gently pushed Matilda forward and used the small pool of water between her legs and Matilda's bottom to re-lather the pouf. Then she smoothed it over all of Matilda's back and shoulders causing Matilda to break out in goose bumps. Matilda groaned with pleasure as Chase began to scrub a little harder in little spiraling circles, leaving no part untouched. Matilda's skin reddened and she groaned once more.

Pulling Matilda back to lean against her again, Chase slowly lathered-up the pouf between Matilda's legs, intentionally stroking at Matilda's pussy with her thumbs as she did so. Matilda giggled at the light tickle. Chase began to wash Matilda's tummy and bellybutton and then each of her breasts with gentle swirls of the soapy little ball. She paid particular attention to Matilda's nipples until each rose into a tightly wrinkled peak.

Pressing the Mesh Pouf between Matilda's breasts, Chase slowly drove the little ball of foaming suds in a straight line, down over Matilda's bellybutton and tummy, over her mound and between her legs. Matilda spread her legs, lifting and draping them over the sides of the bath. Chase held onto the Mesh Pouf with just the tips of her fingers and thumb, working her wrist back and forth to lightly run the edges of the mesh up and down Matilda's sex.

Matilda exhaled with a throaty moan, "Oh, Chase, I can't believe it, but I'm gonna come again."

"Mmm-hmm," nodded Chase, "just relax for me, baby."

Chase held Matilda tightly to her with her free hand while continuing her unrelenting rhythm with the other, gently moving just the fringes of the mesh up and down against Matilda's slit.

Matilda began to breathe more quickly, taking shorter and shorter breaths. Just as she climaxed, Chase pinched Matilda's nipple between her thumb and forefinger, rolling it firmly and skillfully while Matilda let out a long, ardent scream and then panted before her.

Chase leaned forward and lifted Matilda's legs back into the warm water. She wrapped Matilda's arms across her own tummy and breasts. Leaning back against the backrest, Chase folded her arms around Matilda and held her in a secure embrace. She listened to her breathing, waiting for Matilda to recover while whispering reassuringly into her ear.

Several minutes passed as they lay that way. Chase listed all of Matilda's endearing qualities in gentle whispers against her ear, lightly kissing her from time to time; worshipping her.

When the water seemed to cool, Chase motioned for Matilda to sit up. Chase then slipped quietly out of the bath and put on her robe. Picking up a bottle from the vanity, Chase uncorked it and poured a teaspoonful or so of its contents into the bathwater. "Stay there," she requested before moving to the taps and turning on the hot water. Now that Chase wasn't in the bath, there was plenty of room to top it up and rewarm it. Bubbles began to form over the water's surface and Matilda almost squealed her enthusiasm for a bubble bath.

Chase grinned as she stirred the water to even out the temperature for Matilda. "You stay in here and have a good, long soak. You've earned it after that trip away."

Matilda nodded compliance, leaned back and luxuriated in the bath, as ordered. Meanwhile, Chase filled a sink at the vanity and quickly washed and rinsed Matilda's panties. Then she walked around the bath and hung the panties over a hook. Turning back toward the bath, she stooped to collect the remainder of Matilda's clothing before leaving the room.

As the door closed behind Chase, Penny Stick wobbled on her hook and continued to rock for a few moments, keeping Matilda's attention on her. Matilda studied the sex toy and wondered, *Mmmm, would that fit me?*

♀♀♀♀♀

Fifteen minutes later, Chase returned with a soft bathrobe and to help Matilda out of the bath. "You *really* look relaxed, now. I'd better get you out of there before you fall asleep." She pushed the door closed behind her and Penny Stick did another little dance on the back of the door above Chase's head.

Matilda giggled. As she stepped onto the bath mat Chase had quickly placed beside the bath she said, "Just in time. I was about to turn into a prune, I think."

Chase hung the bathrobe on a hook, disrobed herself and led Matilda into the walk-in shower. She quickly got the water to the right temperature and then they rinsed themselves off under the spray.

Then Chase helped Matilda into the fluffy bathrobe and patted her down all over to dry her off, before retrieving and donning her own robe. She took a towel from the rack behind her, shook it open and dropped to her knees to dry Matilda's calves and feet. Standing afterward Chase asked, "Would you like me to get you a pair of slippers?"

"No, thank you, Chase. If it's alright, I'd like to walk about the house barefoot."

"Certainly," Chase agreed and then added, "I've got a meal heating in the microwave for you." She took Matilda's hand and went to lead her from the bathroom, but Matilda stood fast. "Is there a problem?" Chase inquired, her brow slightly furrowed.

"Not a problem, per se," Matilda started slowly. "I was just wondering..." she began to look coy and was starting to lose her nerve for the question she'd resolved to ask while she was soaking in the tub.

"It's okay, Matilda. I do requests." She took Matilda's hands and looked into Matilda's eyes, before adding, "Just ask me."

"Can I use your strap-on." Matilda blurted out with her eyes closed.

Chase chuckled and then answered, "No."

Matilda opened her eyes in surprise and then looked disappointed until Chase added, "I'll give you one of your own to use on me."

Matilda smiled and almost did a little jump of excitement, "Oh, goodie" she whispered and then asked, "is it against policy to share for some reason?"

Chase quietly explained, "It's not a good idea to share a sex toy with anyone, Matilda."

"Oh, of course!" she said smacking herself in the forehead, "I should have thought of that." *It's just that...I keep forgetting you're not my girlfriend. Actually, I keep forgetting that you're a Gigola.*

"And usually," continued Chase, "I wouldn't re-use Penny Stick, either. I'd generally wear her, use her and then discard her. The next time we're together with her, she'll be brand new out of the packet. It's just that...I wasn't really expecting to have company...so, I've been caught short and that's why I've had to sanitize her."

Matilda nodded her understanding, "I'm glad to know that, really." Then asked, "So when will I get my own to use?"

"Tonight!" Chase answered immediately to reassure, Matilda. "I have several to fit me." Then elaborated, "I prefer a larger size to you, Matilda." She smiled broadly at Matilda's look of excitement, amazement and then wonderment, exhibited all in one smooth series of expressions. "Now, let's go eat dinner."

♀♀♀♀♀

After dinner, Matilda sat on the lounge in front of the fireplace with a glass of red wine in her hand. She watched with great interest as Chase set the fireplace and got it started.

Chase stood and collected her glass of wine from the mantel. She turned to Matilda and asked, "Have you ever toasted marshmallows?"

"No," Matilda responded. "Never."

"Well then," said Chase, "you're in for a treat." She went into the kitchen and searched through the cupboards until she found where Matilda had stowed the bag of marshmallows. Then, she looked through the kitchen drawers and quite noisily located the roasting fork. Heading back to the little lounge room she said, "There's a knack to it, but I'm an expert, so I'll show you." She knelt in front of the fire and took the poker from the stand next to the fireplace to reposition a few pieces of the wood. Then she exclaimed, "Oh, shoot! I left my wine in the kitchen." She stood and almost ran to the kitchen, fetched her glass and returned.

Matilda watched her with great amusement. Swiveling her head about to keep Chase in view as the woman jumped about like a jackrabbit. She giggled a little, getting caught-up in Chase's excitement. *Where does she get all this energy?* Matilda wondered with a bemused smile.

Once Chase had the fire burning substantially enough, she crawled to the lounge and took two of the cushions, placing them on the floor in front of the fireplace. She sat on one and opened the marshmallows, poking one onto her fork. She looked up at Matilda seated on the lounge, all rugged up in her bathrobe. Matilda was watching her intently a pleased expression on her otherwise tired face.

"Come down here and sit with me, Matilda." Chase patted the other cushion.

Matilda moved to sit with Chase and Chase showed her how the marshmallow needed to be threaded onto the fork. Next, she held it above the flame, "You can't put it in the flame, otherwise it will just burn and go black and horrible." She began to twirl it, so as to keep it evenly heated over its exterior. "All we really wanna do is get it hot and mooshy." Matilda watched the little ball hover above the flame. Suddenly it looked to droop a little from the fork. "That's it," said Chase, "Now it's ready to eat." She removed the marshmallow from the flame and blew on it a little before offering it to Matilda. "Be careful it's not so hot as to burn your tongue, Matilda," she warned as Matilda opened her mouth to accept the treat.

"Mmmm," said Matilda, "It just collapsed over my tongue, that's quite different, isn't it?" she said delightedly around her mouthful.

Chase was glad to see Matilda suddenly revitalized and offered her the fork to try her hand at toasting a marshmallow.

Matilda accepted the fork and watched carefully as Chase threaded another marshmallow on to it. Then she held the marshmallow over the fire, although somewhat lower than Chase had. After a few moments the marshmallow caught alight and Matilda grumbled with disappointment.

"Not to worry," said Chase using a piece of kindling to knock the charred goo from the end of the fork and into the fire where it crackled and sparkled as it burned away. Chase held Matilda's hand and moved the fork into position for threading another marshmallow. Then she sat back and watched quietly as Matilda reinserted it over the flames. A better position this time, but soon it started to brown on its underside, "Twirl it, Matilda," Chase said patiently and Matilda complied. As soon as it began to sag between twirls, Chase indicated for Matilda to remove it from the flame. As Matilda went to put it in her mouth, Chase reminded her, "Blow on it a bit first, Sweetheart." Matilda nodded, blew and then removed the pliable little ball with her teeth; tentatively chewing at first to check its temperature, then chewing more quickly with a smile. She nodded her delight as she handed the fork back to Chase.

Chase took the fork and toasted a marshmallow for herself. Handing the fork back to Matilda she watched as her student correctly threaded the next ball before poking it above the flame. When it was toasted to perfection, Matilda withdrew it and proudly offered her prize to Chase. Chase blew on it and caught Matilda's gaze as she slowly, sensuously took the treat between her teeth and prized it from the fork.

Matilda felt a stirring between her legs. Her lips parted and her tongue peaked between to moisten them.

Chase swallowed and copied Matilda's example before leaning across to kiss Matilda's lips. Her heart beat fast and her skin tingled. When her lips met Matilda's she lost her breath and her heart skipped a beat. *What the fuck?* she wondered for a moment and then was lost in the passion of that kiss.

The fork clinked onto the hearth when Matilda dropped it and they each wrapped the other in an embrace. The kiss deepened and their tongues twirled together in a sugar-induced wetness.

Chase broke the kiss, opened Matilda's robe and fondled her breasts. Matilda's chest was heaving with her sexual excitement, as was Chase's. "I think we should go to bed now."

Matilda nodded a silent agreement as Chase leapt to her feet and then helped Matilda to stand. Taking Matilda's hand, Chase led her down the hall and into the bedroom. She bent to remove the covers from the bed; tossing them over the wrought iron lacework at the base of the bed and onto the floor. Then she stood and removed her robe, throwing it onto a nearby chair. She helped Matilda out of her fluffy bathrobe and that too, was tossed onto the chair.

Standing before each other, they took a moment to appreciate each other's bodies. Chase's chest was still heaving, her breasts moving up and down with each breath. Matilda's gaze moved lower, eyeing the faintly muscled, sculpted abdomen; then the closely cropped triangle of pubic hair. Lower still, she scrutinized the strong, shapely legs. Then, briefly looking toward the bed, Matilda appreciated the red sheets and asked, "Are you still bleeding?"

"Just barely spotting, really. I'm not needing a tampon," answered Chase honestly trying to gauge Matilda's opinion on the matter.

"So," said Matilda, "where's my strap-on?"

"Oh, right!" Chase exclaimed and moved to open a drawer in the bedside cabinet behind her. She pulled out a brand new dildo and pitched it onto the bed while she bent over still further to find another blister pack. This one held the harness which she opened quickly while turning back to face Matilda.

Chase fiddled with the adjusters to an approximation of Matilda's body size, before bending in front of Matilda to fasten the clasps and adjusted it to fit perfectly. She put her fingers under the straps and tested their tension and seating. Then, she reached onto the bed and retrieved the dildo from its wrapper, holding it up for Matilda to inspect for a few moments before bending down to fit it to the harness.

"My," said Matilda, "there is no way I could deep throat that."

Chase laughed and tugged on the phallus a few times to check its connection.

"Ooh!" said Matilda in delighted surprise. "Do that again."

Chase laughed again, reached down between her own legs and scooped up some of the wetness inspired by that bombshell of a kiss in front of the fire. She smeared it over Matilda's phallus before taking it in her fist and sliding her fingers up and down the staff.

"Mmm," said Matilda, "I'm beginning to understand the attraction."

Chase lifted her free hand and lightly ran the back of her knuckles over Matilda's nipple. She stepped closer and pressed her lips to Matilda's.

Matilda murmured, "Bed," against Chase's lips and started pushing Chase backward. When the backs of Chase's legs made contact, she sat down on the edge and took Matilda's cock into her mouth. She held Matilda by her hips and gently worked them back and forth. Matilda was thrilled at first, to watch as Chase took her cock into her mouth. Soon, she found herself becoming overwhelmed by the sensations of the cock pressing against her throbbing clit and the vision of Chase sucking it. Her legs began to shake and weaken and she knew if she didn't get Chase to stop soon she would come, and Matilda didn't want that to happen just yet. Her fantasy in the bathtub had been about coming inside Chase. She had to get Chase and herself onto the bed and she had to do it now!

"Do you have a name for this one as well?" Matilda asked breathlessly.

When Chase released her oral grip on Matilda's cock to answer, Matilda took the opportunity to push Chase back onto the bed, climb over the top of her and lay on her side next to Chase. She propped herself up on an elbow and lightly smoothed her palm over Chase's torso as she awaited a response.

"Penny." Chase answered, smiling wryly as she laid back. Tucking one arm under her head as she allowed herself to be pushed back onto the bed.

Matilda screwed up her face a little at the name, "Do you call all your tools, Penny Stick?"

Matilda asked as she drew slow swirling patterns over Chase's tummy with her palm.

"No," said Chase. "This one is Pretty Penny?"

Matilda stopped, looked puzzled for a moment and then studied her cock as it rested against Chase's upper thigh, "Do you really like the look of it that much?"

"No." said Chase, shaking her head, "I call her that because she cost a pretty penny."

Matilda laughed and lightly slapped at Chase for teasing her.

Chase caught Matilda's hand, hugging it to her chest as she laughed too thinking, *there's that delightful sound again. I love it when she laughs.* She smiled to herself, pleased at evoking such a delightful comeback from Matilda and then, shock set in, *Love?* She shook her head and closed her eyes for a second. *Shake yourself out of this and get back to work,* she chastised herself. She removed her hand from behind her head and reached up to clutch the back of Matilda's neck; pulling her down for a kiss. Parting her lips, she caught Matilda's bottom lip, gently sucking it into her mouth and playing her tongue over it. Parting her lips again, she caught Matilda's top lip for an instant before searching out Matilda's tongue with her own.

Matilda bit down lightly on Chase's tongue, eliciting a groan. Chase's legs parted and her hips rose slightly. *She definitely likes that,* thought

Matilda, biting down lightly on Chase's tongue again to test her theory. Chase's hips gently lifted a little again. Matilda cupped her hand over Chase's mound and pressed her fingers through her slick folds.

Chase groaned and pushed her pussy against Matilda's fingers as they traced a circle around and then sunk lightly into her opening. Fingertips coated with slick fluids moved upward to separate and moisten the swollen drapes that covered Chase's clit. Chase groaned and pressed her tongue deeply into Matilda's mouth as Matilda's fingertips again dipped lightly into her pussy.

"Oh, fuck me, Matilda!" Chase breathed as she moved her head to kiss Matilda from a better angle.

Matilda rolled over onto all fours placing her hands either side of Chase's head allowing her nipples to brush over Chase's chest as she repeatedly kissed and bit down gently on Chase's tongue.

Chase began breathing more deeply; running her fingers up and down Matilda's back, lightly scratching with her nails. Her other hand hovered, waiting to catch and support Matilda should she begin the climb between her legs.

Matilda kissed Chase's chin, then her neck and her chest before lifting a leg over to rest between Chase's legs. Chase held Matilda firmly by her shoulders and noticing Matilda's tongue reaching toward her nipple, slowly lowered the little woman to allow her to suck a hardened peak into her mouth. Matilda's cock hung low and rested heavily on Chase's groin.

"Mmm, Matilda, that feels so good. Suck it, baby." Chase was panting so heavily now, that every word was breathy and labored. Matilda sucked hard on Chase's nipple, and swirled her tongue over its apex. She lifted her head and stretched Chase's breast up by the nipple, making a popping sound as she released it to go in search of its twin. As she sucked the other nipple into her mouth, she supported herself with her arms either side of Chase's upper body – now on all fours and straddling Chase. She lifted her other leg over, and nestled herself between Chase's legs. She pressed her face between Chase's breasts and reached down with one hand to guide her cock toward Chase's pussy. Chase ran her hands down Matilda's back, reaching down to take hold of Matilda's ass cheeks – one in each hand – preparing to help push when Matilda's cock prodded her opening.

"Down a little lower, honey," Chase guided, "Yes, baby, right there. Mmm, push into me." A little yelp escaped Chase's throat as Matilda pushed. When Matilda stopped for fear of having caused her pain, Chase grasped her ass cheeks tighter and pressed the little woman hard into her rising hips. "Mmm, yeah, Matilda. Fuck me!"

Matilda attempted to comply, but found she was slipping backward, losing her grip as she pressed her knees into the bed. Lifting herself higher, attempting to climb a little further up Chase's torso for stability, she pressed in with her hips again. She had a little more success with this strategy but still, was not satisfied. So she straightened her legs and dug into the bed with her toes. She pressed her hips into Chase and sensed the cock slide a little further into Chase's pussy.

Struggling, knowing she would soon fatigue and fail, she said, "I'm having trouble with this Chase, I think I must be too small to do it properly."

Chase pulled Matilda tightly to her, wrapped her legs over the back of Matilda's and tucked her feet in under Matilda's shins, effectively clamping the pair of them together. "How's that?" Chase said dreamily, betraying her enjoyment of the penetration thus far.

Matilda pressed down again with her hips and her cock slid easily into Chase. The stability offered by Chase's entwined legs made her feel like she could do this all night if she needed to. Another pump of her hips and she could sense that her cock was richly coated with Chase's juices. It easily slipped into Chase with each thrust and she could gauge Chase's wetness by the sounds her cock made as it glided in and out. It also pressed delightfully against Matilda's clit each time Matilda pressed down with her hips. Even the withdrawal from Chase's pussy caused a delectable sensation. All these sensations and sounds served to arouse Matilda; reawakening her clit once more.

"Oh, yes, Matilda. That feels incredible," Chase encouraged.

Matilda kissed Chase's breasts and bit at their well-rounded flesh as she attempted to continue pumping. She found it a challenge to maintain her rhythm when her concentration was disrupted by the sensations on her clit as well as her attempts to suckle at Chase's nipples. She smiled up at Chase and said, "This isn't as easy as I thought it would be." She giggled a little and added, "I have a whole new sense of respect for your talents, darling."

Catching Chase's gaze Matilda was compelled to kiss Chase on the lips, only to find she couldn't reach. She was too short.

Chase kissed her fingertip and then pressed it to Matilda's lips before she wrinkled her nose and said, "I can fix that." She reached for the pillow next her and positioned it against the bedhead. "Hold on tight," she instructed as she pressed both of her strong arms into the bed and slid the two of them up until she was resting her shoulders high on the pillows. Her head was considerably closer to Matilda and a kiss was now within comfortable reach. More than that, Matilda discovered, it was an extremely pleasant reach when coupled with a downward thrust of her hips.

This not only drove her cock into Chase's wet pussy, it also pressed delightfully into her own slit, moving her clit up and down with each movement in and out.

"Mmm," she moaned into Chase's mouth as she began to find her rhythm. Chase moved her hands up and down over Matilda's back, which helped signal a constant rhythmic action for Matilda to follow.

Chase feasted hungrily on Matilda's mouth, murmuring encouragement and hissing her pleasure against Matilda's lips. She became drunk on the ecstasy of being fucked by such an eager and appreciative student.

Matilda began breathing heavily. The deeper she pressed her cock into Chase, the longer the strokes delivered to her clit by the base of the cock. The faster she pumped into Chase; the quicker the strokes across her clit. The sensations soon clouded her awareness until she could imagine it *was* her clit thrusting within her lover. The sucking sounds now doubled by her own wetness, thrilled her, further heightening the sensations she was feeling.

She began thrusting in and out of Chase more rapidly; overcome by her own need and by the sensations on her clit. Her whole body seemed to be abuzz. Breathing heavily, hyperventilating, feeling light headed and oversensitive. She felt – intoxicated.

She couldn't kiss Chase any longer. She needed to suck air into her lungs through both her nose and mouth as she pumped her hips faster and faster. She stared into Chase's eyes, mesmerized with the movement of her eyelids. Chase's eyes would half-close each time Matilda drove her cock in to the hilt. Her cock was pounding wetly, noisily into Chase; in and out, faster and faster.

Chase held Matilda's gaze with those depthless blue eyes, her lips slightly parted to moan her delight at the penetration. The look on Matilda's face as she grew closer and closer to orgasm had Chase fascinated, awe-struck. She lifted her hips to meet Matilda's every downward thrust; their pussy's slapping together with abandon.

Then Matilda's eyes closed and the thrusts of her cock became more deliberate, timed to the rhythm of Matilda's pulsating clit. Her face flushed and her expression softened as her lips parted widely in an unspoken scream. She was coming. And it was good.

Matilda breathed in deeply as her hips twitched, almost completely withdrawing from Chase before pressing against her again. Chase watched Matilda hold her breath, her lips slightly parted, her face flushing deeper still as her upper torso curled in a further throe of orgasm.

Groaning loudly, Matilda collapsed on Chase's chest, breathing rapidly and still twitching her hips. Slightly pushing her cock in and out while also moving the base of the cock quickly back and forth over her clit. She groaned long and languid as Chase wrapped her arms around Matilda's ribs. Chase held her close and could feel Matilda's heart pounding against her chest. Matilda was brushing the skin of her cheek back and forth over Chase's shoulder. Her locks of curls tickling under Chase's chin while her quick breaths tickled the skin on Chase's shoulder and upper arm.

Chase felt her heart swell for this little lady as she held her closer still, turning her head to lightly kiss the back of Matilda's head as she lay still panting; gasping for breath.

After several minutes, Matilda lifted her head and asked, "Did you come?"

"No," Chase admitted.

Matilda looked a little disappointed. "Sorry, I…"

"Don't be," Chase returned immediately. "I would gladly forgo another orgasm just to watch your face again, as you come. It was just…exquisite. The intimacy. Being able to gaze into each other's eyes while you fucked me, it was…" Chase began to twirl Matilda's wayward locks of hair, "…fabulous."

Matilda smiled, "Yes. I felt that way with you. The first time we were together and you sat on a chair and fucked me while I sat in your lap. Except…" she tilted her head and looked to the side as though recalling a memory. "…I did come." She giggled before adding, "Excitable girl," and then giggled again.

Chase smiled genuinely as she enjoyed Matilda's candor and humor while they lay entwined in each other's arms. Matilda's cock still was stretching the walls of her pussy as it delightfully jiggling inside her with Matilda's laughter.

"So, what of your first experience with a strap-on?" Chase asked.

"Well…" Matilda started slowly. "I'm glad I've tried it, but…honestly, I don't think it's for me." She giggled again. "I already know that by tomorrow, I'm going to be walking like I just got off that damned horse in Mongolia again," she laughed heartily. "I don't know how you manage it."

"Runner's legs," Chase enlightened her.

"Ah!" said Matilda nodding. "Well, I think it's time I retired Pretty Penny for good."

Chase nodded and relaxed as Matilda moved slowly backward and withdrew her cock. Kneeling between Chase's legs, Matilda looked down at her soon to be discarded appendage. The light glistening on its wetness as it wobbled there before her. Matilda noted there was no blood, *Oh well, all good things come to an end,* she thought as she unclipped the buckles and removed the harness. Then, she sat back onto her heels and contemplated Chase's pussy – studying each nook and cranny.

Chase reached down with both hands and pulled herself open fully to Matilda. "See anything you like?" she asked provocatively.

"Mmm," nodded Matilda, continuing to stare at the glistening platter of goodies before her.

"Penny for your thoughts?" Chase asked as she reached for the strap-on with a broad smile.

"Oh, enough with the Penny's already," Matilda said in mock flatness as she handed over the now unwanted apparatus, following it with a wave of good riddance.

Chase took the cock from Matilda and dropped it onto the floor beside the bed. Then bending her knees she lifted and spread her legs wide, again opening her sex open with both hands. She looked up at Matilda and said, "Help yourself."

Matilda's gaze flitted back and forth from Chase's pussy to Chase's eyes, smiling her pleasure at the bawdiness of the offer. She knelt forward and slowly laid herself down between Chase's legs. Holding Chase's gaze while she opened her mouth, stuck out a flattened tongue and lapped from Chase's opening up and over her clit with indolent deliberation.

"Mmm," Chase exhaled and continued to watch Matilda with half-lidded eyes. Matilda had by now discovered that this was Chase's look of genuine enjoyment. She pointed the tip of her tongue and slowly backtracked back to Chase's opening. Flattening her tongue again, she slowly licked upward, rewarded by the sweet flavor of renewed juices from Chase's excitement. Pointing her tongue, she allowed the very tip to investigate Chase's clitoral hood, pushing it back and away from Chase's clit. When Chase made to raise her hips into the pleasure of it, Matilda ran her tongue slowly downward and poked just the tip of it into Chase's pussy. Chase groaned and adjusted her grip on herself; pulling herself up higher, exposing more of her clit to Matilda. Flattening her tongue, Matilda slowly drifted up and over the engorged nub and surrounding folds.

"Yeah!" Chase whispered hoarsely and shivered slightly as Matilda's tongue pointed and circled her clit before moving downward again and dipping a little deeper into her pussy.

Matilda's tongue was hot and rough as it dragged up over Chase's clit again. She stopped for a moment to savor the flavor on her tongue before swallowing and then lightly pinching Chase's clit between her lips.

Chase moaned a little louder and pushed her hips up to catch Matilda's tongue. As Matilda circled Chase's clit again, Chase groaned loudly, "Matilda! Mmm." Then when Matilda poked her tongue deeply into Chase, her wetness gushed over Matilda's face. Chase groaned again before renewing the hold on herself, spreading her engorged lips wider, inviting Matilda into her most sensitive areas.

Matilda flattened her tongue and lapped at Chase's clit. Now she concentrated her efforts, with slow swirls over the hard, raised bunch of nerves, causing Chase to exhale and then inhale sharply.

Matilda pinched Chase's clit between her lips again and quickly moved her tongue from side to side across it.

Chase let go of herself and clasped hold of Matilda's head, pressing her face into her pussy. "Make me come!" Chase demanded. "Lick it! Matilda, I'm gonna come," Chase pleaded.

Matilda sucked Chase's clit into her mouth and ran her tongue over and around it with increasing speed. She sucked harder as Chase's hip and thigh movements began to make it difficult for her to maintain a seal with her lips. She immediately chased after Chase's undulating pussy, recapturing her clit and swirling over the top of it with her tongue.

Hearing the sounds of Matilda's mouth on her pussy drove Chase over the edge and she jerked her hips in excitement, pushing her clit deeper into Matilda's mouth.

Matilda flattened her tongue and swirled it over the enlarged nub just as Chase growled throatily, "Oh, yes, you got it. That's it! That's it, baby! That's.....ohhhh." Matilda sucked harder and rested her hands heavily on Chase's thighs in an effort to hold her steady. She sucked and licked and swallowed quickly as Chase came in her mouth; her post menstrual come was thin, hot and sweet on Matilda's tongue. Matilda rolled her head back and forth with the enjoyment of that flavor until Chase let go of her head and then gently pushed Matilda's mouth away from her pussy.

"Oh, wow, Matilda! Fuck, that was good." Chase looked down at Matilda's face. Seeing it glistening between her thighs she summonsed, "Come up here and let me suck your face."

Matilda smirked and made her way forward, resting her hot body on Chase's cool skin. Each woman reveling in the transfer of body heat between them.

Matilda kissed Chase on the lips and then moved her face incrementally, a little at a time, to allow Chase to lick off every last morsel of come. She enjoyed the feel of Chase's tongue on her skin and felt her own clit twitch with the thought of that tongue working on it, as it was on her chin. She instinctively pressed her hips down against Chase's body as she lay atop her. She groaned as the pressure and strain of her movements stimulated her clit; resulting in the need for her to strain and press herself against Chase again.

Chase held tightly to Matilda's buttocks with each downward motion of Matilda's hips. When Matilda climbed up and straddled her abdomen and began rubbing her wet pussy back and forth against Chase's skin, Chase groaned thinking, *I can't believe how incredibly sexy this woman is.* She held Matilda's hips and helped her to maintain a positive contact against the skin of her abdomen; rocking Matilda back and forth, back and forth, more and more rapidly.

Matilda's hands were exploring her own body; running her fingers through the hair on the back of her head; tickling down her neck, crossing over as she brushed over her shoulders and then slipped her hands down to caress her own breasts. She opened her eyes and found Chase staring directly at her with a satisfied grin. *Somebody's enjoying the show,* she thought watching Chase's eyes flicker now, unable to keep from watching the movements of Matilda's hands. Watching Matilda's fingers move down her body and between her legs. Matilda closed her eyes and let her lips part slightly, moistening them with her tongue.

"You need to sit on my face, Matilda?" Chase offered quietly.

Matilda stopped rocking her pussy against Chase's abdomen and immediately began shifting her body up toward Chase's head.

Quickly, Chase grabbed the pillows from behind her head and threw them to the floor. Smiling broadly as she threaded her arms through, under Matilda's thighs as Matilda straddled her face and lowered her pussy onto Chase's open mouth and waiting tongue.

Matilda held onto the wrought iron lacework in the bedhead and looked down at

Chase. She reached down with her other hand and began stroking Chase's forehead.

Chase flicked her tongue back and forth across Matilda's clit and was rewarded by the sounds of Matilda's moans each time she exhaled heavily. She had to hold Matilda in place when Matilda let go of her bedhead to lean back and try to watch Chase's tongue flitter across her clit. Concerned at the level of Matilda's fatigue, Chase decided to help steady the little diva. She ran her hands up Matilda's back and then to Matilda's sides. Taking a moment to steady Matilda again before she slipped her fingers around Matilda's biceps and pulled her arms back, encouraging Matilda to reach behind her body. Chase pressed Matilda's wrists together and positioned Matilda's palms downward against her rib cage. Matilda leaned her body weight back; locked her elbows and rested all her weight against Chase's ribs.

Matilda was much more comfortable like this. Her lower body, fatigued from her earlier efforts with the strap-on, merely draped around Chase's face. Better still, Matilda was able to see more of Chase's ministrations. She could see Chase's top lip as it worked and shaped itself over Matilda's salty lips. She could see Chase's tongue from time to time as it flitted about her clit.

When Chase tucked-in her chin and drove her tongue into Matilda's pussy, Matilda growled quietly, "Oh, yeah!" and pressed her pussy down onto Chase's tongue. She found that her legs had recovered enough to allow her to lift and lower herself onto Chase's face. The extra weight being taken by her arms made easier work for her hips and also, offered her directional control. She could lift her hips forward slightly to give Chase a better angle of attack. She could even control the pace of the tongue-fucking she was receiving from Chase. As well, she could also choose to direct Chase's tongue to swipe over her clit from time to time if she so desired. She was sitting on Chase's face and, she was in total control of everything Chase did.

Chase was well aware that Matilda was enjoying herself. It was evident in Matilda's breathing and constant moaning of, "Oh, yeah!" and further evidenced by the slick trail of juices that coated her face and chin.

Confident now that Matilda could hold herself atop her body, Chase moved her hands over Matilda's arms and began to gently fondle Matilda's breasts. Matilda gasped in a quick breath and moved her hips a little quicker.

Her pussy now dripping wet, Matilda moved her hips back and forth against Chase's face faster and faster. "Oh, Chase….oh, yeah!" was all she could manage to say. Inwardly, she was thinking, *Fuck, I'm wet. I am so turned on. This is so good. Fuck, I'm wet…*

Chase cupped her hands over Matilda's breasts and gently squeezed and played her fingers over them. As she lightly brushed her fingertips over Matilda's nipples, Matilda hissed and groaned, "Oh, fuck yeah!" while breathing even more rapidly. "Oh, Chase," she whispered.

Chase pinched Matilda's hard, taut nipples between her thumbs and forefingers as Matilda dropped her hips back a little and then thrust her clit into Chase's mouth.

"Oh fuck, Chase! I'm coming!" Matilda shouted.

Chase sucked as much of Matilda into her mouth as she could and squeezed and massaged Matilda with her lips while her tongue searched for and lavished attention upon Matilda's clit.

"Oohhhhh……" Matilda groaned long and loud while her hips jiggled and trembled. She was lost in her orgasm as Chase played her mouth and tongue over her clit. Matilda began to crumble, losing control of her arms and legs and Chase had to quickly catch her. With one arm around the small of Matilda's back and the other arm between Matilda's shoulder blades, Chase held her woman fast as she continued to suck and lick; surprised at the length of Matilda's orgasm. All the while Matilda continued to groan, "Oohhhhh…."

When Matilda moved herself back a fraction from Chase's mouth, Chase intuitively released Matilda from her lips. Matilda's head slumped forward, her eyes remaining closed. Sweat beaded on her body and she sat motionless except for her heaving chest.

Chase lifted Matilda by her arms, easily strong enough to pick her up and gently lower her to the bed beside her. She reached over the side of the bed and retrieved the pillows. Matilda's eyes remained closed as Chase lifted her head and positioned the pillow for best comfort. Tenderly, Chase lifted and realigned Matilda's limp body before covering her with the bed covers.

Lying beside her in the dimly lit room, she watched as Matilda's breathing slowed and steadied in a deep sleep.

♀♀♀♀♀

The next morning, Matilda awoke to an empty house. She sat up and draped her legs over the side of the bed. She stopped for a moment to listen for any sounds of Chase and what she might be up to – nothing. Looking out the bedroom window, she could see the birds fluttering amongst the foliage of some flowering bushes. *This is such a beautiful location,* she thought as she took a few minutes to take in the view.

She took in a deep breath, touched her feet to the floor and stood before stretching her arms up above her head, and yawned. Breathing out deeply she dropped her arms to her sides and began to walk around the bed to the chair where her robe lay. *Oh! I knew my legs were going to be stiff again this morning.*

237

She tied her robe and then opened the bedroom door. Immediately she smelled it and smiled – *coffee*. She made her way to the kitchen where a percolator cared for a pot of freshly brewed coffee. In front of the machine was a mug and under the mug; a note. Matilda looked up at the clock on the wall and was shocked as she noted the time, *Ten o'clock! Golly, I can't remember the last time I slept that late. Oh well,* she shrugged to herself, *I must have needed it.*

She picked up the coffee mug and read the note Chase had left for her, '*Gone for a run.*'

Matilda breathed in deeply and smiled. *Wouldn't that be nice*, she thought, *to wake in the mornings to little love notes all of the time.* She poured her coffee and shook her head as she considered that no woman would want to share a life like that with her; not with her gone from the country more often than she was in it. And no woman would want to travel with her to the remote and insect ridden areas of the world that she sees. There was no holiday in her travels – just work, hardship and loneliness. *I don't even want to do it most of the time,* she thought as she pushed open the fly-wire door to the verandah and walked around to the rocking chairs. She carefully sat and rocked herself, stopping from time to time to sip at her mug of coffee. *It's so lovely here. I hope we can make a habit of this.*

When she had finished her coffee, she returned to the kitchen and rummaged in the freezer for one of the ham and cheese croissants she'd placed in there the day before. She quickly read the instructions and heated it accordingly in the microwave. She poured another coffee and took an apple from the fruit bowl. She popped the fruit into her robe pocket and carried her bounty to the dining table to eat her breakfast and await Chase's return.

♀♀♀♀♀

Chase jogged up the steps of the verandah and then bent over where she stood, locking her elbows and placing her hands above her knees so she could rest her weight against them while she caught her breath. After a minute or so, her breathing slowed and she began to perform her warm-down routine. By the time she had finished, she was breathing at her normal rate and the burn in her legs had been replaced by a feeling of limberness.

Spying Matilda sitting at the dining table through the window, she waved and quickly walked around the verandah and in through the kitchen. Her skin was covered in shiny beads of sweat and her clothing was marked with dark shapes depicting her sweat saturation.

"Good morning," she greeted as she bent to kiss Matilda on the cheek. A few droplets of her sweat ran quickly down her temples and dripped into Matilda's cleavage.

"Eeeww!" grumbled Matilda, "you're all sweaty."

"Mm-hmm," nodded Chase, "just like *you* were last night. Have you showered?" Matilda shook her head and Chase retorted, "Then the only difference is that yours has dried and mine's still wet." She giggled at her cleverness and lent in for a quick kiss on Matilda's lips.

"You're incorrigible!" Matilda giggled.

"Owh!" exclaimed Chase disappointedly, "Have you eaten breakfast already?" She was looking at the apple core resting in the center of plate of crumbs situated on the table in front of Matilda.

"I was famished." Matilda defended. "I didn't know if you had eaten or not."

"I never eat before a run," Chase informed Matilda. "It doesn't sit well. But now I'm starving."

"What's on the menu?" Matilda asked with true interest.

"I'd like a Japanese-style breakfast," Chase stated with a tone of voice that Matilda had learned to recognize as impending naughtiness.

Matilda looked up to find Chase's eyebrows wiggling suggestively, "Uh-oh."

Chase chuckled low and lent in for another kiss. This one pressed softly against Matilda's lips and when those soft pink lips parted, so did Matilda's. Chase played the tip of her tongue over Matilda's lips. When Matilda's tongue touched hers she withdrew it, as though playing hard to get. Matilda chased the fleeing organ, pressing her tongue deeply into Chase's mouth. Chase bit down softly, in the same way Matilda had done to her the night before. Matilda groaned and then stopped kissing Chase just long enough to lean back and take in dark-blue eyes that danced while she smiled. Chase leaned in again, pressing her lips to Matilda's while she undid Matilda's robe. She pushed the fluffy material away from Matilda's shoulders and ran her palms over warm, smooth skin. Sliding the robe down Matilda's arms until it fell; draped around Matilda's chair.

Matilda was naked from head to toe. "A perfect platter for my breakfast," announced Chase as she took a small step back to take in the view.

Matilda's brow furrowed in contemplation for a moment before they widened with understanding, "You mean….?"

"Nyotaimori? Yes."

"Oh."

Chase stooped low, grasped slender arms and indicated for Matilda to wrap them around her neck. Kissing Matilda deeply again, Chase reached around and under, grasping Matilda by her rear while she stood, lifting the petite frame up and against her. Matilda yelped into Chase's mouth, surprised by the sudden display of strength and agility. Chase chuckled with pleasure at Matilda's acknowledgement of the power in her arms and legs. Matilda wrapped her legs around Chase's waist as she again became distracted by Chase's deeply probing tongue. Turning, Chase carried Matilda to the kitchen bench and lifted her up onto it. The kiss continued right through until Chase had gently laid Matilda prone on the cool stone surface. Immediately Matilda's nipples reacted to the cold sensation on her back; standing erect and painfully hardened. Chase took one of the hard peaks into her mouth, soothing and warming it while Matilda groaned from the intensity of her touch and the cold beneath her. Chase moved her attention to the other nipple and elicited a pleasure-filled sigh from Matilda. When Matilda began to run her fingers through Chase's hair, Chase caught them and motioned for Matilda to keep her arms straight and by her sides as is the tradition of Nyotaimori.

Chase stood and took in the sight before her. Matilda's soft milky skin outlined by the dark stone of the kitchen bench. Matilda's rate of breathing was causing her small breasts and shoulders to heave with excitement. Chase spent the next several minutes touching, admiring, kissing, licking, biting and stimulating every part of Matilda that was exposed to her. Moving around in a logical progression from the dining room side of the bench, to the kitchen side working her hands and mouth over all of Matilda as she went.

Matilda's heart was pounding in her chest. She was so turned-on, it was all she could do to keep from touching herself, or pulling Chase to her pussy and demanding relief. Her thighs were pressed tightly together in an attempt to squeeze firmly against her clit. Her hips would regularly lift upward, silently begging for Chase to press her hand or face into her slit. Small cries of frustration escaped Matilda's lips throughout this process.

Chase stopped, quickly turned and opened the refrigerator door. She was back in an instant with a small tub of fruit salad. With artful deliberation, she placed the mouth sized portions of fruit on Matilda's body. Then returning to the fridge, she produced a small tub of yoghurt, "I like a healthy breakfast," she smirked as she opened the tub and allowed its contents to slowly drizzle in artful swirls between the chunks of fruit. Matilda shivered, anticipating that Chase would soon begin moving her lips and tongue and teeth over her skin. "Of course I am supposed to do this with chopsticks," said Chase as she stood with her hands on her hips and assessed her talent at culinary art. "But I haven't got any up here." She twisted her mouth as if in contemplation, before adding, "What's a girl to do?"

Matilda groaned loudly with sexual frustration, "Oh! You're also supposed to use sushi, not fruit. Fuck me!" she cursed, holding her arms tight against her sides as Chase had motioned she should. She pressed her hands against her outer thighs, trying to apply more pressure against her clit and ease some of the tension of her arousal.

Chase laughed aloud at the sight of Matilda squirming and took a step closer to the bench. "You're supposed to remain absolutely still and quiet." When Matilda looked at her with pleading eyes, Chase bent forward and licked and lapped at the yoghurt on her tummy. Matilda moaned every time she exhaled. Waiting so long for the touch of Chase's tongue made for an exhilarating sensation on her skin, when it finally arrived. Her lips parted as did her legs, as she gave herself over to this…Nyotaimori.

Chase picked up a strawberry with her teeth and carefully smoothed it over Matilda's nipples. When the engorged nubs were well ladened with the fruit's juice, she quickly chewed and swallowed the portion. Then she plunged her tongue into the pool of yoghurt in Matilda's bellybutton before returning to one of Matilda's nipples and sucking it deeply into her mouth. The juice and yoghurt mingled delightfully on Chase's tongue and she salivated copiously, creating the need for her to suck and swallow and purse her lips about the hardened little nipple. Matilda's hips began to work lightly up and down again with these sensations. Her lips dried from her rapid breathing and she quickly moistened them with her tongue as she watched and felt Chase eat her breakfast.

Chase picked up a piece of pineapple and used it to draw the symbol of infinity around Matilda's breasts. She then sucked the fruit portion into her mouth; chewing and swallowing with such enjoyment that her eyes were temporarily forced to close. When she opened her eyes again and began lapping at the yoghurt, she noticed a small amount was about to trickle down Matilda's side at her waist. She quickly dove onto the trail and licked it away.

Matilda groaned at the tickle on her skin. She found each stroke of Chase's flattened tongue incredibly arousing. When Chase began systematically licking and biting at her, from her shoulder toward and over her breast to suckle at her nipple, she felt herself becoming very wet. Her breathing deepened and her skin goose-pimpled. Chase licked completely down one side of Matilda's body, collecting and eating the fruit as she went. She carefully refrained from licking near Matilda's mound as she rounded the kitchen bench and began licking and eating her way up the other side of Matilda's body. She paid particular attention to Matilda's nipple after she had licked the fruit and yoghurt from her breast. Then she continued upward, finishing at her shoulder. Matilda's breathing was ragged, knowing that Chase had left a thin strip of fruit and yoghurt down the very middle of her body.

Chase kissed her lips and Matilda enjoyed the flavor and scent of the fruit and yoghurt on her lips and tongue. Chase finished her kiss and began to eat and lick her way down Matilda's body. She worked her way downward in a straight line from Matilda's mouth, down her neck and between her breasts. Chase stopped and paid particular attention to licking all of the yoghurt from Matilda's bellybutton before licking and lapping ever lower, toward Matilda's pussy. Matilda's pulse was racing. She could hear her heartbeat pounding in her ears. Her hips were twitching uncontrollably, impatient for Chase's impending arrival.

When Chase reached Matilda's mound, she pushed her arm under Matilda's knees and encouraged her to bend her legs. Then she moved to the end of the kitchen bench, looking at Matilda's face from between her raised knees, Chase reached forward, grabbed Matilda by the hips and pulled her closer. Matilda slid easily on the smooth countertop. When Matilda's feet rested close to the edge of the counter, Chase bent forward and licked Matilda's pussy from her vagina up to her mound. Lifting off, she stuck just the tip of her tongue in Matilda's vagina before licking her way upward again. She repeated this maneuver several times with Matilda breathing quickly, gasping out little groans of pleasure. As Matilda seemed to be getting closer and closer to orgasm, Chase began to spend more time fluttering her tongue quickly over Matilda's clit. She moved back to Matilda's vagina; poking her tongue in a little and tenderly working her flattened tongue back up to Matilda's clit. Then, she would again flutter her tongue about over the swollen little button of nerves.

Each time Chase lifted off to drive her tongue into Matilda's vagina, Matilda would raise her arms and stretch them out toward Chase in an attempt to catch her and drag her tongue back to her clit. Chase would smirk at these attempts, knowing that her antics were driving Matilda wild. The next time Chase began to flutter her tongue over Matilda's clit, Matilda took hold of two handfuls of Chase's hair and firmly held her head in place. Chase had no choice but to continue with the random fluttering of her tongue from just above Matilda's clit.

Matilda sucked in a gulp of air and pulled hard on Chase's hair. She lifted her feet from the bench top and tucked her knees up high, either side of her arms; exposing all of her sex to Chase's flittering tongue. Matilda groaned loudly as she exhaled and then quickly hissed in another deep breath and held it. When she came, she exhaled with a low gruff tone, "Oh, fuck yeah!" Working her wrists up and down in opposition to her hips. Driving Chase's head and directing Chase's flickering tongue to every sensitive nook that required attention.

Matilda's orgasm was lengthy and consequently painful for Chase who began to feel the burn on her sensitive scalp from Matilda's relentless tugging. *I guess I asked for that,* Chase thought resignedly.

Matilda suddenly let go of Chase's hair and collapsed back onto the bench. "Oh, Chase, you're incredible," she panted, delirious with euphoria. She laid her forearm over her forehead and breathed in deeply a few times, trying to catch her breath. She looked down at Chase and seeming not to notice Chase rubbing furiously at the sides of her scalp, Matilda said, "You know, there's just one more thing you could do for me right now, to make this morning perfect." She began to struggle to sit up on the bench.

Chase held out her hands and helped Matilda to sit with her legs hanging over the bench. As Chase reached behind Matilda to grasp her butt and pull her close Matilda finished. "Give Penny Stick another work...Oh!" Matilda exclaimed in delighted surprise as Chase pressed her bulging crotch against Matilda's pussy. "You run with her?" Matilda asked as she looked down at the bulge pressing against her.

"I like the way it feels when she bobs up and down," Chase answered as she assisted Matilda down from the bench top.

Matilda looked back at the kitchen bench behind her and then down at Chase's crotch, before giving Chase a puzzled look. "I thought you might..."

"I have another idea." Chase stated and smiled broadly.

She tugged Matilda along by the hand through the kitchen door and out onto the verandah. Chase kicked off her runners near the kitchen door and then pushed her shorts down her legs and stepped out of them as she walked. Matilda watched her do the same with her briefs and thought, *Well, she's done that more than once.* When Chase reached the first rocking chair, she sat, pulled her tank top and bra off over her head and so, was completely naked. Penny Stick sprang upright between Chase's legs as though bobbing a 'hello' at Matilda.

Matilda stood amused at the sight for a second, not knowing what on earth she was meant to do next.

Chase tugged at Penny a few times and positioned her legs to achieve the best orientation for contact with her clit. Then she looked up at Matilda and said, "It's okay, Matilda. Step up here." Chase pointed at the seat of the rocker, between her legs. "I'll support you. Climb up. You're going to love this."

Matilda frowned and shook her head a little, not at all confident that this was going to be a good idea. But when she looked into Chase's excited eyes, she felt compelled to comply. Matilda held Chase's hand and also the arm of the rocker and stepped up as she'd been instructed. The chair dipped only slightly forward as Chase held it fast with her strong legs.

"Now, support yourself on the arms of the chair and thread your legs under, through these gaps," Chase pointed and the openings under the arms of the rocking chair and Matilda realized now, she was to straddle Chase's lap. She slowly lowered herself into position while Chase held her steady by her waist.

"Tuck your feet in near the back legs of the rocking chair, rest them on top of the rockers." Matilda followed Chase's instructions while Chase carefully lowered Matilda's still dripping wet pussy onto her cock. Penny Stick slid in easily and Matilda thrilled to the sensation; closing her eyes and relishing the shiver of delight that swarmed over her body. Her feet quite naturally found the supports as Chase had described, and with her arms resting loosely on the armrests of the rocking chair, she was surprised to find that she was extremely comfortable.

Chase held still for Matilda for a minute, letting her relax and find confidence with the position on her lap. When Matilda opened her eyes she smiled and looked into Chase's dark blue ones. She thought, *I don't think I've ever seen a more beautiful shade of blue. They darken whenever she's aroused, I think.*

Matilda's pussy pressed Penny Stick's base delightfully against Chase's clit. When Chase ran her arms around Matilda's waist and interlocked her fingers, Matilda felt completely secure. She let go of the arms of the rocking chair and began to run her fingers over Chase's shoulders. Then she followed the outline of Chase's pectoral muscles with her fingers before taking a breast in each hand. She moved her palms up and down and around and felt Chase's nipples harden against them. Chase's breaths deepened and her skin flushed a little. *Another sign of her arousal, I think.*

"Are you ready, Matilda?" Chase asked quietly.

Matilda looked back up into Chase's eyes and Chase slowly began to rock the chair. When the chair rocked forward, Chase would loosen her grip on Matilda a little, allowing the inertia to move her back and away from Chase slightly. When the chair rocked back, the opposing inertia would press Matilda's pussy down against Chase's, and Chase's hands would slide up Matilda's back some and tickle her skin. Matilda opened her mouth, but could not say a word. Still, her eyes managed to express a silent appreciation for the feeling of floating onto and off of Chase's cock. The feeling was quite simply – erotic. There was a quiet amatory expression on Matilda's face as she was transfixed by Chase's gaze.

Each stared back into the eyes of the other while the chair rocked back and forth, back and forth with a slow, steady rhythm. Each had their lips slightly parted, in silent awe of the exquisiteness they were sharing.

Matilda was so wet that her juices trickled down under the base of the cock and were smeared over Chase's clit. The velvet touch of each stroke within her were the most heavenly she'd ever experienced. Her skin was electrified. Her hands on Chase's breasts moving to excite her even more. There was nothing, nothing except her and Chase and the intimacy flowing between them.

Chase lengthened the swing of the rocker to enable longer strokes of her cock in and out of Matilda's pussy. That also provided longer strokes back and forth across her own clit. She moaned a little, attempting to refrain from orgasm too soon. She wanted to make this last. Hell, she wanted it to last forever. Matilda was a beautiful and appreciative lover. She made Chase feel strong, sexually empowered and so very, very glad to be a woman.

Matilda moved her hands back up Chase shoulders. She clutched Chase's neck and slowly leaned in for a kiss. Matilda pressed her lips to Chase's, closing her eyes. Now she truly felt as though she were floating. Gliding effortlessly back and forth on Chase's cock. She could hear little slapping sounds as her wet pussy collided with Chase's. A small cry escaped her lips. No. It wasn't hers. It was Chase's. She opened her eyes and stopped kissing Chase. It took a moment to get her face into focus. Chase's skin was flushed deep, her eyes half-closed. The look on her face proving her total absorption for their connection – their bonding.

To Matilda, Chase's cock felt as though it were reaching some new part of her. Touching on some sacred zone that was linked directly to her clit. Even her nipples were buzzing as though somehow coupled to the activities below. She felt exhilarated and leant in again for a kiss from Chase. This time she stabbed her tongue into Chase's mouth and when she withdrew, Chase's tongue followed hers out. She withdrew marginally to permit a tiny gap between them so that their tongues could dance together in the open. Each seeking the other out, twirling one about the other, tasting the sweetness of each other in the open air.

Chase was relentless in her rocking of the chair. The base of her cock stroking her so close to orgasm, she had to groan each time her clit was caressed. Matilda's response to Chase's groans was yet another gush of juices; making everything even more slippery than before.

Matilda pressed her lips to Chase's and her cold tongue pressed deeply inside Chase's mouth, seeking out the warmth there and playing over Chase's tongue and teeth.

Chase knew that she was about to come and desperately wanted Matilda to come at the same time. She bit down on Matilda's tongue in the same way Matilda had done to her the night before with such pleasurable results. That did the trick.

Matilda gasped audibly and sucked in a breath and then groaned deeply as she exhaled.

"Oh…" was all Matilda could manage as she slowly drifted back from Chase's lips. Her eyes were closed and she was panting out little moans with each change in direction of the rocking chair.

Chase closed her eyes, the throbbing between her legs now almost too much to bear. Another few strokes over her clit and she was coming too. Her chest was heaving as she struggled now to maintain the constant rocking motion of the chair. Her head slumped forward and rested against Matilda's breast. Matilda's taut nipple tickled back and forth on her cheek and gave her the pendulum she needed to maintain her rhythm while she came.

Matilda slowly returned to an upright position. Draining every last ounce of pleasure from her orgasm by slowly repositioning her body backwards: changing the angle of penetration for Chase's cock; titillating the walls of her vagina.

All the while Chase continued to rock the chair. Her orgasm was still coming in spasms as she listened to Matilda's gasps for breath, then groaning lightly each time she exhaled. When Chase lifted her head to look up at Matilda, Matilda's eyes were still closed and she looked as though she may collapse at any moment. Chase watched the changing expressions on Matilda's face, *she is so beautiful after she's orgasmed; so serene.* Gradually, Chase slowed the rocking of the chair. When it rocked slowly enough that Chase's cock no longer worked in and out of Matilda's pussy, Matilda slumped forward, rested her head on Chase's shoulder and quietly shed a few tears. Not because she was sad or in pain, but because the sensations she'd felt were so overwhelming that she needed to release some of it. When Chase became aware of Matilda's tears via the jiggling motion of Matilda's shoulders, she held her tightly to her, kissed the side of Matilda's head and ran her fingers through Matilda's hair. They stayed there like that for some time. Chase comforted Matilda with a gentle massage of the skin on Matilda's back and neck.

When Matilda sat up again, she looked into Chase's eyes and said, "I have never felt anything even close to that before. Not ever!"

Chase looked longingly into Matilda's eyes as her own eyes watered a little. She said nothing. What was there to say? She placed her palms against the sides of Matilda's face and gently pulled her in for a kiss. A gentle, sensuous kiss that gave way to another emotional gaze into each other's eyes.

Matilda smiled and then tentatively lifted herself from Chase's lap.

Chase held the rocking chair fast and lifted Matilda by her hips to help her alight.

Matilda tested the steadiness of her legs and said, "Good grief! Will I never recover from that damned horse ride?"

Chase chuckled and stood to offer her arm and walk Matilda inside and into the shower.

♀♀♀♀♀

"All ready?" Chase asked as she entered the kitchen, having just packed up the Jeep.

"I can't find my shoes." Grumbled Matilda kneeling on her hands and knees to look under the couch.

"They're under the other rocking chair, where you left them yesterday. I'll get them." Chase returned quickly and helped Matilda to slip the high heels back onto her feet.

"Thank you for washing my underwear. There's nothing worse than wearing dirty undies when you've just had a shower."

"You're welcome," said Chase standing and reaching out to help Matilda up from the couch. "It's time to go now, I'm afraid."

Matilda took one last look around the bungalow. "I've loved it here, Chase. Will we be able to do this again? I know it's your *Getaway*, so don't let me intrude if it's a problem...."

"Sure!" Chase gestured toward Matilda, as if to sweep away her concern. "I'd love to share this place with you again."

Matilda smiled broadly and accepted Chase's offer of a hand-up from the couch. As they left, Matilda asked, "Don't you ever lock up?"

"No," said Chase, "the cleaning lady will take care of that."

Chase helped Matilda into the Jeep Wrangler and closed the door.

After Chase got in and started the motor, she turned to Matilda as she reversed around the side of the bungalow and said, "Tighten your seatbelt, Matilda."

Matilda looked concerned and quickly complied.

Chase gunned the motor and took off at a wheel spinning pace. Rounding the stand of trees, the little sports Wrangler swept up the side of the embankment.

Matilda squealed and held onto her seat so tightly her knuckles went white. As they neared the crest, the Jeep had slowed enough to make a comfortable climb over the ridge and Matilda realized she needed to start breathing again. She'd been holding her breath – petrified.

"There! Now, that wasn't so bad was it?" asked Chase.

Matilda looked at her and smiled politely as she placed her hand on Chase's knee. It was then she noticed that Chase's crotch wasn't bulging. "Has Penny been retired?" she asked sadly.

Chase looked down at her crotch and then at Matilda. She looked back at the track when she hit an unexpected bump and decided she'd better keep her eyes on the trail while answering, "I thought it best, since we don't really have time to…pull over…on the way back to the city."

Matilda laughed loudly and nodded, "Good call."

♀♀♀♀♀

Chase drove down the laneway behind her house and pressed the button on her garage remote. She parked and pressed the remote's button again to close the door back down behind them. She got out and quickly walked to the passenger side to help Matilda alight, "Let me help you out. You'll break your neck in those high heels."

Matilda did as instructed and waited for Chase's assistance. Then she followed Chase out of the garage and up the garden path to the back door of Chase's house. When they reached the door, it opened and standing just inside, was Suzette.

"Ah! Mademoiselle, Matilda. It is good to see you again." Suzette tilted her head low and stepped back to let the two women into the house. Then, she led the way through the kitchen offering, "Should I put de kettle on for coffee?"

"No, no! Thank you, Suzette, but I can't stay, I'm afraid. I have a meeting to attend," Matilda explained.

Suzette nodded and scooted down the hallway to the foyer. When the women reached the foyer behind her, she had pulled out the little table and arranged the eftpos machine and business cards, ready for payment.

Chase nodded to Suzette and said, "I've got it from here, Suz. I've got bags in the Wrangler."

"Oui, mon amie." Suzette curtsied and hurried back down the hallway.

Matilda operated her card in the machine as she had done before and settled the account. Then she turned to Chase as she tucked one of Chase's business cards into her handbag and said, "I'm going to be flat out for the next few weeks. I'm not sure when we'll see each other again, but I can't wait."

Chase took Matilda in her arms and kissed her. The heat between them still easily rekindled, as the kiss threatened to turn into another torrid session of love-making.

Matilda broke the kiss, breathing heavily. She whispered against Chase's cheek, "I'd better go."

Chase nodded and as she walked Matilda to the front gate she asked, "Should I have called you a taxi?"

"No," said Matilda. "I'll take the train." She pulled the wrought iron gate closed behind her and leaned across to kiss Chase one last time before leaving.

As she walked to the station at the end of Chase's street she smiled broadly as she thought to herself, *There's no better means of preparation for an important meeting than coming on a woman's tongue.*

The End

The Good Host

"Welcome girls! How was your trip?" asked Jamie as she greeted the couple parked in her driveway and began to help lift suitcases from their trunk.

"We made good time this time around actually – just over thirteen hours," Jacque replied as she knowingly allowed the larger, stronger woman to help herself to the largest and heaviest of the baggage. She considered Jamie to be the best compliance manager she could have been given to work under, but instead of the respect and gratefulness that was due this amazon of a woman, all Jacque had to offer was greedy manipulation and absolute jealousy. She made use of Jamie's capacity to help with business difficulties and was intensely jealous of the woman's personable and popular management style, as well as her physical prowess. "Of course it helped that the Gascoigne wasn't threatening to break its' banks like it was the last time we trekked down this way," Jacque added as she watched Jamie's arm muscles ripple under their load.

"I'm glad you've got here early enough to take a refreshing dip before dinner," Jamie said with a broad smile for Yvette, the passenger of the vehicle. Jamie bowed a welcome to the petite blonde, while walking effortlessly past her in the drive with a large suitcase in each arm.

"What do you want me to carry in?" Yvette asked her partner of four years.

"You're make-up," replied Jacque in a sarcastic tone.

Yvette reached for her cranberry-colored, briefcase-like make-up bag and matching vanity bag from the trunk and walked toward the front stoop of the house. As she reached the door, Jamie was coming back out and stopped to hold the door open for her and welcome her in.

"Let me hold the door for you, Yvette. I've set you up in your usual room. You remember the way don't you?"

"Yes, thank you, Jamie. You're so charming, you know that?" Yvette struggled slightly with her load as she stepped up over the threshold.

"You need help?" offered Jamie.

"No, no. I'm fine," Yvette smiled back toward Jamie before making her way to her room.

Jamie stood holding the door and took the time to appreciate Yvette's fine-boned stature in her hip-hugging dress. Her eyes followed the shapely line of Yvette's legs, right down to her court shoes and then slowly back up again before the little woman disappeared through a side doorway.

"Thanks for holding the door for me, mate," Jacque brashly stated as she pushed past and through the entry.

"Sure!" returned Jamie quickly, having been surprised by Jacque's sudden appearance. She'd completely forgotten that Jacque was still in the driveway. "Any more bags?"

"Nah! This is it," Jacque called back as she followed in Yvette's wake.

"I'll have refreshments ready out by the pool when you two are settled," Jamie called out to Jacque's receding form.

♀♀♀♀♀

Jamie sat on a banana lounge with her pina colada and watched, while grinning from ear to ear, as Yvette squealed-like-a-schoolgirl with each small step she took down into the cool water of the pool.

Yvette was breathing rapidly in and out, straining from cold. The strain accentuating her plentiful bosom and tightening her stomach muscles to the point where the lines of her ribs were showing easily through her fair skin. Her long blonde hair was tied up into a bun atop her head and held in place with an aqua-colored Scrunchie, which precisely matched the color of the scanty little bikini she was wearing.

Almost wearing, thought Jamie as she sipped her cocktail and pretended to be listening to Jacque, who was sitting beside her.

"....I've managed to decrease our monthly overheads by a full five percent, simply by outsourcing the night-fill to a local company...."

Jacque was a dogged store manager, not at all popular with her staff and it seemed to Jamie, getting more and more unpopular with each change she made to save money on her aunt's franchise. Jamie could influence the way in which the little franchised store appeared, its opening hours, the policies it employed when dealing with its customers as well as many other policies. However, human resources and service contracting were solely the responsibility of the store owner.

Jacque made it clear to everyone that her aging aunt was expected to leave the store to her in her will and so, Jacque tended to behave as though she already owned it.

In Jamie's opinion, Jacque was the sort of manager who created a 'sick workplace.' A work place that oppressed and demoralized its staff and caused them to seek work elsewhere for the benefit of their health. Consequently, staff-turnover was a constant concern, especially in an outback town where the pool of human resources was already limited. This resulted in poor customer service which, in Jamie's opinion, was the sole reason for the store's inability to sustain its market share in what could ordinarily be considered a 'cornered market.'

"Outsourcing is a good idea for your store, Jacqueline. It'll save you on staff interviews and induction training," Jamie stated, still fixed on Yvette, now swimming breaststroke in the pool. *Breast stroke. Yes, I'd like to stroke...*

"So. Still no woman in your life, huh?" Jacque asked smugly.

Jamie's gaze suddenly hardened. She slowly turned her head in Jacque's direction and then raised a single eyebrow.

Jacque immediately became coy and quickly looked down at her feet as she added meekly, "Not that it's any of my business."

Jamie said nothing as she looked back toward Yvette and thought, *How did a complete ass like her, end up with such a wonderful woman as this?* When she considered her silence had made the required impact, she offered sharply, "I'm still dating," and Jacque knew better than to continue with the topic further.

Jamie stood and walked to the Webber barbecue where she had a full roast and vegetables slowly cooking and almost ready to serve. She spent some time checking and maneuvering the food inside. In actuality, she was using the activity to provide some space and time to calm herself. Jacque had hit a nerve with that comment. *Yes*, she was having problems finding a good woman to spend her life with. And, *no*, she wasn't really dating anyone. *No one*, seemed to be quite the woman she'd hoped for. *No one*, seemed to have the qualities she found desirable in a woman. *No one*, was quite like, Yvette.

Jamie contemplated the food arrangement for much longer still as she felt the return of that sadness – that acknowledgement – Yvette would never be hers. She stopped, sighed, and stared aimlessly for more long moments as she recalled Yvette telling her just that, the last time the couple had stayed with her. She took a deep breath and straightened her posture. She was bewildered by Yvette's rejection of her when it was so obvious that Yvette had not been happy in her relationship with Jacque for a very long time. She closed the lid on the barbecue and forced a smile as she turned her attention back to her houseguests.

Yvette was now floating on her back in the pool. Her pert breasts rising high from the water and her taut nipples acting as though rigid tent poles under her bathing costume. Jamie felt a stirring between her legs as she took in that view on her way back to her pina colada.

"That sure smells good," complimented Jacque when Jamie had sat down again.

"I'd like to give it a bit longer before serving. Should be long enough for Yvette to finish her swim," added Jamie, not really expecting any kind of answer.

Jacque nodded and removed her T-shirt, revealing the full piece suit she was wearing underneath. "I'll see if I can hurry her along a bit," she said and then dove into the pool next to Yvette causing the water to splash-up and over the bathing beauty. Yvette began to choke as she stood up in the pool; coughing, spluttering and wiping the water from her face. Jacque soon broke the surface of the water and after taking in the view of a disconcerted Yvette, began to laugh as though somehow, victorious.

"Jesus, Jacque! Was that really necessary?" Yvette snapped.

"Awh! C'mon, Yvette. Where's your sense of humor?" Jacque laughed as Yvette turned and made her way out of the pool. She quickly toweled dry and went inside the house.

Jacque shrugged in Jamie's direction and then started swimming overarm laps of the pool, causing further splashing.

Arrogant ass! thought Jamie as she took a pitcher of pina colada from the pool's bar fridge and refilled her cocktail glass.

♀♀♀♀♀

"Dinner is ready, Yvette," Jamie said softly through the closed door of Jacque and Yvette's room. After a short wait she raised her hand to lightly knock just as the door opened. Yvette stood dressed in a lacey top and tailored shorts. Her long, wet, honey-blonde hair combed back behind her ears.

"I took the opportunity to shower and change. I hope I haven't kept you waiting."

"Not at all," comforted Jamie. "I've only just decided the barbecue is ready to serve." Jamie smiled warmly at Yvette and resisted the urge to take her in her arms and press their bodies together.

Yvette smiled up at Jamie and their eyes met. Their chemistry was undeniable. For Jamie, it was as though the world had stood still. She was lost in Yvette's gaze and would be happy to spend the rest of her days just looking back into those silvery-gray eyes. Yvette stole herself from the compelling gaze enough to smile politely and look away. Jamie blinked repeatedly and tried to get her head back into the present.

"Would you like wine with your dinner?"

"Actually, I was thinking one of your pina coladas would be nice with barbecue," Yvette requested as she took in the pleasing view of Jamie's muscular arms and shoulders. Jamie was wearing a white one piece bathing suit under a long, cool cheesecloth top. Its neck chord tied in a bow creating a teardrop-shaped hollow through which Yvette could clearly see Jamie's tanned cleavage. The sheer, cheesecloth fabric allowed Yvette a filtered view of Jamie's trim and athletic body and tanned skin.

"Of course," said Jamie, struggling to take her eyes from Yvette's lace covered bosom, "I'll get that for you now." She turned and led Yvette back out to the pool area.

♀♀♀♀♀

"That was delicious, Jamie," complimented Jacque. "Tomorrow night, you'll have to let me take *you* out for dinner."

"What about Yvette?" Jamie sounded concerned that Yvette might be left out.

"Yes, of course, Yvette as well," corrected Jacque, "that goes without saying," she said with a dismissive wave of her hand in Yvette's direction.

"Perhaps we should wait for the outcome of our negotiations before organizing a celebratory dinner," Jamie cautioned, with a little of her annoyance showing through.

"Oh, you'll get me through it okay," scoffed Jacque. "You got me through the last time, Jamie. You can do it again."

That was true. Jamie did help Jacque to renegotiate the franchise agreement three years earlier. Jacque's aunt had taken ill and the business had slumped alarmingly under Jacque's first 12 months of management. Jamie had thought at the time, that Jacque simply needed to find-her-feet in what was her first managerial role. And so, had assisted Jacque in getting the franchisor on side to give the little country business some time to get back into a position where it could meet its obligations under the franchise agreement. The little business would go under if it did not qualify for continued operation under the franchise umbrella. Three years had passed since then, and the store was still not quite able to meet all of its requirements.

Jamie was certain that she could convince the franchisors to continue with this little business now that it was beginning to show a small return. Especially, in the interests of providing a service to a community that would otherwise be disadvantaged. Her 'trump-card' would be to suggest that a refusal for continuation of the franchise could bring poor publicity to the national operation. None-the-less, she would not be able to play *that* card forever and Jacque would have to address the shortfalls in her managerial style, if she were to still be in business after the next three years.

Jamie sighed, "Let's not count-chickens. You shouldn't assume that I can keep bailing you out, Jacqueline."

Jacque cringed at the use of the name she so hated. No one dared to call her that – no one, except Jamie.

Jamie caught sight of Jacque's discomfort and although she felt some small amount of satisfaction for it, her professionalism would never allow her to show it. "If, and I do mean 'if' you get a shot at a further three years under the franchise, there will have to be some changes made in-store. And *you* will need to be the biggest change of all, Jacque," Jamie finished pointing a stern finger at Jacque.

Jacque looked horrified as she began to stutter and bluster at her own defense.

"No! I mean it!" Jamie said pressing her point home with a thumping finger to the table top. "*You* have to start treating people better. *You* have to reduce your staff turnover." Jamie held Jacque's gaze and stared her down. Jacque relented and looked down at her dinner plate; her eyebrows knitted and her teeth grinding. "If you can't do that, say so now, so's you don't waste any more of my time," Jamie finished almost bitterly.

Jacque pouted as she considered the ultimatum.

"Well?" Jamie raised her voice to an imposing level and Jacque jumped slightly from the shock.

"Okay." Jacque whispered staring at Jamie's hand still pressing a finger into the tablecloth. Then she nodded and looked up at Jamie, heavily breathing out a full breath, before following up with another, louder, "Okay."

Yes! thought Yvette. *Mom and Pascal will be pleased.*

Yvette's mother, Bridgette, had taken a job with Annie, Jacque's aunt, in the twenty-year-old store when it first opened. Annie and Bridgette shared the common experience of the loss of their husbands in a catastrophic flood the year before.

Bridgette's husband was a truck driver and didn't have any life insurance, but the insurance Annie received for her loss was enough to open a little corner store under a franchise agreement. Approximately ten years ago, Pascal, Yvette's intellectually disabled elder brother, also started working there. The two of them managed to bring in enough money to put Yvette through a nursing degree. Yvette qualified as a Registered Nurse just eighteen months before Annie had a stroke and needed in-home nursing assistance. Annie had insisted that Yvette provide for her personal nursing needs and that was when Yvette met Jacque, Annie's only living relative…

Yvette brought her thoughts back to the two women at the table with her. The atmosphere was tense and Yvette was beginning to feel uncomfortable at being privy to a heated conversation in which she had no involvement.

Jamie was taking a risk. She wasn't supposed to get involved with staffing issues, but she knew her role in representing Jacque with the franchisor would never come to a successful end unless this issue was rectified.

"I will be working closely with you on this and you *will* do as I say. If you don't, I *will not* help you with any future franchise negotiations. That's my offer, Jacqueline. Take it or leave it?" She stared coldly at Jacque across the dinner table – waiting for an answer.

Jacque scowled down at her plate for a minute before forcing her contorted face out of its grimace and looking up at Jamie. She studied Jamie's serious expression and gave the only answer she had option for, "Whatever you say, Jamie."

Yvette took the opportunity to escape the potentially heated conversation and quickly collected up the dishes and headed for the kitchen. When she returned to the dining room for the remainder of the dishes, no one was there. She looked out the window to the pool area and could see Jacque aimlessly wondering about in deep contemplation. Jamie, it seemed, had gone to her room.

♀♀♀♀♀

Yvette snuck out into the hallway in a tank top and thin cotton pajama pants. She wore nothing else and hoped like hell that she wouldn't run into anything or knock something over in these dark and unfamiliar surroundings. She didn't want to wake Jacque and bring attention to herself, not when she was on her way to Jamie's room. She felt half-naked, excited and terrified.

She made it only a short distance from the door of the guest room before she began to doubt her decision. She stopped to stare at the closed door at the end of the hallway, the door to Jamie's bedroom. *Behind it, she lays, probably sleeping,* thought Yvette, *Am I really going to chance waking her up?*

She had almost talked herself out of everything when she noticed movement at the top of the staircase, across the hall from Jamie's bedroom. She turned to look and was startled to find herself staring into the blue eyes of her craving. Jamie wore a tight singlet and boxer trunks stretched over her bulkier frame.

"Hey," Jamie whispered, moving toward Yvette.

Yvette continued down the hallway as Jamie approached, stopping when she met her in the middle. They stood in front of the open doorway of the bathroom.

"Are you okay, Yvette? Do you need something?" whispered Jamie.

Yvette gave her a nervous nod while licking her lips. *She wasn't in her bedroom. She wasn't asleep. She had been lingering at the top of the stairs, almost as if she had been waiting for me,* Yvette mused. She let out a nervous breath and opened her mouth as though to speak, but said nothing.

"What do you need?" Jamie asked leaning down in a quiet whisper. She kept her eyes locked onto Yvette's.

Yvette closed the distance between them, rising up onto her tiptoes and snaking her arms around Jamie's broad shoulders. "A kiss," she whispered. She didn't allow herself to stop and experience her terror. She leaned in and brushed her lips over Jamie's, whimpering at the unexpected softness she found.

Jamie barely hesitated before wrapping her muscular arms around Yvette's waist and pulling her tight against her body. Her tongue eased out and played over Yvette's lips for only an instant waiting for Yvette to part them and invite her inside. When Yvette did part her lips, Jamie pushed her tongue into Yvette, licking the inside of her mouth while walking her backward to press her shoulders against the wall next to the bathroom door.

Before Yvette knew it, she was pinned between Jamie and the wall. She gasped at the restriction of movement, her excitement intense, her breathing rapid and labored. Jamie was stroking Yvette's tongue with her own. Jamie's tongue was like liquid and moved in needy strokes, entwining with Yvette's like flames in a fire.

Yvette moaned into Jamie's mouth, closing her eyes at the flood of wetness between her legs. Jamie seemed to sense Yvette's need and eased her thigh between Yvette's legs. Her boxer shorts riding up to expose bare skin to the damp cotton pajamas covering Yvette's arousal. Yvette gripped Jamie's back with frantic fingers and thrust her needy pussy against the hard muscle of Jamie's thigh.

Jamie pulled away from the kiss gasping, "I don't know if I should…"

"Not in the hallway," Yvette interrupted. She didn't wait for Jamie to finish her sentence. She didn't even think before she stepped to the side, grabbed Jamie's hand and pulled her into the moonlit bathroom next to where they had been leaning. "Come in here."

"Eve…" Jamie groaned as Yvette kissed her again. Jamie brought her hand up to tangle in Yvette's long blonde hair, tightening her fingers when Yvette pushed her back against the bathroom door to close it behind them.

Jamie lost her momentary doubts as she growled, forcing Yvette to take a step backwards. Jamie's hand was still roughly grasping Yvette's hair as she swiveled them around one-hundred-and-eighty degrees, again pinning Yvette's body with her own, this time against the back of the bathroom door. She gave Yvette a rough kiss and then pulled away to whisper, "I don't want to hurt you, but I need you so much, I'm afraid I can't help myself." Jamie's hands moved down over Yvette's body and squeezed her hips before cupping her buttocks roughly and thrusting her pelvis hard into her, demonstrating her need.

Yvette whimpered at Jamie's dominance. This was exactly the way she had fantasized she'd be.

Jamie used her hold on Yvette's hair to turn her head so she could lean in to kiss her again. She bared Yvette's throat to her eager mouth and when she found the tender skin of her neck with gentle teeth, Yvette moaned with pleasure.

"It's our first time," Yvette whispered, "but I'm no virgin, I can take it."

Jamie didn't say a word as she continued to lick and suck at Yvette's neck while driving her pelvis forward and into her. Letting go of Yvette's hair, Jamie reached up to disentangled Yvette's arms from around her neck, seizing her wrists and holding them against the door over her head. A quiet groan escaped Jamie's throat as Yvette put up a mock struggle, inciting Jamie to tighten her grip on the tiny wrists.

Jamie pulled away from Yvette's throat and held her mesmerized with dark blue eyes. "You're liking this, aren't you?" she asked, squeezing Yvette wrists, holding them even tighter against the door and pushing her heavier body hard against her. "You like me taking you, like this?"

Yvette nodded. "Yes," she whispered and met Jamie's heated gaze. "I've wanted to feel your body against mine for a long time now."

Jamie ground her hips into Yvette's again, "I've never made a secret of wanting you. You've known that since the first time we met. Nothing compares to the need I feel for you, Evie." Jamie sounded cautious, as if she wasn't sure of Yvette's limits.

Yvette dropped her eyes to her breasts, which were pressed against Jamie's. Her nipples were so hard they hurt. "Show me," she challenged in a whisper as she looked up, straight into Jamie's eyes.

Jamie blinked and Yvette could see the shattering of some resolve in her eyes. "Okay," she breathed.

Just as Yvette was going to ask Jamie to take her to her bedroom, Jamie groaned and captured her mouth in a long, wet kiss. She released one wrist so that she could bring her hand down and squeeze Yvette's breast through her tank top. Yvette kept both of her wrists pressed against the door above her head and surrendered to Jamie's control.

Jamie pinched Yvette's nipple between her fingers, breaking their kiss to breathe heavily into Yvette's ear, but rather than saying anything, Jamie found Yvette's earlobe with her teeth and nibbled on the tender skin. She moved her hand from one nipple to the other, sliding her palms over their tips, pulling and tugging them into painful hardness. Yvette's pajama bottoms were soaking wet against Jamie's thigh. Yvette closed her eyes and moaned; thrilled by the touch she now couldn't get enough of.

Yvette inhaled as if to speak, but Jamie released her nipple from between her fingers and stopped her with a rough hand over her mouth. Yvette whimpered with the shock of such a forceful move.

"You want me to show you?" Jamie whispered, pushing her heavier body hard up against Yvette. It was becoming obvious to Yvette that it wouldn't be much longer before Jamie lost all control.

Yvette nodded and Jamie removed her hand, stepping away and taking Yvette by the shoulders. She pulled her away from the door and turned her around to face the bathroom mirror. The lights were off, but the bathroom was illuminated by the full-moonlight that shone in through curtained windows.

"Raise your arms," Jamie whispered from behind her. Yvette found Jamie's eyes in the mirror; glistening as though excited beyond all reason. This was better than any fantasy she'd had ever had of this Amazon. She raised her arms into the air, as instructed and Jamie pulled her tank top up over her head, tossing it onto the floor beside them. Jamie stared at the bare breasts in the mirror for a moment before reaching around to cover one with each hand. She raised her eyes to meet Yvette's again and then bent down to nuzzle her neck.

Yvette reached her hands back behind her head to weave her fingers through Jamie's hair and pull her closer. Her manner was a little rough, eliciting a groan from Jamie that made Yvette's clit tingle.

"These are so beautiful," Jamie murmured into Yvette's ear. She took hold of Yvette's breasts once again with her large hands, gripping and massaging them as though claiming ownership of them. Then she ran her finger tips over them before gripping Yvette's nipples and applying pressure to them between her fingers.

"I love your hands," Yvette whispered. "Your hands feel so good."

Jamie nipped at Yvette's earlobe. "They'll feel even better in a minute," she said. Leaving Yvette's breasts with one last tug for each nipple, she slid her hands down Yvette's sides to rest on her waist. Keeping the fingers of her left hand curled around Yvette's hip, she moved her other hand up to press down between the blonde's shoulder blades. "Bend over!"

Yvette swallowed hard and her throat went totally dry. It was as if Jamie had tapped into every fantasy she'd ever had about her. Her legs shook as she obeyed Jamie's whispered command – bending over to rest her arms on the bathroom counter, next to the sink. Yvette kept her head up, looking into Jamie's dark blue eyes reflected in the mirror before her.

Without a word, Jamie grabbed the waistband of Yvette's pajama bottoms and tugged them down until they fell to pool around Yvette's ankles. She was completely naked, vulnerable, dripping wet with excitement. Yvette's breathing picked up until she was nearly panting.

"Step out of them," Jamie commanded.

Yvette did as she was told, still bent over the vanity. She watched Jamie drop her gaze and kick away the pajama bottoms, sending them and the tank top across the floor to the wall. When Jamie's eyes looked toward Yvette again, it was to stare between Yvette's legs.

"Oh Evie! You're *so* wet for me," Jamie murmured.

Yvette gasped and her eyes widened as Jamie dropped to her knees and used her strong fingers to grasp Yvette's buttocks; pulling them apart and opening Yvette to her heated gaze.

Yvette felt exposed and would normally shy away but for Jamie, it felt so special and instead, allowed her back to arch, lifting her ass into the air for Jamie to be able to see all of her. *I want her to want me*, she thought. "I've been thinking about *you*," Yvette whispered, "that's all it takes to get me wet." Yvette wriggled her torso over to improve her line of sight until she could see the reflection of Jamie's face in the mirror again.

"I was thinking about you, too." Jamie's voice was low and throaty, unlike Yvette had ever heard it before. All of the restraint between them had vanished. In its place was a raw hunger, driving both of their actions. "You're so beautiful, Evie."

Yvette dropped her head down to the sink as two searching fingertips traced down and around her labia, then found and entered her vagina with absolute ease. Jamie pulled Yvette open again with her thumbs and Yvette could feel the caress of her breath over her buttocks, followed by her lips placing open-mouthed kisses on her butt cheeks and upper thighs. When Yvette felt Jamie's hair brushing between her thighs and then the sucking sensation on her labia, she almost lost herself to orgasm. Her legs shook and she felt the first surge of divine surrender.

"Not yet!" Jamie hissed in a low, muffled command. She continued to milk Yvette's clit: sucking it into her mouth, swirling her tongue around it, flicking slowly up and down and over it firmly before speeding up and buffeting Yvette's clit from side to side. "Your taste turns me on so much, Evie," said Jamie through her mouthful.

She sucked Yvette's outer lips into her mouth, removing her fingers from Yvette's vagina and gripping her ass. Jamie lapped up the slickly lubricated inner folds before continuing on to swirl her tongue around Yvette's opening. She pushed just the tip of her tongue into Yvette, swiping it from side to side and pushing in little by little. She gripped Yvette's butt cheeks even harder and pulled her open wider so she could go deeper with a low growl.

Withdrawing her tongue, Jamie placed open-mouth kisses along her way upward as she stood, and drove just one finger inside of Yvette from behind with excruciating slowness.

Yvette lifted her head, opening her mouth as she was filled, searching for and finding Jamie's eyes in the mirror again.

Jamie stared at Yvette's face in the semi-darkness as if to memorize it. When she was inside Yvette completely, she leaned down over her back and kissed her shoulder. Her breast brushing against Yvette's back as she thrust her hips up against her from behind.

"You feel so good," Jamie whispered into Yvette's ear as she pulled her finger out and then thrust it inside again while sliding her left hand up Yvette's back between her shoulders to grip the back of her neck. The third time, she entered Yvette with two fingers, forcefully.

Yvette kept her head down, arching her back and pressing her ass back against Jamie's every thrust. She kept her feet planted wide apart to give Jamie easy access. Jamie reached over and lifted Yvette's head; holding her gaze in the mirror in front of them. Yvette uttered soundless cries into the night, slipping once and allowing a loud whimper to escape her.

Jamie wrapped her left arm around Yvette, across her chest so as to hold her more firmly against the sink. Then she increased the strength of her next thrust so that it lifted Yvette forward over the vanity, lifting her feet slightly off the ground.

"Oh, yes!" breathed Yvette.

"Quiet!" Jamie warned in a hissing whisper while tilting her head and raising an eyebrow at Yvette's reflection in the mirror. She squeezed the flesh she held in her left hand, giving Yvette a stern look.

Yvette nodded, silencing her pleasure by forcing it deep inside her belly. Without an outlet, it soon overwhelmed her, causing her thighs to tremble as Jamie continued to pump her hand and hips hard against her. On the edge of orgasm, Yvette searched Jamie's face and found exactly what she was hoping to find. Interest. Desire. Affection. All the things she never saw in Jacque's face anymore. This face was strong but not overpowering and the love-making was forceful but not vicious. Well, if Jamie liked to play the part of the dominant lover and was looking for a submissive mistress; then Yvette found that to be an extreme turn-on.

"Please let me come?" Yvette whispered. She gasped as Jamie's hand left her chest, snaking down Yvette's belly and between her legs, seeking out her swollen clit with her masterful fingers. Yvette's thighs trembled even more violently at the added sensation.

"Quietly!" commanded Jamie in a harsh whisper.

Yvette obeyed, stiffening and shaking on Jamie's skillful hands. Yvette's mouth fell open, but no noise escaped her. She pushed up with her hands on the bathroom counter, arching her back and riding the wave of pleasure until she collapsed, trembling, next to the sink.

Jamie didn't leave her there for long. Withdrawing her fingers from Yvette and murmuring her appreciation, Jamie wrapped both arms around her front and pulled her standing. Yvette felt weak and Jamie seemed to sense that because she held her with strong arms and encouraged Yvette to lean back against her body. Jamie kissed Yvette's neck, inhaling deeply, with her nose buried deep in Yvette's hair.

"I can't wait to do that again," Jamie whispered in Yvette's ear.

Subtle, but the message was received. As far as Jamie was concerned, this was not to be a one-night stand.

"But it's not over yet," Yvette murmured. She turned around in Jamie's strong arms and pressed her naked body against the taller woman. She reached up and captured her lips in a long, lingering kiss, and then pulled back with a teasing grin. Just as Yvette was about to drop to her knees and beg permission to taste and pleasure her lover, her heart stopped. She caught her breath and listened intently to noises coming from the hallway.

The sounds of Jacque's footfalls nearing the bathroom had them both holding their breath. When Yvette recognized the sounds of Jacque descending the stairs she sighed in relief and uttered, "She always wakes in the night looking for water when she's been drinking heavily. I better get back to bed and let her assume I was using the bathroom." Then, without further warning, Yvette swiftly collected her clothing before whispering, "Good night, Jamie," and leaving the bathroom.

Jamie was stunned – speechless – as she watched Yvette disappear into the dark hallway.

♀♀♀♀♀

"I propose a toast," said Jacque, raising her champagne flute high above their table at the restaurant, "To Jamie, you're one hell-of-a negotiator. Thank you for saving our little store, once again."

"Yes, thank you, Jamie," added Yvette as she too, raised her glass in Jamie's direction.

After a short pause, Jamie raised her glass as well. Then, staring at Jacque over the rim of the glass, she took a small sip of the bubbly beverage. She savored the flavor before swallowing and licking her lips.

Yvette watched her and squirmed in her seat, *I'd like to lick the champagne from those lips,* she thought as she studied Jamie intently.

Jamie continued to stare at Jacque. "Another toast," she offered, "To Jacqueline's new management style. May it work so well, it saves me from further negotiations in twelve-month's time." The franchisor had issued a temporary franchise, dependent on the store achieving a specific set of mile-stones over the next twelve months. Not the three years of continued operation that Jacque had hoped for, but in reality, providing better leverage for Jamie to force Jacque's compliance with her plans.

Jacque stared back at Jamie with her eyebrows knitted together for a long moment.

Yvette felt a shudder of fear course through her – her look was one of concern as her eyes flitted back and forth from one woman to the other. She breathed a sigh of relief when Jacque broke into a forced laughter.

"Of course! That's the deal," Jacque acknowledged, raising her glass before gulping the remainder of her champagne. As she did so, she noted Yvette's lingering looks in Jamie's direction. She replaced her glass to the table before lifting the champagne bottle from the bucket-stand next to her. She refilled her glass and then topped up the other two on the table. As she did so, she noticed Jamie offering similar looks toward Yvette. Jacque smirked as she thought to herself, *Looks like the two of you are going to fuck each other again tonight, then.* Jacque returned the champagne bottle to its bucket and sat well back in her chair as the waiter served their meals. She gazed at each of her dinner companions once more as she thought to herself, *Good! I'll have the leverage I need to force Jamie to help me with the next lot of negotiations as well.* She smiled broadly and announced, "This looks delicious."

"Yes, I agree," countered Jamie with a smile in Yvette's direction.

Yvette blushed slightly and squirmed in her seat again. She picked up her knife and fork and decided it would be best to study her plate for a while.

♀♀♀♀♀

Yvette slowly opened the door to the bedroom across from the stairwell and quietly slipped inside the partially moonlit room. As she neared the bed she reached out and gently ran her hand along the full length of the reclined form under the bedcovers.

Jamie stared up at her with dazed eyes. She lay there, still and quiet, wordlessly appreciating the show Yvette was making of stripping off her pajamas. Even in the near dark, Yvette could see the way Jamie's pupils were dilated and her nostrils flared with arousal. Just as she was ready to slide her body over Jamie, she halted, studied the hungry gaze in Jamie's eyes and asked, "May I?"

Jamie hesitated only a few moments before nodding as she pushed her pillow onto the floor.

Yvette lifted her leg and mounted Jamie's face; lowering her center to Jamie's lips with excruciating slowness. Jamie opened her mouth wide and took in as much of Yvette as she could; licking and sucking and savoring Yvette's wetness. Yvette situated herself for comfort and took hold of the rail across Jamie's bedhead to help steady herself. Jamie began to move her tongue in circular motions around Yvette's clit, stopping to delve into the exquisite pool of slick juices in Yvette's pussy. Yvette tasted sweet and the heat of her body carried the smell of her sex to Jamie's nostrils. Jamie breathed in deeply and Yvette's scent made her mouth water. She swallowed hard and then sucked Yvette's pussy into her mouth again. She pushed her face forward as she bared her teeth and began to nibble on the sweet tasting folds. Yvette's body shuddered and her breathing became ragged as she let her head fall back in an effort to breath in as deeply as she could. She allowed her arms to straighten and held all her body weight at their length. She let her body gently swing from side to side in sync with the flowing movements of Jamie's head.

"Oh! Fuck you're good!" breathed Yvette, between gasping breaths. "That's feels incredible," whispered Yvette as she let her head loll forward. Her blonde hair slipped over her shoulders and tickled at her erect nipples in time with the flow of movement.

Jamie began to munch a little harder as she concentrated on sucking on Yvette's clit.

"Oh! Fuck me!" exclaimed Yvette, shuddering from her hips as she began to orgasm.

Jamie firmly held the blonde by her hips and pulled her in close and tight to her teeth. Continuing to nibble even when Yvette's body had ceased to shudder.

"Oh! Yes!" Yvette murmured deep and low as she was consumed by a second orgasm. Her hips did not shudder for this one. She rode this intense orgasm without another word, her head tilted forward, her mouth open and her body still as though mesmerized by every pass of Jamie's teeth over her clit. One last prolonged bite had Yvette collapsing into the bedhead; her body heaving under the strain to draw a breath.

Jamie reached up and swept Yvette backward, lowering her back until she was lying on top of her long, strong, athletic legs. In an amazing show of strength, Jamie sat up and guided Yvette's legs over her shoulders. Yvette hooked her feet together behind Jamie's neck to help hold her legs in place while Jamie leaned in and fucked Yvette's pussy with her tongue. Holding Yvette steady by her shoulders, Jamie licked and sucked up as much of Yvette's come as she could.

Yvette began to moan and quiver with each thrust of Jamie's tongue into her pussy. *If she can keep this up, I'm gonna come again,* thought Yvette.

A moment later, Jamie wriggled them both down further in the bed and as she lay back down, she grasped Yvette by the hips, skillfully flipped her over. She pulled Yvette's pussy back up and onto her face.

As Yvette pushed back the covers and tugged Jamie's boxer shorts down, Jamie exhaled with a low, pleased growl and placed a controlling hand on Yvette's head.

Yvette could smell the heated aroma of Jamie's arousal and it made her clit swell as she stared at the short dark hair that glistened in the moonlight. Pushing Jamie's singlet up over her stomach with one hand, Yvette leaned in close to the source of the scent. Nestling her nose into a thatch of dark pubes, Yvette breathed in deeply to enjoy the heady aroma. She inhaled deeply again and then sat back on her haunches, admiring the rock-hard abdomen under her fingertips. She pumped her hips and enjoyed the tongue-fucking Jamie was giving her. Then she brought her lips to the flesh beneath her fingers and began kissing at the muscles on Jamie's stomach, smiling when they flinched to her touch.

"Don't tease me!" Jamie growled from under her. Jamie reached up, her fingers tangling in Yvette's hair and pulled her face closer to her wetness. "I want to feel your mouth, your tongue. Now Evie!"

Yvette leaned down, muffling her moan into Jamie's flesh as she covered her center with her lips. She traced her tongue along swollen ridges and folds, never staying very long in one place. The restrained sounds coming from Jamie were compelling; inspiring her to take her time and enjoy the thorough exploration.

Yvette could feel Jamie's muscular thighs trembling against her forearms as she lay against her and enjoyed that hint of vulnerability. She also enjoyed the increased wetness she felt as evidence that Jamie was appreciating her touch. She moaned into Jamie's skin, circling her tongue around Jamie's swollen clit in lazy movements.

Jamie began to stroke Yvette's hair with her hand. "God, Eve, that's so good," she whispered quickly between licks at Yvette's clit. Yvette strained hard to hear the quiet words, delighting in Jamie's reaction to her. "That feels so, so good, sweetheart. Nice and slow. Just like that," stated Jamie in a whispered plea.

Yvette kept up her licking and sucking, closing her eyes and inhaling deeply of Jamie's scent. She pushed her face into Jamie's wetness, groaning as her cheeks, nose and chin grew slick from it. Jamie's hand tightened in Yvette's hair once again.

"Harder!" was the next demand and Yvette complied by pressing her tongue down hard against Jamie's engorged clit.

"Circles!" whispered Jamie, harshly. Yvette swirled her tongue around and around the hard nub of nerve endings.

"Faster!" demanded a deep, low whisper from behind her. Unthinking, she strove to obey every command, driving her hard, swirling tongue around Jamie's clit as quickly as she was able.

"Now Yvette! Now!" Yvette heard while she sucked Jamie's clit into her mouth, Yvette moved her lips over the distended shaft and lapped at the hard tip with her tongue. Jamie jerked and groaned as her orgasm crashed down upon her.

When the shaking of her body suddenly ceased, Jamie pulled Yvette's face away from her pussy with two hands and struggled to whisper through her heavy breathing, "Woman, you'll kill me," she gasped.

Yvette giggled as she sat back on her haunches again and used her forefinger to collect the come from her face so she could lick and savor every morsel before leaning down for one more long and tender kiss to Jamie's center. Lavishly coating her face with yet more come before accepting the hands that Jamie now offered to pull her around and into a tender hug. Jamie found Yvette's mouth with hers, kissing and licking at the slick juices that covered Yvette's lips.

Yvette gave her another lengthy, lingering kiss, just like the one she had delivered to her pussy moments earlier.

Jamie broke away from their kiss so they could both gasp for air, and then immediately began lapping at the wetness on Yvette's cheeks and chin. "I'd hate to have to explain that to anyone else," Yvette whispered.

Jamie pulled away, looking at Yvette with confused eyes, "Explain what?" she asked in a nervous voice.

Yvette gave her a reassuring smile, "Killing you."

"Oh," Jamie said, smiling as she remembered her entreaty. After a moment her smile faded and she looked over Yvette's shoulder to the closed bedroom door. When she brought her eyes back to Yvette's, they were sheepish. "Um, Yvette."

Yvette shook her head, covering Jamie's mouth with her hand. "Please don't," she whispered. "I wanted this to happen. I can't wait for next time, either."

Jamie's eyes sparkled as she removed Yvette's fingers from over her mouth. She dropped a quick kiss on them before she pulled them away. "Me, too, it's just... I mean, I wasn't planning to just fuck...," wincing, she released Yvette's hand and shifted ashamed eyes toward the moonlit window. "I mean, uh..."

Yvette chuckled at Jamie's discomfort. "We both wanted it," Yvette whispered to her, curling her fingers around Jamie's chin and lifting her eyes to meet with hers. "Don't feel bad about it now, okay?"

"I'm just thinking that...someone...would probably kick my ass if they knew what I just did to you," Jamie whispered.

Yvette was not so certain that was true anymore. Her relationship with Jacque had never been an easy one. But in a country town, the pickings were slim. Besides, Jacque seemed to 'go-easy' on her mother and brother from the moment they'd started dating. Yvette had felt concern over being trapped in their relationship almost from the beginning, but what could she do? In truth, she hadn't really liked Jacque all that much at first – for all the same reasons no one else really likes Jacque very much. However, when Jacque alluded to having to lay off staff from the store, it was evident, that Yvette's attentions were the only means by which Jacque would allow Bridgette and Pascal to remain in her employ. Yvette felt bound to make a sacrifice for the benefit of her family. They had, after all, made sacrifices of their own for her sake when putting her through university. Yvette's mother and brother had no idea that this was the case. No one knew – not another living sole, except of course, Jacque. Yvette simply learned to accept her lot in life and make the best of things. It was really only during Jamie's regular visits to her home-town, and the occasional stay-over at Jamie's house, that Yvette would come question that decision.

"She's asleep. She finished off the last of the pina coladas out at the pool before she came to bed. She'll never know I've been missing," assured Yvette.

Jamie nodded sadly, sensing that their interlude would soon be ending. "I...wish I could... I mean...I'm not...just after..."

Yvette pressed her fingers to Jamie's lips to silence them once more and whispered, "I know." She climbed over Jamie and stood next to the bed while holding the back of Jamie's neck and pressing their lips together. One last lengthy, passionate kiss with each holding the other as though desperate to never let go.

♀♀♀♀♀

"Have a safe trip, you two!" Jamie called from the top of her driveway. "And tell Annie 'I look forward to staying with her next month.'" Jamie had made arrangements to stay with Jacque's aunt for the first week of each month, for the next twelve months, while she helped Jacque install and then oversee the required changes at the store.

Yvette was waving frantically from the passenger seat as Jacque reversed the car onto the roadway. "See you in a fortnight," Yvette called excitedly. *I can't wait to hold her again. I sure hope Jamie has cause to be at the house during Annie's afternoon naps,* Yvette thought and then realized with alarm that she was giggling out aloud.

Jamie walked down to the end of her drive as Jacque backed the car out onto the roadway. In a fortnight, she would be staying for a week as a business guest at Annie's house. Her first call of business would be to discuss with Annie, the outcome and concerns of the franchisors and her ultimatum to Jacque. However, she would be doing more than that. She would also discuss with Annie, her concerns for Jacque's ability to comply with and implement the necessary changes to satisfy either the franchisor or Jamie's ultimatum. A 'Plan B' was required. She sighed heavily as she pondered, *Even if it adversely impacts on Yvette, I have to fix this ongoing problem with Jacque, one way or another.*

Jacque looked back for a moment, also waving a quick farewell before pulling away. She'd noted the looks between the two covert lovebirds all morning and the closer they came to the time for departure, the more evident the feelings between them. Jacque wasn't concerned though, *Pascal will never find another job in that little backwater town. Yvette won't do anything to jeopardize* his *job*, she thought with confidence.

Jamie watched the vehicle pull away and continued with her own thoughts as Yvette and Jacque's car drove out of her street. She intended to negotiate a six month plan with Annie. *If Jacque isn't up-to-scratch by then, Bridgette,* (Annie's previous deputy and longtime friend), *already has a proven ability in the job*. She knew that Annie would be prepared to give the role of manager to Bridgette, if it became apparent that the future of the store was in the balance.

Jamie walked back up her driveway shaking her head. She couldn't believe Jacque's behavior. *How many ultimatums do I have to issue that woman before she takes it seriously?* Then, walking through her front door, she reminisced over Yvette. In her mind's eye she saw Yvette walking through the house with her make-up bags. Jamie smiled warmly as she reminisced over the many interludes between her and Yvette in the last two days. She walked out to the pool area and as she looked into the water, she imagined Yvette relaxing and floating on her back. She breathed in deeply and sighed her contentment. *Finally, things are looking up*, she thought as she stripped off naked and dove into the pool. *At least now I know how she feels about me.*

Breaking the surface of the water after her dive, she recalled Yvette doing breast strokes up and down the pool. *Yes the next two weeks might drag, but at least I'll have some fabulous moments to relive until I see her again.*

She knew it wasn't a perfect arrangement, being 'the other woman.' A few days ago she would not have seen herself in such a role. She would much prefer to have Yvette to herself but in the absence of any other choice, it was a situation she was now prepared to leap into. Anything! Any way! Any where! Any time! Whatever it took to hold that little woman in her arms once more – she would gladly do it.

But what of the store? she thought to herself. She began biting her lip as she considered her dilemma. *Annie is still too weak to take on Jacque, the way I can. Will Yvette still let me touch her if I cause Jacque to lose her position as Store Manager?* She released her lip from the hold her teeth had upon it. Frowning to herself and pouting slightly she thought, *Surely she will understand that I'd only cause that to happen if Jacque leaves me no other choice. In any case, if Jacque continues down her current path, the store will not qualify for a continued franchise agreement and I'll never see Yvette again anyway.*

She sighed heavily, *What to do? What to do?*

Then her face turned serious and she made a solemn vow to herself. *If it's the last thing I do, I will save that little store for Annie.*

The End

Double-Date

Matilda drained the last of her coffee from its cup and savored the richness of the flavor before swallowing. She held the cup aloft while she read the last few lines of a document on her tablet. Smiling, evidently pleased with what she read, she placed the cup on its saucer and powered down her tablet. She tucked the device into her handbag and withdrew her wallet. Catching the eye of the waitress at her favorite café, she waved a few notes in the air before placing them on the counter, next to her cup and saucer.

"Will you need anything more today?" the eager young waitress asked as she collected the money.

"No, thank you. Please, keep the change," Matilda added with a smile as she slipped her wallet back into her handbag. She took a deep breath and prepared herself mentally for the evening ahead as she slid from the stool and made her way out the door and down the street toward her office.

The evening was warm and the traffic light. She noted how relaxed she felt as she walked along the street and pondered how at-ease she was with herself since meeting Chase. *Sex is the best method for de-stressing,* she thought. *I'm so much better at my job since I've started seeing Chase.*

She crossed the busy road at a set of lights and walked to the top of the hill. Still looking relaxed and pleased with herself, she turned and entered the office building situated there.

Alighting from the elevator on the fifth floor of her office building, Matilda wound her way through the empty reception area to her office suite. *Hmm, it's quiet here – that's good. I'm glad everyone's gone home on time. It'll help me to keep my mental preparedness if I don't have to have unnecessary conversation.*

Her personal assistant, Tammy, was waiting for her and stood from her desk to greet Matilda and follow her into her office. Even this late in the day the room was well lit from a large window across from the entrance. It was a pleasant and airy room, not too large and tastefully furnished. Matilda's desk and several chairs were on one side with a compact lounge area and coffee table on the other. Behind the desk and off to one side was a doorway leading to an executive bathroom. In the corner, off to the other side of the desk, was a coat and hat stand. Hanging on the stand was an evening gown still wrapped in the protective plastic the drycleaners had delivered it in.

"I got that black dress – the one with the silver threads here and there through the bodice – dry cleaned for you for tonight, and your favorite black high heels. I wasn't sure which clutch purse you'd want with it; so I've got both the black one and the silver one here," explained Tammy as she held out a clip board and pen for Matilda to sign some papers. "Your travel summary," Tammy informed her.

Matilda nodded, signed the document and handed it back to Tammy, "Thanks, Tam. I think the silver would go well," she handed her handbag to Tammy who immediately began fishing through it for the things needing to be transferred to the silver clutch bag.

"Did you want me to get the bathroom ready for you?" asked Tammy distractedly as she quickly finished up with the bags.

"No thanks, Tam. I had a shower before I caught the train back. I'm refreshed and ready."

"The car is in the garage. Strip off and I'll put your excess things in it while you change." Tammy's manner was one of practiced professionalism. It was her job to get Matilda where she needed to go, in what she needed to wear, with everything she needed for success. They'd worked well together for the past five years and had become a most effective team.

Matilda complied, stripping without a moment's thought, and while Tammy left with her discarded outfit neatly folded into a bag, Matilda dressed in her evening gown and heels before going into the bathroom to complete her make-up and fix her hair.

When Tammy returned, she was carrying another pair of high-heels, for herself, "Ready?" she asked.

"You bet," said Matilda as she quickly reapplied her lipstick. "Did you get the name of that engineer Goldie was so taken with in Argyle?"

"Yes. Patricia Maize," answered Tammy. "Oh, and Legal made some changes to those contracts you put together for Goldie."

"Mmm," acknowledged Matilda with her lips pressed together to even out her lipstick. "I read them while I had a coffee up the road. They're all good. We're as ready as we're going to be for The Gold Digger."

Gold Digger, was just one of the nicknames they shared for Goldie Galore – a rich and influential mining magnate. Goldie had made her start in business on the strength of her first husband's gold mine in Kalgoorlie. When they'd divorced, Goldie walked away with half of a highly profitable gold mine and, all the contacts she needed to bump elbows and rub shoulders with the big boys. One of whom became her second husband. His interests in Argyle diamonds became solely owned by Goldie when he was killed in an ultra-light helicopter crash while surveying a potential mine site in the east Kimberley. *She has to be given her due though*, thought Matilda as she straightened her dress and inspected her look in the mirror. *She is a formidable business woman.* Indeed she was. Goldie now had sizeable interests in gold and diamond mines around the world. Her latest acquisition was a gold mine on a high mountain in central Mongolia. *Most prospectors would have considered themselves lucky if they found copper in Mongolia. Goldie finds the mother-load of gold,* Matilda mused, shaking her head as she looked back into the mirror to touch up her hair. *I swear, that woman must be able to smell the stuff.*

"How do I look?" Matilda asked as she turned toward Tammy.

"Thin," said Tammy honestly. "You've lost weight on that Mongolia/China trip. But then Pussy likes that look, so you're dressed for success."

'Pussy Galore' was another of Matilda and Tammy's pet names for Goldie. Yes, she had been married twice, but even then she was a notorious womanizer. As the years went by and the billions amassed; Goldie began to be seen only with women as her personal companions.

Tammy smiled as she gave Matilda a final look up and down. She decided not to make any further changes to Matilda's appearance. Her boss's look was exactly the one needed to give them the edge with this feisty billionaire.

Tammy pulled on her own high heels and picked up Matilda's silver clutch. Handing it to Matilda she said, "Now, one last meeting to gel all your hard work, Matilda." Tammy walked to office door, opening it with great ceremony and motioning for Matilda to exit, "Shall we?"

"It's in the bag," Matilda said as she tucked her clutch bag under her arm and walked through the door with an air of utmost confidence.

It was not unusual for Tammy to accompany Matilda to these dinner meetings. In fact, it made a lot of sense for her PA to be on hand. They had even devised a code should Matilda be uncertain of any information discussed. Tammy could signal Matilda under the table as to whether she knew the information to be correct. She could also signal to let Matilda know when information was incorrect or needed to be challenged.

The drive to the restaurant was a quiet one. Matilda going over, in her head, the selling points she wanted to convey to Goldie to have her agree to do business with the Mongolian and Chinese governments. The contracts Matilda had negotiated and poured over would outline the manner in which Goldie's mining company would conduct themselves in both countries and also bind China and Mongolia to making certain trade provisions. Tammy knew to keep quiet at this point in her boss's preparations. She drove in silence.

Tammy had booked the restaurant in the same hotel where Goldie was staying. One of the pricier restaurants in the city; the intention was to impress Goldie while also keeping her comfortable. Perhaps even comfortable enough to lower her guard a little and become easier to do business with. She pulled the car into the valet parking area of the hotel and left the engine running as she quickly slipped her high heels back on and got out. She greeted the attendant who had just opened the door for her with a smile.

Matilda was smoothing her evening gown and waiting for Tammy near the door of the hotel by the time Tammy had swapped the keys for a valet ticket and caught up with her. One knowing look at each other, and in they went.

♀♀♀♀♀

Matilda and Tammy were shown straight to their table upon entering the restaurant. They said very little to one another while they awaited Goldie's entrance. The ambiance of the restaurant was perhaps a little darker than Matilda would have expected and the background music would be easily dismissed while conversing; so that was good. The décor was refined as was the conduct of the wait staff. All-in-all, an ideal location for their meeting.

"You've done well selecting this place, Tammy. It's perfect," Matilda complimented her PA.

"The rooms are exquisite as well," Tammy assured Matilda. "Goldie should be well pleased with the suite she's in."

Matilda nodded and returned to her introspection.

Tammy had sat them at the table so as to have a view of Goldie as she entered the restaurant and so, was happy to sit watch over the entrance while Matilda continued her mental preparations for the meeting.

Tammy enjoyed her work. Sometimes she and Matilda would travel together – generally for meetings similar to this one – where her skills as a PA were most needed. Mostly though, Matilda travelled without her. Tammy would coordinate business from the office while Matilda would travel with hired consultants. *Lonely work for her,* thought Tammy, *with very few opportunities for lasting friendships.*

Tammy was married with children, so the idea of travelling as much as Matilda did was completely unappealing. Besides, her wife wouldn't stand for it and her four year old son wouldn't understand.

"How's Jo-Anne and Little Ben?" Matilda asked, causing Tammy to wonder for a moment if her boss was psychic.

"They're both well. Ben asks about you all the time," Tammy smiled and nodded at her.

Glancing back to the door, Tammy noted Goldie entering with another woman. The Maître'D recognized Goldie and immediately began escorting the pair toward their table. "She's here," Tammy said as she started to rise from her chair.

Matilda stood too and watched as Goldie walked toward their table, followed by someone in a tuxedo, both lead by the Maître'D. As Goldie neared the table, Matilda stepped forward and held out her hand. Goldie took it and Matilda greeted, "Goldie, good to see you again. You remember my assistant, Tammy."

"Of course, I remember Tammy. She's one of the few who's actually turned down a job offer from me. No hard feelings, I respect your loyalty to your boss," Goldie said as she reached over and lightly shook Tammy's extended hand.

Matilda smiled at the double-edged compliment. *A good start,* she thought. As Goldie reached over to take Tammy's hand, the woman that had been standing behind her came into Matilda's view. *Chase?!*

Chase looked shocked for a few seconds; a reflection of Matilda. She forced herself to recover and dipped her head slightly at Matilda in recognition.

"Chase, allow me to introduce Matilda and her assistant, Tammy. Chase will be making up our four tonight, ladies." Goldie sat as the Maître'D helped to position her chair.

"Of course," said Matilda attempting to regain her composure.

"Nice to meet you," Tammy added.

They all sat and were attended to for drinks and menus as they made small talk. Matilda had pre-selected the wines for each course based on her knowledge of Goldie. This was just one of many such meetings they'd had and bringing a date with her was not unusual for Goldie. *In fact, she's never brought the same woman twice,* thought Matilda as she quickly glanced up at Chase who was declining a wine in preference for water. *It shouldn't surprise me that Chase would have clientele such as Goldie,* Matilda reasoned. *It makes perfect sense really.* Matilda watched as Chase sipped from her glass of water and then dabbed at her lips with her napkin. She forced herself to look away as she thought, *I've got to stop looking at her, Tam and Pussy are bound to notice.* Almost immediately, she looked over at Chase again, *Fuck, but she looks hot in a tux!* When Goldie spoke, Matilda almost jumped out of her skin.

"I intend to have the most expensive thing from each course," said Goldie, "since you're buying, Matilda." Everyone laughed politely.

Matilda closed the menu in front of her and handed it to the Maître'D. "Well, in that case, we will be staying with the menu I pre-ordered, thank you, Redwin." The Maître'D nodded and collected the menus before leaving.

Goldie laughed out loud and said, "See, Chase. This is why I don't mind coming 3,000 kilometers out of my way to see this woman. She studies her prey and has the confidence to let you know you're being hunted." She laughed again, heartily, before adding, "Too bad you've let your game slip recently, though."

Matilda stared and flicked a quick look in Chase's direction, *Are you a spy?* she thought.

Chase's face was one of growing concern.

Matilda could hear her own heart pounding in her ears and felt as though she were losing her breath. "What do you mean, Goldie?" she asked politely.

"Do you really think I'm gonna spring for a road in those windswept mountains?" Goldie's face was hard, her lips thin and taut. "Do you have any idea how much that's going to cost me? What am I saying, of course you do." Goldie smiled almost menacingly for a moment before adding, "You of all people would know exactly how much, right down to the last penny."

Matilda felt the color rise a little in her face, *Penny! Have I been set up here?* Matilda cleared her throat, "Well, the road trains from your mine will be the only *real* traffic on that road, Goldie."

Goldie cut Matilda short, "Governments build roads, Matilda. Not businesses – you should know that!"

As Matilda opened her mouth to retort their first course arrived. Tammy touched her lightly on the leg, code for '*not now.*' Matilda smiled and said calmly, "Well, let's have our meal and discuss that on a full stomach, shall we?"

Goldie nodded, "You're right. Let's not spoil the meal."

By the time they'd finished the first course, Matilda had resolved to press the positives for Goldie's companies should the contract signing go ahead. Goldie seemed to relent somewhat and acknowledged the fact that Matilda had made some real inroads with the many different ministries not only in Mongolia, but in China as well. With Mongolia being a landlocked country, Goldie's mining company would need to transport their product for further refining, through China to reach the nearest port. Something that would be good for China's economy as well, especially if Goldie chose to use China's smelting facilities to complete the processing of her gold.

Dessert was completed with the dinner going better than it had started, but it was inevitable that they would return to the contentious issue of road building.

"China and Australia have committed to building the road through the flatlands. They can use it to satisfy a good portion of their humanitarian and aid policies. Goldie Galore Mining would only be responsible for the cost and construction of the mountain section," explained Matilda.

"The mountain section is gonna cost twice as much as the section through the flats and desert. Why should we be happy with having both China and Australia each, only coughing up just over fifteen percent of total costs of the road? And what about Mongolia? Why is Mongolia getting a free ride on this venture? That's not right!"

The two women quieted as the Maître'D approached. Under the table, Tammy moved her foot to lightly tap against Matilda's – their signal to challenge with information from Tammy. Matilda looked down as though she might be able to see Tammy's leg movement through the table. Then, looking sideways at Tammy, she ran her fingers through her hair while shaking her head marginally. Tammy understood this to mean, *not yet.*

"Would you like the coffees to be served now, madam?" Redwin asked quietly.

Matilda looked to Goldie and when she nodded, replied, "Yes, please, we're ready now." Matilda exhaled deeply as the Maître'D walked away. She needed to diffuse the situation. Goldie was digging her heels in and Matilda knew if she continued to push, the entire negotiation would collapse. Goldie was rich enough to afford to be stubborn and allow that to happen, if she so wished.

"I'll take a bathroom break before the coffees arrive. Please excuse me, Goldie." Matilda nodded at the other two women seated at the table before leaving.

Chase watched her walk away. *This isn't going well for her and it's all my fault. My presence here has undermined her confidence.*

313

Goldie couldn't have planned it better. I wonder if she knows about us?

Matilda caught up with the Maître'D on her way to the rear of the restaurant, "Give me an extra fifteen minutes before you serve that coffee, okay, Redwin?"

"Certainly, Madame."

Matilda pushed her way through the self-closing door into the hallway leading to the restroom. When the door swung closed behind her, she slowly walked toward the restroom door as she pieced together her next plan of attack. She pressed open the door marked, 'Women' and stepped into the recently refurbished facility. *Hmm, nice,* she thought for an instant and then walked up to the mirror to check her makeup and hair.

The vanity was a long bench with two sinks at the center, leaving plenty of bench space for her to open her clutch bag and shake out her lipstick, mascara and comb. As she worked on her appearance, she heard the door open behind her but didn't take too much notice as the restaurant had been well patronized all that evening. She leapt with fright when a strong hand rested upon her shoulder.

"Sorry, Matilda. I didn't mean to give you a fright."

"Chase! What the hell are you doing here?" Matilda asked in a tone lost somewhere between relief and anger.

"I was worried about you. I didn't know Goldie was meeting with you tonight. Honestly! If I'd known, I would have declined," Chase quickly blurted in explanation.

"I was just wondering if maybe she'd employed you to pick me up from my favorite café and work me for information," Matilda said almost bitterly.

"Oh, Matilda, no!" Chase shook her head and looked hurt. "It's not like that. I assure you, Goldie has no idea we're...acquainted."

Matilda closed her eyes and sighed with relief. There must have been ten or twenty times during the evening's discussion with Goldie when Matilda had thought she was making references to her interludes with Chase. Matilda had convinced herself that Goldie had inside information on her most intimate weaknesses. She had felt out-maneuvered, manipulated and played for a fool. Mostly though, she had felt betrayed – humiliated and exposed by someone she had come to trust and feel safe with. The thought of having lost that relationship had made her feel sick to her stomach.

"So, you're not her spy?" Matilda needed outright confirmation. Taking in Chase's reflection in the wall-to-wall vanity mirror, she looked Chase in the eye and scrutinized her for the slightest sign of untruth.

"No! Absolutely not!" Chase was frowning through her concern for Matilda. She looked back at Matilda's face in the mirror. Matilda's eyes were sparkling with tears.

"Oh, Matilda," Chase pressed her body against Matilda's back and wrapped her arms around Matilda's little waist before bending to kiss her on the neck.

Matilda shivered at the tickle of breath against her skin. She hugged Chase's arms and tilted her head to the side to give Chase greater access to the flesh of her neck.

Chase brushed her lips lightly on Matilda's skin and pressed her hips gently against Matilda's ass. This resulted in Matilda's pussy being pushed against the vanity, making Matilda groan. The evening's anxieties had left Matilda predisposed to arousal. That groan, so well-known to Chase by now, sparked her into action. She reached down for the hem of Matilda's evening gown, sliding her hands up the sides of Matilda's legs and carrying the thin fabric upward.

Matilda groaned again and leant back against Chase as she watched the show in the mirror. She watched as Chase lifted her dress up to her waist line and then slipped a hand under her stockings and into her panties. Another groan escaped Matilda's parted lips as Chase pressed her fingers into Matilda's folds and massaged the wetness she found there.

"Mmm, yes," said Matilda. She looked up and found that she could see Chase's hand delving into her panties from the mirror on the ceiling

316

above the vanity. She groaned again and pressed herself against Chase's fingers. She looked back and forth into the mirrors on the side walls at either ends of the vanity and could see a number of reflections in the play of the mirrors. All were of Chase working her wrist up and down and in and out of her panties. Matilda flooded with wetness and was desperate for Chase to penetrate her with her fingers.

"Oh, I could come if you fucked me, Chase," Matilda said as she squirmed in Chase's embrace.

Chase pulled her hand out of Matilda's panties and quickly turned Matilda around. Now they were face-to-face. She kissed Matilda as she picked her up and placed her on the vanity bench with her dress still up around her waist. She quickly pulled Matilda's stockings and panties down, slipping off one of her shoes and freeing her leg. Then she positioned Matilda on the vanity to rest her back against a mirrored side wall. She moved Matilda's untethered leg up onto the vanity and without delay, went down on the little diva. She breathed in deeply adoring her scent, her flavor.

Matilda took hold of Chase's head and pulled her close to her pussy, "Lick it, Chase! I need to come." Matilda watched in the mirror above the vanity as Chase pressed her face between her legs. "Oh, this is…Oh! Fuck me with your fingers, Stud!" Matilda demanded.

Chase stabbed three fingers home and moved them back and forth, quickly thrusting in and out of Matilda's pussy. Matilda responded with a gushing of fluid that filled Chase's palm and dripped from her wrist.

Matilda reached down with both hands and pulled her outer lips up and open for Chase. Looking up into the overhead mirror again, Matilda panted, "Oh, Chase, I can see your tongue licking my clit in the mirror." Matilda's breathing became ragged and heavy as she managed between panting breaths, "That's...just *so*...fucking hot!"

Chase ran the tip of her tongue over and over the top of Matilda's clit, feeling it grow, tasting it sweeten as Matilda drew closer and closer to orgasm.

Matilda looked into the large wall mirror and for a short while it seemed to her that another couple – the spitting image of them – were fucking too, on an exact replica of their bench. She breathed heavily and looked into the side mirror across from her to imagine that there were numerous other couples also fucking with similar abandon. Matilda felt as though she were in the middle of an orgy. Everywhere she looked, lipstick lesbians were being tongued and finger-fucked by their butch lovers. She groaned loudly, her breasts heaving as she began breathing in faster and shorter breaths.

"Fuck me, Tough Guy! Fuck me hard!" Matilda demanded and Chase obeyed, forcing her spearhead of fingers in and out of Matilda's pussy with every ounce of strength she had to offer, while continuing to lash her tongue back and forth over Matilda's clit.

Neither of them heard the door open. Neither of them saw the figure standing frozen; watching them in their throes of passion. Not until Matilda looked into the vanity mirror for a sideways view of Chase's tongue-play, did she notice the reflection of a woman standing near the doorway, silently watching.

Matilda quickly reached down as if to push Chase's head away, but just at that moment, her orgasm coursed through her. It engulfed her so overwhelmingly, she no longer cared that she had an audience.

"Oh, yeah!" she moaned and held Chase's head in place against her. "Oh, fuck yeah!" she exhaled into the next wave of all-consuming ecstasy. "Ohhhhh....!" she finished as she touched Chase on the forehead with her palm. An indicator Chase had by now learned to mean, Matilda no longer wanted her clit to be touched.

Chase leaned back and plunged her fingers deep inside Matilda, stroking the walls of her pussy; milking the last of Matilda's orgasm from her. Matilda closed her eyes and hummed throatily with appreciation for the unexpected pleasure.

Then, as if snapping herself out of a trance, Matilda caught Chase's eye and gestured toward the door. Chase looked around, saw the woman and smiled.

"Whoops!" said Chase and she smiled, stood and shrugged with good humor. Chase tried valiantly to use her body and tuxedo coat as a shield while Matilda pulled her panties and stockings back up.

Matilda appreciated the gesture but giggled at the futility of it. Not only had this woman watched their sex show, she could still watch from almost every other angle in the mirrors of the vanity.

Chase understood Matilda's humor and laughed uncontrollably. She struggled to be of much use to Matilda because she was laughing so much.

The stranger giggled too, as Matilda indicated a need for assistance from Chase, to climb down from the vanity. At the same time, Matilda was awkwardly clutching her bag and its wayward contents.

Then as they started to walk out, Chase realized Matilda was limping. Quickly, she dashed back to the vanity and collected Matilda's shoe for her. Everyone laughed again as Chase supported Matilda in her gauche attempt to slip the shoe back on.

Their voyeur by now was laughing unashamedly. As the naughty pair began to move past her, she questioned Chase, "I don't suppose this is a queue, is it?"

Chase reached into her pocket and presented a business card for the woman. Gently, she inserted it into the woman's cleavage and then winked at her, saying, "Call me."

All three women were in raptures of laughter as Chase and Matilda stumbled out through the door and into the hall. Matilda stopped for a moment to recompose herself and straighten her clothing properly. She looked up at Chase and said, "Please tell me I don't look like I've just had sex."

"You look all aglow," Chase said honestly wiping Matilda's come from her face with a handkerchief. "And as usual your hair and makeup are flawless." Chase looked her up and down slowly and when she gazed into Matilda's eyes again, she nodded her approval.

Matilda forced herself to lose her smile and straightened. One sideways look at Chase was the last thing she needed before straightening her shoulders and lifting her chin high. "I'm ready," she said determinedly as she re-entered the restaurant.

♀♀♀♀♀

Goldie looked a little unnerved as both Matilda and Chase returned to the table together. She looked down at the tabletop contemplatively as Chase sat in the chair next to her. Then Goldie cast a glance sideways at Chase, with some suspicion. When Goldie looked back across the table, Matilda was smiling broadly at her.

Redwin arrived with the coffees. Each of the adversaries stared directly at the other as he served them and set the table with after dinner accompaniments.

Matilda took a sip from her coffee and cast a determined look at Goldie before starting, "You should be jumping at the opportunity to build that mountain road, Goldie. It gives you total control over the construction and maintenance of the most crucial piece of infrastructure to the success of your project. The winds in those mountains are so fierce, that road transport is the only means you will have available to service your mine. Dig up as much gold as you like, it won't be worth a damn if you can't get it down from that mountain and into a processing plant."

Goldie removed her elbows from the table and leaned back in her chair; subconsciously distancing herself from Matilda. As is Matilda's expertise, she picked up on the subtle sign of acquiescence and re-grouped for her next assault.

"It also gives you the chance to employ the expertise you're already confident and familiar with to build that essential life-line for your venture." Matilda was now stabbing her fingers into the table; forcing her words home with her body language.

"You've been throwing money at Patricia Maize for months now, trying to keep her under contract to you. Well, here's your opportunity to keep her close for years. She's not motivated by money, Goldie. She needs a challenge and this is a challenge she won't be able to refuse."

Goldie pursed her lips and narrowed her eyes. She began to watch Matilda's fingers as they pressed home each point against the surface of the table.

Matilda stopped talking! Stopped moving! Intentionally manipulating Goldie! Forcing Goldie to look her in the eye! Distracting Goldie from thought! Eliminating Goldie's chances of discerning a flaw, finding a loop-hole, or clawing back a foothold for rebuttal. Matilda smelled the blood in the water and the instant Goldie looked up at her, she moved in for the kill.

"The Mongolian government is prepared to assist in constructing the mountain pass. They will source and supply all of the unskilled labor required for the build." Goldie snorted at the meager offering and Matilda leapt, "If you put one of your human resource specialists on the team you can use this as an opportunity for pre-selection from local resources. That way, you can profitably comply with the Mongolian trade policy of hiring 'indigenous labor only' for all entry-level jobs, from day one of your mining operation." Matilda studied Goldie, intently. She knew that she was winning the negotiation, but wasn't certain if Goldie was yet completely convinced.

Goldie was studying her in return, in obvious contemplation, as she ran her tongue over her teeth. Here and there she squinted her eyes or furrowed her brow. A few more moments went by and Matilda decided to call her bluff.

"Or…." Matilda threw her napkin down on the table to signify finality, "…you can let the whole negotiation fall over: embarrass the Australian government in the face of the hard yards that have been won with the Chinese government; frustrate a notoriously unforgiving Mongol government; waste all your R&D dollars; and, hope that a bunch of claim-jumpers don't move in on you while you spend years trying to undo the political damage."

Matilda again looked Goldie in the eye and Goldie stared back. Both Chase and Tammy were holding their collective breaths, when finally, Goldie burst into laughter.

"Okay Matilda, I get the picture. I've screwed you for as much as I'm going to get. Fine! Fine!" Goldie motioned with her hand, waving away the animosity between them. "Send over your lawyers in the morning and I'll sign your contracts over breakfast." Goldie moved her chair to stand. "I might as well get another free meal out of this before we're done," she chuckled and began to walk out of the restaurant.

Chase stood and waited for Matilda to stand before following the billionaire toward the hotel lobby.

Tammy stopped to pay the bill, so Matilda took the opportunity to speak quietly with Chase.

"Your client isn't going to be happy with you, Chase."

"Client?" Chase exclaimed with a furrowed brow, "Goldie's my mother."

Matilda's mouth opened wide as she gaped with shock.

Chase laughed quietly at the look on Matilda's face before adding, "And she's never happy with me, so don't worry." Chase left Matilda standing in the lobby and entered the elevator with her mother.

As Tammy came to stand by Matilda, Chase waved from inside the elevator just as the doors were closing. Matilda attempted a covert wave back until she felt Goldie's cold stare, looking straight at her. She felt a little embarrassed at being caught out. When Goldie looked sideways at Chase before rolling her eyes and quickly pushing Chase's hand back down by her side, Matilda couldn't stop a little giggle from escaping.

The last thing Matilda saw of them was Chase's naughty smile followed by a wink as the elevator doors came to a close. She was pleased with herself as she turned toward Tammy. She noted the smile on Tammy's face. Tammy was staring at her.

"What?"

Tammy couldn't help her smile of incredulity. "We can just send Legal without any further changes to those contracts you drew-up this morning." Tammy's eyes were wide with wonder for Matilda – the tactician.

"Yes," Matilda nodded proudly. "We can," she confirmed smugly as they headed for the hotel's exit.

The End

Things We Do For Love

My wife's family is Persian. That means she can eat anything she wants and never put on any weight. Her whole family is like it. Me, on the other hand, I only have to look at food and I have to do a five mile run for my penance. Her skin looks as if it would taste like toffee and apart from a head of beautiful, wavy, ebony hair; thin, shapely eyebrows; and a small triangle pointing the way to one of my favorite places on earth, she is completely hairless – she waxes at home.

I, on the other hand, have milky, freckly skin and...*bow my head and sigh...Okay! Deep breath*. I'm a hairy little sucker! There, I said it! It's caused me problems in the past. Like, when I went through a Commando phase a few years back – no underwear – it was....liberating, but dangerous. I loved being able to feel the breeze flow up the leg of my trousers. *Should I have confessed to that? Shoulder shrug*. I also enjoyed being able to have a scratch when the mood took me, and not wearing underwear ensured that I'd do a quick and effective job of that. Nothing worse than having to deal with clothing when an itch needs attending to. *Clearing my throat*. Am I right?

So, getting to the part where it was dangerous… Yep. You guessed it. During a moment of extreme 'need to whizz in a hurry' and get back to work, I pulled up the zip of my trousers and caught an enormous tuft of curly hairs in my zipper. *Bugger! Bugger! Shit! Piss! Fuck!* I immediately tried to lower the zip and free myself but the rotten thing wouldn't budge. The pain made my eyes water so much, I couldn't see to figure out how to get myself free. *Deep breaths! Just calm the fuck down!* I told myself but no amount of effort was gonna fix my problem.

I held myself and my trousers as still as possible with one hand, while struggling to get my phone out from my back pocket. This was another excruciating exercise that left me having to wipe tears from my eyes with my sleeve before I could focus on the phone. Desperately flicking my thumb over the screen to open my phonebook I see my salvation: 'lover' (that's my wife) – dial. I explain my situation, but it was some time before she could stop laughing long enough to confirm that she was on her way to help me. Her laughter made me laugh and that hurt like a son-of-a-bitch which made her laugh all the more, which made me laugh again….*Groan.* It took twenty minutes for her to go to her sister's house and drop off our daughter before coming to my aid. In that time, I'd tried to pluck some of the hairs from my fanny, wondering if pulling some of them out through the zipper would allow it to shift. *Ouch! Ouch! And double ouch!* Nope, that didn't work either.

By the time my wife arrived, I looked like I'd cried a river and my pain was intense. Worse still. I was now embarrassed to the max from having her see me in my predicament and her incessant laughter was no longer amusing me. She took to my tuft of hairs with the scissors. *Why the fuck didn't I think of doing that?* Once she'd slipped her hand in underneath to help hold me and save me from the soreness she trimmed all of the hairs back flush with the zipper. I found the placement of her hand quite a comfort as well as a much needed distraction. She put down the scissors and then looked up suddenly at the ceiling. She knows me so well. *Sucker!* As soon as I looked up at the ceiling she pulled the zipped trousers away from my skin and with one quick, insanely agonizing movement, I was freed at last. Oh, what painful relief, as I massaged the affected area with one hand while drying my eyes on the sleeve of the other. So, by now you've realized that I'm not exactly a 'tough butch.' Keep this knowledge in mind for the remainder of this story, okay?

"I think you need to 'mow-the-grass,'" she says through her giggling.

"Huh?"

"Trim it up so they don't get caught anymore."

So that night, after my run and before showering, I took to myself with the scissors and tidied up the hacked mess left after my ordeal. *George Michael eat your friggin' heart out*. It looked good too, even if I do say so myself. *Chest puffed out like a grinning peacock.*

Not long after that the missus pops up from between my legs and says, "Next time you trim can you take some off from down under?"

"Huh?" I say wondering why she'd suddenly stopped when she'd been doing *so* well.

"I'd just like to be able to see where I'm going."

I turned bright red. I was so embarrassed. Did I mention I was hairy? *Fuck me!*

I became…obsessed…with making certain the hairs didn't grow long enough to get caught in my zip or floss my wife's tonsils. Eventually, I just started shaving. Yup, balder than the proverbial eagle's head. *Big grin*. All went well for some time after that apart from the odd bout of razor rash, which was never a pretty sight. *Ouch!*

Then, one day I just felt the need to start wearing underwear again. Now I didn't need to be quite so worried with the upkeep of my bald pussy and shaving less often meant less risk of razor rash. Makes sense, right?

You guessed it. Up she pops again…*groan*.

"It's giving me stubble rash," she says, "I feel like I'm snogging a big soggy European."

Talk about embarrassment. *Fuck!*

"You should let me wax you," she says.

"What? No fuckin' way!"

"It'll make it all smooth and....yummy," she said as she took an appreciative look down at my pussy and smiled.

My breath hitched and I started to feel really quite warm and sensual. It was the way she said, *'yummy.'* It made my clit really stand up and pay attention. Throb. Throb. Pant. Pant. Throb.

"Okay." *Gulp. Did I just say* 'okay'*? Fuck!*

Well, then I get the history lesson. The tales passed down through her family – from mother to daughter – for generations. *Didn't her mother ever teach her it's impolite to talk with your mouth full?* Strangely enough, the anxiety caused by my imminent peril made for a wonderfully intense orgasm. And she didn't say much more until after I let go of her head with both of my hands to let her come up for air. *Chuckle.*

But wait! There's more! Now comes the story about the family recipe, and then the whole method for waxing, as if it's a science to be proud of. I tried to look interested but I know my eyes were glazed over from post-orgasmic bliss.

"...Apparently my great grandmother would also put corn flour into the mix to keep it pliable," she says as she licks her fingers and runs her tongue around her lips. "...but no one can remember how much she used, so, we don't use the corn flour at all and instead, have to test it all the time to make sure we don't overcook it," She wipes some of my come from her cheek with her forefinger. "Otherwise it will go like the outside of a toffee apple on your skin…" she says just before sucking on her forefinger.

What did she say? Was she talking then? I'm certain that I physically shook my head. *Snap out of it and pay attention,* I chided myself.

"…Actually, I think they used to use molasses back then, too."

"You make it sound edible," I return with a giggle.

"It is!" she exclaims and then comes another lesson, this time on the 'green' merits of making your own body wax. *Sigh.*

I won't bore you with too many of the details, but for those who might be interested; here's her family's recipe:

Wax Recipe

1 part lemon juice
1 part water
2 parts sugar

Melt together in a pot over a low heat.
When mixture is completely melted and begun to brown, test readiness by allowing a drip from the mixture to fall into a glass of water. If the droplet disperses into the water it is not ready yet. If the droplet keeps its integrity to the bottom of the glass, it's perfect.
Remove pot from heat and pour wax into a glass jar.

(Warning - Do not heat wax until dark brown or it will become overly hard when cool and not soften when reheated).

♀ ♀ ♀ ♀ ♀

Now we're in the kitchen and she's cooking up the wax on the stove with a big wooden spoon that she's waving around like a witch at her cauldron while she talks excitedly. She's so happy that I have at long last, agreed to allow her to wax my woo-woo. *Gulp! I'm getting cold feet.*

"Maybe I could just buy a tube of that stuff that Aunty Peggy uses on her top lip," I reconsider meekly.

She stops, dead. *Uh-oh!* And stares coldly at me. *Gulp!*

"That stuff melts the hair away, you know. Just imagine what it will do to tender white skin like yours. Besides, you'll still have a stubbly regrowth in just a few days, using that shit." She's sounding indignant. *Fuck! Fuck! Fuck! I'm not going to be able to get myself out of this, am I?*

She smiles and giggles a little as she returns her attention to the pot on the stove. "You could go and get treatments, like Bokah does."

"What laser, no, electrolysis? Which one is it?"

"Oh, I can't remember, one of them," she says as she tests her brew in a glass of water.

"He says he almost vomits from the smell of the hair burning," I realize that I have my face all-screwed-up as if I've just sucked on a lemon.

She takes a long look at me, "Mmmm," she says as she returns her pot to the heat, "He said it's pretty expensive as well."

"Yeah, but you don't have to worry about them growing back either, do you?"

"No. Actually, waxing reduces the amount of regrowth too, because it often pulls out the root and follicle as well." *Don't let her see you rolling your eyes.* "…So, it gets easier and less painful with time. And," she looks at me and wriggles her eyebrows, "the regrowth isn't so prickly."

I closed my eyes, "This is gonna kill, isn't it?" I can feel my clit shriveling to the size of a pin head and I'm squirming in my seat.

"Don't be such a baby!" she scolded me. "It would have been worse last week when you'd just stopped bleeding." I blinked, looked at her and then double blinked a number of times while I waited for her to qualify her remark. She again dripped her brew from the wooden spoon into the glass of water; this time looking pleased with the results. She began scooping her mixture into a glass jar as she continued, "You're always more sensitive just before and just after your period." Somehow that comment didn't feel very comforting to me.

"Right! We'll leave that to cool for a bit," she said with her hands on her hips and looking about as if pleased with her efforts. I tried to smile with her but it just wasn't happening for me. "C'mon, I'm gonna give you a shower." *Things is looking up. Big toothie grin.*

My wife is taller than me and whenever she has a notion to take me into the bathroom and give me shower, I always feel a bit like a child she's taken charge of. She helps me to remove my clothing and clucks her tongue at me if I throw my clothes onto the floor instead of into the laundry hamper. She always gets into the shower first and checks the temperature of the water against her skin before she holds out her hand to invite me in.

I don't mind how long she takes because it gives me a chance to admire her form. Her body is beautiful, lean, not overly muscular, and very, very feminine. Her hair hangs in thick bundles of ebony ringlets that I find particularly captivating, when wet. *Whoa!* I get hot just thinking about that. Her eyes are an intriguing mix of amber and caramel. My wife says they're typical of her Persian heritage and shrugs off any attempt I make at a compliment. But, I often notice others staring at them, just as I do; as if mesmerized by them. *Ahem! Back to the shower.* She reaches out and takes my hand to pull me into the cubical with her. There's nothing better than watching the water form into rivulets as it travels over the curve of her breasts and down her tummy. The curve of her hips compel me to reach out to touch them. Once I've done that the impulse to run my fingers up her sides and cup her full breasts is irresistible. *Oh, by the way, that sound you would be hearing about now – that'd me getting my hands slapped away.*

She gets me wet. Under the running water. *Giggle.*

She soaps me up and washes my body, gently slipping her hands over my skin and swirling the suds all over me. She must consider my ass and tits to be particularly dirty because she seems to spend a long time washing them. *Eyebrow wriggle.*

On this particular night, rather than just handing me the towel to dry myself, she dried me as well. Next she took a bottle from her side of the vanity cupboard and smeared its contents through my pubes and between my legs.

"What are you doing?"

"Baby Oil."

"I think I need more Baby Oil." *Big smirk.*

"Nope, that'll be enough."

"Well, it needs rubbing in, then, I think." *Big pout.*

She laughed and said, "Trust me. You don't wanna rub that in. It stops the wax getting too much of a grip on your skin."

"Won't it stop the wax gripping the hair as well?"

"It doesn't really seem to." She pours more oil into her hand and massages it into her own pussy. I look at her a little confused. *Is she gonna wax hers as well?* I wonder. Then she says, "It helps to stop ingrown hairs."

"Oh, okay." So I'm starting to think this might not be so scary after all.

"The waxing doesn't always pluck out all of the hairs. You always have a few stubborn hairs that need to be pulled out with the tweezers. And, we have to be careful about not getting any wax on your bits." My *bits* did their best to climb up inside of me with that comment, and I couldn't help but let out a little anxious squeak.

"Don't worry," she tried to reassure me, "I'm an old hand at this."

♀♀♀♀♀

She leads me to the bedroom and quickly takes an old shopping bag from the floor of our wardrobe. She pulls out a large towel from it and lays it on the bed.

"Lie down and I'll be right back."

"Hey! These are my old jeans in here! I'd wondered where they'd gotten to." I reached into the bag and pulled out pieces of what obviously used to be my old jeans. She'd cut them into strips. "What the–?"

"I needed waxing strips and you'd worn through the knees of those old jeans anyway."

"Yeah, but...they were really comfortable."
I look up at my wife and she's got her hands on
her hips. *That's code for 'don't mess with the
Prom Queen.'* I quickly shut my mouth with an
audible clash of my teeth and throw the bag back
onto the bed before quickly lying down on the
towel as I'd been instructed. When she returns,
she's got that jar of wax she'd cooked up sitting in
a bowl of hot water in one hand and the spatula in
the other.

"Okay," she says, "Now you need to decide
what kind of wax-job you're gonna have."

"Huh?"

"Mine's called a Bikini Line. That leaves
just a little triangle of pubes that I trim down to an
attractive length." She points at her pubes and then
lifts one leg up to place her foot onto the edge of
the bed, giving me a...distracting view. "All the
hair underneath is waxed off, leaving just smooth,
bare skin."

Just then I realized I'm licking my lips and
staring. I have just enough time to think, *I'd better
look at her face soon or she's gonna get pissed*,
when she clucks her tongue again and returns to
her original standing position next to the bed.

"Hopeless!" she said, shaking her head and
rolling her eyes.

I couldn't help it. I looked back at her pubes
again and took in the view of that arrow pointing
the way to paradise. Of course, I didn't really need

the directions because I already knew the way to that mouthwatering honey pot. *Hummer, hummer.*

"What are you smiling at?" she's asked in an annoyed tone while inspecting her little thatch of pubes.

"Oh...well, um..."

"Never mind," she said dismissively and stirred her pot of wax. "Or we can do just a rectangular strip; that's how the French do it. I've heard it called a Landing Strip," she said marking out the shape on my pubes. "Oh! And I've heard it called The Hitler, as well." She looked me in the eye and realized that I was taking far too much enjoyment from her touch and once again, rolled her eyes.

She's gonna put her hands on her hips again in a minute and then I'll really be in trouble. "Okay. That one," I nodded in an attempt to save myself from getting into strife. *The less technical and the less hair removed, the less painful.* Of this, I was certain.

"Yeah?" she replied, almost in disbelief.

"What?"

"I felt certain you would have gone for the Brazilian."

"What's a Brazilian?"

"The lot off."

I felt my bits start to make that retreat inside of me again. *Fuck, but I'm a wimp!* "Why would you think that?"

She shrugged, "You used to shave the lot off."

Mmm, she has a point. "Okay. A Brazilian."

She smiled broadly. Now I love my wife's smile. Nothing makes me feel more complete than knowing that I'm the reason for her flashing those pearly whites, but…this smile was different. I felt like 'Little Red Riding Hood' to her 'Big Bad Wolf.' *Gulp!* But then she starts smoothing her hands over my pussy and I relax. After a few moments, I realize she's been talkin' again. This time she's saying something about the direction of growth as she's petting me and getting all the hairs running in the same direction. She spreads a little of her wax on with the spatula and it looks to me like she's glued my pubes down flat onto my skin.

"Not too hot for you, is it, lover?" she asks. I shake my head to answer 'no' as she lays a strip of my old denim jeans on top of the wax and smoothes it down into place. I watch as she petted the hairs down against my skin in readiness for the next line of wax and then presses down another thin strip of denim. *Mmm*, I think, *so far, so good.* And it did smell mouthwateringly good. *I bet I'll taste like a boiled sweet after this. Grin.* What? Yes. I have sex on the brain! And your point is? You can't blame me for thinking I might get a reward for letting her do this, surely?

"Ready?" she asks as she lifts the tab end of the first strip of denim to test how well it's adhered.

"Huh?" was all I got to say before I screamed the house down.

She tore the denim away in the opposite direction of my smoothed down pubes. The honey-like wax had thickened and seemed somewhat hardened in place; literally gluing my pubes to the underside of the denim strip.

"Faaarrrk me!" I yelled and pushed her hands away from my burning pain.

"Shush!" she insists just as our two-year-old calls out. I'd woken her from her sleep. My wife leaves me writhing in my silent agony while she goes and quickly settles our daughter. Telling her that, "Mama was trying to sing," and, "...she's not very good at it, is she?"

When my wife returns she immediately takes the tab of the next strip of denim and rips that off as well. I'm struggling to contain my scream as I bear another stinging, burning assault on my pussy.

"Sorry," she said, "I couldn't let it sit on there for too long."

I'm gasping and writhing again as she begins to giggle. I register her laugh and I can't believe she would find humor in my agony. I toss her my best 'miffed-look' over my shoulder, not certain if I should roll back onto the towel and trust her to work on me any longer.

"You're such a pussy," she says, "but that's the worst of it done now." She starts stirring her wax again with the spatula and talking to me as though nothing is out of the ordinary. My head is throbbing and I look down to see that I now have just a thin strip of short and curlies running down my center.

"Is that a Landing Strip?" I asked, holding my head.

"Pretty much," she says.

I wipe the tears from my eyes as I say, "My head hurts."

"Stop holding your breath," she says as if it's my fault I'm in so much pain.

She's petting me again. Smoothing the hairs down against my skin. Then quickly applies another thin layer of wax and a clean denim strip from the bag. This time she's holding down the skin near my clit while her other hand is holding the tab and testing the stickiness of her wax. To my surprise I immediately become super horny. I reach down and press her hand against me and lift my hips to increase the pressure. *Such relief.*

"Do you ever stop?" she asks, huffing and shaking her head at me with disbelief.

"I couldn't help it," I offer feebly in my defense. But the true answer is *No, not really. I'm always a little horny when you're so near to me.* But everyone's like that when they're laying naked on a bed before a beautiful woman, aren't they? I mean, really! What a stupid question!

"It's ready," she lightly announces and then adds, "Try not to hold your breath." Rip!

Faaaark! BREATHE! Breathe, breathe, breathe, breathe!

I'm sweating, crying, writhing and trying my damnedest not to further traumatize our child with my screaming. And what's my wife doing? Yup, she's laughing.

"I thought you said we were through the worst of it?" I gasp through the burning sensation. I look down and notice little specks of blood here and there where my hairs used to be housed. "I'm bleeding!" I exclaim.

"Yes," she says matter-of-factly, "that can happen the first couple of times you wax." She's talking as if it's really nothing to worry about, "Eventually, you get used to it and that doesn't happen anymore. And, it hurts less with each treatment, as well." She dabbed the blood off with the other side of the denim strip and tossed it into what was becoming the 'used' pile.

"Spread your legs."

"Get fucked!"

"It's not so bad down here. It gets less sensitive the further under we go," she says as she pushes my legs apart. "Stop being such a baby."

She mixes up her sugar-wax again, chatting away about something our daughter had done that week. She'd distracted me enough that I didn't notice she had finished preparing the next two strips until she said, "Ready?"

I took a deep breath and exhaled fully before nodding, "Okay." There, now how fucking brave is that? I might be a real butch after all. *Self-satisfied grin.*

"Don't hold your breath," she reminded me while simultaneously ripping the strip up from my skin. She was right. That one didn't hurt anywhere near as much. But I still wanted desperately to scream the house down. She continued her applications right the way around to my butt. I didn't even know I had hairs there. I did though, and I know this because I felt every one of them little fuckers being torn from my flesh. *Ouch!* But again, not nearly as bad as those first three times. When she was done there, she returned to do a reapplication and so, basically repeated the process. Again, not so bad as most of the hairs had been taken with the first application. Until...

"You've got rather a thick growth in the top of your slit."

"Huh?"

"Just in under here." She ran her finger in the groove just above my clit. "You'll have to spread your legs wide so I can get in there."

I clamped my legs shut.

"What the fuck?"

"It's okay, I'll make sure I don't get any on your bits."

"Wha...you....ah... No fuckin' way!"

"C'mon honey, we're nearly done. It's really looking...yummy." I could feel my resolve melting and when she looked at me with those soulful dark-amber eyes; my legs parted before I'd even acknowledged I done it.

She worked quickly and carefully. She firmly held her fingers down flat against my clit, keeping it and the rest of my bits well out of the way while she applied a thin layer of her wax.

Then she pressed the denim onto the wax. "This will be the last one, babe."

"We'll be done after this?" I asked with great hope and a quiver in my voice.

"Just a few hairs to tweezer out and we're done. It's only taken fifteen minutes."

"Feels like fifteen fuckin' hours to me."

"Okay. Ready?" she asks as she wriggles her fingers in under the tab of the denim.

"What are you doing?"

"I'm holding the important stuff out of the way while I rip this last strip off."

"Feels like you're taking advantage of me."

"Okay. I won't keep your bits safe, then," she stated and quickly removed her fingers from under the strip. "Ready?"

"No! No! No!" I yelled out.

"Shush!" she snapped, not wanting me to wake our daughter, again.

"Please, baby, please don't wax my junk!" I pleaded in a half-whisper.

"Okay," she said and wriggled her fingers back in under the denim. I decided I quite liked her wriggling her fingers about under there. "Ready?" she asked.

"Not yet, not yet!" I whispered, wanting to enjoy her touch for as long as I could.

"Now?" she asked, looking as though she might be getting wise to my ploy.

"Just a bit longer," I pleaded.

She rolled her eyes and ripped off the strip.

I writhed with the pain, rolling over and away from her. This was the most sensitive place of the lot. The burning pain was intense and all I could do was hold myself in both hands, my mouth open wide for a silent scream.

"All done," she said as she gathered up the pile of denim strips. "I'll just throw these in the laundry while you get yourself ready for me to use the tweezers."

I groaned loudly, feeling totally over this whole exercise. *Will the torture never end?*

"Shush!" she says as she leaves the room.

By the time she gets back I've rolled back into position on the towel. I'm looking down at my new and polished pussy and I'm liking the look. She sets to me with the tweezers and takes care of the last few stubborn hairs. Ordinarily, this would have seen me jumping about like a wild thing, but compared to what I'd just been through – having thick hairs pulled out of my pussy with tweezers was nothing. Her hair brushed over my thighs as she did this close work on me. It was slipping about like silk and tickling my skin. I can tell you, it was a most welcomed distraction.

She reaches back into the shopping bag and pulls out a tube of cream, which she smears over my baldness.

"What's that?" I ask.

"Aloe Vera to soothe the skin."

It soothed the skin all right! My skin was hypersensitive and the feel of her touch was something different to anything I'd felt before.

"I can't believe how good that feels," I tell her. It was as if the pubes and their roots had been preventing her from ever really being able to touch my skin. How was that possible? I'd shaved and noticed a better sensation on my skin for it, but, nothing like this. This felt deeper, velvety. This was...magic. It felt so clean, so hygienic, so super-sensitive.

She looks up at me and smiles as she lays her cheek on my baldness. "Mmm, feels yummy."

"Yes, it does," I agree.

"No more pain?" she asks.

I was about to say *no* and then thought of a better idea. "N... You...could...kiss it better for me?" *No harm in trying.*

She closed her eyes and turned her face into my pussy. "Mmm, smells *yummy*."

I'm thinking that word – *yummy* – must be directly attached to my clit somehow. Maybe my clit's name is Yummy, because each time she says it, my clit stands at attention. I breathe out a low groan and lift my hips as she breaths in my scent.

Please lick it. Please lick it. Please lick it, I'm thinking over and over in my head as I watch her hover over me. Then she lowers her head and presses her face between my legs; kissing me. Every touch of her lips is like heaven to me. I lay back and relax and let her tantalize me with every little touch of her mouth and every touch of her hair brushing over my stomach and between my thighs. *Oh yes. This is definitely the reward I deserve.*

"Oh, baby. We gotta do this more often," I say as I hold her head gently.

"Every six weeks," comes her muffled answer as she positions herself between my legs. *Nice.*

I can feel her breath on my skin, like I've never felt her breath on my skin – the feeling is so intense – so arousing. I can feel the touch of her mouth on me in a way I've never felt it before. *I love my new woo-woo*, I'm thinking, *The pain was worth it.*

Her lips are wolfing all of my bits into her mouth and I can feel her breath pass over my skin as she breathes out through her nose. Her hair falls forward and brushes over my new hairlessness. *Wow!*

Her tongue feels bigger, closer, and slipperier. *Is that a word? OMG!* "I can't believe how good this feels... Everywhere," I murmur and she groans in agreement.

She starts to lick me as if licking an ice cream. "Oh yes, baby. Lick me like that." Her head's bobbing up and down on me and her shiny, cool hair is tickling my skin. I hold her head gently with my fingertips and groan with every lap of her tongue. I'm lost in incredible sensations. My clit feels the biggest it's ever been and the feeling is *awesome*. "I'm gonna come," I say and then realize this will be the second time tonight and add. "…again." Is she laughing at me? Who cares? Fuck this feels good! *Blow!* Best orgasm in a long time, my friends. *Fucking big grin.*

She comes up for air and climbs up my body to kiss me. She slips her tongue into my mouth to share my flavor with me and slips a leg in between mine. I can feel her skin against my bald, slick pussy and I'm thinking, *I could probably come again.*

She kisses around to my ear and says, "That was *so…yummy.* And no pricks. Just the way I like it." I had to laugh at that.

I hold her hips and push my pelvis up against her. She takes my cues so well. She begins to move her thigh up and down between my legs. I'm so slippery and wet with come. "This is just *beautiful.*" I'm thinking it doesn't matter if I don't come because this sensation is just *so* good. "*You* better not stop…." She kisses me on my mouth, deep and wet. *This is code for 'shut the fuck up before you wake the kid.'* When I get chatty and loud during sex, she finds something to fill my mouth up with. She's so ingenuous. *Silly-looking grin.*

She starts groaning as loudly as I am and that's when I realize I'm holding her ass really tightly. I let go and do my best to rub the sore spots better for her. But, it's difficult to concentrate because I start to come again. This one didn't last all that long but hers went on for some time. She arches her back and lifts her shoulders high and I just happen to be at the right height to get my mouth on a nipple. Yep, that made her move even more quickly against my leg and that wet patch is feeling more like a pond.

She collapses on me and shoves her other nipple into my mouth. She's stroking my hair and breathing heavily on me as she watches me. She's studying me sucking on her breast.

I'm running my hands over her body and next thing, she straddles me. Yup. She brushes her wet pussy against my hairless one. I grab her hips and lift myself against her again. I know I'm not going to come again just yet, but she might. *Eyes wide with excitement.*

"Wow! But this feels so good," I tell her. She nods and starts playing with my nipples. "Are you gonna come like this?" I ask.

She opens her eyes and says, "No. I'm gonna come like this," and climbs up to sit on my face. As I watch her moving closer and closer toward my face, I smile because there's that arrow again, showing me the way. It says, 'insert tongue down here.' *No problem*, I'm thinking.

I lick and suck on her with a new appreciation for what she must have felt every time I've made love to her like this, because she's always waxed this area of her pussy. And she's right. Sex *is* better with no pricks. *Chuckle*.

The End

The Challenge

Matilda finished reading the last of the contract continuation proposal from the Australian Department for Foreign Affairs and Trade and placed it on the pile of documents in front of her. She looked at her watch – another two hours before the Minister arrived for the meeting. This would be her final opportunity to modify and tweak the contract to her favor. But first, she'd have to convince the Minister that she was the best choice for continuing in Mongolia and China. Given the hard yards she'd already forged in both those countries, that shouldn't be too hard. Especially given her skills with regard to logistics and negotiation. She also knew no one could match her expertise with regard to systems analysis and resource procurement. Additionally, she had proven contacts with both governments, an in-depth knowledge of both cultures and the ability to fluently converse in most dialects of Mandarin. Her Mongol needed some finesse, but she had time to work on that, if need be.

As she leaned forward to activate the intercom, she let out a sigh that made her realize she was tense and anxious. She paused at the last moment, her finger hovering above the intercom switch as she considered her options. She chose instead to pick up her cell phone and quickly punch in a number from memory. She breathed an inward sigh of relief when the ringing tone ended and a soft, warm voiced answered her call.

"Hello, Matilda."

"Hi, Chase. Are you busy?"

"Not particularly. What did you have in mind?"

"A challenge. You up for it?"

"What sort of challenge?" asked Chase, her tone suggesting some reservation.

"Get it in 20 or it's free," Matilda replied and let go a naughty giggle before quickly pressing the 'End' button.

She sat back in her chair – self amused. Her eyes drifted back to her desk and she sobered slightly as she looked at the pile of bound contracts in front of her. She reached out toward the intercom again, "Tam, you there?"

"Yes, Matilda."

"These are perfect, just as you assured me they would be. Can you take them to the conference room and make certain that everything is in readiness there? And then…you may as well go for an early lunch…just make sure you're back here when the Minister arrives."

"Okay, Matilda," said Tammy. A second later Tammy was opening the door to Matilda's office and retrieving the contracts from Matilda's desk. "You want me to bring something back for your lunch?"

"No, thank you, Tammy, I've just ordered a delivery," replied Matilda with her best act at nonchalance. "Can you leave the door ajar, so I can see when it arrives?"

"Sure," agreed Tammy and she left the room with her arm load of documents.

♀♀♀♀♀

Chase fumbled in her haste as she pulled on her running shoes while yelling out to Suzette, "...better book me out for the next couple of hours," then she reconsidered when she thought of how tired she was after the last few interludes with Matilda. "No! Suzette, book me out for the rest of the day, okay?"

She pushed her cell phone into her back pocket and tucked the tail of her purple tank-top into her faded jeans before hurriedly making her way out the front door and down the stoop. When she'd vaulted the little gate at the front of her house she broke into a jog and set off down the street. She rounded the corner at a main road and adroitly dodged a near collision with a little old lady pushing her carry-all trolley-bag.

"Sorry, Mrs. Sullivan," she called behind her.

"S'ok, dear," she heard vaguely as she upped her jogging pace and headed toward her favorite café. Her muscles were complaining about the cold-start and the slight cramp near her groin made her wonder if jumping the gate instead of stopping to open it was really such a wise idea. She scooted between two turning vehicles as she crossed a side street and then ran into the busy Café where she and Matilda had first met.

She stopped abruptly at the doorway she looked around the crowded shop. Matilda wasn't at her favorite spot by the counter. Chase's brow furrowed and her chest was heaving as she tried to catch her breath while looking about at the tables and wondering if Matilda were simply playing 'hard-to-find'. *Should I check the rest rooms?* she wondered.

"Hi, Chase," the waitress called, "I'll find you a table."

"No!" puffed Chase and then she swallowed hard to prepare to ask her question, "Have you seen little Matilda?"

"No, not today," replied the waitress with a knowing smile.

"Thanks," replied Chase and waved as she turned and left the café.

She stood on the sidewalk with her hands on her hips and looked down the street toward the supermarket. *Okay. So, it's either the tampon isle at the store...or...her office!* Chase broke into a run back up the street, back-tracking in the same direction she'd just come from. She ran across the side street, dodging a taxi with its horn honking and its driver yelling for to complete her death-wish anywhere but on the front grill of his cab.

She neared her own street and considered running home to retrieve her car. *No, by the time I found a park, it'd take me even longer.* She continued to run past her own street at full speed, once again passing Mrs. Sullivan who almost yelped from the fright of Chase's flight past her.

"Sorry again, Mrs. Sullivan," she called back and then bit her lip at the pang of guilt she felt for not stopping to help the little old lady with her load. She sighed to herself. Then stopped, turned, and ran back, "You need any help Mrs. Sullivan?"

"No, child. I need the trolley to lean on or I'll fall over on these poorly kept sidewalks. You go on and get your exercise, I'll be fine," insisted the old woman with a dismissive wave.

"Okay." Chase smiled. "Bye," she added as she hurriedly turned to again launch herself into a full speed run.

She had to get across the busy main street and so she watched the traffic forward and then over her shoulder as she ran; looking for a break she could use to scoot across to the other side of the road. She looked back to the sidewalk in front of her just in time to see the council rubbish bin she was about to plough directly into. She leapt into the air and did a hurdle over the obstacle with such little room for error that she found herself squealing from the scare. Shaking her head at herself over the close call, she decided to wait and use the pedestrian crossing at the next set of traffic lights just a few hundred meters ahead.

She jogged on the spot to keep her now limbered muscles warm while she waited for the crossing light to let her negotiate the four lanes of busy traffic. She was feeling the futility of having run at such great speed only to reach a place where she would be forced to stop and wait. She reached out and repeatedly jabbed at the button as she willed the signal to turn green.

"C'mon, c'mon," she said out loud just as the green light alarm bleated out its permission for her to cross. She broke into full speed once again – dodging pedestrians and leaping over a wayward pooch on a long lead, to get to the sidewalk on the other side. She could see her destination now. A tall, imposing building that appeared to be made mostly from glass, sitting at the crest of a hill – Matilda's office building.

She groaned as her legs began to burn from the uphill climb. *Why does Matilda's building have to be at the top of the only hill in this area?* She breathed heavily, her chest heaving from the strain of gulping in the air needed to keep up the pace. *So's she can have that fabulous view of the river, of course,* she answered herself, more to keep her mind from the burn in her legs than anything else. She ran into the lobby of the office building just in time to see the doors close on the only elevator. *Crap!*

She stopped for a moment, bent and placed her hands on her knees while gasping for breath and resting the weight of her torso. She looked about the lobby. '*Stairs*,' she read on the sign above the door and walked quickly to it. She opened the door and ran up the stairs, more often taking two at a time. Seeming to rapidly reach each landing to turn in the opposite direction and bound up the next stretch of stairs, two at a time. *Of course her office has to be on the top fucking floor*, she lamented, *Fucking 'view thing' again.* Finally, climbing to the door that led onto the fifth floor, she reached out to grasp the doorknob. It slipped in her hand as she turned the knob. The failed attempt made a loud thud as the door refused to open. She tried again but found the doorknob difficult to turn because her hands were slick with sweat. She pulled the tail of her tank-top out of her jeans and used it as a glove, allowing her to grip and turn the doorknob.

She opened the door with great haste and stepped through with a rush. Her noisy, brash entry caused a few of Matilda's employees to stop and look in Chase's direction. She held her head high and tried to look as though she belonged, deciding it best to walk swiftly instead of running. As she wound her way through the labyrinth of office cubicles she realized the tail of her tank top was still hanging out of her jeans, from when she'd used it to grasp the doorknob. *Shoot! I must look like a vagrant.* She quickly tucked it in as she looked about, hoping no one had noticed. She was so relieved when she was finally able to push her way through the door to Tammy's office and waiting room.

The door to Matilda's office was ajar and she felt a pang of anxiety. Tammy was nowhere to be seen, *Shit! Don't tell me I should have gone to the supermarket.* She stopped at the threshold to Matilda's office, panting audibly. Her heartbeat was pounding in her ears and the sweat was dripping from her hair onto her bare shoulders. She leaned forward, and peered in.

Matilda was sitting against the front of her desk looking at her watch. "You've got just a minute left to get your mouth on me or I'm getting a freebee."

Chase leapt forward into the room and fell to her knees before Matilda. She reached up the inside of Matilda's skirt, tucked her thumbs under the leg hem either side of Matilda's panties and swiftly pulled them down to Matilda's ankles.

Matilda leaned back and grasped the edge of her desk. Bearing her weight, she lifted her legs just enough for Chase to sweep the underwear over and away from her high heels.

Quickly sliding her hands up Matilda's thighs Chase pushed the fabric of the skirt up and out of the way and Matilda accommodated by lifting her buttocks and allowing her skirt to bunch about her waist. Without a moment's hesitation, Chase opened her mouth and licked Matilda's pussy from as deep between her legs as she could manage in her rush and then up and over Matilda's clit.

Matilda's jaw dropped open and she groaned as she allowed her head to fall back. She moved her hands out to rest her palms on the desk top behind her, hoping to better stabilize her weight against the desk front. She spread her legs wide to provide better access as Chase headed back down with another sweep of her tongue.

"Oh, Chase. I'm so fucking horny. I need to come," Matilda implored. Her immense need only too apparent in her voice.

Chase moved upward again and concentrated her lapping tongue on Matilda's clit while she moved to moisten two fingers with Matilda's wetness before pressing them into Matilda's pussy.

Matilda groaned loudly and rolled her head forward to watch Chase work her magic. She looked up momentarily at the door. It was still open. *Fuck it!* she thought, *Let the world watch if they want to.* The risqué thought added to Matilda's excitement and her arousal heightened.

"I need more than your fingers, Chase. Please tell me you've packed our girlfriend before you left the house."

Chase stood to unzip her jeans. With a wiggle of her hips she pushed the lower half of her clothing down to her knees. Then reaching forward, she held Matilda's hips as she pushed

Penny Stick between Matilda's legs. The cock was quickly moistened in its movement against Matilda's wet flesh. Penny slipped into place against Matilda's opening and Chase stopped, looked directly into Matilda's eyes, and pressed her hips forward and upward to easily slide Penny home.

Matilda's eyes rolled and then closed as ecstasy took control of her. Her uncontrolled groan lasting until her lungs were fully deflated. *You ain't felt nothin' yet,* thought Chase as she slid her hands up Matilda's sides and then around to hold Matilda's shoulders while she lowered her onto the conveniently emptied desktop. Once Matilda was lying before her, Chase began a slow fuck and both of them moaned with the pleasure of it.

Chase raised her right hand to her mouth and licked her thumb, liberally covering it with her own saliva and while holding Matilda's pussy open with her left hand, rubbed her right thumb back and forth across Matilda's clit. Matilda's moans began to sound louder as she wrapped her legs around Chase's waist and pulled her forward with her heels, motioning for Chase to start fucking her harder and quicker.

"Play with your tits, Matilda," Chase demanded softly.

Matilda opened her eyes and watched the delight on Chase's face as she slowly unbuttoned her blouse and played her fingertips over her own nipples which were growing more and more obvious through the silk fabric of her bra.

"Oh, fuck me, Matilda! That's such a turn-on."

Matilda smiled and pulled the bra up over her breasts. She cupped and massaged them in time with the thrusts of Chase's hips.

Chase popped her right thumb back into her mouth and sucked on it for a moment, savoring the flavor and then quickly ladened it with saliva before returning it to Matilda's clit.

"Mmm," moaned Matilda. "Harder, Tough Guy. Fuck me harder."

Chase circled her thumb harder over Matilda's clit and pressed her hips forward with greater urgency.

"Pinch your nipples for me, Matilda. Make yourself come, for me."

Matilda caught her nipples between her thumbs and forefingers and twisted and squeezed them as Chase played her thumb around and over Matilda's clit. Matilda raised her hips and her breath hitched as she used her heels to pull Chase in closer and harder to her pussy, forcing her to ram her cock home hard with every thrust.

When Matilda breathed again, it was so she could scream with release, "Oh, fuck me, Chase. Fuck me! I'm coming!"

Chase closed her eyes and concentrated her efforts on fucking Matilda as hard and fast as she could while keeping her thumb in contact with

Matilda's clit. Not easy when her own engorged clit was being pummeled by the base of the strap-on with every forward thrust.

"Oh, Chase!" Matilda cried.

"Matilda," Chase managed, holding her breath as she too, felt the beginnings of spasms over her own clit. She thought she heard a sound over her shoulder. *Is someone watching?* Another clutch of spasms over her clit. *Who fucking cares?* Chase thought as she became awash with orgasm.

Matilda began to slow the thrusts of her hips and Chase opened her eyes to see Matilda twitching against the last of her orgasm on the desk before her.

Chase growled loudly as her own orgasm slowly abated and when Matilda motioned with a hand over Chase's for her to remove her thumb, she slumped forward, laying herself over the little woman. As if by magic, she landed with Matilda's nipple poking into her mouth. She caught the offering with her lips and played her tongue over its tip.

Matilda wrapped her arms around Chase and enjoyed the unexpected thrill over her clit. She moaned softly and said, "Double or nothing."

Chase giggled and slowly slipped down until she was again on her knees with her face buried in Matilda's pussy. Breathing in deeply through her nose, Chase enjoyed the scent of Matilda's recent orgasm – hot and sweet. She pushed her tongue into Matilda's pussy and lapped up the tasty treat held there for her. Then she used just the tip of her pointed tongue to tease and entice Matilda back to sexual arousal.

Chase reached under Matilda's legs and encouraged Matilda to rest them comfortably over Chase's shoulders. Now more relaxed, Chase was able to begin rhythmically running her tongue in circles around the perimeter of Matilda's pussy.

Matilda groaned with pleasure, moving her arms up over her head and holding the edge of the desk she took a deep breath and exhaled heavily. Closing her eyes and relaxing she moaned lightly, as though there was nothing else in the world except for her and the amazing sensations Chase was creating between her legs.

Chase reached under Matilda's thighs and smoothed her hands up and over Matilda's sides toward her breasts. Gently touching and coaxing Matilda's nipples back to full erection.

Matilda let go of the desk and ran her fingers through her own hair. Knotting the curls around her fingers and pulling gently as her hips began to undulate.

Chase smiled at her success. She began to concentrate the circular motion of her tongue over Matilda's clit and Matilda's breathing became labored. When Chase tweaked at Matilda's nipples, she lifted her legs and placed her high heeled feet on Chase's shoulders. She was careful to ensure the sharp heels hooked comfortably over the top of each shoulder and then allowed her knees to spread apart and her legs to fall limply out to either side. Matilda lay surrendered: to Chase's tongue, to Chase's hands, to Chase's breath against her skin, to Chase's lips sucking at her juices, and to the sounds of Chase enjoying the feast before her.

Chase moved her mouth directly over Matilda's clit and then rapidly flitted her tongue back and forth over the little hub of nerves.

"Oh, yes!" Matilda exclaimed. "Just like that!" she implored. Her body shuddered and a low guttural hum exuded from the back of her throat as she came, again.

When Matilda suddenly relaxed, Chase knew to stop her attentions and withdraw. She stood and reached out her hand to help Matilda sit up.

Looking back over her shoulder, Chase noted that the door to Matilda's office had been closed.

Matilda again closed her eyes and softly chuckled as she collapsed into Chase's arms and luxuriated against Chase's chest. "I could live the rest of my life, right here," she said in a voice so tiny, it was as though she were speaking to herself.

Chase smiled as she cuddled Matilda closely and smoothed the ruffled hair on Matilda's head. When Matilda's breathing had leveled out, Chase reached in to cup Matilda's chin with her fingers and motioned for the little woman to look up. Slowly, gently, Chase lowered her lips to Matilda's and kissed her softly for a long moment.

Their eyes sprung open as both heard what sounded like the door to the outer office opening. Both quickly moved to adjust their clothing while giggling like a couple of schoolgirls, anxious at being caught-out during a naughty moment. *Fuck! I hope that's not the Minister, early for our appointment,* Matilda's heart began racing.

Tammy's voice came over the intercom and both Matilda and Chase jumped with a start, "Matilda. The first wave of the Minister's entourage has arrived. They're presently doing a security sweep of the building."

Matilda looked around on the floor trying to remember where she had stowed the intercom. She had to get down on her hands and knees to reach for it under her desk, recalling that she'd quickly shoved the machine under there in her rush to prepare for Chase's arrival. She scrambled for the 'Talk' button and strained to say, "Thanks, Tam." Giggling, she pulled the intercom to her and struggled slightly – due to her laughter – to return it to the desktop. One look in Chase's direction had the two of them giggling like a couple of naughty schoolgirls, once again.

"I'd best be going," Chase suggested as she offered her hand to help Matilda to her feet. Matilda nodded in agreement as she stood and faced Chase.

Chase spent another few moments gently pushing Matilda's curls back behind her ear and softly cupping Matilda's cheek while fleetingly holding eye contact and studying Matilda's features. A moment later, she turned, and left the office.

♀♀♀♀♀

Some minutes after, Tammy entered the office with a brush, a teasing comb and brown paper bag in hand.

Matilda had almost composed herself, having restored her desk top, renewed her lipstick and rechecked the placement of her clothing. She studied her assistant who was preparing to use the teasing comb and brush on her. Just as Tammy raised the comb to put it to use, Matilda asked, "So, how much of *that* did you see?"

Tammy continued with her grooming task without battering so much as an eyelid and replied, "Am I not the best personal assistant you've ever had?"

"Yes, you most certainly are."

"Then you should already know that I didn't see anything."

Matilda smiled a little and looked down at the small brown paper bag that Tammy had tossed onto the desktop.

"What's in the bag?"

"Fresh underwear."

Matilda tried not to let out a little giggle and snorted as a result. She quickly regained her composure and cleared her throat, "When we get this contract, remind me to give you a raise."

"Oh, I've already made a note of that," Tammy said in a light tone as she finished up and took an appraising look at her handiwork. Smiling and with a single nod, she approved of the end result and left Matilda's office, pulling the door closed behind her.

Matilda watched Tammy leave and then breathed out long and slow. She had to be honest with herself – she *was* nervous. This was an important contract and if she got it, she would be very busy and very rich for possibly the next ten years. *Hell*, she thought to herself, *I could comfortably afford to retire after this.*

The nervousness was a good thing. High-stakes professionals need it to keep their edge and deliver their best.

Anxiety however, would have brought her undone. *A good orgasm or two settles that down nicely*, she thought to herself and smiled. *I* will *get this contract*, she had no doubt of that. Just as she had no doubt that Chase had played no small part in helping to make it all happen. *Best money I've ever spent!* she decided pulling on the panties she'd retrieved from the brown paper bag. Then she giggled out aloud when she thought to herself, *Worth every Penny!*

She sat in her chair and swung around to appreciate her view of the river. Taking a deep breath she began her last minute mental preparations for her meeting.

♀♀♀♀♀

"Matilda." Tammy's voice came over the intercom as Matilda sat behind her desk practicing her spiel for the meeting with the Minister. "The Minister's car is pulling in downstairs."

"On my way."

Matilda left her office looking a picture of confidence.

"Good luck," Tammy said watching her boss nod in acknowledgement of her as she calmly marched out of the office.

Tammy had no doubt that Matilda would accomplish everything she had aspired to do that day. She gathered up the things she'd need for her part in the meeting and made her way to the conference room where Matilda would soon arrive; escorting the Minister.

Double or nothing, she mused to herself as she walked briskly into the large room, *I'm gonna have to try that line out for myself.*

The End

The Job Offer

Matilda sat in her favorite café reading her newspaper over her customary afternoon cup of coffee. She smiled as she read the news headline '*Australia Brokers Deal for Mongol Gold.*' Under the headline was a large photograph of the Foreign Ministers from Mongolia, China and Australia; all congratulating each other for a job well done. *A job well done indeed,* she thought, *by me.* She took a deep breath and sighed, as if turning the page on that article was like closing a chapter in her life. But close that chapter, she must. It was time to move on and busy herself with the next phase of the project for Mining Galore International.

"Mind if I join you?" Matilda smiled at the sound of a familiar and welcomed voice. She looked up into the bottomless blue eyes she now knew so well. Those eyes looked her up and down ravenously and Matilda shivered with the hunger of that gaze. She was delighted that those eyes still held the power to make her feel as though their very gaze could caress her flesh.

"Please do," Matilda said, unable to tame the wide smile on her face. Matilda couldn't help checking out the Sex Therapist's form, as she moved to take the seat next to her at the café counter. The well-defined, athletic body, dressed

371

in a black tank top that hugged her ample breasts and fashionably tattered and faded denim jeans with… Matilda almost gasped out loud as she noted Chase's bulging crotch.

Chase followed Matilda's gaze and then smirked back at her. "I packed a friend, on the off-chance that you might be here," she explained in a naughty tone, "I believe you're well acquainted." Chase had managed to fit Matilda into her busy schedule, almost at call, ever since they'd met. The occasional chance tryst, such as this, always excited Matilda into instant arousal.

Matilda blushed a deep crimson and tried to hide her face and smile in her newspaper. "Chase!" she exclaimed.

Chase chuckled as she sat down next to Matilda. She appreciated Matilda's curly, dark hair. It had grown some since they'd first met and was now just past shoulder length. The odd wayward bang compelled Chase to tenderly smooth them back into place for Matilda. She could smell Matilda's shampoo and subtle perfume as she brushed her fingers though the curls. Matilda was wearing a pale yellow sundress and brown sandals; an appropriate outfit for such a warm day. Matilda's trusty cream-colored handbag was resting in her lap.

Matilda moved her head against Chase's touch of her hair and rocked forward on her counter-stool to place a little pressure on her fast swelling clit. She looked down at Chase's crotch now bulging even more prominently since Chase had sat on the edge of her counter-stool.

Just as Chase was about to raise her hand to attract the waitress and order a coffee, Matilda said, "Just take me home and fuck me with her, will you?"

Chase stood immediately, pulled some money out of her pocket and threw it onto the counter without even counting it first. Grasping Matilda by the hand, she tugged her out of the Café, down the street and around the corner to her house. She didn't stop to close the gate, nor empty her letterbox, as was her usual habit. She tugged Matilda straight up the steps and onto the front porch just as the front door opened and Suzette allowed them in.

Chase didn't speak and Matilda managed only fragments of a greeting for the little French housemaid before Chase had pulled her into the living room and closed the door behind them.

Chase took Matilda's handbag from her and threw it onto the couch. Then, wrapping her arms around the smaller woman, pulled her close and kissed her deeply while thrusting her groin hard against her. She breathed deeply as she almost withdrew from the kiss; changed her head position and kissed Matilda deeply once more. She held Matilda by her buttocks and pulled her close, thrusting her hips forward against Matilda again.

Matilda groaned, ran her hands over Chase's back and explored Chase's mouth with her tongue. Their tongues dueled together with a fond familiarity. Each tasting the sweetness of Chase's mouth with the remnant flavor of Matilda's coffee.

Chase fumbled with the zipper at the back of Matilda's sun dress and quickly unzipped it all the way down to her waist. She ran her hands over the skin under the dress fabric before quickly pulling it from Matilda's body. She pushed the dress down and exposed Matilda's braless torso. While the dress fell to the floor, Chase passionately explored Matilda's breasts. Quickly, each of Matilda's nipples rose into tightly wrinkled peaks. When Chase simultaneously squeezed them, Matilda breathed a low groan of pleasure. Chase moved back to swallow Matilda's next groan in a deep and sensual kiss.

Matilda had managed to undo the button and zipper of Chase's jeans and push them down over Chase's narrow hips. Their lips parted and both – frenzied with passion and breathing heavily – removed the last of their clothing and footwear.

Now completely naked, they again sought each other's arms and renewed their kiss as Chase lodged her cock between Matilda's legs. Matilda groaned and rubbed herself against the shaft, seeking relief for her engorged clit.

Chase kissed Matilda's cheeks and forehead. She looked deeply into Matilda's dark brown eyes observing the pleasure Matilda was giving herself, rubbing against the shaft of

Chase's cock. Then she lightly kissed Matilda's nose and eye brows followed by a trail of little kisses toward Matilda's temple before whispering into Matilda's ear, "I'm gonna fuck your brains out, little woman."

Matilda almost squealed, "Yes," and pressed herself closer against Chase's hard cock. Chase kissed Matilda's neck and shoulders causing her to quiver and drive her nails into Chase's bare back.

"Fuck me, Chase!" Matilda begged as she kissed Chase's chest and licked her way to a breast and sucked a nipple into her mouth. Chase held Matilda's head to her breast and began to rock her hips back and forth; rubbing her cock back and forth across Matilda's clit.

Matilda moaned aloud, "Oh, yeah!" she encouraged as she moved to suck Chase's other nipple. Chase felt the wetness between her own legs and at the same time, noticed that Matilda's wetness had not only heavily coated her cock but was now being lathered about her groin as they moved together.

"Faster," Matilda pleaded. Chase had to move a hand to the center of Matilda's lower back to hold her steady while she increased her pace and the pressure of her cock against Matilda's clit.

Matilda breathed in, gasping for breath, no longer able to suckle on Chase's taut nipple. She began crying out with each stroke of Chase's cock across her clit.

"Oh!" Matilda screamed, drawing short panting breaths, "Oh!" she said again as her legs began to shake beneath her. "OH!" she screamed louder still as Chase held her up by a butt check with her free hand, "OH...OH...OH!" shouted Matilda as Chase pounded her groin hard and fast against her.

"Yesssssss!" Matilda growled as she held tightly to Chase's shoulders, her legs now unable to help her stand. "OH, Yessss!" she said just before she bit Chase on the chest and dragged her nails across the tops of Chase's shoulders. "Ohhh, yesssss," she yelled once more and then, became suddenly quiet. She held her breath while still twitching her hips against her lover. At last she offered, "Mmmm, so good," and completely collapsed into Chase's arms – her chest heaving from the effort of her orgasm.

Chase withdrew her cock and bent to pick Matilda up in her arms. "Oh, Chase," breathed Matilda heavily, "I really needed that."

"I'm still gonna fuck your brains out," Chase said matter-of-factly as she kissed Matilda on the temple and carried her to the couch.

Matilda was expecting Chase to lay her on down and fuck her missionary-style. She had visions of Chase's sweat dripping from the sides of her face and chin onto her chest as she drove her hips between Matilda's legs. She imagined the weight of the lower half of Chase's body pinning her to the couch, fucking her fiercely, filling her pussy with her hard and pumping cock.

Instead, Chase draped Matilda face down over the arm of the couch and quickly gathered up the cushions to position Matilda's torso atop a soft pile of them to make her comfortable. Chase kissed the back of her neck and made Matilda shiver with anticipation as she kissed her way down Matilda's back. Chase ran her hands down Matilda's sides, causing her to groan and press her center against the arm of the chair. Her legs were draped over the side of the couch and her feet couldn't quite touch the floor.

Chase spread Matilda's butt checks and moved to stand between Matilda's legs. Then she crouched slightly before slowly, gently, deliberately, driving her cock deep into Matilda's wet pussy. Matilda groaned with the intense pleasure of it. The anticipation of the act heightening the sensations. The penetration filling her with a buzzing, electric feeling that started at her pussy and like a slowly seeping euphoria, washed over her entire body.

Chase leaned forward and kissed Matilda's back with lots of tiny little butterfly kisses and smiled, self-satisfied, when Matilda began to squirm beneath her.

"Oh, Chase! You're so amazing," Matilda said with a shaky voice before burying her face into the lacey cushions beneath her.

Chase chuckled lowly and gently pulled Matilda by the hips, positioning the smaller woman's lower tummy on the arm of the couch. Now Chase could run her hands around the tops of Matilda's thighs and touch her clit if she wanted to. She slowly withdrew her cock and crouched a little lower before making another slow, deliberate entry into the tight, slippery little grotto.

"Tell me, Matilda," she asked between light kisses over Matilda's back, "Do you prefer it this way, or…?" Chase slowly pulled her cock almost all the way out of Matilda's pussy. She straightened her legs so as to stand up a little higher, before slowly pressing her cock home again, "…is this more the way you like it?"

"Oh, yeah, like that, Chase," Matilda said throatily, "It feels like you're fucking my clit from inside my pussy when you push down like that."

Chase kept to the second position and slowly fucked Matilda's wet, hungry pussy while kissing and licking her back and neck. Chase brushed her hardened nipples over Matilda's back and groaned to herself as she slowly pushed her cock deep into Matilda again. The pressure of the base of her cock pressing delightfully over her own clit every time she pushed it into Matilda's pussy. *I hope I can hold off from coming long enough to pleasure her first,* thought Chase to herself as she slowly penetrated the constantly moaning diva beneath her.

"Mmmm, fuck me Chase! A little harder for me now," Matilda requested.

Chase found herself becoming even more aroused by Matilda's requests. *She's found her confidence with me. She can tell me how to fuck her, now. That's so fucking hot,* Chase thought to herself as she increased the force of her re-entries, just slightly. Chase reached out and laid an arm across the back of the couch, holding tightly with her fingers and steadying herself, so that she could push hard against Matilda's pussy and drive her cock all the way home.

"Mmmm, yes! Like that Chase, fuck you're good at this." Matilda was breathing hard into the cushions, muffling her groans and cries.

Chase fucked Matilda hard. She pushed her cock into Matilda forcefully before retreating slow and easy. Each time Chase pushed forward the base of her cock would slide against her clit with equal force. She moaned, more from the exertion of preventing herself from coming than from pumping her hips against Matilda's soft little ass. Sweat began to form on her face and back. She felt tiny rivulets begin to form and slowly trickle down her spine. Her breathing was becoming labored and coming well before Matilda was ready for her to, was becoming a major concern.

Then, Matilda lifted her head to speak again, "Fuck me, Stud. Gimme all you got!"

Chase began to increase her pace. Each thrust rammed home to the hilt of her cock. Each thrust pressing the base of the cock against her clit and making her groan. She wasn't going to last much longer and desperately needed to get Matilda aroused enough for another orgasm. She smoothed her hand over Matilda's hip and slid her fingers around and under to seek out Matilda's folds. Matilda was dripping wet and Chase's fingers became quickly slick with Matilda's abundant fluids. Concentrating hard to continue fucking Matilda, while she fingered Matilda's wetness. Chase spread her fingers and carefully slid them in either side of Matilda's clit. She didn't want to touch Matilda's clit too soon after her last orgasm, as the intensity of that touch might cause her discomfort. She needed to coax that little bunch of nerve endings into erection before another orgasm would be possible for Matilda.

Chase continued her rhythm, fucking Matilda strong and fast. It was intensely difficult for her to concentrate with her own orgasm looming, but Chase forced herself to put Matilda's needs before her own. She pressed her fingers together and as she pushed them further into Matilda's slit, she skillfully pulled Matilda's clitoral hood down and over her clit to protect it from being touched directly. Then she moved her fingers in a circular motion; moving the skin of Matilda's hood around and over her clit.

Matilda moaned. It felt good. It felt as if her clit was slowly reawakening. She wriggled her hands in under her chest and began to fondle her own nipples. The instant she touched them, her clit sprang up into erection.

Chase felt the swelling of Matilda's clit and allowed Matilda's hood to recede a little with each rotation of her circling fingers. She was pushing hard into Matilda's pussy, using her hold on the back of the couch to pull herself harder and faster against Matilda.

She could hear the sounds of Matilda's wet pussy as she slapped hard up against Matilda's ass with each forward thrust. The heady smell of their sex hung heavy in the air. Chase's breasts brushed back and forth over Matilda's back in time with the rhythm of their fucking and Chase struggled to keep from orgasm.

Matilda squeezed her nipples hard and yelled, "I'm gonna come." She yelled out loudly every time the head of Chase's cock pressed into the deepest part of her pussy. "I'm gonna come," she groaned loudly once more.

Chase couldn't hold off any longer. Matilda's throaty warning was such a turn-on – so erotic, that she could not stop herself from coming on the strength of it.

"Oh, Matilda," she cried and buried her cock deep inside Matilda; the base pressing hard against Chase's clit. Chase held her breath and slowly moved her hips to get the best contact for her continuing orgasm. Even so, she managed to continue swirling her fingers around and around on Matilda's clit.

Matilda's tone changed, and instead of yelling a muffled, "I'm gonna come," she began crying out, "I'm coming, Chase!"

Chase was breathing heavily now, enjoying pushing her cock into Matilda until her clit became too sensitive. Then, relaxing a moment, letting her clit recover slightly before pushing her cock into Matilda again. Each thrust giving her a subsequent, fleeting, mini-orgasm.

When Matilda jerked away slightly from Chase's fingers, indicating that her orgasm was complete, Chase collapsed on top of her.

Chase breathed heavily onto Matilda's back and was the first to begin to recover. However, both of them were still unable to speak as they struggled to catch their breath.

Chase managed to slow her breathing enough to allow her to reach over and kiss Matilda on the cheek. Then she brought her fingers, saturated with Matilda's come, to her mouth and began sucking them.....

"Matilda!..."

Matilda enjoyed the tickle of Chase's breath against the skin on her cheek as she watched Chase enjoy her....

"Matilda! You listenin'....?"

Her body was spent and her skin was hypersensitive.....

"Matilda! Answer me, girl....!"

"What, Tony? Can't you see I'm taking a coffee break?" Matilda growled back low. *Trust that jerk to spoil a perfectly good daydream,* she grizzled to herself.

"I don't pay you to sit on your butt, Matilda!"

"I didn't get my break today, Tony. There were too many customers, so I'm using the last ten minutes of my shift to stop and have a coffee," Matilda retorted with restraint. "You might have noticed, that's what I've had to do all week."

"I've noticed you sitting on your butt," Tony scowled at her. "There's a customer waiting, Matilda. Now, get over there and serve or start looking for another job."

Tony was the owner of the Café where Matilda worked. She'd been there for the last four months and it seemed to her, no matter how much effort she put in, it was never good enough for Tony. No matter how hard she worked, he would demand more. She sighed and got to her feet. Resolving to start looking for another job, she turned and pulled her order book from her apron pocket. She took her pencil from her ear as she walked without looking, in the direction Tony had gestured toward when he'd been berating her.

When she looked up and saw who the customer was she smiled broadly and said, "Oh! Hi Chase." *I was just dreaming about you – again.*

"Matilda," Chase nodded her greeting. "He still picking on you?" she gestured with her chin in Tony's direction.

"Uh-huh!" Matilda confirmed. "Espresso?" she asked with her pencil poised, waiting to take Chase's order.

Chase nodded as she added, "You should start looking for another job, Matilda. You're too good to be stuck here with him demoralizing you the way he does," Chase consoled.

"Yeah, I'm gonna have to," Matilda agreed. "He's really starting to get me down." Matilda left to get Chase's coffee.

When Matilda returned with the beverage in hand Chase confided, "I could do with a housekeeper." Matilda stared at her wordlessly, so Chase added cautiously, "If you're interested?"

Matilda continued to stare at Chase, needing a few moments to take in her meaning. Then her brow furrowed and she asked, "Are you for real?"

"Sure!" said Chase. "The counseling business is getting pretty hectic now and I don't have time to clean my house and shop and cook anymore. You're a hard worker, Matilda. I've seen you here, working your ass off trying to please that moron of a boss of yours. I'd be over-the-moon if you'd agree to come and work for me, instead."

"Full-time or part-time?" Matilda questioned as she looked around to see if anyone were overhearing their conversation.

"Full-time. I'd need you to answer the phone and schedule appointments, as well," Chase qualified. "I know your shift ends soon. Just come and take a look at the place and see what you think?" Chase held her breath waiting for Matilda to answer.

Matilda looked around to make sure Tony hadn't heard any of what they'd said. Seeing him busily restocking the fridges with soda drinks, she turned back to Chase and nodded, "Okay, just give me ten minutes to finish-up?"

Chase agreed and Matilda waltzed away excitedly.

♀♀♀♀♀

Chase's house was two blocks from the Café. (One block further than it was in Matilda's daydreams). When Chase stopped in front of a newly restored, Federation-style house, Matilda's jaw dropped. *It's just like I dreamed it,* she thought incredulously. Chase stooped a little to open the low wrought-iron gate and stepped aside to allow Matilda to walk through. *I wonder if the gate squeaks a little as she starts to close it.* Chase closed the gate and sure enough, it made a little squeak, just as Matilda had daydreamed from the first time she'd spoken with Chase.

Chase had been a regular customer at the Café. During the previous four months, she'd told Matilda a great deal about her home-based counseling practice. That was when Matilda's daydreaming about Chase had begun. And why not! Chase was fit, gorgeous, sexy, compassionate and calm. A confident, well educated, soft butch of independent wealth. How could an under-appreciated, over-worked waitress working in a dead-end job resist daydreaming about her.

Chase pushed the gate closed and when she stopped to check the letterbox, Matilda was stunned. *This is getting spooky!*

They turned to walk down the path together. As they climbed the steps to the porch, Matilda began tentatively, "So, this housekeeping job of yours, Chase," she looked into Chase's beautiful blues eyes and dared to ask, "Does it come with a French Maid's outfit?"

The Beginning

A Note from the Author

Yes, yes. I know what you're going to say. 'There's a quirky novelette in this book!' I like to think of it as a hidden surprise. Now before I start getting overloaded with emails asking why I wasted what might have been a good book by dispersing it through *this* collection of stories - let me explain.

The underlying message is that of successful businesswomen, trading their chances at loving relationships for success in their fields of expertise. While their lifestyles are incompatible with long-term relationships, they still need to feel a connection – an intimacy – with someone. The alternative is to drown in loneliness.

Hence, the novelette is about a high-flying entrepreneur and her sex-worker. I felt the story needed 'hot sex' to properly convey the intensity required to fill the void of a loveless lifestyle. But that gives us a tale with too much sex in it to carry the story with dignity in a book by itself. I've done it like this, hoping that by the time the reader has recognized the hidden novelette, they've also begun to look forward to its next installment. That perhaps, this system of delivery might give the story a chance to be expressed before being lost in what could otherwise be considered, a sex-fest.

Please contact me with your feedback. I value the input of others and I really do care what you think.

Eva Reddy

♀♀♀♀♀

Contact Eva with your feedback: eva.reddy@outlook.com

About the Author

Eva lives in a small city in the south of Western Australia where she cares full-time for her terminally ill mother and lives with her soul mate and life-partner of 23 years. They're proud parents of a shepherd-cross who rules the house.

Writing serves as a distraction from her daily humdrum and provides for useful conversation topics when chatting with her best friend and Beta Reader, (who she has never met in person and lives almost 2,500 miles away), via the internet.

Her interests include woodwork, gardening, reading, writing and lovingly renovating her little cottage.

♀♀♀♀♀

Contact Eva with your feedback: eva.reddy@outlook.com

www.ingramcontent.com/pod-product-compliance
Lightning Source LLC
Chambersburg PA
CBHW050903250626
47155CB00001B/81